The SKIN RIPPER

Also by John Dwaine McKenna:

Unforsaken
Colorado Noir
The Whim - Wham Man
The Neversink Chronicles

The SKIN RIPPER

John Dwaine McKenna

East of the Mountains  and West of the Sun™

RHYOLITE PRESS LLC
P.O. Box 60144
Colorado Springs, Colorado

Published in the United States of America by Rhyolite Press LLC
P.O. Box 60144 Colorado Springs, Colorado 80960
www.rhyolitepress.com

McKenna, John Dwaine
The Skin Ripper / John Dwaine McKenna
First Edition   March 1, 2024
ISBN 978-0-9896763-7-3
Library of Congress Control Number 2024939042

Cover and book design/layout by Donald R. Kallaus
Cover graphics inspired by Lora & Dillon Brown
Jake McKern character graphic: *"Firing up a Lucky"* Glenn W. Murray photograph

To Jane and Bob Battle . . .
two people who are always
ready to offer a willing
and helping hand.

Epigraph

I am now of an age which causes me to forsake the dreams of a younger man in favor of the memories of an older one. These are the stories of my life, collected from the journals I have kept through the years . . . and everything of value that I possess. You may take heed of them to become a better person . . . or ignore them at your peril.

My name is Jake McKern.

I was once a cop.

The Skin Ripper

Under a moonless sky in the smallest hours of an ominous March morning, a black Mercedes sedan turned west onto Bijou Street from the dark canyon of unlit buildings on Nevada Avenue in downtown Colorado Springs and crossed the Denver and Rio Grande Railroad tracks, made a second change of direction and headed north on Spruce—as if it had just slipped from the shadows of some sinister, unholy place—then purred over the cracked and patched asphalt as quiet and sure and purposeful as a beast of prey, intent on catching an easy meal.

"How much farther?" The driver said.

"A few blocks," was the answer and the automobile continued up the street in silence.

Moments later a second, more commanding voice said from the rear seat, "Do not stop here. Turn at the next corner and go down the alley. They are upstairs at the back of the little grocery store. There is an apartment where they live."

The car turned right. The driver killed the lights and shut off the motor at the same time. He slipped into the alley, then coasted to a stop at the rear of the two-story wood framed building. No one spoke as they donned surgical gloves and pulled nylon stockings over their heads to obscure their faces. The driver, with the collar of his brown tweed overcoat turned up against the cold, remained on guard downstairs. He watched as the four others gathered the tools for the job, and prepared to make their entrance on silent, muffled feet. There was no surplus movement, no wasted gestures—each of them had done it before—and were ready for the task ahead.

It was going to be wet work . . .

Chapter 1

I was elated, when the ringing of the telephone on the upended wooden crate that served as a nightstand roused me from a recurring nightmare about a character I called the Whim-Wham Man, who sometimes crawls out of my subconscious to visit my dreams, and remind me of odious past deeds which cannot be erased . . . or forgotten . . . nor forgiven.

I picked it up just as it began its second ring, hoping to keep from waking my wife Mo, who was sound asleep beside me. The alarm clock next to the phone read 5:50 a.m. as I croaked, "Yeah," into the mouthpiece and tried to come to life.

"McKern?"

"Yeah. This is Jake."

"It's Wally, on the desk. You're about to pop your cherry, boyo. Your name is up top of the available list and we just got a double, over on Spruce Street."

Fully alert in an instant, I slid out of the covers, sat bolt upright on the side of the bed, and fumbled in the dark for the brass pull chain on the reading lamp that stood on the floor. Once I could see, I grabbed my notebook and ballpoint pen beside the phone and said, "OK, Wally. I'm ready to copy. Did you say a double homicide?"

"I did. At 927 north Spruce Street."

"Isn't that a grocery store?"

"It is. Call came in at oh-five-forty. The butter and egg man reported it when he found the door open and the lights off at oh-five thirty."

"He found the victims," I said, as I lit a cigarette from the pack of Luckys beside the phone.

"He did. The Unies are on scene. They have the place locked down, and await only your presence to make their day complete."

"Cut the crap Wally. I'll be there in a few minutes—the scene's right around the corner from my house. Anything else?"

"Yeah. All sarcasm aside, Jake. Don't eat anything before you go over there. It's a bad one."

Wally's comment kept bouncing around in my head as I got up and headed to the bathroom, where I did my business and grabbed a quick shave, then ran a wet comb through my hair.

How bad can it be? I thought as I dressed in a blue, button-down oxford shirt, striped tie, and gray flannel pants along with polished black cowboy boots. *I've seen it all in the Pacific during the war. I know what a dead body looks like . . . that bastard Wally's just fucking with me . . .* were my exact thoughts as I took my beat-up, brown leather A2 jacket out of the closet and slipped it on. I clipped the gold CSPD detective shield to my belt and snugged the old 1911 Colt .45 auto I'd carried since the battle of Okinawa into the shoulder holster under my left arm. I checked my appearance in the hall mirror on my way out, to make sure I was spit-shined. This was my first case as a detective since Chief Budd had pinned the shield on me three months ago, and I wanted to make a great first impression.

My right leg wasn't fully healed. It ached at the place the broken femur was reset, and the scar where the fractured bone stuck out of my thigh was livid red and itching as I closed the front door of the little house we lived in, over on south Seventh Street. It was just off Colorado Avenue on the city's near west side, and less than a mile from where the murder took place. I limped down the walk and got in the two-year-old unmarked car I'd been assigned, hoping the clunker would start and take me to my first crime scene without any problems. I let it idle for a couple of minutes with the choke halfway out, then dropped it into first gear and took off in a cloud of smoke. The department was supposed to get a new fleet of vehicles in a few months, and they couldn't get here soon enough as far as I was concerned.

I turned east on Colorado Avenue and north on Spruce Street, arriving on scene at 6:25 a.m., where, despite the early hour, a group of onlookers was starting to gather. I guessed they'd either been attracted by the police cars, or were working folks on their way to the job who'd stopped by for a morning paper or a snack. In any case, they were going to be disappointed.

I pulled into the alley and parked behind a couple of marked patrol cars. I climbed out and walked to the back door of the Spruce Street Grocery, where I was met by a uniformed cop I'd once patrolled with named Donald Brearley.

"Hi Jake," he said. "It's been a while. How're you doin' these days?"

"Not bad Donnie, but let's catch up later. Who's here besides yourself, and who's the senior-most man?"

Donnie sucked in a breath and started to give me the stink eye, then thought better of it. He said, "Good idea Jake. There's me, Andy Claypoole, Jim Dunlap and a new guy named Amos Magness. Dunlap and Magness are out front, Claypoole's inside."

"Has anyone else been in there?"

"All four of us, plus the delivery guy."

"Where is he, and do you have a name?"

Donnie pulled out his notebook and flipped it open. "It's Rufus Gerry. He's been selling butter and eggs to the neighborhood grocers since the thirties. He's pretty upset. Been puking his guts out. It's a nasty scene in there."

"Tell me you've kept him here . . ."

"Oh yeah. He's in his truck, right over there," Donnie pointed to a white panel truck parked along the south side of the grocery.

It said, *Canyon Farms* on the door in red and black letters. In my haste, I'd failed to notice it. I reminded myself to *Slow down,* and said, "Thanks, Donnie. You've done a good job. It helps. Any idea what took place here?"

Ma always said, *You get more flies with honey than vinegar,* and she was right.

Donnie smiled, drew in a breath, and said, "Whoever did it parked here, went upstairs right there, and jimmied the back door. Shot 'em execution style, in their bed while they slept is what I think . . ."

I felt Donnie was holding something back, but didn't want to press him about it after the rocky start I'd made. I let it slide. Said, "Has anybody called the coroner?"

3

"Not that I know of . . ."

"Okay. Call dispatch. Tell Wally we need help with crowd control and site preservation . . . we also need a photographer, some crime scene people, and the coroner. Thanks for locking things down out here. We're going to have a lot more folks to deal with in a little bit. Keep everybody back and tell the delivery guy I'll talk to him as soon as I get a look inside."

Donnie nodded and walked over to the egg man's truck, while I started up the outside staircase to meet the victims of my first ever homicide case. I had no idea as I mounted those steps that morning, how much the rest of my life was going to be changed by them.

Chapter 2

I was on the third stair when I saw the blood. It was dripped on the steps, the railing and even the risers. There were smudges where someone had stepped in it, and a few smears and handprints along the white clapboard siding.

Slow down. I reminded myself a second time, as I backed down the stairs to make a better start of the investigation. There was a trail of blood leading to the back door where the deliveries were made. I'd walked right over it in my haste, and decided to backtrack a bit more. I knew there was some resentment among a few of the guys in uniform with seniority on me, that I'd been promoted before them. It wasn't any secret that some of them coveted a detective slot. I hadn't thought Officer Donald Brearley was among the jealous ones, but it was time to find out.

I walked back to where he was standing in front of his patrol car, smoking a cigarette, and pretending he wasn't watching me out of the corner of his eye. "Donnie," I said, "would you mind helping me out? Telling me whatever you can . . ."

"Sure, Jake. Whadaya wanna know?"

"You were the first one here. What did you find, who's the victim? It's the first case I've been lead on, and can use whatever help I can get." *Don't show weakness. Don't let any of them know how nervous you are. And don't apologize,* I told myself as I waited to see what he'd say.

Donnie put his right foot up on the bumper and rested his elbow on his knee. He took a big drag on his smoke and squinted off in the distance, as if he was trying to remember all the words to Hamlet's soliloquy. Then he gave a big sigh, exhaled from both nostrils like a dragon letting off steam and said, "I got here first, then Claypoole. We found the butter and egg man waiting in his truck. He was pretty shaken at first, didn't make much sense. I gave him a jolt from my flask and he got a hold of himself but still wasn't givin' us any more information."

"How big of a jolt? Is he loaded?"

"Not unless he's got his own bottle in the truck. I only gave him a little sip. Not even enough to get a hummingbird hinky. Dunlap and his trainee showed up and I put 'em out front to keep any customers from enterin' the place."

"I thought you said all four of you'd been in the crime scene . . ."

"I'm gettin' to that," Donnie said as he puffed another lungful of smoke in and out while he searched for his next few words.

I could see he was struggling but didn't know why. "Just spit it out man. Whatever it is, I'll handle it . . ."

"Don't be too sure of that," my one-time patrol partner said, as he looked at me with red rimmed and bloodshot eyes that I hadn't noticed earlier.

Donnie was a veteran who'd seen hard action in Korea. I'd always thought him to be steady and tough, willing, and able to handle the worst kinds of situations. It wasn't like him to be emotional. As hard as it was, I waited for him to speak.

After a moment of hesitation, Donnie took a breath and continued. "Claypoole and I went in the back door down here, while Dunlap and Magness cleared the upstairs. Andy and I were still clearin' the store itself . . . there was aisles, shaded spots, and counters to check . . . when Jimmy came back down. He told us that there was a lotta blood up there. Started in the bedroom, then went through the hall, out the back door and down the stairs. He said that the place was tossed pretty hard; drawers turned over, bookcases upended, cabinets ransacked, but no bodies." Donnie stopped speaking and looked down at his feet. I waited, saw a couple of tears spatter to the sheet metal between the front bumper and the grille of his '55 Ford prowl car.

Donnie looked up at me with tears now running down his cheeks. He brushed them away with a thumb and said, "I knew them. I grew up over on Mesa Road, three blocks from here. Abe and Ruth Sorwell. They came here right after the war. Jews, who survived the concentration camps. They helped my mother and me after my dad was killed in a hunting accident up in Kremmling. Mr. Sorwell carried us on credit for a while. Nobody else would. Never asked us for money neither. We paid when we could, didn't catch up until I was drafted in the Army. Sent all my pay home to Ma . . ."

Donnie's voice trailed off again at that point, and while I felt a kinship—my own story was eerily similar—I had to get on with the business at hand. "Is there anything more you can tell me?"

"Go see for yourself. Look in the cold storage locker in back. By the meat counter," he said as he threw his cigarette butt on the ground with all the force he could render, then walked up the alley toward the entrance, where he stopped and stood with his back to me, trying to work out his grief privately. I could see his shoulders shaking as I headed for the back door of the neighborhood grocery store.

I remember thinking, *thirteen months in a patrol car with that guy, and I never saw him act like such a pussy . . . it's no wonder we didn't win the war in Korea if all our troops were so weak . . .*

It was the lowest, most uncharitable, unfair, and mean thing to think about a man who'd answered his country's call, fought for her, and stood shoulder-to-shoulder with me through all the ups and downs of being an on-duty cop. I was ashamed of myself for even allowing such a comment to form in my mind. Thank God I never voiced any of those thoughts out loud. I include them here as a kind of penance, and to honor a man who gave his life in service to his community. Five years later, Officer Donnie Brearley was shot and killed during a routine traffic stop.

For me, revelation came only moments later.

Chapter 3

The back door had been jimmied with a crowbar. *It must have taken someone with a helluva lot of upper body strength and a four-foot bar,* I thought, as I looked at the deep gouges in the frame, the splintered trim, and finger-width dents in the three-inch oak door. It was a stout four feet wide and sported strap-iron hinges that looked to be at least one and a half feet long. The door was formidable, but hadn't stopped the criminals.

Inside, shelves lined the walls and were filled with canned goods and all sorts of household sundries, while display cases, tables and double-sided free-standing shelves created aisles. A check-out counter with a brass cash register stood by the front door, and a refrigerated section towards the back of the store held fresh vegetables, as well as meats in see-through lighted cases. There was a large Toledo scale for weighing bacon, chops or steaks atop the counter, and a roll of white butcher paper in a dispenser stood next to it. At the rear, behind the butcher block and not accessible by the public, was a large walk-in cooler. That was where I headed.

I almost fell over Patrol Sergeant Andrew Claypoole, who was sitting in one of the wooden chairs that were usually found around the big pot-bellied stove, where some of the old men from the neighborhood would gather to gossip, and tell war stories. Claypoole was drinking from a bottle of Coca-Cola and looking like he'd rather be anywhere but here. I said, "Morning, Andy . . . it's been a long time since we've crossed trails."

"Yeah. It has been. This your first case? As a dick, I mean . . ."

"It is, yeah, it is. I look that green to you?"

"Pretty much . . . but not as green as you're gonna be. They're in there," he pointed at the cooler door with his left thumb and took another sip from the cola bottle. Then added, "I'll leave another dime on the register and have one of these Cokes ready for ya. You're gonna want it after you go in there."

"Is it that bad?"

"Worst one I've ever been on," Andy said as he rose from his seat and headed for the front of the store where the soda pop was kept in an old Crosley refrigerator, and sold on the honor system.

I went around the counter, stepped past the butcher block, and took a deep breath, then pulled the latch that opened the thick insulated door to the walk-in cooler, where I found the abomination that still raises bile in my throat as I write this, forty-some years after the fact.

The bodies of an elderly man and woman were hanging from meat hooks that were attached to wooden joists in the ceiling. The skin had been peeled from both corpses with surgical precision, and was nowhere in sight. It was at that point I wanted to puke, and felt the room closing in on me. My heart was thumping out a regimental tattoo in my chest and I could not breathe. I had to get out of there.

I turned and pushed the iron bar that unlatched the heavy door. It clacked open, and allowed me to stumble into the fresh air, where Claypoole handed me a freshly opened bottle of Coca-Cola. I nodded my thanks and took a long pull of the cold, fizzy, sweet liquid. I swallowed, shook my head, and said, "Sweet, suffering Jesus . . ."

"It sure puts a crimp in your point-of-view, don't it?"

"Yeah, Andy. It does. This is Colorado Springs, for crissakes. We ain't supposed to be dealin' with shit like this."

" 'Pears we are though. Like it or not."

I finished the soda and went to work, looking for evidence; trying to find the who, why and how of the horrific murders of two elderly members of the local community while I was sound asleep in my bed less than a mile away. Knowing that gave me the creeps. Even though Imogene and I hadn't been getting along very well lately, I'd be devastated if something like that happened to her, or, God forbid, our ten-year-old son Scottie. I forced those thoughts out of my mind and got on with the job.

After pulling my head out of my ass, I put on a pair of latex gloves I had in my jacket pocket, took a deep breath, and went back in the meat locker. A couple of things came to mind right away. There was more than one person at work in here, and, because the only illumination came from a single forty-watt bulb, they either had another portable light source, or this wasn't the first time they'd savaged a human body. The slash marks in the underlying tissue were sure, straight and without hesitation. I was certain of it.

I poked around in the cooler for a few more minutes without finding anything of significance to the case. Before I left however, I did something I've done in the presence of every victim of every murder scene I've ever investigated. I spoke to the deceased. Told them I would not forget, that I would speak for them, and never give up on the case until it was solved. If there is a hereafter—and I believe there is—I want the departed to know I am their advocate. Just as I would want someone to do for me.

The next thing I need to figure out, I thought as I reentered the land of light and the living, *is why the killers moved both of the bodies down here . . . it defies logic and common sense, and it was done at great risk of exposure.*

I blinked and took a deep breath as the cooler door clacked shut behind me. "Andy," I said, "do you have any thoughts about why the bodies were moved down here?"

Without hesitation, he said, "Sure. Make it easier to skin 'em."

"Of course. That sounds about right to me." I headed out the door and to the stairs, thinking, *I should have remembered what old Professor Blackburn taught us about Occam the Arab and his razor . . . 'The simplest solution is usually the best solution.'*

I was careful, as I went up the outside staircase, to avoid the blood, while admonishing myself for the third time in less than an hour, to *Slow the fuck down, Jake. The dead have infinite patience, but your days are numbered . . . and you promised to speak for them . . . so you'd better get it right.*

Chapter 4

Upstairs, the modest apartment was destroyed. The utter chaos seemed—in my mind at least—to be a match for the depravity that had taken place downstairs, with no apparent reason for it. *If the vandals were trying to find something, they sure did a thorough job of searching. I wonder if they found it . . .*

The blood trail led to the bedroom, where it appeared the elderly couple were murdered in their bed. That much at least was apparent from the powder burns on the sheets and one of the pillows. *I hope for their sake that they were asleep when the triggers were pulled.* I was careful not to touch or move anything until the Medical Examiner got here, along with the photographer and fingerprint techs, but I was anxious to see where, and how, the deaths took place. After a brief look through the bedroom, I did the same in the bathroom, living room and kitchen, but nothing stood out. I closed the door and went back downstairs to talk with the butter and egg man, Rufus Gerry.

I found him sitting in his truck, right where Donnie Brearley put him an hour ago. "Mr. Gerry . . . my name is Jake McKern. I'm the lead detective on this case. Thanks for your help. I want to ask you a few questions about what you saw when you got here, but first, are you comfortable? Can I get you anything?"

Rufus Gerry looked to be in his mid-to-late-fifties, and judging by his face, hands, and clothes, he was a man accustomed to hard work and a life of toil. He pushed his brown fedora up high on his forehead and squinted at me with hard brown eyes behind rimless wire-framed glasses, then said through the driver's window of his truck, "You can get me outta here sonny. The ice is meltin' in the back, and butter don't keep in the heat. I still got a dozen more deliveries to make and people'll be wonderin' whereinthefuck I am . . ."

"I get it," I said. Then the Rage Monster who lives inside of me flew out of his cage, and before I could stop myself, I added, "But two old folks who ain't done anything to anybody are lying in there, dead, and butchered. They're depending on me to catch the sick sons-a-bitchs who done it. So, lose the fucking attitude and help me. I'll getya outta here as soon as possible. Otherwise, I'll clamp your nasty old ass in that patrol car over there and we'll do this downtown. That'll take all day. Call me 'sonny' again and I'll slap the bejeezus outta ya, just on general principles. We clear on all of that?"

Gerry looked at me for a moment, as if he was undecided how to take or give it, but then he got just a fraction of a smile, tugging at the corners of his mouth. He said, "We understand each other perfectly. I was outta line and . . ." He grinned, in spite of—or maybe because of—the circumstances, and continued, "Be damned if anybody's chewed my ass out like that since I was drafted into the Marine Corps, back in nineteen and seventeen. Was you by any chance a member?"

"I was."

"In the war?"

"I was."

"Well, *Semper Fi,* Detective. *Semper Fi.* Ask away."

At that point the attitude adjustment was over and done with and we got right down to the business at hand. In the end though, Rufus Gerry wasn't able to provide anything of value. The perpetrators were done and gone by the time the delivery man arrived . . . or else there might have been a third killing to deal with. I got his contact information, then cut him loose after giving him one of my business cards and an admonition to call if he remembered anything else. He promised he would. I doubted I'd ever see him again.

By 8 a.m., reinforcements began arriving, and word of the crime was spreading. The group of onlookers was growing bigger by the minute, and I could see a few of the newshounds I got to know as I convalesced from the Colorado Commercial Bank robbery, sniffing around, and trying to get the attention of Dunlap, or his trainee, Magness. The first cops to arrive went on crowd control. I told 'em to move the gawkers and rubberneckers back at least fifty feet and keep them there. They used their cruisers as barricades, and I left Claypoole in charge of everyone. He had the stripes of authority on his sleeves and the foghorn voice of an old drill instructor—which he once was—to go with it. He was perfect for the job. Pretty soon after he went out, the gawkers were backed off and we had containment, as well as better site preservation. The crime scene itself had been FUBARed—*fucked up beyond all recognition*—long before I arrived, by the five people who'd tromped all over it.

The coroner arrived. The man himself, not one of his minions, who were real physicians with a license to practice medicine. In an odd twist of the state laws at the time, the position of County Coroner, or Medical Examiner, was an elected one, and did not require a medical degree from an accredited university. Harry Bucklin, the El Paso County Coroner from back then, was just such a one. He was an ambitious little prick, a political operative with a sharp eye for ever higher office, and a publicity hound of the first magnitude. If he was here, it could only mean one thing. Someone in the Colorado Springs Police Department had called him. I remember thinking when I saw him drive up in a cherry red Buick, *If I ever find out who tipped this guy off, I'll personally rip his nuts off and stuff 'em down his throat.*

Coroner Bucklin pulled past the cops guarding the street entrance, drove into the alley from the south side, and parked where the butter and egg man's truck had been. He got out of the car with his trademark half-smoked cigar butt clamped in his teeth and waved to the crowd. He hitched up his suit pants and took a small black doctor's bag out of the trunk, then came over to where I waited by the back door. I started to say "Good Morning," but he cut me off.

"Where's the body?" Bucklin said. "I have an important meeting with the County Commissioners in a few minutes and I need to do this quickly."

"Of course. And just so you know, there are two bodies. A man and his wife." I told him nothing else, gave him no warning about what he was walking into. *We'll just see what those prissy patent leather shoes and that oh, so cute, red bow tie looks like in a little while.* "Come this way," was all I said.

Chapter 5

The self-important and officious token Democrat in a county dominated by Republicans was right on my heels as I navigated through the aisles and shelves, past the deli counter, the scale and butcher's block to the door of the meat locker. I grabbed the latch, and said, "They're in here," pulled it open and stood aside, allowing the official and duly-elected El Paso County Coroner to enter first.

He gave me an unctuous smirk as he brushed past, and was fully inside the cold storage room before realization of the horror within hit him like a fist to the face. He gasped, and turned to me with his mouth working up and down, but no words were coming out. The cigar came loose and tumbled down the front of his immaculate black silk suit, leaving a trail of dirty gray ash and smoking pinholes every place the burning tip made contact, before it finally hit the floor in a shower of sparks. Harry Bucklin stumbled sideways, mewled like a baby kitten, and blew chunks all over his shoes, suit, and my crime scene. I had no words as the dead looked down at him with contempt and the puking seemed to go on forever.

When he finally stopped ralphing, Bucklin was bent over at the waist with his hands on his knees and gasping for breath, as he spit out the last of the bile in his gut. I stood there dumbfounded, still holding the door like an ignorant Irish fool, straight out of the peat bogs.

A few more moments and Himself had caught his breath. He stood, retrieved a hankie from inside his pocket and wiped his face. Then, with as much dignity as he could muster, the petty bureaucrat drew up to his full height—still ten inches shorter than me, even in his elevator shoes—and said, "You'll pay a price for this McKern." Then he squished past me, dripping vomitus with every step he took, all the way back to his car. I heard the V-8 motor come to life and roar down the alley, slinging dirt, rocks, and gravel at everything in sight, with Donnie Brearley taking the worst of it. I could hear him cursing, even though the back door was closed. I sighed, and started to re-establish the murder scene as best as I could.

When I opened the cooler door, a wave of stink rolled out and washed over me like a tsunami. It was touch and go for a few seconds, whether or not I was going to lose my cookies too, but I held it back and started breathing through my mouth. That helped. Under the unblinking eyes and the ravaged bodies of Mr. and Mrs. Sorwell, I eased back in to see what I could see . . . and find what I could find that might bring us closer to the who of this heinous crime.

Not much . . . as it turned out . . . other than the black doctor's bag Harry Bucklin had carried—for nomenclature—I guess, so those who saw him would think he was doing something useful. When I looked inside, all it contained were some cigars, a Playboy Magazine and an unread, day-old copy of *The Denver Post* newspaper. Even with gloves on, I didn't want to touch any of it. I stuffed everything, vomit, and all, into an evidence bag and made a mental note to drop it off at the Coroner's office . . . after letting it ripen for a few days in the trunk of my car. I carried the bag in a bag out to the old unmarked I'd been assigned and did just that. Then I went to check on the apartment.

I found Doug Sikes, the CSPD photographer, and a pair of finger-print techs upstairs and asked, "How much longer?"

"I'm done," Sikes replied.

"Come with me then. Did you get shots of everything in here?"

"Yeah. The stairs, too. And all the blood on the walls. I tagged the bedclothes, the sheets, and the pillows. There just wasn't much else to find. No shell casings, no knives . . . and no fingerprints either. This looks like a professional job."

"It could be . . . but we don't know yet. I want you to take pictures of the crowd out there without being too obvious about it. Okay?"

"Sure. I can do that."

"Good. Come downstairs. I want you to get photos of everything, from the tool marks on the door, all the way in, to where the bodies are."

"This isn't the first time I've done this Jake . . ."

"I know, Doug. I know that. But it's mine. The crime's about as nasty as you're ever gonna see, and the scene's been fucked up and over, six ways for Sunday. Brace yourself before you go in there."

"I got it. Here. Put some of this on your upper lip."

"What is it?"

"Vicks Vapo Rub. It helps to take the smell away."

"Good. The Coroner blew his guts out down there a few minutes ago."

"Where's that?"

"Downstairs," I said. "Where the rest of the crime took place. In a walk-in meat locker."

I put Sikes to work in the cooler, then went to find Andy Claypoole. My right leg was complaining from all the trips up and down the stairs by then, so I swallowed four aspirins from the tin of them that I carried in my shirt pocket. I'd have to find something stronger pretty soon if I was going to be on my feet much longer. The pain from my old wounds wasn't going to go away. I walked out front and found Claypoole, standing behind one of the wooden barriers, where he was smoking a cigarette and talking to a newspaper reporter for the *Gazette-Telegraph* named Lenny Bragg.

I'd give my right nut to have a partner right now . . . I feel like there's too many holes in the dike all of a sudden, and I don't have enough fingers to plug 'em. And just what I don't need at the moment, is a nosey-assed reporter in the middle of this fucked up multiple murder. The city keeps on growing; the developers get fatter and richer, while the growth advocates and real estate worshippers on City Council rubber stamp 'approved' on plat after plat, annexing every square foot in sight and still expect all of us in the police and fire departments to make do with the same number of cops and firemen. In a pig's ass . . . something's gotta give. And soon . . .

Chapter 6

I stopped and fired up a Lucky Strike, then walked over to where Claypoole and the newshound stood on either side of the barrier. I nodded and said, "Morning, Lenny. What's the news?"

Leonard Bragg was a young and eager preppy type who'd graduated from an eastern college, failed his physical for the draft due to poor eyesight, and then—against the wishes of his blue-blood Yankee parents—followed the advice of Horace Greeley and came out west. He'd caught on with the paper a few years ago, and now his investigative column entitled *Bragg About,* was a fixture that many in town, including myself, followed avidly. Lenny pushed his heavy black-framed glasses back up his nose, shrugged deeper into his navy-blue pea coat and said, "Hiya Jake. The news, as always, is full of nothing other than the bad, the evil, and the nasty shit that people do to each other. . . which, when you think about it . . . makes it impossible to be optimistic and well-informed at the same time. Wouldn't you agree? And hey, could I bum one of your smokes? I'm all out."

In spite of our semi-adversarial occupations, I liked Lenny. We were about the same age, early thirties, and even though our backgrounds couldn't be more different, we tolerated each other's company. I grinned as I shook one out for him and said, "Shit Lenny, you're always smoking O.P.s. Long as I've known ya, I can't ever remember you having any, or giving any away."

"That's because other people's cigarettes always taste better," he said, as he accepted a light from Andy Claypoole, who'd been silently watching our repartee with a grin on his face.

While Lenny sucked down a big lungful of fine tobacco smoke, I said to Claypoole, "Andy, as usual we ain't got enough manpower to take care of everything here. I'm gonna call and talk to Lieutenant Patterson, see if he can shake out a few more troops for us. Meanwhile, would you kindly set Dunlap and his rookie to knocking on doors? See if anyone saw or heard anything out of the ordinary last night. You know the drill . . . we're gonna be up shit crick without a paddle if we don't get some kind of clues . . ."

Claypoole nodded and went to find the others.

I turned back to the reporter and said, "Lenny, can you keep a lid on everything you're hearing right now. We're strictly off the record here. Okay?"

When he looked at me, Lenny's cobalt blue eyes were as cool and detached as an Old West gunfighter, out in the street with the sun at his back. He said, "I would if I could Jake, but there's no way. Look around. The cat's out of the bag. Word-of-mouth is spreading and rumors are flying. The stories are getting more and more lurid with each retelling . . ."

"Such as?"

"Oh, for christsakes, Jake. Just strolling around in the crowd and eavesdropping, I've heard that there's anywhere from two to five people murdered, and they've been tortured, chopped into pieces, or skinned. That the killer was A., an escaped madman, B., a group of devil worshippers, or, C., and get this . . . cannibals. And, just in case you haven't had time to notice, that hot new young blonde chick from KRDO is somewhere around here."

"Isn't she the one who interviewed the Bavarian woman who's going to run the new ski area down on Cheyenne Mountain, next to the Broadmoor Golf Course?"

"The very same," Lenny said, "she's wearing a bright red Loden coat. You can't miss her. Which, I suppose, is exactly what she intended . . . ambitious young woman that she is."

I took a last pull of my cigarette, knocked the fire off with a fingernail and began field-stripping it. As I rolled and scattered the unburnt tobacco with my hands, I said, "Did I detect some animosity, Lenny? Some petty jealously perhaps?"

Lenny Bragg blew smoke out of both nostrils, then shrugged at the same time. He shook his head and said, "And why-ever would I be jealous of such a one as she ... who is endowed with the body of Venus, the heart of a lioness and all the brains of a barnyard goose? She's only using her assets the best way she knows how. And I don't think that commotion, catastrophe, confrontation, conflagration, or the casting couch will prevent her from attaining her goals."

"Well, let the alliteration begin," I said. "What's her name?"

"Agnes," Lenny said and waved over his shoulder as he melded into the crowd. "Agnes Bedwell."

I wrote her name on the last page of my notebook and went back to the grim work I'd been assigned.

As I walked back to the grocery store's delivery door, the who and why of this terrible murder fell on me like the weight of the world. The awesome responsibility for catching what appeared to be a team of professional killers now rested entirely on my shoulders . . . and I wasn't sure I was up to the task. Abraham and Ruth Sorwell deserved, no, I thought. *Mr. and Mrs. Sorwell's case demands justice. It screams for it . . . because this is America, where ordinary folks are supposed to be safe in their homes while asleep in their beds at night . . . and because this is Colorado Springs. My home. And my sanctuary, where my family lives, where my son is growing up . . .* I stopped moving as I reached for the door handle, shook my head, and chuckled to myself. *That was the corniest thing that's ever run through your head, Jake. Thank Christ you didn't say it aloud, in front of anybody . . . even if it is the God's honest truth.*

I pulled the door and went inside. I needed to find Doug Sikes, to see if he and the fingerprint guys were through yet. The coroner's men were waiting in their unmarked black panel truck to remove the deceased and transport them to the morgue. I was determined to show the couple all the dignity and respect they'd earned over the course of their life's journey. No one should ever come to such an ignominious and evil end of their days. Certainly not in the Springs.

Chapter 7

I found Doug Sikes sitting on the checkout counter eating a Hershey's chocolate bar. He had the same haggard, *I can't believe what I just saw,* look that each of us who'd been in the store's meat locker came out wearing. I said, "Are you doing okay, Doug?"

When he raised his face, his eyes had the same hollowed out stare I'd seen before, on the faces of the survivors of some life-threatening event . . . the ones who couldn't believe that they were still alive. It was a face I'd seen on myself a few times.

Doug looked like he'd aged a hundred years in only a few minutes when he said, "I've been to war, and fought in combat. I've seen the bad things we're capable of doing to each other. But never such as this. Never have I looked at pure evil. Not like what's over there, in that re-frigerator. Only an honest-to-God monster is capable of doing what's been done to those poor old folks."

I waited a bit, before I said, "Are you done taking photos?"

Doug bit into the last piece of his chocolate, chewed, swallowed, and said, as he wadded up the wrapper and stuck it in his camera bag, "Yeah. I am. Unless you want the inside of the store, shelf by shelf . . ."

I thought about it for a moment, then said, "No. I don't think that's necessary, as long as you've taken general interior shots."

Sikes nodded. "I have."

"What about the fingerprint techs?"

"They're done too. Once we figured out the killers wore gloves, there wasn't much point in doing any more dusting."

"Yeah. I agree. Is there anything else you can think of that we should do . . ."

He paused, reflecting about it, then shook his head. "No. I don't believe there is."

"Okay. Would you get the pictures to me as fast as possible, and let the coroner's men know that they can take the bodies out now. Better give 'em a hint about what they're in for too."

The seasoned old investigator looked at me with what I thought was pity in his eyes. He said, "This is going to be an enormous and controversial case Jake. It's the kind of situation that can make or break your career . . . and it's the kind of crime that can destroy you from the inside out . . . because it gets so deep in your head that it tortures you until you go nuts. It'll also go political right away. Those asshole politicians at the City Council will cut you up for chum as soon as they smell blood in the water . . . when the story gets out. As soon as the press starts stirring the public up, those fuckers in City Hall will look for a scapegoat. You. As the lead, you'll be the one in the headlines Jake. I wish you all the luck, 'cause you're damn sure gonna need it."

Doug hopped off the counter and started to collect his gear.

I said, "Thanks for telling me that. It helps to know somebody has my back, and I won't forget what you said."

Sikes was disappearing into the interior gloom toward the back of the store. He stopped, turned to face me, and said, "Oh, I ain't got your back son. My run with the CSPD is about over. But yours is just startin' and I wanted to pass on some advice I got from a hard old copper, back when I was a young buck like you. Be careful who ya trust. Things ain't always what they seem around the department." And then he turned again, and was gone.

I stepped behind the counter to get the telephone, located on a shelf under the register next to the paper bags and pulled it out . . . called HQ over on east Kiowa Street. It was time to get hold of Lieutenant Patterson. I needed reinforcements. I needed a clue. And I needed some kind of a break, if I was ever going to catch whoever was responsible for the abomination that had taken place here.

When Patterson answered, I said, "Loot, it's McKern. I'm over on Spruce Street, at a double homicide. We're having issues with crowd control and the press. I've got six uniformed officers and could use that many more. I . . ."

Lt. Patterson cut me off. He said, "I know you're up to your cajones in crocodiles, Jake. The phones been ringing off the hook ever since I got here at six-thirty. We've been goin' nuts all day. Tell me what you've got so far."

I took a breath, then another. I jammed the phone between my shoulder and neck, so I could use my hands to light another smoke while I reported. "We have two victims, a man and a woman named Abraham and Ruth Sowell, ages are undetermined, but they appear to be in their mid-sixties. They were killed in their bed upstairs with a small caliber handgun. Both were shot execution style: two rounds in the chest and one in the forehead. The bodies were stripped, rolled in blankets, and carried downstairs, where they were hung in the storage cooler and flayed. I'd guess that at least three-quarters of the epidermis is gone, and both bodies are mutilated; his genitals; her breasts. The apartment was tossed, but no apparent thefts. The killers appear to be a team of professionals—who've done it before. There are no fingerprints, nothing left behind and no witnesses. The reporting party found them hanging in the cooler. That's it, except for this. Harry Bucklin showed up and promptly puked all over himself, the victims, the meat locker and then tracked his puke through the grocery and all the way out to his car." I thought about mentioning the threat Bucklin made, but kept it to myself.

"How in God's name did HE get there?"

"You tell me. The whole scene is compromised Loot. Everybody's walked around, in or through it."

"Okay Jake. Tell the newsies that we'll have a press release for them early this evening. I can't send ya any more help. We're up against it over here too."

"I figured as much, but thought I'd ask anyway."

"Good. I'll brief Captain Duncan, and let him know what's going on over there. And Jake . . . welcome to Robbery-Homicide."

The dial tone let me know that Lieutenant Patterson had hung up, I sighed, put the black Bakelite handset in its cradle, and went back to work.

Chapter 8

The only useful thing I came up with after rooting around in the bottom cash register drawer, was a list of suppliers and a ledger of accounts receivable. I took both of them, planning to contact each of the entries, in hopes of learning any information about the Sorwells. After tagging the pair of books I bagged them as evidence and went to check on the morgue attendants to see if they'd finished with the removals.

I caught up with them outside, just as they'd begun to back their panel truck up and leave. I quick-stepped over and tapped on the passenger's window to get their attention. When he rolled it down, I recognized Keith White from a traffic fatality we'd worked together this past summer. The driver was unknown to me, but all of our departments, like the city itself, were growing like mushrooms after an overnight rain. It wasn't unusual to meet strangers on the job.

Keith recognized me. Said, "Jake, it's good to see you up and around. I thought you were gonna be my next customer the last time I saw you, laying in the middle of Tejon Street with your leg all torn up. You were a mess. I thought you were deader'n a door nail."

I grinned for the first time in what seemed like a long while. "Well, to tell ya the truth, I damn near was. I didn't even know you were on the scene. Last thing I remember was seeing that bone sticking out and a corpsman stickin' a needle in me."

"It was one helluva damn day," Keith said. He pointed to the driver beside him and added, "This is my associate and helper, Reggie Kelley."

I nodded a greeting and Keith continued. "And this guy's a hero, Reggie. Jake's the one who shot it out with a gang of ex-cons that were tryin' to rob the payroll for the Air Force Academy construction crew last fall . . ."

"YOU'RE THAT GUY?" Kelly said.

"'Fraid so."

"This is the toughest lawman since Gary Cooper came to town in *High Noon*," Keith said. "He's the real deal. It's a fact."

"Jeeze, Keith," I said, "knock it off. I ain't no big deal."

"Sure Jake."

"I could use your help though. I got into a ding-dong a little while ago with Harry Bucklin . . ."

"He's an asshole."

"He's also the coroner, and the one who barfed all over the crime scene. It upset his plans for the rest of the day and I think he took it personally."

"I'll bet he did," Keith White said with a grin. "How can we help you?"

"Expedite the autopsies and make sure the reports don't get lost or held up."

"I'll do my best Jake."

"Much obliged. Do you happen to know who the cutter's going to be?"

"Not off hand, but if I had to make a guess, it'll be the newest one, Dr. Chapin."

"Never heard of him."

"Her. She's a licensed Forensic Pathologist. First name is Alta, and she just graduated from the University of Montana with honors."

I took a last drag on my coffin nail, bent down and stubbed it out on the sole of my right boot. I stood up and said, "How come you know so much about her?"

Keith blushed, and said, "She's hot. All the docs and lab technicians are talking about her . . . and all the secretaries are jealous because she's so good-looking. She's nice too. Not stuck-up or snooty."

"Why Keith White . . . have you got a crush on her?"

"Me? Oh, No. No Jake. I've heard folks talking is all."

I squinted at him as I pulled out one of my cards and handed it through the window, "Give this to her, would you please . . . and ask her to call me."

"What if she's not the one who gets the autopsy assignment?"

"Give it to whoever does. I need the results ASAP. Got it?"

"Yeah."

As I watched them drive away, so very slow and carefully down the alley and disappear into the flow of downtown traffic, I found myself wondering if they were doing that out of respect for the victims . . . or because they were being paid by the hour. *Such is the inherent cynicism of the law enforcement professional*; I thought as I walked up the street to find Andy Claypoole. *Jesus, Mary and Joseph, Jake . . . get ahold of yourself . . .*

Claypoole had moved over to the sidewalk by the time I found him, where he was in an animated *tête-à-tête* with an attractive blonde woman in a red wool coat that sported a hood, and wooden toggle buttons. Andy was facing away from me as I walked up behind him, so I couldn't quite make out what he was saying. But I couldn't miss her answer.

"Why Sergeant Claypoole, that's so interesting and helpful too. May I quote you on it?"

"Quote him on what?" I said as I came near and interrupted them.

"Just some background stuff," Claypoole said.

"Such as . . ."

"Wait a minute," the woman said, "who are you?"

"Jake McKern," I said, showing her the gold shield that was clipped to my belt.

"I'm the lead investigator here. So, who are you and what are you doing here?"

"Agnes Bedwell. My job."

"Which is what, Madam?"

"It's Miss, not Madam. I've never been married. And I'm a reporter for KRDO News."

"Well, isn't that special," I said, only then noticing a small microphone in her left hand and the thin black wire connecting it to a miniature battery-operated tape recorder in her coat pocket. "Are you recording this . . . is that a tape recorder?"

"Maybe . . ."

"Maybe my ass. Give it to me or . . ."

"Or what? I'm allowed to . . ."

"You can either hand it over, or I'll run ya in for interference. Impeding a criminal investigation and obstruction."

She bit her lip, and I felt bad. Then a fat tear escaped one eye and I almost relented. I felt so damn bad . . . but then she reached in her pocket and withdrew a small Motorola tape recorder. She turned it off and handed it to me. I was only going to remove the tape reels and give it back, but she leaned in close, said, "Bastard," and stalked off.

I didn't know it at the time, but I had just met one of my future ex-wives.

Chapter 9

I stood there, holding the confiscated recording device, and feeling like an asshole, when I noticed the smirk on Claypoole's face. "I expected more professionalism from you, Andy. How much did you spill to her?"

"Just what I told you, Chief. Background."

"Well," I said, hefting the recorder in one hand and wiggling it back and forth, "we'll soon know for sure, won't we."

Claypoole snorted derisively and busied himself lighting up a smoke.

I tried to save as much face as I could and reassert control at the same time. "I'm through here. You secure the building, lock it, and have the place sealed. Do you think we need to post a guard on it?"

"Short-handed as we are . . . I doubt the brass will let that stick."

"We can try. Leave a car out front and a uniformed officer for the rest of the shift. Nail the back door shut if you have to, else we'll have a ton of vandalism going on before you know it."

"Okay. Anything else?"

"Yeah," I said. "Where's Dunlap and his trainee? I set them to canvassing a while ago."

"Dunno," Claypoole said. "I've been too busy out here to pay much attention."

"I see," I said. "Let's wrap it up then. Post someone out front and put the others back in service."

A laconic nod and surly wave was all the response I got. Claypoole turned one way at the same time I turned the other, and we both started our different tasks.

I reentered the store and checked that the keys I'd picked up in the apartment locked the front door; which they did. I gave them to the fingerprint guys, who were hanging around without anything to do; told the pair to tag the whole bunch into evidence and lock the upstairs door, then seal it with crime scene tape. After that was done, they were free to go back to the lab. I took a last glance inside, hoping I'd be able to think of a new idea, or somehow re-evaluate the scant bit of information we'd gathered thus far and, like Sherlock, be able to use deductive reasoning skills to figure out who did it . . . but nothing came to mind. I got in my beater of an unmarked car, tossed the tape recorder on the seat, and left in a cloud of blue smoke to find Dunlap and Magness, the new guy. I remember thinking at the time, *This sure ain't like the movies . . .*

I stopped at the end of the alley to tell Donnie Brearley that we were done here and see if he knew where I might find the pair of door-knockers. He pointed toward Mesa Road with his thumb and said, "I believe they're working their way up to Walnut Street and back. I saw them a little bit ago."

"Thanks. Take care of yourself."

"You too Jake."

I watched Donnie in the rearview mirror as I drove out of the alley and turned west on Mesa Road . . . he looked like his best friend had just died and he was in the middle of the worst day of his life . . . which it truly was. But I thought it was something else too, something more, something that happens to every one of us who pins on a badge and swears to protect and serve. And that something else is this: at some point in every cop's life he—or she, because lady cops are on the way sooner or later—will be in such close proximity to evil that they feel touched by it. It makes you want to go home and scrub yourself with kerosene and a stiff brush to get the awful stink of evil off your body. It's the one case you can't ever forget. It's the one that makes you awaken in the middle of the night and question God.

I made a mental note to look Donnie up on our off-duty hours and have a beer with him. Somehow, I never found the time. Then he was KIA and I never got the chance. I regret that very much.

I cruised the short block that made up Mesa, and turned around on Walnut before I saw the pair of CSPD officers emerging from the side yard of a two-story gray house that had seen better days. I coasted over to the curb and met them at the sidewalk.

Jim Dunlap gave me a nod by way of greeting and got in the front seat. Amos Magness climbed in the back, blowing into his hands to shake off the cold. I left the motor running and turned on the heat to help them warm up. In typical March fashion, some dark clouds had blown in over Pikes Peak, the temperature dropped twenty-plus degrees—down into the mid-thirties—and it looked like it could start snowing any minute.

I cracked open my wing window and fired up a smoke, figuring to give them a few moments to warm up, but Dunlap had other ideas.

Without preamble, he said, "We ain't havin' no luck gettin' any information Jake. Either the suspects were ghosts of some kind, or demons, that dug themselfs up outta the ground an' done their dirty work, then went back where they come from. I ain't ever seen so damn many cases of no see-ums, no hear-ums, and no speaks-ums since St. Mary's boys basketball team got caught on a panty raid in the girl's locker room back in nineteen and forty-nine."

In spite of the dire circumstances, I couldn't suppress a grin . . .

Magness chortled in the back seat.

"Somethin' funny?" Dunlap said

"No suh," Magness managed to croak out with his body rigid and his brown eyes facing straight ahead. "No suh. Nuthin' funny at all."

I caught the brief flash of anger that crossed the young man's face in the rearview mirror, but let it pass. I wouldn't be around later, keeping Dunlap in check, and I didn't want to make things worse by calling him out about his treatment of the rookie. I had enough on my hands to deal with . . . and from the look of him, Amos Magness was willing and able to handle whatever came his way. He was a smart, polished, and tough new recruit . . . and exactly what we needed on the CSPD at that time.

Chapter 10

After a few more minutes of chit-chat and general bullshitting with Dunlap, during which time I learned nothing of any value about what would soon be called *The Skin Ripper Case,* I had to move on. I'd had my fill of Dunlap's peckerwood philosophy and general commentaries on all that was wrong with our country and how to fix it. By then, my right leg was sending a pain message to my brain that was increasing in frequency and intensity with every passing hour, despite the many aspirins I'd been swallowing throughout the morning like candy. The combination of being on my feet all day and the cold front moving in was taking a toll. I had to find something stronger pretty soon if I was going to continue functioning and still be able to do my job.

When Dunlap finally paused long enough to take a breath as I was putting my cigarette out in the ashtray, I said, "Okay Jim, I gotta go. You and Amos check the rest of the neighbors to the south, on both sides of the alley, all the way to the end of the block. Call me if you get any hits and I'll take it from there. And thanks for the help."

"It's the middle of the afternoon. You gonna authorize overtime for me?"

"Sure, thing Jim. Absolutely. Amos, I'm pleased to meet you. Welcome to the department."

"You too, Sir." The young man was stone faced as he climbed out of the car and went back to work. If Dunlap heard the purposeful change in speech, he didn't indicate it . . . but I did. I thought that Magness was more than he appeared to be. I decided to stay in touch with him in the future.

My gut was reminding me that I hadn't put anything other than caffeine and aspirins into it for almost twenty-four hours when I pulled into the Pancake House parking lot at Walnut and west Colorado Avenue. Despite the name, it had a full menu, plus, it was fast, cheap, and filling. All of us cops ate there, and it was close to my current location.

I had barely sat down in the last window booth—with my back to the wall so I could stretch my right leg out and watch the front door at the same time—when Maggie Johnson brought me coffee and a mimeographed sheet with the daily specials on it. I pushed the paper back to her and said, "Hi. Beautiful. I know it's between dining hours, but do you think I could get a hamburger steak with some home fries and a large glass of milk?"

Maggie, a stocky woman about twice my age who was supporting herself after her husband was killed in a mining accident, said, "Jake Honey, flattery like that'll getya the whole damn kitchen. Hell, I'll cook it myself if I have to . . ."

"Thanks. Sometimes I forget my own powers of persuasion."

She finished writing my order on her pad, stuck the pencil in her hair and said, "Oh, it ain't persuasion Honey, it's all that manliness just-a-boilin' right off of ya that makes a girl's heart go pitter-pat, pitter-pat, pitter-pat."

I blushed, and Maggie smiled as she walked away, chuckling to herself, and clearly one up on me in the sass department. I got to my feet, headed for the washroom and the pay phone to see if Nurse Gloria was around. I had to get something to relieve the constant throbbing pain in my right femur, where it felt like a whole squad of demons was beating on me with sledgehammers. Aspirin just wasn't up to the job.

I sat down in the mahogany paneled phone booth and closed the folding door. The light came on and I took the phone off the hook, dropped a dime in the slot and heard the dial tone begin after the silver coin tinkled down into the built-in coin box. Then I dialed Nurse Gloria's number from memory. Lady Luck—or maybe it was old Mephistopheles himself, considering the path that that fateful call started me down—was with me. Gloria answered on the third ring. I said, "Hello, Nurse Gloria . . . this is your old patient, Jake McKern."

"Jakey . . . the man on the flying trapeze . . . I'll never forget you, Honey."

She was referring to the traction tower my right leg was held in for almost three months. It had weights, ropes on pulley wheels and a stainless-steel bar that hung down on two chains for me to pull myself up on. I smiled and said, "Yeah. How well I remember that. It hurt like a sonofabitch."

"It's supposed to. Otherwise, one leg would be shorter than the other. And crooked too. You still married to, uh . . . what's her name?"

"Imogene. Yeah, 'fraid so."

"That's too bad. How's the leg . . . and why haven't I heard from you in so long?"

I thought a bit before I said anything, because there were two or three ways to screw this up. I didn't want to make things any worse than they already were with Mo, and I didn't want to start something with Nurse Gloria. But I had to get some pain relief without going through the regular channels and procedures. Then it would have to be reported. It'd go into my work file . . . and I'd be unemployed. You can't be less than one hundred percent or on heavy duty drugs and remain on the job. I'd be suspended . . . or fired. I said, "To be honest, I've been trying to keep it together with Mo, and it ain't goin' too red hot. My leg is hurtin' so damn bad I almost want to cry. I was hoping you could help me out from that secret stash of yours, because it's the only way I'll be able to stay on the job, or . . ."

I could hear her moving around, then the flaring of a match as she lit one of those nasty menthol cigarettes Gloria liked so well. She inhaled, and said, "Are you telling me that you're back at work already?"

"Yeah."

"Are you nuts or something? Didn't the doctors tell you to stay off of it . . . ease back into full-time duty . . . around June or thereabouts?"

"Yeah. It's what they recommended, but we're really short of personnel on the department right now. I'm on my first case as lead detective . . . and to tell you the honest-to-God truth . . . being around the house all day wouldn't be a good idea, if you know what I mean."

"I do. And you're a damn fool, Jake McKern. A stupid, stubborn, hard-headed imbecile."

"Hey. I'm Irish. Dumb-assery runs in my genes."

"You're right about that. Come over to my place. I'll see what I can do…

Chapter 11

I hung up the phone and limped back to my seat by the window, just settling in at the same time Maggie appeared with a steaming platter of food. She leaned over and put it on the table next to the tall glass of milk that had arrived while I was away from the booth. As she straightened back up, she said, "You ok hon? You're favoring that leg pretty good."

"Oh, yeah, Mags. I'm as right as rain."

"Bullshit, sonny. I know pain when I see it . . . Ed used to come home from work covered in coal dust, all stooped over and limpin' like that from workin' in the seams for twelve hours, all underground."

I put a dose of ketchup on my meat and potatoes, plus some butter on the roll that came with dinner and said, "It's still healing and I've been on it since early this morning. It's why I'm eating so late, but I'm okay. Really. I am." As if to add emphasis, I dug into my meal and went on with a cheekful of food, "Thanks for this. It's really good."

Maggie was adding up my check. She finished and flopped it facedown on the table, said, "People's been in here all day, speculatin' and askin' me about the going's on over there on Spruce Street. It's all they've been talkin' about. You ain't on that case by any chance, are yuh?"

I cut another piece of meat, slid it through the condiment and forked it in to give me time to think. Chewed, swallowed, and washed it down with milk before I said, "Yeah. I am."

"Can you tell me what's happened?"

"Some. Not much . . . it's an ongoing situation and we're still investigating. I can tell you though, that two people were murdered.

33

There's gonna be a press release from the police department this evening. It'll be on the news."

"Was it the Sorwells? Abe and Ruth? I know them. Nice folks. Oh, don't tell me it's them. They come in here all the time. He kids me about this not being a kosher kitchen . . . that they shouldn't eat here, where milk and meat come from the same refrigerator, *and pork,* he'd laugh and say, *ye Gods . . . go ahead and give me the waffles with ham and eggs over easy on the side. I'm really hungry.* Please don't tell me it's them."

I nodded.

Maggie coughed, hiccupped, then turned and walked away without another word. I looked down at my half-eaten meal, but couldn't touch another bite. I stuck a five under the plate for a tip and a couple of singles plus some coins to cover the bill . . . then got up and left.

Nurse Gloria lived in a one and a-half story Sears kit home that she'd inherited from her parents. It was located over on west Kiowa at Seventeenth Street, in the part of town known as Old Colorado City. It was the territorial capital for a short time in 1859, before it was moved to Denver, and the whole area was swallowed up and annexed into the bigger city of Colorado Springs in 1917. In any case, it was less than a mile from the restaurant, and I pulled over and parked beside her garage in the alley behind her house, less than ten minutes later.

I took a deep breath and got out of the car—trying not to think too hard about the ethics of the line I was about to cross—then limped through the back yard and up on the little porch, where a discarded wringer washing machine and an abandoned green velour couch with a big orange cat in residence, all sat waiting for judgment day. The husky feline looked at me for a second, yawned, then curled into a tight ball in one corner of the sofa and went back to sleep with a paw over its eyes. I smiled. Knocked. Waited for Nurse Gloria to come and answer. I shifted my weight from one foot to the other . . . nervous as the groom at a shotgun wedding, with fatherhood imminent.

I was about to knock a second time, when Nurse Gloria, all five feet of her, appeared and stood there, framed in the entryway glass. "Well look what the cat dragged in," she said, as she stood aside and opened the door. "It's that big old Irish laddie I remember so well. Please. Don't be shy . . . come in."

I hesitated, torn inside by an emotional hurricane. I couldn't deny the allure I felt for this tiny woman with the raven's wing black hair that fell past her hips. It was she who'd nursed my broken body back from the point of no return to its present state of near health. But I was still married to Imogene, a woman I'd wedded impulsively when we met in college after I came back from the service and the war. We'd only known each other a few months, were only man and wife for a couple of months more when Scottie was born. We no longer cared for each other—if we ever did—and once the sex wore off, the infatuation did too . . . but I still felt compelled by some misguided sense of honor to keep our wedding vows, even though I'd broken them before. All of that flashed through my mind in less than a second. Then I stepped across the portal, into the first circle of my own individual Hell. Looking back on it now with the perspective of forty some years, I can honestly say that the ride was brief, the penalty steep . . . but sweet suffering Jesus . . . the thrill was indescribable.

As I walked into the neat little galley type kitchen, Gloria said, "It's okay Jake. I ain't gonna bite ya. Come on in and have a seat." She pointed to a table for two that sat under a side window and overlooked the driveway and porte-cochere that was built on after the house was assembled. Back in the 1920s, the do-it-yourself homes that came in a box on a railcar from Sears-Roebuck or Montgomery Wards were all the rage. They were peppered throughout the westside, where hard working folks demanded the most for their money. Gloria's father, a millhand at the Golden Cycle Crusher, was one of them.

I sat and said, as I fumbled through my pockets for a cigarette and matches, "I'm sorry, but I can't stay. I'm AWOL right now, and I've gotta get downtown before the brass realizes I ain't where I am supposed to be."

"Where's that?"

"A double murder over on Spruce Street."

Gloria sat in the other chair and put a ceramic ashtray in the center of the Formica table. She said, "Why you?"

"I'm the lead investigator. It's my first case too. I'll be working late."

Gloria lit a cigarette of her own, took a big drag and exhaled a long thin stream of mentholated tobacco smoke without ever taking her eyes off me. Finally, she said, "So, if I understand you right, all you want from me is to mooch some drugs and go. What do I get out of it?"

Chapter 12

Nurse Gloria's question caught me so unprepared that I was struck dumb for a moment. I couldn't have been more surprised if Rita Hayworth herself had flown in the door on a broomstick, stark naked.

Gloria was leaned back in her chair with her legs splayed out in front, her left hand cupping her right elbow as she smoked and watched me with all the intensity of a necromancer, waiting for the spell to work . . . and the dead to rise.

The silence dragged on for most of a minute, while my brain scrambled to find purchase enough to cause my mouth to open, and my voice to speak. I said, "That depends, I guess, on what you want. Do you know?"

She looked at me with her glittering, almond-shaped Sino-Hispanic eyes. Eyes that held such intensity in them, it looked like they could bore holes in half-inch steel plate, and said, "Yeah Jake, I know what I want. I know exactly. I want to see more of you . . . and I want your respect. You never even said good-bye to me when you checked out of the hospital. Never called, never looked me up at work, treated me like shit. Jakey hit-and-run. Mr. love 'em and leave 'em himself . . . until he wants something. Then he comes slinking around like a mangy old coydog, mooching for a free meal."

I was careful with what I said next. I didn't want to complicate her life, or inject it with my problems . . . plus I couldn't handle a romantic entanglement on top of everything else that was going on in my world at the time. It was a revelation to me that Nurse Gloria had taken what happened between us when I was laying in the hospital so much to heart.

All those thoughts crashed through my brain like a summer thunderstorm before I collected them together. I said, "Until this very moment, I had no idea you felt like that. And I want you to know, I'd cut my arm off before I would hurt you on purpose. I honestly thought you were just having a fling—a dalliance—with me at a time when we were both lonesome and needy. I was wrong Gloria, and I'm sorry for assuming so much. I came here as a friend, because I knew you had that hoard of drug samples and could do it off the books. I shouldn't have." I put out my cigarette and started to stand, adding, "I'll go now. I hope you'll accept my apology . . . and forget this ever happened."

I wasn't quite to my feet when Gloria stopped me.

She put her hands on my shoulders and said, "Sit. Down."

When I did, she sat on my lap with her legs outside of mine, pressed her chest against me and put her arms around my neck. She laid her head on my shoulder and nuzzled that tender spot below my ear as she kissed me there and whispered, *"I love you, Jake."*

At that point all my resolutions, all my reservations . . . and every bit of my resistance . . . flew right out the window and disappeared.

All the way downtown to the police department in City Hall, at 212 east Kiowa, with six lovely gray and ivory colored *pain-be-gone* capsules inside an aspirin tin in my shirt pocket, I wondered about myself. *Do I lack ethics? Am I morally corrupt? Maybe I'm just weak,* I thought as I turned off Weber Street, into the cop-car parking lot in back of the station. Behind me, I was still laying down a thin smoke screen from the worn-out motor in the sorry-assed old beater I'd been assigned to drive. *But whatever it is, the guilt is overwhelming. It's crushing me.*

It was six o'clock when I came in the front door. Counting the time I'd taken to eat, I'd been out-of-pocket for almost three hours. I got to my desk upstairs, where there were five pink message slips waiting. One was from Dunlap, another from Magness, and three from Imogene.

I took the path of least resistance and called Dunlap first. His voice sounded slurred when he picked up the phone on the fifth ring. "Jim, it's McKern, getting back to you. Did you do any good canvassing the area?"

"Not a damn bit. I ain't even sure they wudda told me anythin' anyhow."

"Anything else?"

"Nah. Was a waste of time, ya ask me . . . what about my overtime?"

"Put it in through the regular channel is all I can tell you. I gotta go." I hung up before he could answer. Then I dialed his trainee, Amos Magness.

"Hello," he said, in between the first and second rings. "This is Amos."

"Magness this is Jake McKern."

"Yessir, Captain. I wanted to report back to you about the door knocking I did this afternoon."

"Okay, but my name's Jake and I ain't a captain. I'm a plain old P-3, just the same as Dunlap and most the rest of us on the force who aren't sergeants. So, what can you tell me?"

"Dunlap's a prick . . ."

In spite of the mounting tension, the job pressure and personal stress I was under, Magness's candid comeback hit me square in the sense of humor. I couldn't stifle the giggle that turned into a chuckle, then an all-out gale of laughter. I couldn't help myself. And for a few seconds, I let it go. When I got myself back under control, I said, "Truer words were never spoken, Amos. But let's keep it between you and me. How much longer are you probationary?"

"First of the month, if I make it that long with that cracker motherfucker."

I cradled the phone between my shoulder and ear, used both hands to light one up. "I hope you do. It's a good job, steady pay and not everybody's like Dunlap. The Department needs men such as yourself. I can't walk in your shoes, but a couple of weeks ain't so awful long."

"So, you say. But you ain't never been treated like Step'n'fetchit neither."

"Best I can tell ya is, we ain't all like that Amos."

"Oh, shit," he said, as I heard him light one of his own, a cigar by the sound of it. "Call me 'Rags,' like all the rest of my friends do . . ."

"Why Rags," I said.

"Cause I'm always on the rag about somethin' or other, according to them. But let me tell you about the canvas . . ."

And just like that I was back up to my ass in butchery.

The images of those two bodies hanging in a meat locker still haunts me today.

Chapter 13

Amos "Rags" Magness said, "Dunlap and I went up and down both sides of the alley behind the Spruce Street Grocery Store without turning anything up. It was all no answer, not home, nope, no see or hear, just like Dunlap said. But, after Sergeant Claypoole closed the place up and everybody left, Dunlap told me to keep on door knocking, while he went for a nap in the squad car. I went back to all of the no answer addresses, thinking some of them might have been in the group of onlookers and got a few more responders, but no leads. Then, as I was about to give it up, a negro man walking his dog stopped me. He asked what I was doing and I told him. He said he was worried about the Sorwells after he saw an unknown car leaving about four in the morning. He said it was black and he thought it looked like one of them German staff cars in the war."

"He say anything else?"

"No. That was it."

I felt Magness was holding back on me but I let it go for the time being. I got the good citizen's name and contact information and thanked Magness for going the extra mile.

After I hung up the phone, I went down to the break room, pumped the last of my change into the machines, and got a Coca-Cola, along with a Baby Ruth candy bar for my supper. Then I went back to my desk, and tried to call Mo. I was relieved when she didn't answer. *Must be in the yard,* I thought at the time, and got busy calling every person in the accounts receivable ledger, followed by all the store's suppliers.

Four hours later, all I had to show for my efforts was an ashtray full of Lucky Strike butts smoked right down to the nub, five pages full of random doodles, condolences, and unsolicited comments about how well-liked and respected the Sorwells were, as well as many promises to 'Help in any way we can.' *Yeah,* my own cynical self kept whispering in the back of my head. *Fat chance of that ever happening . . .*

By 10:30, the pain meds I swallowed at Nurse Gloria's place were wearing off and my leg was throbbing in sync with each beat of my heart. The pain was ramping up so much that it was starting to drive every other thought out of my head. I put the murder book I'd started to assemble, along with the store receivables, in my desk drawer, locked up and packed it in for the day . . . exhausted.

I'd gotten lucky. There wasn't much activity around the station that night. I hadn't had to account for my whereabouts, or go over the case details three or four times with any of the other guys who had seniority on me. I snuck out the back door and hobbled over to the sorriest ride in the entire Colorado Springs Police Department and slid in . . . while my right leg kept singing a dirty little ditty of pain, over and over, and over. I fired the engine and headed for home, leaving a thin trail of smoke in my wake.

There were no lights on when I rolled up in front of the little two-bedroom house we rented on south Seventh Street. There wasn't any light from the street either, so I stumbled up the steps to the walk and onto the porch . . . cursing under my breath the whole way . . . thinking, *Why the fuck didn't she leave a light on?* I had to light a half-dozen matches to get enough illumination to find the right key and get the damned front door open. I got in after a bit, found the light switch and flipped it on. I shut and locked the door, closed the curtains, and took off my jacket before I realized something didn't feel right. I went in the kitchen to get a beer and scrounge around in the icebox for something to eat, but the pickings were slim. I dug out a bottle of Coors and a dried-up pork chop from supper several days ago. I nudged the door shut with my hip, stuck the chop in my teeth and opened the beer with a metal church key from the silverware drawer. It was only then that I saw the note from Mo, laying on the kitchen table.

Oh shit . . . was all that went through my mind as I pulled out a chair, sat down and started to read. There was no mistaking Mo's fussy handwriting . . .

Dear Jake,

I've been trying to reach you all morning. I've called and called but you've never called me back. There's been an emergency. Mother and Daddy are missing. They were down in Louisiana somewhere looking at some oil prospects Daddy was thinking of buying. They were supposed to be back in Houston last night but they never made it. They were in that funny looking airplane Daddy likes so much. The one with the V thing in back instead of a regular tail. Mr. Grinder called me early this morning from Daddy's office and delivered the news. They want me in Houston right away. He arranged a charter flight for Scottie and me. I'm taking a cab to the Colorado Springs airport. I'll call when I know more. I hope I can reach you.

Your wife,

Imogene

I dropped Mo's note on the table and swallowed some beer, tossed the pork chop bone at the sink. Almost made it. Watched it drop on the floor with total indifference. When I went to take another sip of Coors however, it was all gone somehow. I got up and fetched more, re-read the message several times as I nursed the brown bottles from Golden, Colorado and thought about family and things.

Mo—Imogene—and I were just a pair of drunken, hell raising college kids in Ft. Collins, Colorado when we met in the late summer of 1946. She was an Art Major about to start her senior year and I was a freshman on the GI Bill, trying to forget the war. A little less than three months later, we were married by a Justice of the Peace in an anonymous ceremony, hardly knowing each other at all. And while I was a dirt-poor Colorado ranch kid, she was Texas Royalty . . . her father was rich.

His name was Big Jim Curdy and he was a legendary wildcatter whose rags-to-riches story was the stuff of every oilman's wet dreams. Back in the twenties, as a young roustabout, Big Jim had partnered up with the father of one of his deceased combat buddies from the first World War. He had the title and mineral rights to a thousand acres of mesquite and snake infested wasteland that sat about forty miles southwest of Big Spring, Texas—the soon-to-be beating heart of the Permian Basin oil region—that he'd won in a poker game. Somehow, through 'Pluck, luck and good fortune,' according to Big Jim, they managed to acquire the pipe, casing, and timber to spud in a well using an old cable drill and walking beam. Five months later, in a last-ditch effort, they brought in Jody Belle Number One, named for Big Jim's wife . . . and Imogene's mother. At 1850 barrels per day, the prodigious well was the beginning of the Chaparral Oil Company and the basis of Curdy's fortune. They were now one of the biggest producers in the Permian Basin, and had gone international, with interests in Saudi Arabia and down in South America.

And now Big Jim and Jody Belle are missing, I thought, and drained the last of the beer, then swallowed another one of the gray and ivory no-more-pain capsules as I wobbled, staggered, and weaved my way toward the empty bedroom. *I hope they're still alive . . .*

I detoured into the bathroom and hit the pot . . . I think I hit the pot . . . I hope I hit the pot. After that I stumbled in and passed out on the bed with all my clothes on.

It was a fitting end to day one of my first-ever murder investigation. My last conscious thought was, *it can't get any worse, can it . . .*

At least I had no nightmares.

Chapter 14

Somehow, I awoke just as the sun was sliding up over the eastern plains with all its usual enthusiasm . . . dazzling us mortals with a sky that was stuffed full of puffy, backlit cumulus clouds and pastel colors . . . proving that the world was still turning and didn't give a shit about McKern or any of his problems. I sighed and rolled out of bed with hammers going off on my skull, eyes that were almost glued together, and a mouth that tasted like I had licked the Devil's ass.

I showered, shaved, and got myself to the PD by seven o'clock, where I was greeted by Wally Bailey from his seat behind the front desk.

"Jake McKern, the man, the myth, the legend in his own mind. I left ya a present, Boyo. On your desk. You're in the news . . . again."

I flipped him the bird, said, "Piss off, Wally," and hustled up the stairs to my desk with his laughter ringing in both of my ears and my right leg beginning its drumbeat of dull pain. *Good thing I ate one of Nurse Gloria's magic capsules when I brushed my teeth,* I thought, *or there's no way of telling how bad it'd get.*

A moment later I wished those gray and ivory beauties worked on mental anguish too, after I saw the morning paper, smack-dab in the center of my gray metal desk where everybody could easily read the screaming twenty-four-point type.

SKIN RIPPER STALKS THE SPRINGS

45

Under Lenny Bragg's byline the text began:

Sometime in the darkest part of the night before last, a vicious, blood-thirsty fiend crept through the streets of our fair city and murdered two innocent, elderly, and beloved residents of the Springs near west side. Abraham and Ruth Sorwell were sleeping peacefully in their bed, secure in the knowledge that the modest apartment that they called home above the neighborhood grocery was their castle, when the slayer broke in and shot them as they dreamed. Then, compounding the horror, the skin was torn from their bodies.

Are we dealing with cannibals? Flesh eating monsters, or Satanists pursuing some kind of cabalistic rite, an evil black mass of some sort? A ceremony known only to themselves and the dark angel himself?

Rookie detective and lead investigator Jake McKern was tight-lipped and unresponsive to this reporter's questions. He looked as if he was confused and wished he were somewhere else . . . (turn to BRAGG ABOUT, pg 6)

All of that was above the fold. Below and in a sidebar, was a photo of me with a cigarette in my mouth as I stared off into the distance, looking bewildered. The copy underneath recapped my shootout with the Lee Roy Morgan gang during the attempted armed robbery of the Air Force Academy payroll from the Colorado Commercial Bank, and the subsequent explosion of the getaway car that broke my leg. All of that took place last November, about five months ago, and ancient history now. *Then I was a hero. Now I'm a zero. So much for fame,* I thought as I dropped the paper into the trash can.

I was retrieving my case notes from the desk drawer when Lieutenant Patterson came by and said, "We're wanted in Captain Duncan's office."

"Right now?"

"Sooner. Bring whatever you have about the Sorwell case."

"It ain't much."

"That doesn't matter. It's your attention to detail and devotion to duty that's the most important."

In other words, I thought to myself, *it don't matter if you catch the kidnapping and mother raping, axe-murdering sonofabitch, so long as your hair's combed, shoes are shined and there's plenty of paperwork, neatly done . . .*

Aloud I said, "Activity don't mean progress, Loot."

He looked at me as if I'd just dropped in from planet Whatthefuck and said, "Yeah. Better step on it. Cap'n's waiting."

Lieutenant George Patterson was a fair and decent man . . . braver than a pack of Siberian wolves too . . . he'd fought his ass off from North Africa to Austria . . . all the way through the mountains of Italy and had almost as many medals as Audie Murphy himself. But, damn. He sure wasn't the brightest brass in the CSPD arsenal . . . which made him, I suppose, the ideal subordinate.

I said, "Lay on, MacDuff, and damned be him that first cries, 'Hold, enough!'"

If George caught on to Macbeth's last words, he didn't say so, and neither of us spoke again as we trudged into Captain Duncan's office like teacher and truant to the school principal.

Without looking up from whatever he was so intent on, Captain said, "Last one in, shut the door."

I compiled and Lt. Patterson and I stood there, waiting for whatever was coming next. It didn't take long.

Captain Duncan finished reading the last page of the papers he held, initialed them with a flourish and tossed everything in the OUT basket on the credenza behind him.

The light caught and flashed on his old-fashioned octagonal eyeglass lenses for a second, before he looked up and pinned me with his steely blue-eyed gaze. "I'm already hearing shit from the Chief this morning about the Sorwell murder you're assigned," he said, without introduction. "And I'm hearing from him because he got roused at six this morning by the mayor, who's hearing from the whole damn city. All of which means that you're gonna hear a whole lotta shit from me. What have you got so far?"

Still standing, I opened my notebook and ran down the entire chain of events, starting with Rufus Gerry, the butter and egg man, and leaving nothing—other than my interlude with Nurse Gloria—out, finished up with the final phone call at 10:20 last night, and shut my trap.

Captain Duncan and Lt. Patterson both listened without interrupting . . . Duncan leaned back in his chair with his hands on his head, and George standing at parade rest with his hands clasped behind his back.

Finished, I said, "That's all for day one."

"Well, it's, not very much," Captain Duncan said, adding, "but I'd like to have seen that asshole Harry Bucklin, puking his guts out after he caught a glimpse of those two hideless Hebrews . . . I'd paid five bucks to see that . . ."

Without caring about the potential repercussions, or damage to my budding career as a detective, I said, "It wasn't quite so funny or entertaining, sir. In fact, I think what was done to those two old people was hideous. It was the act of a monster. A demented, disgusting act of depravity."

Duncan gave me a look that could have impaled an insect to a specimen board . . . and held me there in silence for several long uncomfortable seconds. It was a moment that seemed almost like a lifetime to me. "You done?"

"Yessir," I said, maintaining eye contact with him.

"Nothing more to add?"

I shook my head. "No sir."

"That's good. Because I do. From now on until this case is resolved, and by that, I mean with a suspect in jail, I want your smiling face and insubordinate Irish ass in here first thing every morning, giving me a complete, full, and accurate report of your previous day's activities and progress. You so much as take a shit; I want to know which hand you wiped with. You understand?"

"Written or orally, sir?"

"Both, you smart-mouthed young dickweed. Get out of my sight."

I about-faced and walked out, with Lieutenant Patterson a step behind.

I was halfway to my desk when George said, "Jake . . ."

"Yeah, Loot?"

"Are you nuts? You got a death wish or something?"

I stopped, took a deep breath, and then another, before I said anything. After a few more seconds of silence, I said, "I'm sorry Lieutenant, for not acting better. But that remark he made was just too damned insensitive, callous, and crude. I couldn't not say something back in the face of such bigotry. If you saw those old folks hung there like butchered animals, you'd know."

Patterson didn't say anything else. He just shook his head, patted me on the shoulder and walked away.

As I watched him go, I wondered if I'd still have a job by this time next week.

Chapter 15

I spent the rest of the day going over each and every detail in my notes, no matter how insignificant or minor they appeared. I re-canvassed Spruce and Walnut Streets, Mesa Road, and the alleys in between with no results. Even Amos Magness's lead—the man walking his dog—when asked about specifics, had nothing. He said, "I was sittin' on my back porch drinkin' beer and talkin' to myself and just tryin' to stay warm."

When I asked him how much he'd had to drink, he didn't know exactly, "But a lot. It's the only way I can sleep. The war, y'all see, keep on comin' back at myself."

When I asked him what time it was, he didn't know, 'too dark to see and no watch to keep track of anyways,' were his approximate responses. By then I wasn't bothering with my notes any longer. He was too unreliable. And that's when he came out with the gem, the one tangible thing that was a solid lead I could hang my hat on.

He said, "I remember the car though. Couldn't see it but I could hear it. And I'm pretty sure it was one of those German ones like the officers and dignitaries all ran around in. The engines are real precise. They sound like sewin' machines. And I think it was black. All black. Yessir. Black. I'm sure."

"A Mercedes?" I said.

"Yeah. I believe so. There was several of 'em in it too."

"Do you know how many, exactly?"

"Four men at least," the man said, "maybe as many as five."

His house was on the east side of the alley and had a four-foot-high chain link fence around the backyard. It was five houses south of the grocery and had leafless lilac bushes along the sides, as well as various sizes of barren elm trees that dotted the property and throughout the whole neighborhood. As I noted all of that, I said, "Did the vehicle come down the alley this way?"

"Yeah."

"So, you got a good look at the car and the occupants?"

"No. I didn't," he said, as he looked over my shoulder and started reaching into his pockets for his pipe and tobacco. "When I saw they was headin' this way, I hit the deck and hugged the ground for fear they'd see me and shoot."

"Whatever made you think that?"

"Sixth sense." He said. "It's a survival skill folks my color develop right after we're born."

I looked to see if he was kidding. He wasn't. I handed him one of my cards, asked him to call if he thought of anything else. He pocketed the information and promised he would. I nodded my thanks and left him standing in his front door. His name was Thomas Benham . . . and he was the only witness I had.

When I looked at my watch, I was surprised to see that it was already mid-afternoon. Captain Duncan had notified me, there was a press briefing scheduled for four o'clock at City Hall. He said, "You WILL be there, McKern, as will Mayor Eldridge, Chief Budd, and My-self. You may or may not be at the podium answering questions. Be prepared. Dress appropriately. Look sharp. You'll be representing the entire Colorado Springs Police Department. And whatever you do, for crissakes, be on time. Understand . . ."

Since I was already in the neighborhood, I ducked by my house to put on a fresh shirt and grab a quick shave. I was determined to be as presentable as possible. And, after the hatchet job he'd done on me in the paper that morning, I had hopes of having a few words on the down-low with Mr. Man-About-Town himself, Lenny Bragg. I wanted to look dead-perfect if that opportunity presented itself.

I made it into the station with half an hour to spare, looking like a whole new man with the help of my next-to-last capsule of whatever that stuff was that Nurse Gloria had given me. Trouble was . . . I only had one left . . . and my leg still hurt like hell. I checked for messages, expecting to hear from Mo, but there was no word from her, so I headed to the press conference.

I was stunned when I walked into the meeting area. It was stuffed. Every seat was taken and a standing-room-only crowd was filling the sides and back of the whole room and looked to be four to six people deep. News organizations from every city along the front range were in attendance, and they all started shouting questions at me the moment I stepped foot in the door.

"Hey Jake, tell us about the Skin Ripper."

"Is he a cannibal?"

"How big is he?"

"Where'd he come from?"

"You got any leads?"

"How many are there?"

"Are you close to catching him . . ."

It felt like I said, *No comment* at least a hundred times as I pushed my way through a throng of reporters and a sea of microphones. Flashbulbs were going off in my face every few seconds and the constant click, clack, and whir of SLR auto winders assaulted my ears like a swarm of cicadas hunting for mates, while I made my way up to the podium, where a copse of microphones, Lt. Patterson, and several other suits I didn't recognize, all awaited me.

George nodded a greeting as I climbed the steps leading to the dais, where the speakers would address the crowd. I said, "Jeeze Loot, I feel like an endangered species after running that gauntlet."

He pointed to the side door behind the curtains alongside the stage and said, "Next time, come through there. Makes it much easier." I shrugged, gave him my best silent 'who knew' gesture, and at that exact moment the door opened and hizzoner The Mayor, Robert Eldridge came in. Mayor Bob, as he was known to his constituents, was followed by Jasper John "JJ" Budd, The Chief of Police, who had four silver stars adorning each side of his blue uniform collar. The third and last one in, was the Robbery Homicide Division's own Captain Fred Duncan, whose totally polished and spit-shined appearance made him look just like the desk jockey he was. He strutted in as if he were *the cock o' the walk,* as Ma would say with her soft Irish lilt, *surveying the place for possibilities?*

Mayor Bob wasted no time. He strode up to the microphone and said, "Thank you all for coming. We're here to give you the pertinent details of the double homicide which took place a couple of days ago on the city's near west side, in the area known as Old Colorado City. Our purpose here today, is to clear up some of the misconceptions and plain old mendacities that are being promoted by a certain irresponsible member of the press corps and his editors at a certain newspaper. It's got to stop. Right here. Right now. My office—and all the other City Council members, plus the police department—has been swamped with calls from angry and concerned or scared citizens. You're creating a panic. I'm asking all of you to act responsibly in the public interest. So here, without further jawing from me, is Chief JJ Budd, of the Colorado Springs Police Department."

The Chief got up and put in a few good words for the mayor, then promised to 'Turn the full resources of the CSPD loose on the miscreants who dared to commit such a foul and disgusting crime in the most beautiful city in America . . . his city . . . on his watch. "Make no mistake," JJ said, "it is my solemn vow here, today, that this department, my department, will leave no stone unturned, nor any dark and dank corner un-illuminated until this monster is run down and brought to justice. He will then face the full weight and might of the law. And now, I'm pleased to present Captain Fred Duncan, who's overseeing the actual investigation."

Captain Duncan looked like he'd been chosen by central casting to play the part of the ideal heroic cop when he strutted to the microphones with his ramrod posture, polished accoutrements, and iron demeanor. He stood there for several moments with his hands on the podium's edges, silent, commanding the rapt attention of every individual in the room. Only when he felt everyone watching did he begin to talk.

Damn, I thought, *he's really good at this . . . pay attention Jake, and learn something . . .* I had no idea that I was about to become the sacrificial calf at a wolf, coyote, and crocodile convention.

Chapter 16

When Captain Duncan began his spiel about the who, where and when of the crime, his voice was deep, sonorous and resonate . . . as if he was at ease in front of a crowd . . . but his tone and inflection, as well as his delivery, had an odd metallic cadence and ring to it that I couldn't quite place. It was very slight, nearly undetectable, and so vague that I forgot about it almost immediately, because after he gave a brief rundown of all the publicly known facts of the murder, Captain Duncan said, "So here without further delay, to answer all of your questions, is the lead investigator of the tragedy, Detective Jake McKern."

And just that fast, I was up to my neck in newshounds . . . all of them barking and howling, braying, and snarling, snapping their jaws and just itching to be the first to sink their teeth in my ass.

After a half-hour of questions and answers, during which the questions became more and more repetitive, disrespectful, and outrageous, as well as downright stupid, Chief Budd finally stepped up to the mic and announced that it was over for the time being. He said further announcements would be made as the situation developed in the coming days, the case progressed and events warranted.

If I can make any headway, I thought to myself as I limped out the side door behind all the others, who outranked me. With all the anger and adrenaline I'd dumped into my bloodstream, I'd been able to suppress my hangover and leg pain thus far, but now it was wearing off. And after the workover I'd been given by the press corps, plus the canvassing, the brown bottle flu, and the stress of the situation with Mo, it felt like I'd been mugged by Mighty Joe Young and left to die alongside the road somewhere. I decided I couldn't take any more, and packed it in for the day.

I stopped twice on my way home, to buy a six-pack of Coors and a hamburger sandwich to go. I ate the thing—grease and all—drank most of the beer, then crashed and burned on the couch in front of the TV, right after I'd swallowed the last one of Nurse Gloria's magic pills. I'd have to call her in the morning to see if I could get resupplied.

There was still nothing from Mo. *Hope she and Scottie are all right. Wonder too, how the search for her mother and dad is going . . . I knew that damned Mooney was too much airplane for Big Jim to . . .*

Next thing I knew, it was six o'clock in the morning. The television was still on, buzzing with a target-looking screen image thing. I was stiff, cold, and sore from laying uncovered on the couch all night . . . and had to piss so bad that my tonsils were singing *Anchors Aweigh* . . . I hopped to it and got busy.

Forty minutes later, I was sitting in a booth at the Pancake House with a steaming cup of black coffee in front of me and a hot breakfast on the way. The long-distance calls I'd made to Houston had been un-productive. I talked to Mirabelle Johnson, a live-in housekeeper at the Curdy's, who said she had instructions to refer all callers to the Chap-arral Oil Company Headquarters. When I pressed her about it, about whether Mo and Scottie were there or not, she said, "Mr. McKern, I have been given specific instructions, as I've already told you, to refer any and all callers to the company by Mr. Grinder himself. That is all. That is what I am doing. Goodbye." I heard the phone disconnect, then a dial tone buzzed in my ear.

After that, I tried the corporate phone number and got pretty much the same treatment, except the receptionist did take my name and phone number. She told me she'd relay the message and bid me 'Have a pleasant day' before she too disappeared into the electronic haze. I could tell that something was going on down there, and what-ever it was wasn't good. The only question was, *who was engineering it . . . Mo, her father and mother . . . or that snakey-assed lawyer, Preston Lee Grinder?*

As I sat there smoking, drinking coffee and waiting for my meal, I didn't think it was Big Jim. He and I always got along okay. Jody Belle was another story. She flat-out didn't like me. Thought I wasn't good enough for her Jeannie, Mo's preferred nickname, and it was a major disappointment when her debutante daughter, "Got herself knocked up higher'n a kite, then run off and married the white trash sumbitch what done it."

Like a lot of newly rich folk, I thought, *Jody Belle was so busy adopting the ways and means and airs of the wealthy, that she forgot where she and Big Jim came from.* Personally, I don't give a tinker's damn about their money. The truth is, they fell in shit and came up smelling like roses. They could've just as easily gone bust and lived out the rest of their lives in a ten by sixty-foot trailer someplace . . .

Then, a young lady whose name tag said 'Florence Sue' on it, brought out a steaming platter of ham, eggs over easy, toast and hash browns and put it right in front of me. She said, "Enjoy," filled my coffee mug, dropped the check on the table and sashayed away. I watched the white bow of her apron flutter against her hips like butterfly wings as she walked . . . and appreciated it very much . . . although I don't think that's what she meant. I put out the cigarette and got down to the serious work of eating, knowing it would be the last quiet and pleasant moment of my whole day.

While I ate my first real sit-down meal in what seemed like a long time, I took out my notebook and jotted down the synopsis of my activities from the previous day on some napkins in preparation for the first of my daily ass-reamings from Captain Duncan. *He wanted a written report. I'll give him one. He didn't specify on what, so he'll get 'em on whatever I've got,* I thought, as I ate the last bite of breakfast.

Good thought . . . bad idea . . . one of the most dumb-assed things I ever did in my police career as it turned out.

There were so many cars at the curbs in the 200 block of east Kiowa Street, that the man in the gray Volkswagen had to park on the top of the hill by the First Baptist Church, more than a block away. He got out and took great pains to see that the little car with the high-performance Porsche engine was fully secured. The nondescript man who emerged, matched the commonplace automobile so well that they were almost invisible in a group, able to blend in and just . . . vanish. And, like the vehicle, the driver too was a wolf in sheep's clothing. He was a well-traveled spy, an accomplished assassin and a merciless adversary who'd practiced his craft all over the world. There was a price on his head in several countries, where he was known by a host of different names. So many names, so many places, so many times, he wasn't sure any longer, what his real name ever was. It didn't trouble him though, not in the least. He never cared. He was amoral. He had no conscience, no remorse, and no regret after the fact.

Today his mission was simple.

"Go to the police press briefing and find out what is known about our activities with the juden on Spruce Street," the leader directed.

He was eager to obey.

In the crush of the large crowd, no one, not Jake McKern, nor any of the other trained professional observers took any note of the anonymous man—the average, plain, ordinary man standing at the back of the room next to the door, wearing the brown tweed topcoat and slouch brim hat—who was taking copious notes in his own secret shorthand.

Chapter 17

I thought it was my lucky day when Wally Bailey wasn't at his post to annoy me when I blew in the front door of the station at a few minutes past seven.

That thought didn't last too long. I met him on the stairs. As I was heading up, he was coming down and seemed to be in a good mood for once. He had a slight smile pasted on his face, even gave me a mock salute as he passed by and said, "Mornin' Jake. How's it hangin'?"

Caught by surprise, I mumbled "Hello," and then we'd passed by each other and refocused on our own destinations. I knew why he was so jolly as soon as I saw the *Colorado Springs Gazette* on my desk.

SKIN RIPPER STILL AT LARGE

Screamed the headline. Under Lenny Braggs byline, the text began:

> *No clues. No leads. No suspects. No ideas. No help. No how. Know nothing.*
> *That paragraph sums up exactly what this correspondent learned in the two-hour press conference at City Hall yesterday. After enduring Chamber of Commerce-like civic endorsement speeches by the Mayor, the Chief of Police and the Commander of the Robbery-Homicide Division, lead Detective Jake McKern went to the lectern to "Answer any and all questions about the murders of Abraham and Ruth Sorwell," according to Captain Fred Duncan. McKern responded however, not with informative answers, but more evasions than*

*a drunk preacher, caught in a house of ill repute with a
naked woman on his lap.*

*Meanwhile, the Skin Ripper is still out there, lurking
in The Springs somewhere . . . plotting his next victim
perhaps?* (Turn to BRAGG ABOUT, Pg 5)

I sighed and dropped the paper into the trash, where it belonged,
then headed down the hall for Captain Duncan's office. George Patterson intercepted me.

"He's not there Jake. Come with me."

"What's going on Loot, what's the news?"

"Couple of things," he said, as we headed for his tiny office. "First,
tell me you've got something in writing to show for your activities
yesterday."

"Yeah, I do," I said, as I struggled to maintain his pace with my
bad right leg hurting like a sonofabitch. It wasn't fully healed, and a
greenstick fracture of the femur would've required amputation in the
not-so-distant past. It's the largest single bone in the human body, the
hardest to break and the hardest to heal.

I'd give my right nut just now, for another one of Nurse Gloria's pills,
I thought to myself as we entered George's office and he pointed me to
a chair beside his desk.

"That's good, because Captain Duncan and Chief Budd are both
in Mayor Bob's Office for an off the record butt-chewing. All three
of them are highly peeved about the bad publicity that Bragg guy's
directing against the CSPD. Now it's being picked up and repeated by
newspapers and television stations up and down the front range."

"I didn't know. I don't have time to look at the TV."

"You sure as heck wouldn't like it if you did. They're making all of
us look like a bunch of incompetent fools . . . with you at the top of
the list."

"Do you think maybe that's because I keep getting thrown to the
wolves by my own bosses?" I said, as I took out my pack of Lucky
Strikes and offered one. Lieutenant Patterson took it and I lit us both
up.

We smoked for a bit, then he said, "Do you ever think about how easy you make it for them to do it?"

The question stumped me. "What's your point?" What do you mean by that Loot?"

He looked me in the eyes and said, "Remember smarting off to Captain Duncan the other day?"

"He's a fucking bigot . . ."

"That he is. But what good did it do to call him on it? Think you changed his mind, or his thinking?"

George had me there. I knew he was right but I had a hard time admitting it. The world isn't a perfect place, but it won't ever get any better if no one tries to improve it . . . and how are we supposed to deal with someone like Duncan, when they hold the power of life and death over us? I said, "I know, you're right Loot. It wasn't thought out very well. I shouldn't have popped off like I did."

Patterson took a last puff of his cigarette and stubbed it out. With smoke coming out of his nose and mouth, he said, "Give me your report and clear out of here before the captain gets back. Do you have anything at all to follow up on?"

"Truthfully, no," I said, as I pulled the crumpled pile of Pancake House napkins from my jacket pocket and put them on his desk. "This case is already colder than a mother-in-law's kiss . . . and without some kind of a break, I don't know if it'll ever be solved."

Lieutenant Patterson looked at the pile of napkins that comprised my report and said, "Really Jake? Really? This," he nudged the wad with his index finger, "you're submitting THIS, as your report . . . I can't believe you make it so easy for him. Go. Get outta here."

I didn't say another word. I just stood and left the room before the floor cracked open and swallowed me. I have never since felt more embarrassed and ashamed of my personal behavior. I should have been arrested for criminal stupidity and conduct unbecoming.

As I hurried out the back door that morning, I knew Lieutenant Patterson was sorely disappointed in me, but not as disappointed as I was in myself. All I'd ever wanted after becoming a cop, was to be a detective, and now here I was—after struggling so hard to achieve that goal—in danger of pissing it all away, three days into my first murder investigation

Chapter 18

Without any other ideas, I decided to revisit the crime scene and sift through it with the proverbial fine-toothed comb. *What the hell,* I thought. *I've got everything to gain and nothing to lose . . . and about as much chance of success as finding a diamond in a goat's ass . . . but I still think it's worth trying.*

The Spruce Street Grocery already had a forlorn and forsaken look of abandonment when I drove by it in a spring snow squall. The streets were wet, the heavy flakes melting as soon as they touched down, but at the same time, they were sticking to the tree limbs and lawns and rooftops, covering all else in a mantle of virginal whiteness. As I went around the corner and pulled to a stop at the back door of the closed store however, the allure of the new snow was destroyed by a couple of inches of thick red mud, oozing up from several sets of fresh tire tracks. A few cars or light trucks had passed down the alley and mixed the heavy wet snow with the clay-rich soil which was so prevalent in that part of town, into a slimy red sucking gumbo that was lying in wait to trap the unwary. I moved the unmarked car to the side of the store, hoping for better footing. I was fussy about my clothes back then, and vain about my appearance—as some young people are wont to be—and I was anxious about getting my dressy cowboy boots in the mud . . . or slipping and falling on my ass in it either.

I got out of the car and pussy-footed over to the back door. It had been nailed shut and barred with a couple of two by six planks that were fixed in place with a dozen or more sixteen-penny spikes in each. The door was also posted with paper signs that read, "KEEP OUT.

61

CRIME SCENE. BY ORDER OF CSPD. JJ BUDD, COMMANDING."
in big bold letters. Since all I had with me to gain entrance was the
keys, I'd checked out of the property room where the PD kept all our
evidence, I decided to start in the living quarters on the second floor.

I made my way up the steps with extreme caution. The boots I was
wearing had leather soles that were slippery as shit in the snow, and
the last thing I needed was to go ass over tin teacup back down the
stairway . . . and break my damn leg again.

Fortunately, I made the landing without incident and got inside.
First thing I did was to find the telephone and see if it still worked. It
did. I operated the rotary dial, entering the numbers for Nurse Gloria
with my pen, because my finger wouldn't fit in the little hole, and she
answered on the second ring. "Wow," I said, "that's the fastest I've ever
had anybody pick up . . . were you nesting on it?"

She laughed. "No. I was passing by is all. How are you doing Jake?"

"That's a real saga. You want the long or the short version?"

"Better make it the quick one. I'm on my way to work."

"Without a lead, the murder case I'm on is starting to look like it's
unsolvable. Wife's gone, took my son with her. I'm in trouble with my
boss. I'm being torched by the press. My leg's killing me and I'm out
of those pain capsules you gave me. How're you doing?"

"Waitaminute. Did you just say you've taken ALL the meds I gave
you, just two days ago?"

"Uh-huh. Yeah. I was hoping I could get s'more of 'em . . ."

"Jeezus Jake, those are only supposed to be taken on an as-needed
basis. And even then, no more than one every twenty-four hours.
What I gave you was at least a week's worth. They can do significant
things to your liver and kidneys, and none of 'em are good."

I was sitting in one of the kitchen chairs and had my foot up on
another one. The phone was mounted on the wall next to the table,
with a long cord attached to the handset, I guess so that Mrs. Sorwell
could talk to her friends while she was working in the kitchen. There
was a tin ashtray in the middle of the table—just like at my house—so
I fired up a smoke as we talked. I said, "Well, it just hurts all the time.
What else can I do . . ."

"Stay off it more. The doctor only released you for light duty, as I recall. Why are you going at it so hard?"

"Because it's my first case. Because everyone else is working other crimes. We're short at least two dozen men at the department . . . and because it's what I've always wanted to do, ever since I pinned on the badge. But most of all Gloria, it's because I promised the victims I'd never quit looking until I found their killers."

"Jake, I think that sometimes you're too noble for your own good. Listen, I've gotta go. I'll get you fixed up, but you have to understand, those kinds of drugs are the hardest to get, even the samples. They're painkillers and they're tightly controlled. Everybody keeps an eye on them. Call me tonight. Take aspirins until then. Eat something and drink water. Bye."

I sighed, hung up the phone and went to work . . . trying to find what I didn't know was missing, couldn't define, and might not even exist. *But somewhere in here, I thought, there might be a clue of some kind, a motive perhaps, or even a reason for someone to creep in here at night and kill two harmless old people who didn't appear to be a threat of any kind. I only hope I'm smart enough to know if and when I do see it.*

I started in the kitchen. Since the whole place had already been ransacked, I had to move it all again while I searched, and hope whoever was here first might've overlooked some things I'd find useful. I was methodical and thorough, but five hours later, I had nothing . . . only what I'd started with . . . which was squat.

Tired, sore, and discouraged, I sat down in the middle of the wreckage of two innocent lives and tried to think. My right leg was now white hot with pain. So much so that it was getting harder by the hour to keep my mind focused on what I was doing. I hobbled to the kitchen and threw down a half-dozen of the aspirins I'd pilfered in the bathroom, then cupped my hands and drank from the faucet to wash them down.

In the remains of what was once a neat and orderly galley, I dug around and retrieved a plastic bag. I limped to the refrigerator in search of ice cubes, intending to put them on my leg. It was surprising, but the ice box wasn't ransacked and purred along, doing its intended job of keeping the foodstuffs cold. But the white, round-shouldered Kelvinator also held a cold secret I only found by accident. In the end, it was the key to solving the grisly murders . . . as well as part of the reason for committing them. Even now, some forty years later, as I recreate these events from my old journals, I get a shiver of excitement thinking about that fateful discovery.

Chapter 19

When I tried to pull the aluminum ice cube tray from the freezer compartment however, it wouldn't budge. It was one of those contraptions that had a lever running down the center of it which had to be pulled in order to release the ice cubes. I thought maybe it was stuck somehow, but couldn't see where. There were two of the damned things sitting side-by-side on top of what looked like a big piece of steak, or a roast of some kind, wrapped up in brown waxed butcher paper.

I searched around the room until I found a wooden rolling pin and a pair of flat butter knives, went back to the fridge, and started trying to pry on the ice trays and dislodge them. In a moment of almost blinding insight though, I realized that both trays, and whatever was underneath them, was frozen in place and thought, *Damn Jake, why not do this the easy way* . . . I tracked the power cord to the wall outlet and unplugged it. Retrieved a bottle of root beer from the open door of the refrigerator and popped the cap off on the countertop. Then I sat in the kitchen chair, lit a cigarette, and drank pop while the defrosting process took place.

I couldn't quite imagine what the motive was for the murders, much less the aftermath. It couldn't have been robbery. Looking around the apartment, it didn't seem like there was anything worth stealing. Love, revenge, jealousy . . . it didn't appear to me that any of those applied, and even if they did, it wouldn't account for the butchery after the killings. A feud . . . unlikely . . . but possible. After that, nothing else came to mind.

I picked up the phone, called the department and reported in to

Lt. Patterson. "Loot, it's McKern. I'm at the Spruce Street crime scene, sifting the victims' personal effects. Seeing if we missed anything on the first go-round."

"Anything turn up?"

"No. I've been here all day, going through the upstairs apartment . . ."

"Downstairs?"

"Not yet. But I don't think there's much prospect for discovery. Too many contaminants to be honest. Seems like everybody in town walked in, over and through it before it was blocked off. I'll give another look, just to be sure, but it'll be a real surprise if there's anything to be found."

"I agree. Do what you can. And Jake . . ."

"Sir?"

"Be careful around Captain Duncan. When he saw your activity report on those paper napkins, he went through the roof. Then he chuckled. Said he didn't tell ya how to submit them. I can't tell what he's thinking. But you'd better watch your step. He may be looking to ax your butt or demote you back to patrol."

"I will. And thanks for the warning."

"Be here at oh-eight hundred, all bright and shiny."

"Yessir," I said, but he was already gone. I dropped the rest of my cigarette in the empty soda bottle and went to check the ice trays, hoping to numb my leg pain a little bit.

When I put the old-fashioned table knife under the nearest tray and tapped it with the rolling pin, both it and its mate popped up and slid forward with ease. But when I reached for them, my hand bumped across the wrapped package the ice cubes sat on top of, and realized something was odd. It was off, didn't feel like anything meant to be cooked . . . I was pretty sure it was metal. A box of some kind. I knocked it loose and yanked all three items free.

I plugged the ice box back in, then secured the freezer compartment and the door, and left it humming quietly to itself. After that, I wrangled the ice into a plastic bag and applied it to my aching thigh. I couldn't find anything to keep it in place, so I sat down again and put the bad leg up on the second chair, balanced the ice bag where it hurt the most and started to look at the mysterious brown package marked "Kosher Pork Loin" with a black grease pencil. I got the joke right away and chuckled to myself as I started unpacking it.

It turned out to be a rectangular metal box, about eight by ten inches and four inches thick. It reminded me of the kind of containers movie film comes in . . . the ones where the top slides precisely over the bottom and the contents are protected from most ordinary kinds of damage. When the thing finally came apart after a minute or so of trying, I found a leather-bound, handwritten book. It was wrapped in cotton batting, inserted into a water-resistant oilcloth pouch, and padded in place with tissue paper. I recall thinking at the time, *This must be really meaningful to someone . . .*

I had no inkling I was holding in my hands a piece of national treasure belonging to a newly formed nation, evidence in an international war crimes trial, as well as the solution to a murder case I was working to solve in Colorado Springs. None of that even crossed my mind, because I couldn't understand a single word and I didn't know what to make of it. It was all written in stick-like words . . . a form that reminded me of the Norse mythological legends called the Elder Edda. I'd taken a course on them in college and learned that they were done in a primitive form of early written language known as runes. Runes were believed to have magical powers and were sometimes etched on Viking swords to give the warrior supernatural powers in battle. I thought the book in my hands looked just like them. I've never believed in superstition, paranormal events, or the occult . . . but something, some hunch compelled me to rewrap the hand-written volume and enter it into evidence.

After I tagged and bagged the mystery book, I looked around one last time, then locked the place up and headed for Nurse Gloria's house . . . just as the sun was about to slide down behind the shoulder of Pikes Peak.

I was sitting on the old green couch on her back porch, smoking and petting the orange cat—who was purring on my lap—when she came home with twilight as her close companion.

"His name is Buddy-Boy," Gloria said. "Come on in . . ."

Chapter 20

I was in the house at my desk doing paperwork by six the next morning, feeling really good about myself—and not just because of the new batch of pharmaceuticals Nurse Gloria had laid on me the previous evening, which were working mighty fine, thankyouverymuch—but on account of the fact that together, we'd come up with a plan for mollifying Captain Duncan; second, I hadn't broken my marriage vows last night . . . We'd had a quiet supper together and I was home, alone, in bed and asleep by 8:30 . . . and third, Mo called me early this morning.

Imogene and I talked for about ten minutes, and while she wasn't overly friendly, she wasn't mean, or unfriendly either. Businesslike, I think, best described her. She said that things were really hectic down there, the search was still on for her parents, Scottie was doing fine and she'd write to me in a few days. It didn't register until later . . . that Mo had never asked about me . . . or how I was doing.

By a quarter to eight when George Patterson came in, I had typed log sheets for everything I'd done regarding the Skin Ripper case, from the time of Wally Bailey's call-out four days ago, to the discovery late yesterday, of the arcane, handwritten leather book.

I waited at Patterson's open office door and knocked on the trim, just as he was taking his jacket off and hanging his Tyrolean style plaid hat on the coat tree that stood in the corner of the closet-like space. *If it wasn't for the picture window looking out on the bullpen where all the dicks are,* I thought, *this place would be claustrophobic. It's airless, there's not much light and there's barely enough room for his desk and chair. I wonder how he stands it . . .* "Morning Loot. Something turned up at the apartment on Spruce Street after I talked to you yesterday. It's interesting, but I don't know if its significant or not."

Lieutenant Patterson looked up from his seat behind the desk, "What is it?"

I showed him the book and said, "This was concealed in the freezer compartment of the refrigerator. It looked like Mr. Sorwell went to great lengths to protect, preserve, and hide it. I only found the place where it was secreted by accident, and then it took me a half-hour to chisel it out. It was in plain sight, where it was wrapped up like a roast and frozen in place—I think on purpose—but left to look like an accidental spill of water from the ice trays."

Lt. Patterson handed the box and its contents back to me without opening it. He said as he stood, "Well, whatever it is, it's going to have to wait. Cap'n wants you—and me—standing tall in his office at oh-eight hundred. I hope you've got your act together, because I think you can be a great asset to the force. The city's growing faster than we can keep up with and I don't want to lose you. Whatever you do, keep your smart-assery to yourself. Understand?"

"Yessir. I do. And I will. And thank you for being on my side."

George nodded and started moving. "Let's go," was all he said.

I led the way to Captain Duncan's office, carrying my log sheets and the metal box with the unreadable journal in it . . . hoping for the best, expecting the worst . . . and no longer having even a shred of doubt about how Louis XVI felt when Robespierre's henchmen frog marched him to the guillotine.

I took a deep breath, said a quiet *Hail Mary,* and stepped into Captain Duncan's office in response to his silent gesture at exactly eight a.m. As we entered the generous office and workspace of the CSPD's man in charge of the city's Robbery-Homicide Division, Captain Duncan hung up the phone and said, "Shut the door, George, and have a seat. YOU," he pointed a manicured index finger at me, "stand right there and tell me why I shouldn't bust your sorry-assed self down to the unemployment office, hunting for a new job."

I stood proud, looked him in the eyes, put every one of my chips on the table and went all in. I said, "With all due respect Captain, the reason for giving you my case notes like that was because this is my first-ever as lead, and I was in a hurry to get back to it while everything was still fresh and potential witnesses might still be found and interviewed. Since then, I've typed all of them for you, up through yesterday evening when I found a curious, handwritten ledger—which may or may not be relevant—because it's unreadable." I put the folder with the daily log sheets and the evidence bag with the journal in it on his desk.

"That all?"

"No sir. It's not. For what it's worth, I don't think disagreeing with you philosophically is grounds enough for firing me. I made a solemn promise to the corpses of two elderly and revered citizens of the city and my own neighborhood that I'd never stop hunting for their murderers and bring them to justice. It's what I'm paid to do, is my duty to do, and my intention to do . . . come hell, high water, or the apocalypse. Sir."

Captain Duncan leaned forward over his desk with his arms outstretched, his hands clenched and his eyes blazing. He said, "Always ready with a smart-mouthed answer aren't you. Got any idea who defines the difference between philosophy and insubordination . . . me. That's who. Want to know what'll lose that gold shield you're so goddamn proud of, faster than you can say, *Oh shit* . . . one word . . . insubordination. What do you think of that, you stupid mick pain in the ass . . ."

His attempted bawling out was outrageous, insulting and so bigoted, it proved my beef against him without uttering a single word. A few years ago, the rage monster who lives inside of me would have been out of his cage by then . . . howling, and snarling, and breaking things into small pieces . . . starting with the good captain's face. Age and experience, combining to form wisdom, kept my temper in check and me out of life-altering trouble. So, I said nothing, and held his gaze until he looked away.

At that point, a profound silence—thick as a London fog and heavy as private grief—fell over the room.

It took Lt. George Patterson to break it. He said, "Captain, are we dismissed?"

"Yeah," Duncan said, as he spun his chair around to watch the traffic on Weber Street. With his back to the pair of us, he added, "And McKern, be here first thing tomorrow, activity report in hand. Leave today's. Take your may or may not be, unreadable, so-called evidence with you."

Chapter 21

As we headed for the stairs that would take us down to the bullpen where my desk and Patterson's office were situated, I thought, *it's an unjust world that grants a man like Duncan such authority.*

Like he could read my mind, George said, as we reached the detective's lair, "I guess old Fred forgot, that mine is also an Irish name and heritage. You're right Jake. He is a bigoted sonofabitch."

It was one of the only times in all the years I've known him, I ever heard Patterson curse or disrespect a superior officer. Then, after that quick peek into his inner secrets, it was back to business.

Lt. Patterson said, "Bring the book to my office. I want to look at it."

I trudged after him, into the closet-like space he'd been assigned, carrying the hard-worn, underappreciated, and as yet undeciphered leather journal. I took it out of its metal box, unwrapped it with care and passed it over, "Here you go."

I noticed that he handled the battered, leather-bound tome with something almost like reverence, when Lt. Patterson laid an ironed handkerchief on his desk before he opened it. After he'd viewed it for several minutes and read through a number of pages, Patterson looked up and said, "Who else has seen this?"

"Just you, me and whoever wrote it, so far as I'm aware."

"It appears to have been written over a period of time. See the numbers over here on the right? I think they indicate dates . . ."

"Why?"

"They're in ascending order, but they're not consecutive. Like a calendar."

"A sequence of some kind . . ."

"Yeah. Maybe. It looks like an organized language to me, and if someone was able to write it, there's bound to be a person somewhere who can read it."

"I think so too," I said, as I shook out a Lucky Strike and offered it, still in the pack. He took one and lit us both up. "But who . . . and where?"

Lt. Patterson handed it back. "Why don't you check over at CC."

"Colorado College? Really Loot? What makes you think they'll be willing to do anything?"

"Because it's a mystery. And if there's anything that one of those eggheaded professors loves, it's finding the answer to something before someone else can. Try the anthropology department. If that don't work, try history. Use your imagination. Some instructor over there who doesn't know it yet, is just itching to assist the CSPD. Your job is to figure out who."

I stuck the cigarette in the corner of my mouth, and tilted my head to keep the smoke out of my eyes, so I could use both hands to repack the journal. Finished, I stood and said, "Thanks Loot. I'll see who and what I can find, but honestly . . . if nothing comes out of this, I'm at a dead end. There's just not anything to follow up . . ."

Patterson put his smoke out in the ashtray on his desk. "Think. Jake. Think. What have you overlooked? Who's out there to talk to that you haven't found? Where's the next of kin? Somebody out there knows more about the Sorwells. Talk to their customers again. Surely one of them has a tidbit of information—some little detail—that can help."

"Okay." I said as I turned to go.

"And Jake . . . don't get your hopes up, but we may be getting a couple of transfers . . . experienced men. You may be having company soon."

"That'd be really welcome," I said, "but I sure as hell ain't countin' on it."

I headed for my desk in the corner, where I planned to get the phone book and start smiling and dialing, looking for a professor with a knowledge of the arcane and a thirst for solving the unknown.

The room was a beehive of activity. I wasn't the only one scrambling to keep up with his caseload, because even back then, in-between the Korean and Vietnam mistakes, the city was growing faster than the infrastructure could keep up with. The post-World War II peace came with a boom in babies, building and bust-assium as a forward-thinking America set out to remake the world in its image. In Colorado Springs, our pro-growth city council was hell-bent on making sure that each and every carpet-bagging land developer who staggered into town with the deed to a newly-purchased ranch in one hand, and a plat plan to split it up into a high-density housing development in the other, got their projects approved by rubber stamping bureaucrats in lickety-split fashion. The result has been an on-going and ever greater rolling disaster, with the Springs gradually losing its charm and its character. Where antelope once played and cattle and horses grazed, we now have endless rows of look-alike houses without storm drains, sidewalks, streetlights, or stop lights. I call it urban sprawl at its nastiest . . . and watch through downcast eyes as more and more of God's own prairie is transformed into asphalt and concrete parking lots.

I was so preoccupied with my thoughts that I didn't pay attention to what was going on in the rest of the room. Amidst all the commotion—phones ringing, typewriters clacking and footsteps thudding over the old wooden floor—three dicks, a pair of Unies and Ann-Marie Fuchs, our shared clerk-typist, were all putting a stealthy eyeball on me, waiting to catch my reaction to the newspaper on my desk, where, for the third time in less than a week I was the subject of scorn.

GUN SALES BOOMING the headline blared above Lenny Bragg's byline. *Suter's House of Guns sells a firearm every 15 minutes, while Lucas Sporting Goods has almost sold out of ammunition in every caliber as citizens arm themselves for protection in the wake of CSPD's failure to catch the Skin Ripper. Where are you Jake McKern? What are you doing to put a stop to the fiend's ghastly activities?*

I put the metal box on my desk, rolled the newspaper up and threw it into the closest trash can with extra enthusiasm. Then I started making phone calls to the college.

Chapter 22

After a couple of hours of prospecting, more dead ends than an abandoned graveyard and a few almosts, I struck gold in the unlikeliest of places when a series of referrals led me to a woman named Gilda Arkady. She was a PhD and an art historian with a special interest in Egyptology, who also spoke five languages. After I explained myself, she agreed to meet for lunch at Michelle's, a chocolate, ice cream and sandwich shop just a few blocks down from the college on Tejon Street. When I started to describe myself however, she cut me off.

"Don't worry detective," she said. "I'll recognize you right away. I've seen your picture in the newspapers."

We agreed to meet at 11:30, in order to beat the lunch crowd and rang off. That left time enough for me to make a couple more phone calls.

First, I dialed the number on the pink message slip that was left on my desk by Ann-Marie while I was in with Captain Duncan. It connected me to the Coroner's Office. I asked for Dr. Chapin.

"This is she," a voice said.

"Jake McKern, Doc. Returning your call."

"Hold on for a sec . . ."

I could hear something metallic clanking against the porcelain, imagined surgical instruments going into stainless steel pans. Then a match flared as she lit a cigarette.

"Thanks. I called to let you know I'll be doing the Sorwell autopsies this afternoon. Should start at two o'clock."

"I'll be there."

"Have you ever attended one?"

"No. Why does that matter?"

"It doesn't," she said as she exhaled. "I always ask if I don't know the cop. Are you squeamish around blood and gore . . ."

I hesitated for a moment, then said, "No, Doc. I'm not. I grew up on a ranch. We did all of our own meat processing in the fall, and I also hunted big game to supply meat for our family, plus elk and antelope steaks for a restaurant up in Palmer Lake."

"All that's well and good. But carving into a human body's a lot different than cutting up a critter."

"Point taken. Let me put it another way. I appreciate your concern and I promise I won't mess up your workspace. I was a grunt in the Marine Corps from 1940 to 1945 in the Pacific."

"Where, if you don't mind me asking."

"The Canal, Okinawa and a couple of others in-between."

"You are a lucky and tough man."

"Well, maybe, I . . ."

"My older brother Tom is buried on Iwo. He was killed on Mt. Suribachi."

"Then he is a hero, Dr. Chapin. *Semper Fi.* I'll see you at two."

I don't like talking about the war, or my part in it. And other than on a few rare occasions with other vets, I never have. I think about it. I have nightmares about it, more often than I like admitting. I did my part. It's in the past. Let it stay there.

I lit a coffin nail and smoked it some, then I dialed the Curdy's number down in Houston. As before, Mirabelle Johnson answered. I said, "Hello again Mrs. Johnson. This is Jake McKern, Imogene's husband. I'd like to speak to her please. I know she's there and I want to talk with her or Scotty."

"I'm sorry Mr. McKern . . . they ain't here. They done gone somewhere with Mr. Grinder . . ."

"I see. When will they be home?"

"Late tonight or early tomorrow. They went down to Galveston, but I ain't sure why . . . they ain't said neither."

"Okay," I said, as I ground my teeth and sucked in a double lungful of cigarette smoke before adding, "has there been any news about Big Jim and Mrs. Curdy?"

"No. Nothin'. It ain't lookin' good."

"Is the search still going on? Are there people out there, trying to find them?"

"Yeah. Mr. Jim has a lotta friends high up in gov'ment and bidness. They all worried and lookin' for them."

"Thanks for letting me know. And would you tell Imogene that I'd like to talk to her?"

"Yessir. I will. And Mr. McKern . . . I apologize for my rudeness when you last called. Mr. Grinder and Imogene was listenin' an tellin' me what to say."

"I understand. And no apology is needed or expected. Have they said much about me?"

"Not that I've heard."

"Would you tell me if you did?"

"I might. But probably not. They wouldn't let me. And I need my job."

I took a last puff of Lucky Strike and said, as I crushed it in the ashtray on my desk, "That's the most candid answer anyone's given me in at least a month. I appreciate you being so honest."

"I always tell the truth Mr. McKern. 'Cept when I don't."

I thought about her answer for quite a while after that. It made me smile whenever I did.

I decided to walk over to Michelle's. It was only a couple of blocks and I wanted to stretch my legs . . . plus the day was perfect for it. Cool but not cold, with a bright sun sailing high in a cloudless cerulean sky.

It was just past 11:30 when I entered the chocolatier and sandwich shop on north Tejon Street. As I made my way past case after glass case, piled high with an astonishing variety of Old-World chocolate maker's art, the smells and sights were mouth watering. I sidled past the soda fountain and headed toward the booth where a small middle-aged woman with short, silvery blonde hair, eyeglasses with turquoise cat-eye frames and a pair of midnight blue eyes was waving at me. "You must be Dr. Arkady," I said, as I slid into the seat opposite her and laid the tin box with its mysterious contents on the table between us.

Her cherubic face broke into a hundred-watt smile as she extended her right hand and said, "I am. And you," as we shook, "are the brave and handsome detective Jake McKern. Such a big one too. I can only wish I was twenty years younger."

I blushed. Stammered out something like "Thanks for the compliment, but I'm not really."

"Ooh. And modest as well. We're going to be friends Jake McKern. Good friends."

"I hope so. In my line of work, I need all the friends I can get."

Chapter 23

A waitress came with two glasses of water and a menu, but we went ahead without looking at them and ordered club sandwiches and coffee for both of us. Then we got right to it.

"The journal I'm about to show you is something that was found during an evidence search in an investigation I'm conducting," I said. "It may, or may not be relevant. The trouble is, it's undecipherable. No one can tell what it says. I'm hoping you can either read it, or identify the language for us." I handed the book to Professor Arkady.

She received the volume with both hands and carefully examined the front, back and sides. She cleared the space to her left and laid the diary down while she rummaged in her purse for a bit and came up with a pair of white cotton gloves. As she was putting them on, Dr. Arkady said, "Are you at liberty to tell me where and how this item was found?"

"Certainly Doctor. I . . ."

"I'd like to dispense with the *faux* formality. Kindly call me Gilda from here on, and I shall use your given name—with your permission—and all flirting aside."

"Consent given Gilda. I answer to Jake. Anytime and everywhere."

"Good. Tell me, Jake . . . about the journal's discovery."

"I was looking for evidence in an apartment where two people were murdered . . ."

"The Skin Ripper Case that's been all over the news?"

"I can't say. It's confidential, not public information. If this book turns out to be material to a case, we wouldn't want the suspects to know we have it."

"Why not?"

"Someone, I believe it was the victim, went to great lengths to conceal whatever's written in there," I said, then went on to tell her the how, where and when of finding it.

Gilda gave me her full attention, listening without interruption and never taking her eyes off me. When I finished, she said, "Most intriguing. Do you think the murderers had any idea of the book's existence?"

"The place was ransacked, so they were looking for something. But whatever it was, is known only to themselves. I have no inkling . . ."

"Well, I have several observations already . . ."

"Just a moment," I said as I pulled out my notebook and pen. I opened it to the first clean page and started to write. "Okay Gilda. Go ahead."

She pushed her glasses back up the bridge of her nose and began. "First, the book cover, the binding and its pages are all made by hand. The workmanship is coarse, but well-crafted . . . as if the bookbinder knew the process but didn't have the proper tools and materials to do the job right."

"Any idea how new or old it might be?"

Gilda opened the cover and looked at the flyleaf and endpaper. She glanced toward the ceiling and said, "I wish the light was a little bit better. It's hard to see very well."

"Here. Maybe this will help," I said, and pulled out the small flashlight I keep in my jacket pocket and shined it on the page for her.

"Thanks. That's much better."

The waitress appeared with two mugs and a carafe of coffee. She told us she was sorry for the delay, but she'd had to wait for the stuff to brew in its big industrial urn. "But it's really, really fresh and *muy caliente*. Your sandwiches will be coming right up."

I nodded and said thanks for both of us, then busied myself with cream and sugar while the Professor continued her inspection. As I stirred with my left hand and held the light in my other, she leafed through the pages and checked the spine several times.

Just about when my arm was ready to surrender to gravity from the weight of the black Eveready, Dr. Arkady looked up and said, "Okay

Jake. I've got it. You can put that away." She didn't have to tell me twice.

Gilda took a last glance at the book's cover, closed, and handed it back. She sipped her coffee, then said, "I don't think it's more than a few decades old. Some of the pages are a little browned, but the paper used to make the book are a hodge-podge of different bonds and types. It looks to me like it was made from scraps. But it's not very old. I'm certain of that."

I made a lot of notes as she savored her coffee and watched. Our lunches arrived while I was repacking the journal. As Gilda started to nibble on a potato chip, I said, "What about the contents . . . any help there?"

She shook her head. "Unfortunately, no. I think it might be Hebrew, but if so, it's a form I don't recognize. It may even be a dead language of some sort that the modern language is based on . . . or vice-versa. In any case, I have a friend who's an expert in Middle Eastern, Babylonian, and Persian cuneiform writing. I'd like to consult with him, if you don't mind."

I thought for a moment while keeping a close watch on the pair of club sandwiches. "No," I finally said. "I think it's a good idea . . . but how do you propose to do it?" Then I grabbed one of the triangles of turkey, swiss, bacon and avocado on toast and bit it in half.

Without hesitation, Dr. Arkady said, "He's in Denver, attached to the archdiocese up there. He's lecturing at Regis, the Catholic College, as a visiting scholar for ancient Mesopotamian history, culture, and language. His name is Alphonso Gianette. He's a Jesuit priest who normally lives and works in Vienna, Austria . . . and he's a confidant . . . as well as an adviser to Pope Pius XII. The kids all call him 'Father Al,' by the way, and just adore him. His classes are always full . . . and hard to get into as well." After saying that, she pulled her plate in and began eating.

"How are you planning on showing him the writing," I said, as I was polishing off my third sandwich triangle and the last of my chips. "It's logged in as evidence. I have to return it to the station."

"It's not a problem. I'll write the first page out when I get back to my office and mail it to him. We'll talk on the phone."

I swallowed the last bite of my club sandwich and tried not to stare at hers, most of which was still on her plate. "How, might I ask, can you do that?"

"Help yourself to a couple of these if you're still hungry Jake, I can never eat more than one or two. And to answer your question . . . I have perfect memory. I close my eyes and see it in my head, then write it down. It's what makes me such a good art historian. I never forget a brush stroke."

I flipped my notebook to the next empty page and turned it around to her. "Would you show me . . ."

Gilda took my ballpoint, and in less time than it took me to eat half of her lunch, she filled the page with the same kind of rune-like scritches as I'd seen in the mysterious journal. I didn't want to unpack and repack the thing again in the restaurant, but when I did so later that evening at my desk, it was a perfect match. All I could say to her at the time was, "Amazing. I'm in awe. Wish I could have done that in college . . ."

She smiled. "Thank you. It is a rare talent, bequeathed to only a few. I try not to waste it."

Our waitress came back at that moment and asked if she could get anything else for us.

Professor Arkady looked at me and said, "Would you like to split a dessert? Then I have to leave. I have a two o'clock class."

I shrugged—while my sweet tooth was muttering *OhboyOhboyO-hboy! Yes! Yes! Yes!* in some crevice somewhere, deep inside my brain—and said, "Sure. You decide though. I'm overwhelmed."

"Do you like chocolate?"

I grinned. "Everybody likes it. But some of us love it. Which includes me."

Gilda nodded and said something to the young woman serving our table in rapid fire Spanish, and the result was a pair of white china plates, two forks, and a mammoth piece of four chocolate cake with chocolate icing.

"It's a kind of Bavarian treat I call *Death by Chocolate*," she said, as she took a mouse sized bite. I was forking it down like a hungry hound at the moment, and could only nod in happy acknowledgement.

81

"I have two other observations to give you," Dr. Arkady said, as she chunked off another nibble of the rapidly disappearing treat. "The first is that the writing took place over an extended period of time with a blunt stylus—a matchstick perhaps—and it was done with a number of different mediums . . . but mostly in charcoal or soot of some kind . . . and what will undoubtedly be analyzed as blood. Whether it's human or animal however, will have to be determined by lab analysis."

Then she put down her fork and pushed her plate away. "The second, and last thing is this. Although I haven't seen or handled enough of it to be 100 percent positive . . . I'm pretty sure that the leather covering is made of human skin."

I'm glad I was taking notes at that moment instead of eating cake. I'm not sure I could have kept it down.

Chapter 24

I waved to Professor Arkady as she rode away on her Schwinn Black Phantom, then hoofed it back to the station at forced-march pace with the journal packed inside its metal box in my right hand. I had about half an hour before the autopsy was due to begin. Lucky for me though, back in the late fifties it was still possible to get from anywhere to everywhere in the Springs in twenty minutes or less. I stepped it up a little anyway.

A petite blond woman wearing a blouse and slacks under a crisp white lab coat was pulling on surgical gloves when I stepped into the autopsy room with only a few minutes to spare before 2 p.m. "Dr. Chapin, I presume?"

The woman looked up from the surgical instruments she was laying out on a folded hand towel and gave me the once-over with a pair of cornflower blue eyes. They went from my brown cowboy boots to my leather A-2 jacket and red necktie before looking at my face and into my eyes. She said, "Y'know, that line was lame when Henry Stanley used it on Dr. Livingstone in Africa, eighty-five years ago. And yes. I am she. You're McKern I suppose."

"Yes'um. At your service," I said, and snapped off a half-bow like the Japs do.

"Oh, jeeze, it's getting pretty deep in here. My name is Alta."

"Jake," I said, as we shook hands.

"Before I start, would you happen to have a cigarette? I left mine in my pickup."

"Unfiltered, okay? Lucky Strikes are what I have."

"Fine. Beggars can't be choosers."

I tapped one out for her, another for myself, and lit us both up. We puffed in silence for a moment. Then, as she blew out a lungful of tobacco smoke filled with carcinogens, tars and nicotine, Alta said, "Now tell me Jake McKern, what exactly did you do to so piss off himself, the right honorable and most supercilious Harry Bucklin?"

I'd just inhaled, tried to chuckle, but wound-up coughing, choking, and laughing until tears ran down my cheeks. Alta watched me with clinical detachment, her left hand cupping her elbow and the burning cigarette stuck between the index and middle fingers of her right hand. When I finally got a grip on myself and began telling her why Bucklin was so teed off, the image of the prissy little County Coroner bent over at the waist, urking his guts out hit me right in the funny bones for the second time, and I started to crack up again . . . and this time it was infectious. Neither one of us were able to stop hooting until our sides ached.

Thinking about it now—our laughter at that moment wasn't because we were being disrespectful of the victims—it was our attempt to release the tensions we both felt from having to deal with the aftermath of such a vicious crime. I think Mr. and Mrs. Sorwell would have understood . . . I hope so anyway. And my commitment that I would find the criminals who murdered and desecrated their bodies was stronger than ever. I quietly reaffirmed my vow to them in my mind, as Dr. Chapin began her work on their earthly remains.

Three hours and twenty minutes later it was finished. Abraham and Ruth Sorwell had made their last formal statements of truth.

I watched as both bodies were returned to their refrigerated vaults on sliding trays and listened as the gasket sealed doors closed behind them with a loud clack that put the final period on two life stories. *Such a sad ending,* I thought *for two persons who endured so much, asked so little and deserved a lot better than what they got . . .* It made me more determined than ever to find the killers.

Dr. Chapin removed her safety glasses and face mask, peeled off her latex gloves and tossed them in a trash bin. Only then did she wiggle out of the lab coat and the disposable booties which covered her white tennis shoes. She went to the sink, washed her hands with soap from a wall dispenser then dried them with paper towels. She stretched, and rubbed her back at the waist before she turned and said, "If you'd like to come have some lemonade with me, and for the price of another cigarette, I'll give you, my findings. They'll be unofficial, of course, but you'll have everything that will be in my written autopsy. Things being what they are, Hell may freeze over by the time the paperwork comes through."

"I hear you loud and clear, Doc. Lemonade sounds lovely. I haven't had any of that in years."

She smiled. "I made it myself. If you go down the hall past the reception area and out the back door, you'll find a path that goes over to a sitting area where there's an outdoor table and chairs. I'll meet you down there as soon as I get my coat and our treat."

"Sounds great," I said as the elevator door opened and let me out on the main floor before carrying the friendly pathologist on up to her office on the second. I followed her directions and found myself relishing the late afternoon sun on an unseasonably warm March day, so soon after it had snowed. *But that's high-altitude Colorado weather. Stick around another few hours and we could be ass-deep in snow with gale force winds,* I thought, as I sat at the wooden picnic table under a leafless ash tree that grew alongside a small half-acre pond, complete with a fountain and more than a dozen wild ducks swimming around. Trees and mossy green rocks dotted the surrounding area, giving it a relaxing and peaceful atmosphere that was in direct contrast to the dissections and other goings-on in the basement morgue behind me. I heard footsteps, turned, and saw Dr. Chapin.

She sat opposite me—put a quart mason jar full of an opaque liquid that had a few lemon wedges floating around in it on the table—and said, "Tranquil, isn't it . . ."

"Yeah. Especially after what we've seen and done for the past few hours." I handed my cigarettes to her and watched as she took one and gave them back. After we both fired up, she unscrewed the old-fashioned zinc and porcelain cap that still had a red rubber ring inside, to keep everything watertight.

Dr. Chapin took a sip, wiped her mouth on the sleeve of her fleece-lined Woolrich shirt, and passed it to me. "Sorry . . . I couldn't find any cups. We'll have to share."

"That's okay," I said, as I took a big swallow—and got the shock of my life as it burned all the way to the bottom of my craw. I added, with tears streaming out of my eyes, and in a voice that could only squeak, "I believe this is about the driest lemonade I have ever tasted, Doc. Mr. Gilbey's recipe, I presume . . ."

Dr. Chapin covered her mouth and giggled like a little girl. It reminded me so much of my sister Catherine, it almost brought me tears. But then the mischievous Doctor said, "Beefeater's actually. The Yeomen of the Guard."

"Damn good lemonade Doc." I took another, much smaller sip, and passed it back.

She tipped in a second tiny taste and screwed the lid down tight. "I come out here," she said, "to find internal peace after seeking such awful truths in there. I know that's an odd attitude for a physician . . . especially one in my field to take . . . but, can you understand?"

"After what I've seen and done in my life Doc, I understand perfectly."

She nodded with a faraway look in her eyes. Then we got down to discussing the sad business which had brought us together at that time and place.

Chapter 25

Dr. Chapin and I sat at the wooden picnic table in the gathering dusk for about four cigarettes worth, ignoring the falling temperature and the lateness of the hour, quietly cementing our newborn friendship while she enlightened me as to the manner, means and cause of the untimely deaths of Ruth and Abraham Sorwell. I took extensive notes as Alta told me, in a dry clinical way, that each of the two victims had been murdered execution style. "Two bullets to the chest and one in the head. There were no defensive wounds and no evidence of a struggle," she said, as she unscrewed the lid from the lemonade jar and sipped. "There is, I suppose, a small mercy in the fact that their deaths appear to have been quick . . . and therefore, most likely painless. I think they were killed while they slept."

"Same gun used on both victims?"

Dr. Chapin shook her head. "No. There were two different caliber bullets. Probably a .22 and a .32, or a .380 caliber is my estimation but it's just a guess. I recovered the slugs for ballistics to have a look at. Then we'll know for certain."

"You're positive about two different weapons . . ."

"Yeah. Mr. Sorwell has a larger entry hole in his skull. There's no question about it."

"Which would imply two different shooters," I said.

"Had to be," she agreed, adding, "there were multiple people involved. I'm certain of it. Mr. Sorwell weighed 237 pounds. It would have taken a lot of effort to move his body downstairs into the locker. Hers as well."

"I think so too," I said, as I closed my notebook and put it in my pocket. "Anything else you'd like to add?"

"Yeah," Alta said, as she put out her cigarette. "Catch these monsters. Between you and me, I'm pretty sure that whoever flayed our victims has done it before, because there was no hesitation and no errors that I found. All the cuts were straight and smooth. The perpetrators are evil. No doubt in my mind."

"Mine either, Doc. You're not the first one to tell me that. Things like this aren't supposed to happen in our part of the world—this is big city crime—I've heard that before as well."

"No. They're not," she agreed. "One other thing Jake . . . both of their bodies show evidence of extensive torture."

I drew in a sharp breath between clenched teeth. "Recently," I said, as I pulled my notes out and started adding this new information.

"No," she said, as she started to reach for another cigarette, then thought twice about it and put both hands in front of her, one on top of the other. Head down, she went on. "It doesn't appear to be anything very new. I'd say their scars and wounds are at least ten to fifteen years old. Both bodies present with multiples of unset, poorly healed bones in the hands, feet, and knees. I believe it was done with hammers and other common tools. The breaks are deliberate. They also look to me like they were done to inflict the most possible harm. It was willful, deliberate, savage, vicious and utterly barbaric. I've never seen anything like it . . . I can't imagine the kind of depravity it would take to do something like what was done to those two people . . ."

I did my best not to notice the lone tear that snuck out of her eye and slipped down her cheek before she slapped it away. I said, "Would like to take a break? We could stop if you want."

Dr. Chapin looked me right in the eye and said, "Don't mistake anger for weakness, mister. If I was thin-skinned or a fragile flower, I wouldn't be here . . . a woman operating in a man's world. I wouldn't have survived medical school."

I dropped my pen and raised my hands in mock surrender. "Hey, I understand what you're saying. I come in peace, Doc. I was only trying to be respectful of your feelings."

The light was fading fast by then, but I could still make out a kind of rueful half-smile on her face. Dr. Chapin said, "Your gallantry is most sincerely appreciated, Jake. God knows, there's little enough of it around these days. I didn't mean to sound peevish. But what was done to those old folks was obscene . . . I'm positive that both suffered constant and chronic osteoarthritis pain every day."

She stopped for a moment, sighed, and reached for the last cigarette in the pack. She fired it up, took a drag and exhaled, then said, "The last thing I have to tell you is this . . . both of the Sorwells were surgically mutilated as well. Someone, somewhere, performed crude operations on them. I think they were experimented on by somebody who didn't know they were doing, but who enjoyed inflicting pain on others."

"A sadist . . ."

She nodded. "Yes. It's remarkable that they survived at all."

"I think they must have been two tough and determined people who lived through all of that in order to serve a higher purpose . . ."

"Divine intervention?" Dr. Chapin squirmed and shifted in her seat as she said it, then went on, "I couldn't say for certain. But I've seen biological complexities that haven't any rational explanation . . . so I wouldn't say that it's impossible either. I guess time will tell. We'll just have to wait and see."

I had no answer.

The temperature was dropping fast. It was getting too cold to stay out of doors in comfort; stars were winking on and lights were starting to show across the city. My leg was stiff and throbbing—a reminder that I needed some of Nurse Gloria's pilfered drugs as soon as possible.

I said, "Thanks Doc for all the insight. It's eye-opening, and a help. I know you're sticking your neck out for me and I'll do my best to return the favor."

She smiled and put out her cigarette in the coffee can of sand that sat in the middle of the table. "Don't worry about it Jake. It's no big secret around here that Harry Bucklin and I don't see eye to eye. But I'd better get a move on. My family probably thinks I've been kidnapped. I never work this late on Fridays."

"I'll be your alibi," I said as I stood up . . . and tried not to gasp as the bolt of *hurts like a sonofabitch* shot up my thigh and backside.

It was a slow stroll down a path that wound around some Ponderosa pines and deposited us in the parking lot, where I saw the doctor to her pickup and we said goodnight.

Chapter 26

I followed Dr. Chapin's pickup truck out of the parking area, watched as her lights disappeared and she went home to the family she'd mentioned. Then, I turned and headed back downtown, to my desk at the station, where I intended to type my daily activity report for Captain Duncan. I could have gone in early, and tapped it out in my two-finger style when I was fresh and rested, but the truth was, I didn't want to go home to an empty house and a take-out supper.

I missed my son, Scottie. Only nine years old and already a pretty good second baseman, I was looking forward to better weather when he and I could go to the park and play catch. Then—after warming up—I'd hit flies and skinners for him to field. Skinners, or ground balls, were our favorites because they're unpredictable and the hardest to field.

Scottie, conceived by accident in the backseat of a borrowed '34 LaSalle sedan, was the best thing about the otherwise unhappy marriage of Imogene Elizabeth Curdy and myself. We both knew it too, and each of us loved him in our own way with a fierce and unconditional devotion. The truth and common sense however, told us that our union wasn't the lasting kind, but neither Mo, nor I were willing to give up our son. Scottie was the center of his mother's and his father's personal universes, and we were at an impasse because of it that we were unable to deal with. It wasn't a unique situation . . . lots of other young couples had tied the knot in haste after the war, trying to get on with life and return to the ordinary . . . many a post armistice hook-up was in the same trouble as Mo and I. And like us, they were unwilling or unable to face up to the facts and do something about it.

My reverie was interrupted at that point by an ongoing gunfight.

I was headed up Nevada, about to cross Colorado Avenue with a green light when a maroon Oldsmobile Coupe—one of those Rocket 88s with a big motor—flashed in front of me and went into a four-wheel drift at high speed, then took off to the north in a cloud of smoke and the stink of burning rubber. Hot on his heels came a brand-new pink and black '56 Ford Crown Victoria with an arm sticking out of the driver's window, firing a big semi-automatic pistol at the first car. I counted four muzzle flashes before the Ford driver realized he had a problem. He'd come into the intersection too hot. He needed to bleed off speed, and a whole lot of it, if he was going to keep pace with the fleeing Olds, because his first problem was . . . he had to make a ninety-degree left turn.

But that driver turned out to be a real wheelman. As I watched with mouth agape, the rear bumper rose up and the front end of the Ford dipped, all four tires locked up and howled in protest as they left two weeks of workman's wages in Firestone rubber on the roadway. The guy jerked the steering wheel to the left, fishtailed three or four times and resumed the chase. I stabbed my junker into second gear and floored it, intent on pursuit, and left a cloud of crappy blue smoke in my wake.

All that took place in a span of mere seconds. I hadn't even had time to call it in. But as I banged into third and reached for the radio, I saw the maroon Oldsmobile duck east on Kiowa Street . . . *right in front of CSPD Headquarters* . . . the pink and black Crown Vic hot on his tail.

When I got there a few moments later, I found mayhem. Kiowa street then, as now, was one-way east, with angled parking into the curb. The Olds coupe was rammed into the left rear quarter-panel of a black and white '55 Ford police cruiser with probationary cop Amos "Rags" Magness at the wheel. It appeared he'd been backing out when the Rocket 88 plowed into him, slewing both vehicles around and blocking the whole street. The pink and black '56 Ford had jumped the curb trying to miss them, and wrapped itself around a light pole. But nothing, it seemed, was going to stop the two suspects from trying to kill each other. They were already out of their wrecked cars and shooting in the middle of Kiowa Street when I came around the corner and skidded sideways to a stop.

I pulled my weapon—an unauthorized 1911 Colt .45 caliber automatic loaded with 225 grain hollow points—and jumped out. Keeping the car between me and them, I jacked a round into the chamber, laid my right arm on the hood and drew a bead on the nearest of the two combatants . . . a medium-sized, dark-skinned man of color who was wearing a faded denim jacket and a glistening red shirt. He was holding a large squarish pistol of a type I couldn't identify in the street-lights. He was the Ford driver.

"Police," I screamed. "YOU. RED SHIRT. DROP YOUR WEAPON AND PUT YOUR HANDS UP. DO IT NOW."

Just when I said that, two high-velocity rounds fired by the Oldsmobile man—a tall African-American in a screaming yellow and white and black checkered zoot suit—slammed into the engine block of my sorry old police car. Then, Amos Magness shot him in the right eye.

Zoot suit man went down in an ugly mess, the back side of his head missing, and gore splattering the street as his life drained away. The long barreled nickel-plated revolver he'd been trying to murder me with clattered to the ground and skittered under the pair of crunched automobiles.

I said "DROP IT," at red shirt, who looked unsteady on his feet . . . the black pistol still gripped in his right hand. "Drop the fucking gun or I'll drop you. Now."

Red shirt gave me a dazed look. I had him center-mass in my gun sight at point-blank range, my right index finger steady on the trigger. He was a dead man if he so much as twitched.

But he didn't

Red shirt's gun arm dropped. His eyes rolled up in his head, he turned a half-pirouette and collapsed on the pavement next to his now destroyed pink and black Crown Victoria.

I hustled around the front of my car and stood on Red shirt's out-stretched wrist, plucked a big clunky looking automatic pistol out of his hand and thumbed the hammer down, then stuck it in my waist-band. I stood over the Red shirt and felt for a pulse on his neck. It was there, but barely. That's when I realized his shirt was saturated with blood. He was actually wearing a long-sleeved white thermal underwear top, the kind favored by those who were outside for extended periods of time. Judging by the man's scuffed work boots and calloused hands, I figured him for a construction worker of some kind or another . . . concrete or drywall maybe. He had the muscular build for it.

I was sure that Red shirt wasn't going anywhere, but I rolled him over and cuffed him anyway. Finished, I yelled to Magness, "Amos, you doing, okay?"

"Yeah. I'm fine. That you, Jake?"

"It's me," I said. "Good thing you ID'ed yourself before you discharged your weapon. That was quick thinking," I was trying to give the less experienced young man a heads-up . . . help him when the higher and mightier started asking questions about who shot whom . . . and when.

My concern was unfounded. Young Amos Magness was as fast on the draw as a nearsighted gunslinger. He said, "Thanks for reminding me. I might have forgotten I said that."

It was a good thing too. Because by then, cops were boiling out the front door of the station house like angry hornets whose nest was on fire.

It's hard to imagine these many years later, but by my reckoning . . . after all that action had taken place, no more than three minutes had elapsed since I first entered the intersection at Nevada and Colorado Avenues. Now, it feels like the longest . . . and at the same time . . . the fastest 180 seconds of my entire life.

Chapter 27

Lieutenant Patterson and Sergeant Andy Claypoole were among the dozen or so uninformed officers who'd emptied out into the street in response to the gunfire and car crashes. They took charge of the scene and reestablished some order into the space where utter chaos was happening only moments before.

Claypoole took responsibility for crowd control and containment. Friday night traffic was heavy and starting to back up with gawkers who, drawn by the noise and commotion, wanted to see what was happening. He put a squad car at each end of the block with flashers on and a cop directing drivers on Nevada Avenue to the west, and Weber Street on the east, to keep moving.

George Patterson, as the highest-ranking man on scene, assumed command. He sent two men over to assist Magness, brought another with him to see why I was calling for a corpsman at the top of my lungs.

"Easy Jake. Are you hit?"

"No Loot. Not me. The suspect. He's bleeding out. His wounds are unknown. He got here this way and passed out. He's disarmed and cuffed. I haven't ID'd him. But I think we'd better get him to the hospital fast—or we'll lose 'im.'"

Patterson looked and nodded. He pointed to Andy Claypoole, who was urging traffic along on Nevada Avenue. "Sergeant, bring that patrol car here. We gotta get this man to the hospital." Then he said to another cop, "Go. Replace him. Help with traffic."

Andy backed the black and white around my unmarked, and together the three of us wrestled the unconscious and wounded man onto the back seat, then slammed the doors shut.

As he was about to get behind the steering wheel and take off, I said, "Hey . . . those are my cuffs. Be sure to bring 'em back, would ya?"

Without a word, Claypoole reached behind his back and pulled a brand-new pair of Smith & Wesson handcuffs and handed them to me. "Take these," he said. "I'll keep the others after I get him sorted out at the hospital." Then he was gone in a blast of light and sound, headed for Memorial Hospital on East Boulder Street. It was a small but kind gesture that I really appreciated, because back in those days we were making around four thousand a year and had to buy all our own uniforms, guns, ammo and equipment. I've always remembered that thoughtfulness and tried to pass it along as my career with the department progressed down through the years.

By that time, things were starting to calm down. The crime scene technicians were arriving and beginning to measure, document, and photograph everything on, in or near the 200 block of East Kiowa Street, while patrolmen were roping off the area and telling curious pedestrians to move along.

George Patterson reached in his shirt pocket and produced a red and white cardboard box of cork-tipped Marlboro cigarettes. He offered one to me. Curious about the new brand I took it and lit us both up with my old Zippo that had the USMC World and Anchor emblem embossed on it. As I did, he said, "What happened . . ."

"I was returning from the Coroner's Office after attending the autopsies of Ruth and Abraham Sorwell," I said, and then told him everything that I had seen and done . . . from the time the maroon Oldsmobile coupe tore in front of me, up to when we loaded the Ford driver into the backseat of the commandeered cruiser Sergeant Claypoole took him to the hospital in.

Patterson said, "Where's his gun?"

I pulled my jacket to the side and said, "Right here, Loot. It's not cleared. I didn't have time."

He nodded. "Go ahead. It's gotta go into evidence."

I stuck the cigarette in the corner of my mouth and tilted my head to keep the smoke out of my eyes. I turned to the left, dropped the clip, and indexed the slide, ejecting a live round. I retrieved it from the pavement and put the bullet, clip and pistol into the open evidence bag

Lieutenant Patterson had produced and was holding for me. I wrote the content information on it and signed my name and badge number. Then, I put the evidence number into my pocket notebook—just to be on the safe side. *Never know when you might need it,* I thought as I wrote everything on the line after the one with the mysterious hand-written book number. That particular habit has saved me a lot of grief over the years, and I recommend it to all who wear a badge.

After that, Magness and I were up to our asses in supervisors, questions, and paperwork. The brass all wanted to know—as Chief Budd himself conducted the debriefing in his office with Captains Duncan and Hoffman, Lieutenant Patterson and a City Attorney named S. William Tournillon observing.

"How'd you get involved?" The Chief said to me.

"Accidentally," I said, then repeated what I had told Patterson.

"How many shots were fired?

"None," I said.

"One." Magness added.

"Why?" Budd asked the rookie who, like me, was standing at attention in front of the Chief's desk.

"Because the suspect was trying to kill Detective McKern. He shot twice with a big nickel-plated revolver before I dropped him, right where he stood."

"That right McKern?"

"Yessir. It is. The suspect in the first car fired at me two times as I was dealing with the other one in the second car. Magness's actions kept me alive."

Chief Budd eyeballed both of us for a few moments before he turned to the onlookers and said, "Any of you have any questions? Want to add anything? Comments?"

His query was met with stone silence and I thought we were done. But then the attorney, Tournillon, chimed in. He said to Magness, "Before you fired the fatal bullet, what happened?"

Magness sucked in a breath and said, "I screamed, "Police! Drop your weapon."

"When did you draw your sidearm?"

"As I was getting out of the cruiser, after the suspect crashed into it."

Tournillon looked like he was about to ask another question, but Chief Budd cut him off. "That's enough Bill. We've got all we need. They've established good cause. It's justified. We'll put the young man on a desk for a week and close the case. Captain Hoffman, that's your responsibility. Officer Magness, you're no longer on probationary status. I'm promoting you to patrolman grade one immediately. I'm also putting a letter of commendation into both of your jackets. You've represented the Colorado Springs Police Department with bravery and distinction, and we're proud of the pair of you. Now, if there are no other questions, we have an important meeting to get to . . ."

Magness and I stood, mute and dying to get out of there.

A few seconds went by before Chief Budd said, "Gentlemen, you're dismissed."

Magness and I couldn't leave the room fast enough.

Chapter 28

Things were a lot different in those days . . . in the department and in the city . . . when both were smaller and more efficient. Back then, the Chief knew every officer by name and ran the Springs Police with absolute authority. His word was law. If he said, *it's justified,* that's all it took. You were exonerated.

As we made tracks down the hallway from Chief Budd's office, I stuck out my hand and said, "Rags, you're gonna be a great cop. Welcome to the CSPD and thank-you for saving my ass tonight."

Magness flashed a rare smile as he clasped my outstretched hand. "And you can be in my foxhole any time Jake. Thanks for having my back in there . . . I figured I'd be the first to get thrown under the bus when Lieutenant Patterson took my gun and hauled the pair of us up here while the stink of cordite and gunpowder was still in the air."

"It was out of our hands, and your weapon is in evidence. Once you're cleared, you'll get it back. We can't be the investigators of our own actions and have any credibility."

"Like Congress does."

"Shit, Rags," I said. "Those bastards wouldn't recognize Veracity if she rode a white mare into the Capitol Rotunda, stark naked. Mark Twain wrote that Congress was the only true criminal class in America. I don't think he was kidding, either."

Magness shook his head and grinned. "You are priceless, Jake. I hope there's only one of you, 'cause the world will never be able to handle a pair of ya."

I took that as a compliment.

We descended to the second floor and prepared to go our separate ways. As we did, rookie-no-more Amos Magness said, "I'm gonna enjoy telling that ofay Dunlop that I ain't his personal nigger no more."

I stopped and looked him in the eyes and said, "I can't even imagine what it's like to walk in your shoes Rags. But if I did, I'd think twice and be real careful about that, because you never know who's gonna show up—or not—the next time you call for backup. Word gets around. Then you're fucked. I'm not saying change your principals or take his crap. I wouldn't either. But God knows, neither one of us needs any more enemies."

"My head hears you, Jake, but my heart's sayin' go after the motherfucker, because there's no way in hell, I'd let that sonofabitch get behind me with a gun."

I shrugged. "It's your choice Rags. I don't blame you either way. But you're the one who'll pay the price."

"As always," was the last thing he said to me.

I hoped the best for my new friend and brother-in-arms, but at the same time, I feared for the worst. Only time would tell about that, because some inner sense informed me that Magness was a man with a bigger destiny.

I got to my desk and thought about writing up the day's activity report, but the adrenalin rush I'd been riding had faded like the aftertaste of cheap whiskey and left me drained. I was exhausted in mind and body . . . barely able to think.

Looking at the big round, black and white electronic Session's clock on the wall gave me another jolt, as I realized I'd been on the job for close to eighteen hours. My right leg was sending an urgent message of pain up to my head with every thump of my heart muscle and I craved rest with every cell in my body. I checked out a black and white patrol car and made it home, where I stumbled over a couple of days worth of junk mail that had been shoved through the slot in the front door, then made my way to the bedroom in the dark. I put my .45 auto on the nightstand, stripped and flopped into the unmade bed . . . asleep, in spite of everything, before my head hit the pillow. The eerie green radium-tipped hands on the alarm clock read five minutes past midnight.

It was a helluva ending to my tumultuous first week on the Skin Ripper Case . . . and I was already a changed man . . . but there was more to come. A lot more.

Chapter 29

Two days later, the doo-whop hit the fan in big steaming chunks that seemed like they'd never stop.

I'd had a pleasant couple of days to myself, an unusual event in the life of a homicide dick, but there weren't any call-outs or new developments in the double murder case that had the whole city on tilt. I'd spent most of Saturday afternoon at Nurse Gloria's, where I stocked up on pharmaceuticals, and Sunday in Palmer Lake, doing odd jobs for Ma.

I was in a jaunty mood as I came into work on Monday at a little after six in the morning . . . well-rested, well-fed, thanks to Ma, and with a minimum of pain, courtesy of Nurse Gloria's illicit pharmacy. Without a hangover, I planned on getting a head start on the ton of paperwork I'd been shirking.

That all ended when Wally Bailey looked up from his burrow behind the front desk. He smirked and said, "Jake McKern, the man, the myth, the legend himself. Your fame is spreading far and wide boyo. You've got a visitor."

Wally watched as a tall man wearing a black leather duster, hand-tooled black leather cowboy boots and a high-crowned, pearl-gray Stetson cowboy hat stood up and said, "McKern? Jake McKern?"

"Yes. I am," I said. "And who are you?"

"Name's Bryan Moore. I'm a Texas Ranger," he said as he reached inside his coat and withdrew a thick bundle of papers folded inside a light blue wrapper. He stepped in close and slapped them on my chest. "And you've been served," he looked at a gold Rolex on his left wrist, "at seven fifteen a.m. central time."

I stood there open-mouthed, clutching what turned out to be my first-ever divorce papers and watched Wally Bailey sign the Ranger's other proffered document as witness, attesting to my humiliation. Wally seemed happy to do it too.

As he nodded at my traitorous co-worker and turned to leave, I said, "Bryan, could I have a word with you? Outside," I added, looking right at Wally.

"Why not," he said. "Lead the way."

I noticed the star atop his left shirt pocket and the big single action thumb-buster he carried on his right hip in a tied-down holster when he moved behind me and thought, *I wonder if this guys for real . . . he looks like he this very moment, stepped out of a Hoot Gibson movie. Then again, maybe he's just another drugstore cowboy, trying to look like something he ain't . . .*

I stuck the divorce papers inside my belt in the small of my back as we came out the front door and down the steps to the sidewalk. I stopped in front of the cruiser I'd had over the last two days and said, "Would you rather sit in the car?"

"Out here's good," he answered from behind me.

When I turned to speak, I'd been flanked by the Ranger, who now had the rising sun at his back and the duster pulled behind him, leaving his walnut gripped pistol exposed and unencumbered.

I raised my hands in mock surrender and said, "Whoa there. What the fuck hoss. You think you're Wyatt or something? This ain't the OK Corral and I ain't Ike."

"Just being careful is all. Wally told me you were in a gunfight Friday night and that it wasn't your first."

"He also tell you I never fired my weapon?"

"No. But he said a man was killed."

"That's true. But not by me. Wally's got nothing to do besides gossip and stir shit up. I'm putting my hands down and getting my cigarettes out. Would you like one?"

"Sure, as long as it ain't one a them filtered kind. I heard those things'll give ya cancer."

"These are good old Lucky Strikes," I said, as I offered him one and took another for myself.

After we both lit up, I said, "Look Bryan, I've no animosity toward you. None at all. You're just the conductor. It's not your fault that I don't welcome the message. The reason I asked you out here was to see if you could, and if you would, tell me what's going on down there. Nobody's talking to me—and I've called more than a dozen times."

The Ranger looked at me and smoked for a bit, as if he was trying to assess my character from the outside. Then, he said, "You ever seen the elephant?"

"Yeah." I said.

"Whereat? Korea, or the Big One?"

"Big One. I was a US marine, from 1940 to '45."

"Got there early. Pacific, I presume?"

"Yeah."

"That's good enough for me. What would you like to know?"

"Anything. Everything. Where's my young son? What's the news about Big Jim and Jody Belle? And lastly, how is Mo . . . I mean Imogene?" I went on, and told him I'd been on the Sorwell murder case . . . going day and night on it.

"That's a whole bunch of questions," Bryan said. "You care what order I answer 'em in?"

"Not really. Any answers more than what I've got."

"It'll make more sense this way. What I'm about to say is on the down low . . . confidential and lawman to lawman . . . understand?"

"Sure."

"Y'all gotta be real damn sure pardner. There's a shit ton riding on this deal . . . not the least of which is my ass. I can't tell ya why I'm sticking my neck out like this for somebody I don't even know, but I will. Just as soon as you convince me your word's good."

I smoked and thought about that for a few moments. "You're asking me to bear witness against myself when you put it that way. All I can say is that my word has always been my bond, because if a man's word ain't no good, then he ain't no good."

"Makes sense," Bryan said. "Tell you what, take me somewhere for breakfast and I'll spill my guts to ya."

"Hop in," I pointed with my chin, as I knocked the fire off my coffin nail and field-stripped it. "I know just the place," and headed for the Pancake House.

Neither one of us talked much on the way over to the westside restaurant, as Bryan was busy gawking up at Pikes Peak, capped with fresh snow and rose-tinted by the dawning of the late March day. But as I pulled into the parking lot, he said, "That is one awesome mountain. Y'all are blessed to be able to look at it every day."

"We are," I said, as I nosed into a parking slot, right in front of the dining room. "The Ute Indians call it *The Shining Mountain Sitting Big.* Mornings like this, I understand why with perfect clarity."

"They got the essence of it for sure," the dark-eyed Ranger said.

Before I shut the motor off, I called in to dispatch and told them I was going ten-seven, out of service for a while, even though I didn't have to. Then we went inside and seated ourselves in the last booth, where Maggie Johnson saw us and came right over with coffee and menus.

Chapter 30

After the introductions, and all the other bullshit and donkey dust was done with, Maggie took our orders and left. The place was filling up by then, and she had other customers to take care of.

Bryan stirred his coffee, and got right to it. He said, "How much do you know about Chaparral Oil?"

"Just what Big Jim told me over the last few years. I know he struck it rich in West Texas and that he's got interests over in the Middle East somewhere . . . that's about it. We never talked of his business all that much," I said. But at the same time, I thought, *I want to see where this is going before I put all my cards on the table . . .*

The Ranger busied himself for a moment, sipping his coffee and lighting another of my smokes from the pack I'd left on the gray table between us. He inhaled, then shook out the match as he exhaled and said, "Chaparral Oil is one of the top fifteen oil producers in the world today, in terms of the amount of barrels pumped. No one knows for sure what the total estimated reserves they hold are, because the company is closely-held and . . ."

"What's that mean," I said as Maggie brought our steak and eggs and hash browns on big steaming platters, and Bryan snuffed out the cigarette he'd just lit.

Maggie said, as she topped up our coffees, "You're livin' high on the hog today, Jake. You win the Irish Sweepstakes or somethin'"

I laughed and said, "No Ma'am. Just the opposite in fact. But this here's my rich uncle. He's buying."

Maggie, at least twenty-five years older than either of us, gave Bryan Moore the twice-over from head to toe and said, "Well damn, darlin' . . .

where've you been all my life? Are you married, by any chance?"

Bryan, busy trying to clear the coffee he'd snorted up his nose after the unexpected outburst, mumbled something unintelligible.

Undaunted, Maggie leaned in and said, "Well you tell her bad weather's on its way Honey, cause a feminine hurricane is comin' right at her. Yes, oh yes indeedy. And I will not be denied." And with that she danced off, looking light on her feet for such a large woman.

I got busy with my breakfast, while Ranger Moore tried to collect himself and regain some composure.

Bryan turned to the side and blew the last of the coffee into a napkin. Finished, he turned to me with a grin on his face and said, "Sweet suffering Jesus . . . I thought Texas women were a handful, but old Maggie there takes the cake. Are all the girls so wild up here?"

"Dunno," I said around a mouthful of food. "But you can see why this is my favorite place for grub."

Then we quit talking for a while, and the sounds of knife and fork on heavy duty restaurant platters was all the noise that came from our booth. Outside, I could see the sun rising up in a pristine sky, where it was a bright and warm reminder of the promise of rebirth that comes with every spring.

I finished eating first, was drinking coffee, and enjoying an after-meal smoke when Bryan picked up the last triangle of toast and bit the corner off. He chewed and swallowed and said—as if no time had elapsed—"A closely held corporation is just that, closely held. It means that all the shares belong to one person or a group of persons."

"Like a family," I said.

"Exactly. In the case of Chaparral, all the shares are owned by Big Jim and Jody Belle Curdy. Because of that, they don't have to disclose or make public their profits and losses like a corporation that's listed on the New York Stock Exchange. You understand?"

"Yeah. I think so . . ."

"What it all boils down to is this, Chaparral Oil is a major player on the world energy stage, only no one knows for sure how big. All the analysts can do is make educated guesses."

I processed that for a bit, then said, "If you don't mind me asking Bryan, how do you know so much about all of this?"

He looked at me with something like amusement, or maybe it was pity. He said, "They really have kept you in the dark about the family business . . ."

"I never have had any money, and never cared about it either. I grew up in the Great Depression and learned to be pretty much self-sufficient and content without it."

The big Ranger looked out the window for a second before turning his gaze on me. He said, as he fired up his own after breakfast smoke, "Well that's good. Because your soon to be ex-wife is about to become one of the richest women in the world. She's the sole heir to all the Curdy's holdings. Oil, ranches, office buildings, automobile dealerships and banks . . . the whole damned empire. Everything goes to her and her alone—except for a trust fund of several million dollars that's set up for your son, Scott James McKern."

Stunned, all I managed to say was, "Jim and Jody Belle . . ."

Bryan shook his head. "Found a day after they disappeared, in New Iberia Parish—what the gators and gar fish left anyway—down in western Louisiana. They were headed for Houston from New Orleans and ran into a line of storms. Went down in the swamp."

All of a sudden, I had more questions than answers. "How come it took so long for me to find this out?"

"Because their deaths and the transition of ownership is going to roil financial markets around the world. Imogene Curdy McKern is a complete unknown to them, and markets hate uncertainty. Billions of dollars are at stake. Plus, there's the problem of you . . ."

"Why? What do I matter?"

"The way I understand it, the divorce had to be started before the Curdy's deaths are made public, so that you have no familial ties, and therefore no claims against the estate."

It was too much information to handle all at once. If I felt stunned before, the only possible way to describe myself at that moment was gob-smacked. I couldn't think straight. My simple little $380.00 per month lifestyle seemed like a farce, and my career the punch line of a crude locker room joke. Finally, I took a breath and said, "How in God's name, do you know all of this Bryan, and why are you telling me?"

"I'm telling ya because I was instructed to do so by Mr. Grinder and Imogene when I picked up the papers I served you with."

Ranger Moore paused then, looked at the check Maggie Johnson had put face-down on the table between us. He took out his money clip, peeled off a ten and laid it on the table, under the tab. Then he looked at me and said, "I know all of this from spending hours and hours in the air with the Governor, T. Wade Gilson. He's a silent partner of Big Jim's . . . along with a certain family down in New Orleans. One with a lot of cash to invest and a bunch of vowels in their last name. *Capeesh?* I'm Governor Gilson's private pilot and bodyguard. I also take care of special missions like this one, where the utmost discretion is needed."

I remember thinking, *It's downright amazing, that for the last ten years I could've lived with, slept with, and engendered another human life with someone, and still know almost nothing about them. I can't believe I was such a damn fool . . .*

I must have looked bewildered, or in shock, stupefied by the revelations of the past hour, because my breakfast companion cleared his throat to get my attention. When I returned to the here and now, he said, "There's one other thing . . ."

"Yeah. Like always. What else Bryan?"

The Ranger looked away for a moment, then said, "Mr. Grinder told me to tell you that the divorce and settlement terms have been in the planning stages for the last eighteen months. A whole team wrote them and they're pretty damned air tight, he said. So don't go wasting a lot of your time and money trying to get around the terms of it . . . because you won't be able to."

"Tell Grinder I said to go fuck himself."

"Sure Jake," Bryan said as he stood up. "Y'all will have to excuse me now. I gotta call a cab. I have a sweet and sexy little twin-engine Beech Queen Air, waiting for me out at the airport. She's all gassed up and ready to go home to Houston and I just love flying her."

"Go with God," I muttered as he left, and I sat there by myself . . . wondering what I was going to do with the rest of my life.

Chapter 31

I made it back to the police station at a little after the eight o'clock shift change, where I was greeted by Amos Magness on the front desk.

"Hello, Rags," I said, "What's the news?"

He looked up from the paperback he was reading under the counter, saw who spoke and shrugged. He said, "Morning Jake. No news is good news, far as I'm concerned. I'm just glad to get through the day without the windows blowin' out."

"You have an economy and an eloquence with words my friend. And have you by any chance seen that sorry-assed Wally Bailey? I want to have a few words with him."

"You're outta luck Jake. Wally hit the door at full waddle and disappeared as soon as I got here, a half-hour before his stint was even over. Told me to punch out for him, but, oh darn, I forgot to do it," Magness said, as he picked up his book and started to find his place. "But Lieutenant Patterson's been lookin' for ya." Then he went back to reading *Go Tell It on The Mountain* by James Baldwin, and a light went on in my head.

"Thanks Rags. Take care of yourself."

He tilted his head and looked at me over the top of his gold wire-rims, "Will do." Was all he said.

I'd started on the stairs to the bullpen and Lt. Patterson's office . . . then turned around and went back to the front desk. "Rags," I said, "sorry to keep interrupting, but are you okay with Friday night? It's a hard thing you did, and if you need to talk or anything, I'm always available for you . . ."

When he looked at me, the overhead lights flashed on his glasses and made them opaque. He said, in a voice that could've knocked a bird off a telephone wire, "He wasn't the first I ever killed. I'm okay Jake." Then he went back to his book and I trudged on up to the second floor.

Patterson was immersed in a blue personnel file when I knocked on his open door frame. "Loot, It's McKern."

Without looking up from what he was doing, my immediate boss waved his left hand and said, "Come in. Sit. Wait just a sec."

I let myself down and watched, while he wrote something in the file, signed and dated it, then tossed it in the pile already in the OUT basket on the credenza behind him. Only then did he look up and into my eyes. "Quarterly evaluations. What a waste of time. I should have stayed at sergeant. Then I'd be in the field, doing something useful, instead of pushing paper that nobody ever reads in this airless closet the city calls an office."

"Well take heart George. The rumor is that Captain Hoffman's gonna run for political office this fall and you can move into his slot. Put Sergeant Claypoole in here."

"Yeah. Maybe. Making plans is the easiest way to hear God laugh too."

"Seems like I've heard that before," I said, as I crossed my legs and started to relax a little. It was a mistake.

Lieutenant Patterson pulled out his cigarettes and lit up without offering me one . . . a bad omen. He exhaled and said, "So. You wanna tell me where you've been for the past couple of hours, instead of at your desk doing your job, and getting your daily reports up to Captain Duncan on time, so I'm not getting my butt reamed out by him?"

I was caught off guard by the way he was chewing my ass. We'd always been on a more or less friendly basis—one combat vet to another—so I was surprised at the rank pulling that was going on. I said, "What's the problem here Lieutenant?"

"I already told ya Jake. The last we heard from you was 'Going out of service.' Then nothing, until you breeze on in here a couple hours later, as if you own the place. Meanwhile, I'm getting my keister handed to me by Duncan. Why?"

"Because I forgot. I forgot to go back in service," I said, as I pulled the blue bundle from my back and thumped it down on the desk. "I was too busy being schooled by a Texas Ranger, about the perfidy of women and lawyers, all courtesy of the governor—a silent partner of my soon-to-be ex-father in-law, now officially dead—and his new quiet partner, the newly crowned empress of oil who used to be wife . . ."

Lt. Patterson leaned forward with both arms on his desk "Whoa. Whoa. Whoa. Stop. You're not making any sense. You need to back up and start over Jake. Quit babbling and go through it in a logical and step-by-step manner."

I took a breath and willed myself to calm down, and quiet down. I'd been unconsciously raising my voice in the heat of the moment. I took a breath, then another and still another one after that, while I pulled out my pack of cigarettes and lit up. Then I told George Patterson everything that had transpired, from the moment I came in the front door of the police station at a couple of minutes past six, until the time I put the summons on his desk.

He smoked and listened to my saga quietly, without comment or interruption. When I stopped talking, he said, "Sorry for your troubles Jake, I'll cover for you with Captain Duncan, but we've still got to do our jobs. Do you have a lawyer?"

I shook my head.

Patterson pulled a flat metal address file from its spot next to the telephone. He found the place he wanted, opened it, and said, "Write this down," then read off a series of letters and numbers. "That's the city attorney's office. His name is Bill Tournillon. He'll help, or refer you to someone who can. He was at the poker game Friday night, asked Magness some questions about the shooting."

I wrote everything in the back of my notebook, then said, "So that's what was going on. I was in such a fog from the autopsy and the gunfight, I didn't stop to wonder how an investigation committee was put together so damn fast. To tell you the truth, I'd lost all track of time, and place."

"I know what you mean, Jake," Patterson said as he stubbed out the butt of his cigarette. "I've done the same thing after a gunfight. It's eerie in the aftermath, when you start to think about what just happened, and your part in it."

Oh, yeah, I thought, while the Loot dug around on his desk for something, I remembered; *George Patterson had landed in Sicily in WWII, fought his way across the island and then up through the Apennines, town by town and mountain by mountain, in some of the toughest fighting of the war.* And like all the rest of us . . . he didn't want to talk about it.

Lt. Patterson found the file he was looking for, then shoved the ashtray and pushed a stack of papers to one side in order to clear some space on his busy desk.

As he opened the folder, Patterson said, "You and Magness lucked out Friday night. The guy Magness killed was on the FBI's ten-most wanted list. He's a contract killer out of Kansas City; name, Elray Robinson Rose, wanted for armed robbery and two counts of murder in the first degree, attempted murder of a police officer, bank robbery, fleeing to elude arrest and etcetera, etcetera, etcetera. Chief Budd said he'll add another attempted murder charge for shooting at you too."

"That was one bad bastard for sure. Any idea what started the whole thing?"

"Yes," Patterson said, "Elray Rose was trying to hold up Mrs. Duncan's Cotton Club over on Colorado Avenue. He stuck a gun in Fannie Mae's face and tried to steal the show proceeds from her. Joe Pierce was moonlighting as a bouncer and bodyguard. He saw what was about to happen and got in the middle of it. Rose slashed Pierce with a straight razor and tried to escape. Pierce went after him, and you know the rest."

"What about the other man, Pierce?" I said, as I leaned over and put my smoke out in the big brown glass ashtray on the desk.

Lt. Patterson opened a second file. "You lucked out there as well. His name is Joseph Johnson Pierce . . . he's a local man and solid citizen. Married to wife Elizabeth, two kids, owns a house in the Hillside neighborhood. He works construction for the road contractor at the Air Force Academy and served in the Army in Europe during the war. Received a bronze star and a purple heart. No priors, no warrants, and no arrests."

"Did he make it? Is he alive," I said.

"Haven't you seen the weekend newspapers?"

"No. I took it easy and stayed out of touch. Kept my head down on purpose," I said.

The Lieutenant turned around on his chair and retrieved the front section of the Saturday newspaper and held it up.

I could read the headline from where I sat . . .

HEROIC COPS BATTLE WANTED DESPERADO

and see Magness's photo on the left and mine on the right, all above the fold, with the full story of how we shot it out with the gangster and saved a local man, by Lenny Bragg, underneath it.

"You haven't seen this?" Patterson said.

"My hand to God Loot. No. I have not."

He handed the paper to me. "Here. Enjoy it while it lasts. And I've got a couple more items for you."

"Do I need to brace myself?"

"Nope. It's all good. First thing is, that junker you were driving was killed by Elray Rose. It took two .44 caliber super vels through the engine block. It's gone to the car crusher. So, because the Chief has been given a brand-new Coupe de Ville to drive, courtesy of Ned Dolan, the Cadillac dealer, an almost new, unmarked '56 Ford with all the options is being assigned to you. Turn in the patrol car and they'll give you the other one . . ."

"For real, Loot? No joke?"

He grinned. "No joke. But the other thing is, you've got to double down on the Skin Ripper. We're getting all kinds of heat about it."

And just like that, reality set in, and just like Icarus, I crashed back to the Earth . . . where the doo-whop was still splattering onto the fan.

Chapter 32

When I went back to my desk, there were several messages waiting for me. Three of them came from Gilda Arkady, so I called her first, and wonder of wonders, she answered. I said, "Hi Gilda. It's Jake McKern, returning your call."

"Hello handsome. How are you, my heroic friend? You were featured on the front page again. Everyone is talking about you."

"I'm denying everything, Gilda," I said and chuckled, adding, "and how may I help my favorite professor today?"

"Ah. So modest. And such a kidder. No Jake, it is I who can help you. Remember my friend up in Denver, Father Al at Regis College?"

"Of course. The ancient language and biblical historian. Did you speak with him?"

"I did. I explained everything and he's quite interested . . . he loves mysteries."

She gave me the contact information for the Jesuit Priest, whose name was Alphonso Gianette. I thanked her, promised to meet her for lunch sometime in the near future and rang off.

I lit up and was waiting for an outside long-distance line, when Ann-Marie Fuchs, the clerk-typist and all-around gal Friday for the detective division came over with two more pink message slips in her right hand. I disconnected the phone with my left index finger, laid the handset upside down on my shoulder and took the memos from her. I said, "Thanks Ann-Marie," and started to go back to trying to call Gianette in Denver.

She said, "Jake, can I talk to you?"

"Sure. What's going on," I said, as I put the phone back on its cradle, then glanced up at her. I saw that her eyes looked a little puffy, as if she had been crying, but couldn't tell for sure. She was a good Catholic girl, fresh out of secretarial school and only about nineteen years old. She came from a nice family and had a spotless reputation. Her father wouldn't have it otherwise, from her, or her two sisters. But I knew too, that as an attractive young woman in a male-dominated environment, she was forever fending off unwanted advances and innuendos from all the old-boy Lotharios whose beer guts hung over their belts, and asses drooped in their pants. Perhaps she came to me on that day of days because I always addressed her by name . . . not honey, sweetie, toots, chickie or babe . . . but she never said, and I'll never know.

Ann-Marie sat down in the battered old gray metal government surplus chair that was placed beside my matching desk. She leaned in close and said, "I have a problem . . ."

"You should talk to Lt. Patterson. He's the one in charge . . ."

She looked at her hands, twisted together in her lap. Keeping her eyes downcast, she said, "It's not that kind of problem . . . it's . . ." and she stopped talking.

I paused for a bit, stayed quiet, waiting to see if she'd start to explain what the problem was.

After a minute or so, she sighed, looked past me, and said, "It's that old guy. Dunlap . . ." and went silent again.

I let the hush play out for a second interval, thinking she'd resume speaking, but she remained mute. This time I said, "Ann-Marie, if you won't tell what's the matter, I can't help."

"It's really hard to say out loud. It's embarrassing . . ."

"I understand, but we can't keep doing this. I've got a ton of work to get to. If you can't explain what's bothering you, that's okay, but I have to get back to my job."

She sniffed, and tears rolled down her cheeks as she said, "He put his hands on me."

"Who? Jim Dunlap?"

The blushing young woman covered her face with her hands and nodded yes as the tears slipped through her fingers.

In spite of everything else that was showering down on my head that morning, the thought of this innocent young woman's distress at the hands of an old creep like Dunlap was burning a hole in me. In truth, she reminded me of my little sister Catherine, murdered by a degenerate and drifter named Petey, almost twenty years ago, I wanted to reach out, take her hand and comfort her . . . but was afraid to do so . . . thinking the last thing Ann-Marie wanted was another male laying a finger on her. So, as the rage-monster who slumbers within me began to stir and mutter, chittering and snapping its teeth as it dreamt of havoc and mayhem . . . I waited.

And then the dam broke.

Ann-Marie looked at me with angry eyes. Without a word, I handed a packet of Kleenex to her from my desk drawer. She dabbed her face, blew her nose, and drew in a gulp of air. In a rush of words she said, "Ever since I got my job here, that man has leered and made nasty two-way remarks to me—and about me to others. I've never, ever responded or dignified his smuttyness by saying something back. I've always just ignored him. He's nasty. And disgusting too . . ."

"You mean Officer Jim Dunlap."

"Yes. Jake."

"I said, "Use his name Ann-Marie."

She nodded and said, "This morning, when I came in to work at 6:30 am, Officer Jim Dunlap assaulted me in the employee parking lot. As I was locking the door of my Nash, he snuck up from behind and pinned me, pressing me against the side of my car with his body. Then he put his arms around me, grabbed my breasts, squeezing them painfully and whispered in my ear; *You know you want it don't cha, you sexy little cock teasin' bitch . . . I'm gonna give it to ya too . . . Soon. Real soon.* Then he stuck his tongue in my ear and left. I spent the next half-hour in my vehicle with the doors locked, crying my eyes out and swabbing my ear with tissues and eye drop solution from my purse. But I can still feel it in there. It's disgusting and I can't stop thinking about it."

I could see she was about to break down again. I said, "Ann-Marie, do you recall anything else?"

"I think he was hanging out in the parking lot, waiting to get off at eight. He had alcohol on his breath. I could tell that he'd been drinking when he got close. He reeked of it."

"Did you see anyone else in the parking area?"

She shook her head. "No. His attack was well planned, I think. There wasn't anybody out there. I'm sure of it."

"Okay," I said. "What do you want me to do?"

"Make him stop," she said as she stood up to go. "And make sure it won't happen again," she added as she walked away.

You can depend on that, I thought, as I reached in my desk drawer and turned off the tape recorder I'd started when I got the tissues.

I went down to the pop machine and bought a bottle of Coke, just to get the bad taste and the thought that that kind of a low-life had wormed his way into the organization I was sworn to support and pledged to honor. Men like Dunlap were a disgrace to the uniform and anathema to all the rest of the good cops who wore the badge.

I stayed in the break room for a few minutes, drinking cola and smoking while random thoughts drifted through my mind. I swallowed the last of my drink, put the bottle into the wooden case of empties next to the vending machine, and headed back to my desk. There, I resumed making telephone calls . . . while the rage-monster slipped out of hibernation and fed my subconscious mind with all the ways I could stomp a mudhole in Jim Dunlap's ass.

Chapter 34

Even with enough anger inside of me to burn a hole in the back of my head, I managed to get some work done that morning.

First thing I did was to make contact with Gilda Arkady's friend and fellow polyglot, the Jesuit Priest, Alphonso Gianette. He was cordial, interested, and expecting my call. It seemed Gilda had filled him in with the known facts of the hand-written book and stirred his curiosity about the mystery of its contents. He was eager to have a look, while I was more than ready to find out if it had any relevance to the Skin Ripper Case. He gave me directions to his office in Denver and we arranged a meeting for late afternoon.

I took a moment then, to glance through the other pink message slips that were piled up on the center of my desktop empire, where they were weighted down with a brand-new box of .38 caliber ammunition . . . a subtle reminder from George Patterson that CSPD management frowned on the .45 ACP hand cannon I had under my left armpit at that very instant. I smiled and pushed it aside. *Thanks for the gift, Loot,* I thought. *But I'd rather be judged by twelve than toted by six . . .* I've said it before—and I'll no doubt say it again—because it's the truth.

Most of the slips were congratulatory in nature, mentioning the weekend article in the Gazette and my part in it. It felt like I was being promoted all of a sudden, as a public personality and face of the Colorado Springs Police Department . . . something that I didn't think would sit well with the other officers. I didn't deserve, nor desire the notoriety. And, as if proving that thesis, mixed among the remaining messages were two from Agnes Bedwell, the TV news hottie, and one sent by the Sultan of Snark himself, Lenny Bragg . . . all seeking to have some time with me. *Sure,* I thought, *just as soon as I finish slamming my head in a car door.* I swept the whole pile of well-intentioned but gratuitous tidings into the trash.

I couldn't put it off any longer. Heaving a big sigh, I pulled my notebook, turned to the back page, and called the City Attorney's Office. After two rings, an efficient, well-spoken female voice answered and told me I had reached the legal department.

I stated my name and asked for Mr. Tournillon, as I stared at the thick blue packet of legal documents that had upended my life a few hours ago.

"Oh, hello Mr. McKern. We've been expecting to hear from you. Lt. Patterson spoke to Mr. Tournillon earlier. He said for you to drop the process papers by here and he'll look them over for you. It may take a few days before you hear back from him. It seems the City's been swamped with mostly frivolous lawsuits lately, but they all take up his time."

"Thanks," I said. "Should I ask for you?"

"Sure. My name is Judy. Judy Ives. I'll take care of it."

"See you in a little while, Miss Ives."

"It's Mrs. Ives. I'm married."

"Beg your pardon, Mrs. . . ." I said, but she was already gone.

I called Ann-Marie Fuchs on the inter-office phone line, asked her for a large manila envelope and J.P. "Jim" Dunlap's personnel file—if she had access to it.

"As a matter of fact, I do." she said.

Five minutes later, I was glancing through the man's personal history as well as his record with the CSPD. It wasn't pretty. I said, "How'd you get your hands on this so quick?"

"Lt. Patterson was just doing quarterly evaluations. I was about to refile them."

I found what I was looking for in the file and transferred the details to the hard worked last page of my notebook. I passed the folder back to Ann-Marie and said, "Are you feeling any better?"

She looked at me with eyes that seemed too old for her face. "I don't think I'll ever be better—I know I'll never forget the feel of that swine putting his hands on me—but I've gone from shame to anger. I'll run over him with my car if I get the chance."

"I don't want you to get put in jail because of his criminality . . ."

"You ever hear of hit-and-run?"

"Damn, Ann Marie, are you sure you ain't Irish?"

"Pretty sure," she said. "But the Celts don't hold the patent on retribution. Ask Otto Von Bismarck . . ."

"The Iron Chancellor? I guess you've got me there. But don't let an asshole and loser like Jim Dunlap rob you of the chance for a long, beautiful, and productive life."

"We'll see," she said, and walked away with Dunlap's file pressed to her chest like a shield.

The Rage Monster didn't even blink.

I lit a cigarette, wrote my name, badge, and phone numbers on the tan envelope, then stuffed the divorce papers inside. With the heavy packet under my arm, I ducked into Patterson's office. "Loot, I'm headed to Denver to meet a professor at Regis College. He's a language and ancient writing expert . . . to see if he can tell us anything about the handwritten book recovered at the Skin Ripper murder scene."

Patterson looked up from the pile of paperwork he was working on, "How'd you find this guy?"

"Through Gilda Arkady, the art professor at Colorado College. He's a priest."

"I saw enough of them when I was over in Italy to last me a lifetime. Good luck getting a straight answer out of him. My experience with the whole bunch of 'em wasn't all that positive . . . most of those religious types will lie just for the hell of it. Even if the truth would've sounded better."

"So, I guess you're not too religious Loot?"

Patterson snorted. "No. I'm not. Get outta here. I'll see you when you get back."

"Will do." I said, and headed down to the basement property room to retrieve the leather-bound journal I'd found in the Sorwell's freezer compartment.

When I got there, Roscoe was nowhere to be found. The evidence room was wide-open and Officer Gifford was gone. Roscoe Gifford was our charity case. He was attacked one night while on patrol, and nearly beaten to death with a three-foot piece of galvanized iron water pipe by a pair of young thugs, who'd been in the process of breaking into a downtown jewelry store when Roscoe interrupted them.

He was on foot, out of his patrol car, checking to see that front doors were locked, over on the South Weber Street and Pikes Peak Avenue business district. As he approached the Knight Jewelers building on the SE corner of the two streets, noises in the alley prompted Roscoe to investigate . . . and that's when he found a prowler with an aluminum ladder back there. Realizing he's caught a burglar in the act, Officer Gifford drew his revolver and commanded the suspect to put his hands up. That's when the second burglar—who'd been up on the roof of the single-story building removing the bolts from the air conditioning unit in order to enter the store through the ceiling—attacked him from above using the piece of pipe he'd scavenged on the roof.

Roscoe Gifford wasn't found until just before dawn, when a paperboy making his morning rounds stumbled across his body and called for help. The young lad thought the policeman was dead. The doctors said it was a miracle he survived. But he did. And seventeen weeks later, in an act of kindness in those pre-disability retirement days, Chief Budd put a seriously handicapped man with a young wife and four little girls at home, in charge of the evidence and property room of the CSPD.

It was a quiet place without many demands, but even those few sometimes taxed Roscoe's abilities and his limited capacity to concentrate. Then he'd forget where he was or what he was doing. He'd wander off somewhere, hide and take a nap. On a couple occasions he was found at home, doing chores in his uniform. Once, he was sitting in his recliner watching soap operas.

And back in those more laid-back days of the late 1950s, when The Springs was a town growing into a city, the police department too, operated on a looser footing . . . so we all made allowances for Roscoe . . . and gave him a lot of latitude because we all knew that *There, but for the grace of God, go I.*

So, if there was no officer guarding the evidence room—like to-day—we operated on the honor system. I let myself into the cage, as the locker was called, found the Skin Ripper file, and retrieved the metal box with the mysterious leather book and let myself out, after leaving a hand-written receipt on the counter for Roscoe Gifford.

It was an act I'd come to regret a few days later.

Chapter 35

I headed over to the City Attorney's Office, where I met Mrs. Judy Ives and dropped off the legal papers I'd been served. She was pleasant, chirpy, and busy, but took the envelope and repeated everything she'd said earlier on the phone. I thanked her and hurried out. I had two more errands to do before I could leave for Denver and my meeting with the priest, Gianette. I needed to step on it.

The unmarked police car I inherited from Chief Budd was a dream come true. It had power steering; automatic transmission and a big V-8 motor. *Black Beauty,* as I called the car in my head, was fast, but she just L-O-V-E-D the taste of gasoline. I needed to fill her up before I left town; and at that time, we had a great system for it.

Each municipal vehicle contained a city-issued credit card in the glove compartment. They came from the same regional oil company with stations all over town—and owned no doubt, by a friend of some of the oligarchs in city government, or one of their relatives—which made it convenient for everyone who was authorized to drive a City of Colorado Springs motor vehicle. And as an added benefit, the city received huge discounts on its monthly fuel bills. It was an arrangement born of bias . . . but it was based on altruism and trust . . . principals that were diminishing at a faster and faster rate, because as the Springs grew ever larger, it cast off more of its innocent ways with every step along the way. Such were my melancholy thoughts as I pulled into the Sinclair station on East Cucharras Street, where Tyler Myers came out to pump gas.

"Hello sir, fill it up?"

"Yeah. And check the tires too, I'm on my way to Denver."

"Wish I was going with you," the young man said as he washed the windshield and rear window, then opened the hood and made sure that the oil, water, and power steering fluids were all full. Lastly, he used the tire gauge he carried in his shirt pocket to check the air pressure in all four tires while I went inside to buy a bottle of root beer and a couple of nickle bags of salted peanuts for a quick, stand-up lunch on the run.

Tyler finished the tires, closed the hood, and topped off the gas tank. He hung up the nozzle, shut the pump off and came in the office, wiping his hands on a red shop rag he pulled from his back pocket. He said, as he walked up to the register, "She took $7.63 worth of gas Mr. McKern, and everything else is okay. I did put some air in the right front tire though."

I gave him the credit card I'd taken from the glove box. "If I get time, I'll bring it in next week, have you check it."

"Sure. Maybe it's got a slow leak or something . . ."

"Could be," I said, "there seems to be a couple of them around all the sudden," as I thought of Ray Dunlap.

Tyler filled out the credit card slip then handed it, and the card, to me. I signed and said, "Ain't you going in the service pretty soon?"

"Yeah. Next month, when school lets out and I get my diploma, I'm enlisting in the Navy."

"Gonna see the world, huh?"

"I hope so. Colorado Springs is great, but I want something new, a change of scenery. Know what I mean?"

"I do Tyler. I damn sure do," I said, as I shook his hand and wished him well, handed him one of my cards and asked if he'd drop me a line or two every once in a while. Tyler was the thirteen-year-old boy delivering newspapers who'd found Officer Roscoe Gifford, bloody, comatose, and close to death on a beautiful summer morning, almost five years ago. I was one of the first responders on the scene and saw how devastated the young lad had been. I did my best to comfort him at the time . . . and I've tried to look out for him ever since. He was a good kid with a bad home life . . . and that was something I knew all about. My old man was a mean drunk who abused our whole family until I put a stop to it.

I was about to get in my car when Tyler came out and said, "Thanks for caring Mr. McKern. It means a lot."

"You're welcome. Be good and make the most of it. It's hard . . . but rewarding."

"Aye-aye sir," he said. Then he came to attention and saluted as I drove away.

From the gas station it was only a short hop over to Platte Avenue and South Institute Street, where Ray Dunlap lived alone, in a little one-bedroom wood-framed house he'd bought at a tax sale during the war. I parked a couple of blocks down the street at The Deaf and Blind School, and walked back to the place with peeling paint, missing front gate and a weed-choked lawn that sported broken whiskey bottles, some soggy newspapers, and a discarded car tire for ornamentation.

I was thinking about Ann-Marie Fuchs and her tearful confession as I came up the neglected walk, getting angrier with each step I took.

With the rage-monster spurring me on, I knocked on Dunlap's front door with a lot of enthusiasm. It took several attempts before there was a response, and by the time Dunlap's shadow flitted like a bat across the peep-hole, I was pounding on the door hard enough to knock it off the hinges.

Dunlap—with his whale-belly flopping over his tiny white BVDs—jerked the door open and stood near naked in the entryway. "What the fuck McKe . . ."

That's when I waded in, swinging an uppercut that came from my knees and connecting with everything I had to that quaking mass of flab and guts he called a bay window. I drove forward, lifting all three-hundred pounds of fat man clean off the ground. He flew backwards for a foot or two, then landed on his ass with a thud that shook the whole house. After that, he rolled onto his back gasping for air, then turned over on his right side and emptied the contents of his stomach.

I closed the door behind me, leaned against it and watched as Dunlap squirmed in pain on his parlor floor. After a minute or so, spitting, coughing, choking, and gagging . . . the wounded man made it to his hands and knees. Through gritted teeth, he said, "I get to my feet McKern, I'm gonna fuck you up. Bad . . ."

"Uh huh," I said, as I took two steps forward and kicked him in the area of his left kidney with enough force to flip him over again. I caught him with the heel of my boot and put my left leg and body weight into it. It hurt. I know it did, because Dunlap thrashed on the floor like a beached fish . . . moaning and writhing in the mess he'd made on the floor.

My voice quivered with rage as I said, "Stay down, Dunlap, and keep your mouth shut, or I may lose control of myself."

The only sounds for a few moments was the big man's gasping. But after a bit, he moaned, rolled over and sat up. "Then what?"

"I won't be able to contain the anger. It'll take over and I'll wind up beating you to death with my bare hands." Saying it out loud like that made me feel like a monster . . . but the truth is the truth . . . it is unassailable and irrefutable.

And the truth is that at times I am in fact a monster. The only question is, whether or not that makes me evil. I have never been able to come up with an answer.

"You're as crazy as a shithouse rat, McKern. You come bustin' into my house, wake me outta a sound sleep and assault me? Make an unprovoked attack, cause me great bodily harm and possible internal injuries? I'll have you arrested and brought up on charges before your shift is over, you cocksucker."

"No, you won't."

"Oh yes I will motherfucker."

"NO. YOU. WON'T. And I'll tell you why you won't. Ann-Marie Fuchs," I said, as I lit a cigarette and inhaled.

That's when the first crack appeared in Dunlap's indignation. He blinked. Said, "What about her?"

"You know goddamned good and well, what about her, you sorry sonofabitch. You sexually assaulted her in the parking lot this morning and threatened to rape her."

I could see I had Dunlap's attention. He shifted in his seat, looked down to his left and said, "Aw, bullshit. Her word against mine. I was on patrol up in the Roswell neighborhood when she came into work today."

"I never said when, Dunlap. I just said 'this morning.'"

"It's still her word against mine, a twenty-one-year CSPD veteran. I'll deny it."

"No, Dunlap. You won't. You're gonna put your papers in first thing tomorrow morning, or else."

"Or else what, McKern? You think you can bully me? You better think twice before you threaten me, asshole."

I licked my thumb and index finger and pinched the ember out on my cigarette, stuck the butt in my shirt pocket. "It ain't a threat, Dunlap. It's a promise."

I pulled the little battery-operated tape recorder out of my coat and played Ann-Marie's confession for him. When it finished, I said, "Even with all your time-in-grade, you're still only a P2, patrolman second class. You've never been promoted. And with all the complaints in your file . . . what do you think Chief Budd will do . . . I put this on his desk and play it? My guess is he'll arrest you himself. Then frog-march you into a cell. No pension for Dunlap. Just public humiliation and loathing."

"Oh, and there's this too . . . you don't go to church, so you wouldn't know . . . but Ann-Marie is a devout Catholic. She was raised that way. What do you think her father would do, he heard this? He's a tough old railroad dick who's been bulling on the Rock Island Line ever since I can remember. My guess is, he'd come over here that same night and beat you to death with an ax-handle. Make it look like a burglar did it. What'cha bet Dunlap? Bet your life?"

The two strong licks I'd put on him and the preponderance of guilt in the evidence against him had taken all the starch out of Dunlap. I could see the acquiescence in his face and eyes as I showed myself the door without another word passing between us.

There was a lightness to my step despite the pain in my right leg as I walked back to my car. I swallowed a couple of white tablets from Nurse Gloria's secret supply and set off for Denver and my meeting with Father Al, secure in the knowledge that I'd just done a good deed, but it triggered old memories. So, with each passing mile, I couldn't stop thinking about my little sister Catherine, murdered when she was only a child by a real-life monster who preyed upon the young and most innocent among us.

Chapter 36

I made it up to Denver at a little after three o'clock, but it took another half-hour to get out to the northwest part of the city where the Jesuit College was located and find Alphonso Gianette's office in the Boettcher Commons.

He was on the phone in a tiny book-filled office on the third floor when I arrived and stood in the open door with the metal box that held the handwritten book in my hand. Seeing me, Professor Gianette covered the phone with his hand and said, "McKern?"

I nodded, and he waved me in, pointing to a metal and wood chair in front of his desk. I sat and soon realized those things were still as uncomfortable for someone my size as when I was attending college back in the late forties. I stayed as motionless and quiet as I could, while the man in the clerical collar kept talking in what sounded like German on the phone.

Dunno what I was expecting, I thought. *But it wasn't a small man who looks like a vampire with an Adolph Hitler mustache, dressed like a parish priest and smoking a fat black stogie that smells like burning trash in a barrel.*

I must have wrinkled my nose or made some kind of unconscious face, because—as he hung up the phone—Gianette said, in accented English that tended to lilt upward at the end of his sentences, "I know they stink. Everyone who comes here says so. But I like them. They are the one vice I cannot seem to shake off. What can you do? I am Alphonso Gianette. You may call me 'Father Al,' as the kids do, or just 'Al,' if that's more comfortable."

"Jake McKern," I said, and reached across the desk to shake his hand.

"The Detective from Colorado Springs. Gilda Arkady told me a lot about you . . . she said that you are a famous and brave man. She also informed me of your investigative prowess, and added that you have discovered a book of some sort, hand-written and undecipherable. Is all of that correct?"

"Yes, as far as the book is concerned. No, with regard to myself. I'm just an ordinary guy doing his job."

Father Al uttered a short bark that passed for a laugh, puffed on his cigar, and blew a cloud of smoke at the ceiling, then extinguished the stinker in a sand-filled metal ashtray that stood on the floor next to his desk. As he did, he said, "She also told me you are a modest man who doesn't yet know his strengths. What do you say to that, eh? I think she is smitten with you."

An uncomfortable silence ensued while I tried to think of what to say next . . . I wasn't comfortable or happy about being discussed in the third-person, nor interrogated in such an intimate manner. It took about a half-minute or so, before my brain sputtered back to life and I said, "That's very gratifying Father, but not to be taken seriously. Madam Arkady is at least a generation older than I and her remarks, while flirtatious sounding, are only meant in jest. I barely know her. We had lunch together and she referred me to you. And that is all. I want to make that clear."

"And so, you have Detective," the Priest said as he made space on his desk and turned on a brass reading lamp with a green Emeralite shade. I took the hint, put the metal box with its arcane contents on the desk and began to unwrap it while Father Al watched me with a creepy and morbid intensity, I found unsettling.

And just like that . . . he changed.

The cloak of respectability came off and an inner Mr. Hyde emerged as soon as the leather covered work was revealed. I heard an intake of air from Gianette when he saw the book's smooth leather exterior, and he seemed almost giddy when I said, "This is it," and handed it over.

The sudden difference was so unexpected and radical, it put me on high alert. I started giving the same level of attention to the scholar and priest as I would to a suspect being interviewed in a murder investigation. I was looking for tells—signs of deception, guilt, or ulterior motives—and I didn't have to wait long before my sixth sense was setting alarm bells off. It was telling me that Father Alphonso Gianette was as hinky as a cheating spouse who'd been caught with their pants down . . . but not why.

My focus was glued to the scene in front of me. As I watched, Father Al opened the book with hands that jittered ever so slightly, and he looked at page after page without saying a word, while I was left wondering if his quiver was due to an infirmity caused by a medical condition of some sort . . . or if he was just so eager to get his hands on it that he trembled. I waited and watched, unanswered questions piling up in my mind.

The man across from me appeared to be in his sixties, but I wasn't sure. He may have been older. *I wonder where he was during the war, and what he was doing. The rumors about the Pope and the Nazis are full of collaboration stories. Maybe Lt. Patterson can shed some light on the subject, because, so far at least, Gianette seems to be a man of contradictions and secrets and unknowns . . . an enigma,* I thought to myself.

Aloud, I said, "Father, would it be okay if I smoke?"

Absorbed as he was in the journal, Gianette gave only a slight nod to indicate if he'd heard me. I wasn't sure, but I craved nicotine at the time, so I went ahead and fired up a fresh coffin nail, inhaled, watched, and waited some more.

It took a while. I'd smoked the cigarette down to a nub that was about to burn my fingers and was getting ready to put it out on the sole of my boot when Father Al pointed to a bookshelf on my right. I looked and found a small ceramic ashtray with the college logo on one side. I took it down and extinguished what was left of the Lucky Strike in silence, not wanting to further break his—or my—concentration. As he poured over the journal, I continued to observe his every move, while my personal alarm bells were ringing off the hook.

I was beginning to squirm on the hard uncomfortable student chair by the time Professor Gianette closed the book and looked at me. He said, "Whoever made those chairs must have been in league with the Devil himself."

"They don't like me for a fact. Feels like I've been wadded up and tossed in the trash to tell you the truth, but I'll survive. What do you think about the journal?"

Gianette paused for a moment to take off his bifocals and massage his temples. Then he put them back on and said, "Tell me please, where did you find this?"

He's dissembling, I thought, *buying time* . . . Aloud, I said, "It was recovered at the scene of a double homicide in Colorado Springs, on the near westside. Why do you ask?"

"Curiosity mostly. It's an unusual document to be found in America, or anywhere outside of the Middle East."

I waited. Gianette remained silent, looking down at the desktop, keeping his right hand on the book . . . protectively or possessively . . . I couldn't tell for sure.

After a few awkward moments, I said, "Father?"

"Oh. Sorry. I was thinking . . ."

About what . . . I wondered to myself.

"I can't read this," the professor priest said, "yet. I can tell you some things about it however."

"Would you hold on to those thoughts for a moment," I said as I reached for my notebook. "I want to write everything down."

When I nodded, he started talking again. "The book is written in Aramaic. It originated in Mesopotamia around 1000 B.C. and is one of the first written languages. It was spoken from Judea to Persia and formed the basis for many other tongues, including Arabic and Hebrew, as well as hundreds of offshoots. That's the problem. I recognize the idiomatic style—and some of the words, enough to tell you a few details—but not the dialect. I need to research it in detail before I could translate the whole thing. A challenge I would welcome."

I was writing and thinking at top speed. As I filled the page and turned to a fresh one, I said, "So what can you tell me?"

Father All hesitated for several heartbeats, looked down and away, then said, "I think what you have here is a jeremiad . . . a lament for the dead."

"Lamenting who? By whom?"

"I'm sorry, Jake. I haven't been able to read enough of it to answer those questions at this point. Why don't you leave the book here and I'll decipher it for you."

I paused, said, "How long do you think it would take to do that . . . translate the whole thing?"

The priest reached in his desk drawer and withdrew another short black cigar and busied himself with the process of clipping the end off and lighting it, while I waited for an answer,

When he finally got it going and puffed out enough smoke to foul the air around us, Gianette said, "That depends, on how long it takes to decipher which dialect it was written in, and how old and obscure."

"How old is the book?"

"Hard to say for certain. At least a couple of centuries, I think. Perhaps more. But once I have the dialect, translating it should not take more than a month or so . . . six weeks perhaps."

". . . After you've ID'ed the dialect," I said as I watched him. I noticed he had his right hand back on top of the leather-bound journal again.

"Yes. That is correct."

"I can't do that Father," I said as I reached over and took the book from him.

"Why in heavens name, not . . ."

"Because it's evidence in a murder case," I said, then began to wrap and repack the hand-crafted journal in its metal box, while Gianette looked on with what I thought was dismay . . . or covetousness.

Two certainties however, were stuck in my head as I left for the Springs. Father Al did not want the mysterious journal to leave his sight . . . and he was lying.

Chapter 37

It was late by the time I parked in front of the house on Seventh Street where I now lived by myself. The drive back from Denver had taken longer than usual because of a storm that began as I was thanking the Professor and Priest, Alphonso "Father Al," Gianette, and taking my leave of him after promising to send a copy of the journal, trading contact information and saying we'd stay in touch.

It was snowing hard as I headed down Federal Boulevard, slowing traffic to a crawl. I turned east on Belleview, then south on Santa Fe and stayed with it all the way out of town. The heavy, wet, and greasy spring snow kept falling too . . . making the roads treacherous and the driving hazardous. I had to pull over twice to clear the windshield, where the wipers had packed the corners so full of it that they stopped working. It made the return to Colorado Springs long and slow, but gave me plenty of time to think about the Skin Ripper.

The case was getting colder by the day. I had no suspects, no leads, and no motive for the execution-style murders of the two elderly survivors of World War II Nazi death camps and the mutilation of their bodies post-mortem. Why? Why a pair of harmless old folks? Robbery? Revenge? Retribution? The why of it kept bouncing around in my head without an answer. The only potential clue was the leather-bound journal that rested on the seat alongside me, packed in a metal box of unknown origin. Now, even it might not be meaningful if Professor Gianette was to be believed. Should I? My head did. But my gut said otherwise.

I stopped in Sedalia—at a liquor store whose neon signs threw a rainbow of colors that blurred in the snowy dark like the echoes from an interrupted dream—where I bought a half-pint of bourbon to wash down a pain pill and keep me warm the rest of the way home.

The next morning, after one of the longest and most eventful days of my life, I was at the Police Department typing several days worth of daily reports at 6:30 a.m. I was a bit on the shaky side from lack of sleep, too much booze and too many pain pills . . . but had it under control with a pot of strong black coffee and a couple of bennies—the stay-awake stuff favored by long-haul truckers—from nurse Gloria's contraband pharmacy. All of that combined meant I was flying right along when I presented myself at Captain Duncan's Office to give him an overdue progress report on the Skin Ripper Case.

The Captain kept me standing while he read my write-ups, leaving me once again, feeling like a delinquent teen remanded to the Principal's Office. When he finished the last page and laid it down, Captain Duncan said, "I see you've been busy, McKern, so why haven't you made any progress? Why don't you have any suspects in mind? And, why are you still standing there? Siddown for chrissakes, so I don't put my neck out of joint looking up at you."

I took a seat on the closest of a pair of brown leather wingback chairs in front of his desk. I was chewing gum to cover up my bourbon breath, thinking like crazy, and hoping he wouldn't notice how bloodshot my eyes were. I said, "I have no suspects, because there haven't been any leads, nor motives, nor clues. The closest thing I have to an eyewitness is a man who was drunk, lying face down in his backyard, who said, 'He heard what sounded like a German car, but couldn't see a thing.' The only tangible item I have is the mysterious journal that's written in some ancient language that nobody can read . . ."

"What is this book? Tell me about it again," Captain Duncan said as he came to full alert, putting all his attention on me.

I gave him every bit of the information that I'd gathered, starting with the discovery of the mysterious journal in the Sorwell's freezer compartment, to the knowledge I'd gleaned from lunching with Gilda Arkady, and finally, everything Alphonso Gianette told me the previous evening.

When I quit talking, Captain Duncan said, "Is that all?"

"Yessir. It is."

"Where's the book now?"

"In the property room downstairs. I checked it back into evidence when I first came in this morning."

Just then, the phone rang on his desk. Captain Duncan picked it up, covered the bottom of the handset with his other hand and said, "Keep me up-to-date about it. That is all."

I heard him say, "Hello . . . Yes Mr. Mayor . . ." as I left the room.

On the way back to my desk, I bumped into Lieutenant Patterson, who looked as overworked as usual, but managed to give me a friendly grin anyway. He said, "Good morning, Jake. How's it going?"

"Slow and confusing Loot. If you have a moment, I'd like your advice . . . go over some details about the Skin Ripper Case."

"Yeah. I can do that, but give it fifteen minutes or so. I'm dealing with some personnel issues at the moment."

"Sure," I said, and headed on to my gray metal desk, which sat to one side of the bull pen, directly across from an identical empty one. It was that way when I got here a few weeks ago, and despite the rumors of transfers and promotions, there was still just three of us in the whole Robbery-Homicide Division at the moment instead of the six we were supposed to have. *Sure, would be nice,* I thought, then put the idea out of my head. We'd get more help when we got it, and not before.

While I was waiting for Lt. Patterson, I walked a block down Tejon Street to Pikes Peak Avenue. I went in the Busy Corner Cafe, bought a couple of sweet rolls and two cardboard containers of coffee with cream and sugar to go. I stood by the cash register and drank a glass of Bromo-Seltzer while my purchase was being wrapped up and put in a paper sack, then paid the waitress, thanked her, and left. Last nights snowstorm had stopped on the north side of the Palmer Divide, bypassing the Springs, so the short walk back to the police department was brisk and pleasant . . . but I couldn't stop thinking about the morning paper that was left on the counter. Over Lenny Bragg's byline, the headline read:

SKIN RIPPER STILL STALKS SPRINGS

Chapter 38

A few minutes later Lt. George Patterson and I were sitting on opposite sides of his desk drinking lukewarm coffee, eating cinnamon sweet rolls wrapped in wax paper and brainstorming about the Skin Ripper Case.

I recounted the previous day's meeting with the professor and priest, Alphonso Gianette, in minute detail . . . including my gut feeling that something was off about his behavior . . . and the oddness of his appearance.

"Are you sure you're not letting his looks affect your judgment?" Patterson said, as he drained his coffee, wiped his lips with one of the paper napkins that came with the sweet rolls, then dropped the refuse in the trash can under his desk and reached for his pack of cigarettes.

I thought about the question—and my answer—as I stuffed my mostly uneaten pastry into the cardboard cup and handed it over to be thrown away. "No," I said, as I lit one of my own smokes, "I don't think so, Loot. It felt like he was withholding some, or a lot, of what he saw in the journal. And then he lied about the age of it. Last of all, it was apparent, plain as day in fact, that he did not want to give it up. I had to literally take the book out of his hands in order to retrieve it."

It was Patterson's turn to ponder for a moment before he answered. We both smoked in silence for a bit, then he said, "I think you need to find another translator."

"I agree. And based on what the two professors told me, I have some ideas about where to look for one, but there's a problem . . ."

"Isn't there always. Tell me."

"I don't want to take any chances with the original."

"Make a copy."

"I was thinking of several, just in case Loot."

"Don't make more than three, Jake. I can't cover the expenditure if it gets too big."

"Understood and acknowledged. I'll take care of it. I believe the journal is the key to solving the murders . . . and I have a hunch that it's why the apartment was turned inside out. The killers were searching for it."

"Maybe. Without knowing what it actually says, we can only guess," Patterson said as he extinguished his cigarette and turned to a stack of folders on his right, where he extracted one from the middle of the pile.

I took a last drag on my smoke and crushed it out in George's ashtray while I watched him open the file.

He said, "Well here's a bit of good cheer. The first of our anticipated transfers has come through. His name is Butch Hernshaw. He's been a cop for six years and a homicide investigator for two. He's thirty-five years old, married, has three kids, and another one on the way. Wife's name is Sallie. He'll start the day after tomorrow. I'm assigning him the desk across from yours."

"Permanent or temporary?"

"Don't know. You'll have him for a little while is all I can tell you. We'll get him here, in Robbery Homicide first, but Captain Hoffman needs officers too. I can't say what's going to happen. The Chief will be the one who decides."

I shifted in my seat, pleased at the prospect of some much needed help, but concerned about what kind of guy he was, because nothing's worse than being stuck working with someone you can't stand. I said, "Where's he coming in from?"

"Pueblo. He's a native Coloradan."

I figured it all sounded like good news as I went back to my corner of the bull pen, but I wasn't counting on it. Only time would tell.

By the time I was seated at my desk and sifting through the pink message slips that had piled up under my phone, I was starting to feel jittery, light-headed, and shaky . . . the result, I guessed, of the five cups of caffeine I'd ingested this morning . . . on top of all the booze, bennies, and lack of anything nutritious to eat for the last two days.

It was the side effects of taking too many amphetamines—along with the appetite suppression—that nurse Gloria had warned me about. She told me, 'You'll think you're Superman for a while, and you won't be able to sleep. But then you'll come down hard. It'll make you feel like something the cat dragged in and chewed up, then urked back out again if you take too much.'

She warned me. I hadn't paid enough attention. Now I was on the verge of paying the price.

I tried to put all of that out of my head as I picked up the phone and dialed the number for Doug Sikes.

A woman answered, "Sikes Photography Studio."

I said, "This is Jake McKern with the CSPD. I need to talk to Doug please."

"He can't come to the phone right now Officer, he's developing film in the darkroom at the moment. Can I help you with anything? This is Rhonda, his wife."

"Thank you, but no. It's about a possible project . . . and it's Detective McKern. I spoke to your husband last week, when he and I were both at a crime scene together."

"Oh. Yes. You're the detective he told me about, on the double homicide over on Spruce Street. What a terrible thing to happen here, in Colorado Springs."

"Or anywhere Mrs. Sikes. Have Doug give me a call."

I was working on a Murder Book compiling all the known information and photographs of the Skin Ripper Case into a three-ring binder when my phone rang about twenty minutes later. It was Sikes.

He said, "I hope you don't have another murder already Jake."

"No. I don't. The reason for the call is to see if you can help me duplicate a hand-written book that was found at the Spruce Street crime scene."

"You mean like a diary?"

"No. It's larger—more like a journal in size, but it's put together from scraps of paper and handwritten, in some kind of ancient language. It's like nothing you've ever seen before."

"What exactly do you want Jake?"

"Three copies. I thought you could make photographs of it. Or something . . ."

"How many pages are there?"

"Around a hundred and fifty."

"Yeah. I think we can do it. I'll make photos and halftones. Then you can print as many as you want."

"Can you keep the cost down? Lt. Patterson's worried about the money part of it."

"Well, it ain't gonna be free. I will keep it as reasonable as I can though, if you're willing to assist me. But I can't tell you exactly how much until I see it."

"Understood," I said as I lit up a Lucky Strike with my old stainless-steel Zippo that still has the brass Marine Corps globe and anchor embossed on it. "How soon could you do it . . . and how long will it take?"

"I assume you want it as quick as possible?"

"It's believed to be the key to solving a double homicide . . ."

"I know. But I have commitments all day today and tomorrow that I've got to honor. I can't put them off. Plus, I'll have to set up some equipment in the studio for this kind of job. How about the day after tomorrow? You can bring the book first thing in the morning."

I said, "If that's all you can do, it'll have to be okay. I'll see you then," and we both hung up. It was disappointing. I was anxious to make some progress . . . to be able to inch toward solving the brutal murders . . . and prove that I was the real deal when it came to crime detection.

Two days later, when I opened the evidence file, the hand-written journal was gone without a trace.

Chapter 39

Thursday morning, I went in to work at a hair or two before seven in the morning, spit-shined, shaved and standing tall. Or so I pretended.

The truth was that I was a little green around the gills and ragged at the edges from carousing, pill-popping, and pouring enough eighty proof down my throat to pickle a walrus. Physically, my leg was killing me, and I was eating pain meds like salted peanuts to stay on my feet. Psychologically, I was devastated by the thought of Mo divorcing me, losing my son Scottie, and my inability to catch either The Skin Ripper . . . or the long-ago murderer of my sister Catherine and her playmate Maddie Brickman . . . a drifter named Petey. I was self-medicating with alcohol because I felt sorry for myself.

I hammered out my daily report and managed to get through the morning bracing by Capt. Duncan with a minimum of fuss. I checked in with Lt. Patterson and told him where I'd be, then went down to the property room to retrieve the journal before going to see Doug Sikes.

When I got there, Roscoe Gifford was nowhere to be found, so I let myself into the cage and pulled the Skin Ripper evidence box, in order to get the handwritten book. When the lid came off however . . . there was no metal container with the precious journal. It was gone.

I know I put it here the morning after I came back from seeing Gianette up in Denver, I thought, *I know I did . . . so where the fuck is it?* I searched all three of the Skin Ripper files, went through blood-stained pillows, sheets, blankets, and nightgowns, all to no avail. Then I looked through several adjacent, unrelated case evidence boxes . . . all with the same results. The book was gone.

Not quite panicked, but definitely pissed off, I went back out front and found Roscoe sitting at his desk, drinking coffee from a thermos, and eating a piece of his wife's home-baked apple strudel.

"Roscoe," I said, "wouldya please look in your log and see who's got the metal box from the Skin Ripper case? I need it, but it's not in the file where it's supposed to be . . . and I know I checked it in when I got back from Denver."

"Sure thing Jake," Roscoe said as he put down the piece of pastry he'd been eating with his hand, adding, "just give me a minute," as he licked his fingers, one-by-one, then wiped his hand on his side, and his face on his uniform sleeve. He shoved the snack off to the right and pulled an old-fashioned ledger book from its place in the desk drawer in front of him.

I watched, as Roscoe made a production out of opening the chain-of-custody register and methodically turning page after page, until he got to the current one. I recognized the loose piece of paper stuck in it, at the same time that he pulled it out.

Roscoe checked, line by line, then read the scrap he held in his left hand. He said, "The last one to remove that book thing was you, Jake. It says so right there."

"Look here," I said, as I reached for the page from my notebook, but Roscoe was holding on like it was a fifty-dollar bill. "That's from a few days ago, when I was on my way up to Denver."

"There ain't no date on it."

I looked. There wasn't. Someone had cut it off. I tried again, said, "If you take a gander at the ledger, you can see where I signed it in and out at various dates and times after that, dammit."

"Well, you can say whatever you want to Jake. But as far as I'm concerned, the proof is right here," Roscoe said, as he tapped the open book with his index finger. "And you're the last one to sign for it," he added as he reinserted the loose piece of paper and closed the book, then put it back in the drawer.

While I stood there, fuming, and embarrassed, Roscoe went back to eating strudel with his fingers, ignoring me, as if I was no longer there. I turned and left without another word. But I wondered, all the way back to my desk . . . *Who in the CSPD was trying to torpedo me?*

And more importantly, why? What was it about an unreadable diary that was inciting so much drama? The questions without answers kept on piling up in my head as I went back upstairs to the bull pen.

The new guy, Hernshaw, was sitting behind the desk across from mine when I got there, putting stuff from a cardboard box into the drawers and arranging some mementos and trinkets on top.

"Hello Butch," I said. "I'm Jake. You look like you're gonna stay for a while."

He looked across the expanse of desktop separating us, a cork-tipped cigarette dangling from the corner of his mouth, and said, "I'm like an old stray cat. Give me a few scraps to eat, a warm place by the stove, and you'll never get rid of me."

I nodded, gave a polite chuckle as I got ready to light one of my own, then said, "Well, I'm damn glad to have you. I think some new blood is just what we need around here."

Butch grunted and went on emptying his carton, stowing almost everything in the lap drawer. There wasn't much, so it didn't take long. Finished, he took a jackknife out of his pocket and cut the box along the seams, then dumped the pieces in the trash can next to his chair.

While he finished his chore, I called Doug Sikes, who answered on the second ring. I said, "I'm having a problem locating the evidence. Someone took it out of the locker without signing the chain file. As quick as I catch up with whoever did it, I'll callya and bring it over."

"Well, I hope you do it soon, because I have the studio rigged up for the job. I'll leave it as long as I can, but if someone calls for a por-trait session, I'll have to take it all apart."

"I understand. I'll turn this place upside down if I have to."

"Good luck," he said and hung up.

"If you don't mind me asking," my new deskmate and possible partner said, "what's the problem?"

"You want the long, or the short version," I said, as I took a long drag on my cigarette and tapped the ash into an empty coffee cup.

"Long. I'm a detail and facts guy."

I nodded and gave him a full briefing on the Skin Ripper Case, starting with the discovery of the bodies, all the way up to the moment I faced off with Roscoe Gifford a little while ago. It took the better part of an hour, during which Butch gave the recital his full attention and never once interrupted the narrative.

When I finally quit talking, he said, "So. You think this diary is the key to the murders?"

"Yeah. I do. Somebody, somewhere, spent one helluva long time creating it, and Mr. or Mrs. Sorwell went to great lengths to preserve and conceal it. And now, the newest entrant in the ever-expanding cast of characters—an odd little man named Alphonso Gianette, the Jesuit priest and visiting professor at Regis College up in Denver that I mentioned earlier—wanted the book so badly, I had to take it out of his hands."

"By force?"

"I pulled it from his grasp. He wasn't gonna hand it back otherwise. It felt like he was lying about it too."

"Lying? How exactly," Hernshaw said.

"I'm pretty sure he could read it. And I also think he concocted a story as to what it was about."

"And why do you think so?" Butch said, as he stood and pushed his chair under the desk.

"Gut instinct."

"I'll be right back," he said. "I gotta go get something out of my locker."

The shower and individual changing room was downstairs, next door to Roscoe Gifford's fiefdom. As I watched my new brother-in-blue disappear, I lit a fresh coffin nail from the stub of the old one and wondered . . . *Someone among my fellow officers had sabotaged me . . . Who was the dirty bastard?*

Chapter 40

Butch came back—just as I was about to go and bare my soul to Lt. Patterson, where I planned to confess my inability to handle the only real evidence, we had in the Skin Ripper Case and eat the consequences—with a dirty towel in his hands and a frown on his face.

He put the soiled terry cloth on his desk and said, as he unwrapped what was concealed inside, "This what you're missing?"

I almost couldn't believe what I saw. Right there in front of me, was the gray metal box I'd dug out of the freezer compartment at the crime scene over on North Spruce Street. I said, "It's damn sure the first half of it. If there's a leather covered handwritten book inside, we're in Fat City."

As Butch passed it over to me, I said, "Where'd you get this?"

"It was hidden in the bottom of the wall locker I decided to take," Butch said as he lit up a fresh smoke and watched me open the sought after container.

I grunted with relief when the journal reappeared in fully intact condition. "Thanks Butch. You just saved my ass. This is the only tangible piece of evidence I have, and so far, at least, nobody can figure out what it says."

"I took a peek, Jake. It looks like Hebrew to me."

"You're the second one to tell me that. The other was a professor at the Colorado College," I said as I repacked the journal. "Did you happen to see who put it in the locker?"

"I had my arms full as I came in the door, and I was thinking about all the stuff I had to do at home, as well as here, so I wasn't paying a lot of attention. But when I came into the locker room, I heard one of 'em shut and footsteps moving away. Then the door slammed. I didn't think too much about it at the time, but now, it looks like I might've interrupted somebody making off with the metal box. They stuck the damned thing in the first open wall locker and took off rather than be seen with it. That's what I'd guess anyways. There was a bunch of old rags and crap in the bottom of it when I went to put a change of clothes and a shaving kit in there. Lt. Patterson told me to take any one of 'em that wasn't being used and put my own lock on it. It was only by chance that I even found the metal box."

"Lucky's better than good in this case," I said. "And I'll take all of it that I can get. Can you remember anything else—any other details—that might help us figure out who it was?"

Butch was quiet for a bit, then said, "I'm pretty sure it was some-body big. The kind of person who doesn't pick their feet up all the way when they walk."

"Do you know about what time it was?"

"Yeah. It was oh-six-thirty."

"Thanks, Butch, I owe ya a beer."

"*De nada*, but I'll take you up on the beer sometime."

I called Doug Sikes and said, "Got it. I'm on my way," and hustled out of the building.

Then it only took a few minutes to get over to Union Boulevard where his home and studio was located. After I was ushered in by his wife Rhonda, I found the irascible photog in his studio, fiddling with some adjustable lights he had clamped to a work table that was cov-ered by a dark green drop cloth. In the center of the table was a tripod with a camera on it that was pointed straight down at a couple of short pieces of 1″x 3″ wood furring strips.

"Sorry it took so long Doug," I said, "but we had a short setback at the PD. Some dirty bastard took this outta the evidence room and hid it. We only found it by accident when a new guy stumbled onto a pile of rags where it was concealed."

"That's okay Jake. It took me a while to get these damnable lamps adjusted anyway. You'd have just been sitting here, listening to me curse at the friggin' things."

"Nothing I haven't done myself on more than a few occasions."

Sikes made another small tweak to one of the lights, tightened a wingnut, then said, "Okay Jake. Let's see whatcha' brought."

I took the book out of the box and handed it to him. Doug looked at the outside, then flipped through a few pages and nodded to himself. He said, "Here's what I need you to do . . ."

And for the next four hours—with only a couple of quick bathroom breaks—all I did was bend over, hold the pages of that arcane diary open under those hot-assed photo lights and listen to the click and whirr of the camera, as we took pictures of the whole book . . . page, by page, by page.

After what seemed like all day and half the night, Sikes said, "Okay Jake. That's it. We're done."

"Those words couldn't come soon enough," I said, as I stood and stretched the ache out of my lower back, then added, "or be more welcome. I don't know how you do it. The tedium and monotony would drive me crazy."

"You get used to it. I guess it depends on what you like to do," Doug said as he pulled out his smokes and lit up.

I followed suit, inhaled, and snapped my lighter shut. "What happens now?"

"I'll develop the film, make halftones, and get prints made and put 'em in three-ring binders. That'd be the fastest and cheapest way to reproduce it."

"Yeah. That'll make the Lieutenant happy. How soon can you get it all done?"

"Couple of days if the printers not jammed up."

"Anything you can do to expedite it would be appreciated," I said, as I rewrapped the leather-clad diary and got ready to leave.

"Thanks for your help, Jake. It made the job faster . . . and easier too. You could be a good photographer if you wanted to."

I looked to see if he was joking. He wasn't. I smiled, said, "Not a chance, Doug." And then I left, with the boxed journal under my arm, wondering how best to keep it from disappearing again.

At a rendezvous in the foothills south of Colorado Springs, the small man in the brown tweed overcoat sat at one end of a long table, smoking an unfiltered cigarette, and watching as the four others who made up the cadre of their elite group filed in and took their seats. They acknowledged each other with slight nods of the head, but no words, for conversation wasn't really wanted, or even necessary. They were all battle-hardened veterans of the late war who'd been tested on the Eastern Front, at Stalingrad, in the deserts of North Africa, the Alps of Italy and the plains of Europe, as well as covert operations in Macedonia, Greece and the Balkans, and some were even on the deserts of the Middle East, where none of them had ever lacked for courage, fighting spirit, or devotion to the Fatherland, Adolph Hitler, and the Third Reich.

> 'Now we are in the home of our greatest enemy, tasked with the audacious and probably impossible . . . to sow the seeds of its ultimate destruction from within . . . while at the same time we prepare for the rise of the Fourth Reich . . . no matter the cost or the time it takes. My only fear,' he thought, as he extinguished the cigarette, 'is that we lose sight of our purpose because of unforeseeable problems like the one we're dealing with now. We cannot withstand exposure, or even the threat of exposure. It was only by pure chance and bad luck that those two old Jews turned up at the same exact time and place as us with that damnable journal. The chances of that happening must be so small that they're almost infinitesimal . . . yet here we are. My only hope is that the little führer has a better solution in mind than her last one . . . because we are doomed otherwise.'

At that point his reverie stopped. The small man in the brown tweed overcoat sat up straight in his seat and gave his full attention to the captain's chair at the other end of the dining room table . . . where the highborn woman herself . . . the unconditional leader of the cell, had just taken the seat reserved at all times for Number One.

Seeing every eye focused upon herself, she opened the folder on the table in front of her and said, "We have averted disaster by only the slimmest of margins. Our operative at the Police Department escaped detection, but failed to recover the incriminating book. It was in his hands, then hidden in haste with the intention of recovering it later that night when there were not so many observers. Unfortunately, as you are all aware, that did not happen. It was discovered, then returned to Detective McKern. We do not know at this time, what he has done with it. Number Two . . ."

The man in the brown tweed overcoat said, "Yes . . ."

"Your assignment is to follow McKern. Find that damnable journal and get it back if possible."

"By any means?"

"No. Use stealth only. Sanction is out of the question at the present time."

"As you wish."

"It is the command of those whose authority far exceeds mine. The rest of you continue with your jobs at the hotel as we get this situation under control."

> 'If only she had listened, we would have done our work and gone undetected,' the man in the brown tweed overcoat thought as he made his way to the guest cabin where he was bivouacking by himself. 'By mutilating the bodies, the murders became noteworthy . . . and notorious . . . all for the vanity of a woman who is most likely insane. And I will probably have to kill her because of that.'

Chapter 41

It was late afternoon when I left the photography studio, which didn't leave much time to get anything done, but all I could think about was how to secure the Sorwell Manuscript—as I'd started to call the leather-bound diary in my head while turning the pages for Doug Sikes—from theft and harm. I had a half-assed sort of plan in mind . . . if I could get to the office supply store before it closed.

With just minutes to spare, I pulled into a parking space in front of the City Office Supply on East Bijou Street and hustled inside. I bought twine, three cheap writing tablets, tape, and a roll of brown wrapping paper, plus a couple of grease pencils—one black and one red—the kind that write on glass, then headed for my rented house over on Seventh Street, where I carried everything inside.

The next thing I did, was to call Lt. Patterson and let him know where I could be reached.

He said, "I'm just on my way home myself. For once it wasn't too eventful of a day . . . the only thing of real interest is that Jim Dunlap quit. Filed his retirement papers, effective immediately, turned in his badge and gun, then scarpered off to parts unknown, as my old Scots-Irish granddad would say."

"So, it was unexpected?"

"Yeah. Never gave any indication he was gonna pull the pin until he laid his service weapon on my desk this morning."

"Guess you never can tell," I said as I started to light one up, then thought twice about it and stuck the smokes back in my shirt pocket.

"He did say one kind of a curious thing though, 'Tell McKern I'll see him around.' You have any idea what he meant?"

"None whatsoever, Loot," I lied.

"I'm asking because it sounded like a threat to me. You have some kind of a beef goin' on with him?"

"Not that I can think of," I lied again. "We've had our differences—his idea of law enforcement is a helluva lot the opposite from mine—and he wasn't a good training officer to Amos Magness in my opinion . . ."

"Okay Jake. Point taken. But you've got more than enough on your plate with the Skin Ripper Case. I wouldn't want to see you overloaded. Know what I mean?"

"Yessir. Perfectly. But you'd better get out of there while the gettin's good. Stick around much longer and some emergency will crop up. You'll be nailed to your desk all night."

"You just make sure I'm the first to know about any goings-on around here Jake. Not the last."

"I hear you loud and clear L.T.," I said, while I thought, *Better grow eyes in the back of your head for a while . . . 'cause Dunlap is just stupid enough to try.*

I turned on the kitchen radio for some noise and a little company, then cleared off the kitchen table and got to work. An hour or so later I was almost done. As I was packing the second cut-down writing tablet into the metal box, the phone rang. When I picked it up, I heard, "Have you had supper yet?"

"Hi there Gloria. No, I haven't."

"Good. I'm making spaghetti and homemade meatballs. Why don't you come over and I'll feed ya."

A glance at my watch told me it was after seven. I'd been working longer than I realized, said, "How soon would I need to get there? I'm not quite done with work."

"Can you get here by eight?"

"I think so. What can I bring?"

"Just yourself honey. I'll see ya in a little while," she said and hung up.

I finished trimming, wrapping, and packing the two Big Chief writing tablets into the metal box the Sorwell Manuscript was discovered in, and thought it was an adequate decoy. Bound in brown mailing paper and sealed with two-inch wide fish tape, they were about the same size and shape as the real diary. I closed the metal box and tied it off with sisal twine—as if it was going to be mailed in the postal system. Then I took the real manuscript and made a book cover for it out of a brown paper grocery bag, wrote, "Sr. Thesis—Cervantes, Chaucer or Dante" on the spine with an old fountain pen and rubbed it with the palm of my hand until it looked old and worn and well-used. I stuck it in the living room bookcase next to all the journals I'd written, starting back in 1940 when I left home and entered the Marine Corps. It blended in perfectly and I was satisfied with the way it was hidden in plain sight. After policing up the left-over scraps and tossing everything in the trash can in the alley, I put the decoy into the trunk of the unmarked, and headed for Nurse Gloria's place. After stopping at Lee's Liquors on Colorado Avenue for a bottle of chianti, I got to her house with about five minutes to spare.

The light was on over the back porch door when I came up the wood steps with the straw-wrapped liter of wine in hand. Nurse Gloria must have heard my footsteps, because she opened the door before I could knock and ushered me into her kitchen, where the smells of spices and sauces bubbling away were mouth-watering.

Without a word she rose up on her tip-toes and kissed me on the mouth. She said, "What took you so long? I didn't think you'd ever get here."

"I stopped for this," I said, as I handed her the gift.

"Perfect. You open it and pour while I get our food. Everything's already on the table."

We ate and drank wine, made small talk, and just enjoyed the moment together. Afterward, I helped her clear the table and dried, while Nurse Gloria washed the dishes. When the last utensil was scrubbed clean and put away, she wordlessly took off her shoes, locked the door and turned off the lights.

I said, "Gloria, I think . . ." and that was all I got out before she covered my mouth with one hand and pulled me into her bedroom with the other. I had no resistance, no protest, no objection—I was weak and compliant—for the allure of that tiny woman was overwhelming to me. I watched without words as she took her slow and deliberate time, removing each article of clothing from both of our bodies by the dim light of a pink boudoir lamp . . .

And then we were together in clean white sheets, locked in an old sweet tango that's as ancient as humanity itself, endlessly rocking, rocking, rocking in a cradle of she and he that has no beginning or end and floats along forever, somewhere outside of time and space.

Chapter 42

I awoke before dawn, in the darkest part of the night to find Nurse Gloria curled up next to my torso and holding the top of my right hand, which was cupping her left breast as we spooned together under a hand-stitched quilt that was made by her mother's mother's mother.

My time sense told me it was only a few minutes after four, so I stayed in place, listening to the rhythm of her breathing as it rose and fell, feeling the steady beat of her heart beneath my hand and inhaling the flowery scent of her raven-black hair, which was spread like a cloud between us. And it was at that moment, when I realized what I was feeling was peace. *It's been a long time,* I thought and dozed off again.

I woke up for good an hour later when Nurse Gloria said, "Honey it's time. We both have to be at work soon. Wakie wakie."

"I'm awake," I said, then sat up and watched, as she climbed out of the iron bedstead and tiptoed to the bathroom in the nude. It was a scene I revisited any number of times in my mind over the next days and weeks, and it always put a smile on my face.

I sighed, then started to retrieve my clothes, which were folded neatly on a wooden rocking chair that sat next to the window, and put them on.

I was just getting to my footwear when Gloria came out of the bathroom, wearing a flannel bathrobe and some fuzzy pink slippers, which made her look downright adorable. As I was pulling my pant legs over the tops of my cowboy boots and starting to stand up, she stopped me.

Laying her hands on my shoulders, Nurse Gloria looked me in the face. She said, "I need to tell you something Jake, and I want you to listen close and hear me. Okay?"

I nodded, saw the concern in her eyes and stayed mum, waiting for her to speak. There were a few heartbeats of silence, then she began saying her piece.

"I know you probably think I'm nothing more than a common slattern after the way I've acted toward you . . . but I'm not. Until I met you in the hospital last fall, I've been celibate for the previous nine-plus years . . . ever since I was molested by a second-year intern at the hospital, right after I graduated from Beth El Nursing School. He cornered me in an empty room where all the graveyard nurses went to nap for short breaks. After he got done with me, he said he'd destroy my reputation and my career if I ever said a word to anyone. I never did, not even when the solution to the problem he left me with took away my ability to have children. I've never told anyone, until now. My father would have disowned me and my mother's heart would have been broken if they had known. It's been my secret, and my shame. Everyone at work thinks I'm the Ice Queen, or a lesbo, and I've done nothing to disabuse them of the notion. It was only when I met you, something gave way inside me that lit the flames of desire again, and they've never gone out. If there's such a thing as love at first sight, it's what happened to me when I laid eyes on you. I'm telling you now, so you know what you're getting into if you keep seeing me. And if you don't." she stopped and looked aside for a moment while a couple of fat tears rolled down her cheeks. She brushed them off and continued. Said, "If you don't, I understand. I'll live. I'll go on, and I'll make last night last the rest of my life. But I'm also telling you—don't just call me when you're horned up or in pain, looking for some drugs—I'll be here if you want me, but I expect the same fidelity and commitment from you that you're getting from me. I'm not some loose woman and I won't be treated like one . . ."

Sitting down, I was only a bit shorter than Nurse Gloria was standing up, with her hands still on my shoulders. Her gaze never wavered and we never broke eye contact as she looked down at me and waited, while I searched for the right words.

I said, "You are dear to me Gloria, the most precious and caring woman I've ever known—the most beautiful and giving too. And I confess that I have not had enough time at this point to explore what I'm feeling and doing with the relationship we have . . . but I do know that it's personal and deep . . . and growing. I don't know where my heart is at the moment but I can tell you with certainty that you have first claim on it, and there's no one else I'd rather be with. That's the truth. I'll never lie to you. I'll never disrespect you. I'll always hold you in the highest regard."

"And just so you know . . . Imogene has not only left me; she took my son too. I was served with divorce papers on Monday. A Texas Ranger flew up here special, from Houston, to hit me with 'em when I came to work. Wally Bailey, the overnight desk clerk, signed off on them as an official witness. The asshole . . ."

"I should say I'm sorry for your troubles Jake," Gloria said—as she wrapped her arms around my head and pressed my face to her chest, comforting me the best she could while some of the stress and worry and grief leaked out of me— "but I'm not. Because as one door closes, another one opens. My mother, who was born and raised in San Francisco's Chinatown, was fond of saying that. I never fully understood what she meant . . . but I think I do now."

"Time will tell Gloria. I know that . . . but all I feel right now is foreboding. It's as if something bad is coming right at me and I can't recognize it."

Gloria kissed me on the top of my head and said, "It's fear of the unknown honey. You're going through some huge, life-changing events that are out of your control. Nobody likes change, especially when it's forced upon them. Add to that the pressure of the Skin Ripper Case, plus your leg pain and it's a wonder you're still functioning at all."

I hugged her closer as I said, "Last night was the first real sleep I've gotten in weeks. I felt relaxed for the first time in what seems like forever when I woke up with you all curled up beside me."

She bent her neck and nipped my ear and brushed it with her lips as she said, "Play your cards right, *hombre,* you could wake up like that every morning."

"I don't deserve you . . ."

Gloria put her hands on my head and pushed out to an arms-length away. She looked into my eyes as she said, "Don't say things like that to me. Deserve has nothing to do with it . . ."

"I only meant that I don't think I'm worthy of you."

"I'm the one who decides where, and with whom, I'm willing to spend the days of my life Jake. I've told you what I feel about you. Now it's up to you to do something about it."

"I will, Gloria. I promise. I will."

She kissed me on the lips and re-tied her bathrobe where it had come undone, stepped away from me and said, "Sorry honey, but the fun's over for now. We both have to be at work in a little while."

I nodded in agreement and headed for the kitchen door while Nurse Gloria went back into her bathroom. It was a quiet ending to a night of tender beginnings, the start of what looked like a promising and lasting relationship.

Only time will tell, I thought, as I let myself out—and the big orange cat, who was merowing at the back porch door—in, to the sanctity of his home and hearth, something I no longer possessed.

Chapter 43

After a pit stop at the house on Seventh Street to clean up, shave and change clothes, I was at work early, typing those pain in the ass daily activity reports that Captain Duncan was so enamored with. He hadn't been quite so insistent over the past two days, that I stand at attention in his office while he read them, so I tamped the sheets neatly together and clipped them in a labeled file folder I placed front and center on his desk, hoping for the best, but fearing the worst, from experience and force of habit. I kept my fingers crossed.

After that, I took the twine wrapped metal box back to the property room and made a big production out of entering it back into evidence under the watchful eye of Roscoe Gifford. In one of his many unusual habits, Roscoe was always two hours early for work. He might forget and wander off in the middle of the day, but he was always at his post by six o'clock in the morning without fail. He was sitting on a metal stool in the cage, drinking coffee and eating a white, powdered sugar donut from the box of them at his elbow when I came through the door at six-thirty. I said, "Morning Roscoe. What's the news," as I put the manuscript box with its decoy contents on the counter between us.

"Hi, Jake. No news," Roscoe said as he pushed the newspaper off to the side. "I was just readin' the funnies is all."

"Some days, they're the best part of the whole damn newspaper."

"Every day, far as I'm concerned. You checkin' that box back into evidence?" Roscoe pointed at it with his chin, while he shoved half a donut into his mouth and chewed.

"Yeah. And I'm gonna want to see it go into the file box on the shelf. No disrespect to you, but I want to make sure it's where it's supposed to be."

"Whatever yuh want Jake."

I watched, as Roscoe entered the manuscript back into the CSPD chain of custody ledger, and together we repacked it into the cardboard file box containing the rest of the evidence from the Spruce Street murder scene, then stuffed it onto its overloaded metal shelf in the physical storage room. After that I left Officer Gifford to his newspaper and donuts, while I made my way back upstairs . . . to where the station house was coming alive for the day.

The shifts were changing. The graveyard guys were signing out and the daylight crew was being briefed by Sergeant Andy Claypoole. Phones were ringing, people were talking and the steady clickity-tap-ta-tap-tapping of typewriters could be heard keeping a contrapuntal undertone in the background. I nodded to a few officers I knew and made my way over to the pair of desks in the corner, where the new guy named Hernshaw was settling down at one of them with a stack of file folders and some coffee. I took mine and said, "Morning Butch. Howya doing?"

"Doing good Jake. Just lookin' over some of the Cold Case Files for Lt. Patterson—see if a fresh pair of eyes can spot anything new in 'em."

"Good luck to ya, but I'll be surprised if you do. They've been gone through more than a few times already."

"True. But there's always a chance."

"Well, when you're out of patience and possibilities, maybe you could take a look at the one I'm on. It's been a couple of weeks and I don't have squat."

"Be glad to. Do you have a murder book started on it yet?"

"I do, as a matter of fact," I said, and pulled it out of my desk drawer. I pushed it across to him and waited, while he gave it the once-over.

After a few moments, Butch looked at me and said, "I've got two questions . . . Is this up-to-date," he tapped an index finger on the open three-ring binder.

I nodded. "Yeah." Then put fire to the unlit cigarette in my mouth.

"And what," my might-be new partner said, "is this," as he held up a hand-written page that was torn from my notes.

"It's where a woman named Gilda Arkady—the Colorado College Art History Professor—was demonstrating her eidetic ability by re-creating the first page of the hand-written manuscript I found at the murder scene."

Butch frowned. "Perfect memory is exceedingly rare in adults. So rare, it's almost non-existent. A few kids have the talent but it almost always fades away by adulthood. Are you sure about it?"

"Yeah Butch. I am. I watched her do it. It's an exact copy. I checked it, scritch by scritch. How do you know so much about human brain functions, by the way?"

"I read a lot. Anything. All the time. I've done it since I was a little kid. As a result, I have a whole junkyard full of weird facts and arcane knowledge rattling around in my head."

"But you don't have perfect recall though . . . do ya?"

"No. No I don't Jake. That'd make me a freak."

I wasn't even going to try and respond to that, but lucky for me, the phone rang. I picked it up, said, "Homicide. McKern."

"Detective, this is Judy Ives at the City Attorney's Office. Can you come over here right now? Mr. Tournillon said to tell you that it's urgent."

"Did he say what it's about?"

"No. He didn't. But I believe it has to do with the legal summons you asked him to look over for you."

"I'm on my way," I said, as I stubbed out my coffin nail and hung up the telephone.

I stood and looked over at the new guy, Hernshaw, my almost, but not-quite new partner and told him I'd be over at City Hall in the Legal Office with the Spring's Attorney. Then I left.

Chapter 44

It was only a hop, skip and a jump, as Ma would say, from the Cop Shop to City Hall—where the City Attorney's Office was located back in those days—so I presented myself at Mrs. Ives desk in less than ten minutes from when we'd ended our phone call. She looked up from her typewriter when I came in the door and said, "Wow . . . you must have wings on your feet to get here so fast."

I was standing in front of her desk like a big awkward schoolboy; I was a little bit out of breath and my heart was pounding like a trip-hammer. I said, "No. No wings. Just anxious is all. Reckoned it wasn't good news and wanted to get it out in the open and over with as quick as I could."

She smiled. "I understand. But worry won't help any."

"Yeah. I know that anticipation's always worse than the event. But it doesn't seem to help at the moment. It's my son, Scottie, I'm concerned about the most . . ."

"Kids are always the center of importance for every parent who loves them. But I'm afraid you'll have to wait for just a little bit longer. Mr. Tournillon is on the phone. I'll let him know you're here as soon as he hangs up."

"Thanks," I said, and took a seat on one of the oak side chairs with arms that lined the periphery of the room. I chose the one at the end of the row that sat next to a free-standing metal ashtray and lit up a Lucky Strike.

I'd smoked most of the cancer stick, read Injun Woody's column, the sports pages and about all the rest of the *Gazette-Telegraph* by the time Mrs. Ives said, "Mr. McKern . . . Mr. Tournillon's off the phone.

He's ready to talk to you now."

I put down the paper, stuck the cigarette butt in the sand at the top of the ashtray, then followed her into the inner sanctum of S. William Tournillon, Esq., and Attorney-at-Law for the City of Colorado Springs. He was sitting in a high-backed, green leather judge's chair behind a walnut executive desk that had a green blotter in front of him, a couple of telephones and a large double fountain pen set on a marble stand which had a bronze statue of a blindfolded goddess of law on it. She was holding the Scales of Justice in her left hand and a sword in her right one. The rest of the desk was as open and barren as the winter plains of eastern Colorado. At first glance, it seemed to me that it was set up to intimidate his visitors, who'd be sitting in front, looking up at the man behind the imposing desk. The effect was diminished however, by the matching credenza along the wall that was piled high with books, file folders and legal briefs that threatened to avalanche at any moment. But even after observing and factoring in those details . . . it was the man in the chair who commanded the visitor's attention. He had the countenance of an old warrior; a hard campaigner whose many courtroom battles had left his hair gray; his face lined and seamed as if by wind and sun and rain; and although he wore a white shirt and tie, I thought he'd look every bit as natural and at ease with a bandana around his neck and a faded denim work shirt on his back.

Mrs. Ives closed the door as she left the room . . . and just like that . . . I was alone in the old lion's den. I said, "Thanks for taking the time to look at my summons Mr. Tournillon. I appreciate it."

"You can call me Bill. George Patterson must think a lot of you to send you over here like this, but it's a good thing for you that he did, because these are the godamndest divorce pleadings I have ever seen in my forty-five years of practicing law. Are you aware that there's two sets of 'em in here?"

"I never opened the blue folder they're in." I said and watched, while the old attorney pulled the packet of legal crap Ranger Bryan Moore had slapped me on the chest with last Monday morning, from somewhere in the mess on the credenza behind him, and opened it up. Spread out on that big desktop, it was a helluva lot of double-spaced, typed pages.

Mr. Tournillon pulled out a pair of black plastic framed reading glasses and put them on. Looking at me over the tops of them, he said, "They're offering you a carrot and a stick. It's a pretty good carrot and a pretty bad stick. You want the long or short version?"

"Do you care if I smoke?"

"Not as long as you give me one—and use the receptacle," he said as he reached in a desk drawer and retrieved a big glass ashtray and set it in the middle of the desk.

"Luckys okay with you?" I said as I pulled a newly opened pack and shook one out for him.

"They're fine. Anything without a filter works for me. I'm not supposed to smoke anymore. Doctors' orders. I find however, that it's easier said than done."

I shrugged. "I never tried. Never even thought about it to tell ya the truth."

"You're still young. You may have to reconsider when you grow older."

"Maybe so. I know you're probably right. But, as far as the legal stuff is concerned, let's go with the abridged version. I never was one for extensive plot details or long, drawn out good-byes."

"Okay then," Tournillon said, "here's the bad news . . ."

"The stick?"

"Yeah. If you don't agree to all the terms and conditions set forth in the other set of divorce proceedings, they'll file this one without any input on your part. In it, they're claiming infidelity, failure to support, desertion . . ."

"Desertion? How the hell can they claim that, for crissakes?"

"Says here you were absent from the household for three months plus, beginning in November of last year and continuing through the end of February of this year . . ."

"I was in the friggin' hospital! Recovering from being wounded in the line of duty!"

Bill Tournillon looked up from the paperwork in front of him, and pointed at me with the lit cigarette for emphasis as he said, "Listen here Jake, I didn't write this fucking thing—I'm only telling you what's in it—and what your options are."

"You're right. I didn't mean to pop off like that either. Please continue."

"Brace yourself, because it gets worse."

I nodded. Took a deep drag on my smoke and put it out in the ashtray. While I sat there seething, my host picked up one of the phones on his desk and said, "Judy, would you bring us a couple of coffees . . . yeah. Sure, if we have any. Thanks."

The tough old lawyer smoked and looked at me for a long moment without saying a word. I wondered . . . *Is he waiting for me to get over my snit and calm down, or is he assessing my lack of character . . .*

I never did find out what he thought about my moral lapses because at that point, he stubbed out his cigarette, cleared his throat and said, "There's a report from a private investigative agency attached as an exhibit to back up their claims, which details your activities over that period of abandonment with a certain woman named Gloria Martinez. It includes photographs. They're graphic."

I was embarrassed. Shamed. And speechless. I wanted to sink through the floor and disappear.

Mr. Tournillon didn't comment or add to my humiliation. He said, "The petition ends with a pleading for one thousand dollars per month in maintenance, plus another five hundred in child support."

I couldn't breathe for a second. Finally said, "That's more than four times what I make in a month."

"They know that, Jake. It's a ploy to get you to look for another way out of your predicament."

"The carrot . . ."

At that moment, Mrs. Ives opened the door with her hip and came in carrying two mugs of coffee and a pair of blueberry muffins on a tray. She put it down on the desk and said, "Sorry fellows, we're out of milk. The muffins are compliments of one of the gals in accounting. Mr. T., you have an eleven-thirty meeting with the mayor about some taxation issues . . ."

"See if you can move it up to sometime after lunch, or anytime on Monday, would you, please?"

"Will do," she said and left.

"Help yourself Jake," the attorney said as he reached for a mug of coffee. "And take both muffins. They don't agree with me. While you do that, I'll give you the rest of the news."

"Thanks. That works for me," I said as I bit one of the little sweet bread rolls in half and swallowed it with a sip of coffee. After three more bites, they were both only a memory and a few crumbs on a pair of paper plates. They were so dainty I could have eaten them in one chomp each, but I didn't want to seem like a pig.

In the meantime, as I was stuffing down pastries, Mr. Tournillon was organizing papers on his desk and getting ready. Then he said, "That was the stick. Now here's the carrot. Your soon-to-be-ex-wife will simply petition for a divorce based on *Irreconcilable Differences*. There's no request for alimony or child support. But in return, you must agree to give up all parental rights and privileges, and appoint sole custody of your son Scott James, aka "Scottie," to Imogene—including the right to change his last name to 'Curdy.' You will also give up the right to ever see him again, unless by his choice, once he's passed twenty-one years of age."

I felt like I'd been kicked in the balls, wanted to stick my head in a trash can and puke my guts out.

The lawyer said, "How about another smoke?"

I shook two more cigarettes out, we lit up, and I said, "Is that all?"

"No. There's two more things in here. First one is a check, made out in your name, in the amount of fifteen thousand dollars, contingent upon you agreeing to the terms contained herein."

"What's the last item?" I said, as I took a big puff of Lucky Strike and exhaled smoke out of my mouth and nose at the same time.

"You have to do it by four o'clock today, or the agreement, and the check, becomes null and void."

I thought for a bit, smoked, then said, "Bryan Moore, the Texas Ranger who served the divorce papers, is also a private pilot and bodyguard for Governor Gilson, who's a silent partner in the Chaparral Oil Company with Big Jim and his wife. The Ranger said that the Curdy's can't be publicly declared dead until the divorce is official, so there won't be any question about Imogene being the successor to her parents in the company. He also told me that there's billions of dollars at stake, as well as properties all over the world.

What if I hold out for better terms?"

Mr. Tournillon looked in my direction with an expression on his face that was as if he'd just taken a bite out of something really bad tasting. He said, "In light of all that's on the line here, why are you even thinking such a thing?"

"Because I don't want to give up my son. Whatever attraction Mo and I ever had for each other disappeared—or never existed—a long time ago. But I love Scottie with all I have. I don't want to lose him. I don't want to be forced away and alienated from him either. The money doesn't mean anything. He means everything."

"Your emotions are understandable, Jake. Were I in your shoes, I believe I'd feel the same . . . but think about the boy. What's best for him? To be in the middle of an everlasting, and bitter fight between his parents, or to have a more normal and stable childhood, one that's removed from conflict and strife. Based on my experience, what you've told me, and what I see here, I think his mother will do her best to poison any love he might have for you. And since she'll have total control, you know the answer without me telling you."

"It's like tearing an arm off . . ."

Mr. Tournillon spun his chair sideways and looked out at The Peak, which was capped with a broad mantle of snow, and gazed for a number of breaths, then turned back around and faced me again. He said, "As your attorney, I urge you in the strongest possible terms. Do. Not. Fight. Them. You will be destroyed personally, financially, and emotionally. They have too much leverage on you . . . and the clock is ticking."

I took a last puff and put out the cigarette, then said, "It's not fair."

The grizzled old courtroom fighter gave me a look of pity. "Fairness has nothing to do with it son. Nothing at all. Do you know why life is like a shit sandwich?"

I shook my head. "No."

"Because," he said. "The more bread you have, the less shit you have to eat . . . and those folks have more bread than you and I can even imagine. Not in our wildest dreams."

I shook my head again—sick at heart and depressed in spirit—but reason prevailed over emotion in the end. I signed the papers. Mr.

Tournillon witnessed them, and Mrs. Ives notarized everything. She gathered all the documents and left to prepare them for being mailed, by Special Delivery at the Post Office.

After she left the room, Tournillon said, "You have to understand something Jake. Those rich fucks don't play by the same rules as the rest of us. They rig the system so they never lose . . . they almost always get everything that they want . . . one way or the other. And let me give you an example. I don't have proof that would hold up in a court of law, but based on my years of experience as a prosecutor, I'd bet next years wages that Elray Rose, the hit man from Kansas City, Officer Magness shot and killed, wasn't in Colorado Springs by chance. I think he was sent here on business. Sent here by someone with interests in the Chaparral Oil Corporation, as a back-up plan, just in case you tried to hold them up in any way. I believe he was here to murder you."

An icy finger ran down my spine when the gray-haired attorney spoke those words. *And I never even told him about the 'Silent partner from New Orleans with a bunch of vowels in his last name' that Bryan Moore mentioned at breakfast on Monday . . .* Out loud I said, "I believe you. And thanks for your counsel. I know I couldn't have navigated all this treachery by myself."

"You're welcome. I'll call down there, let them know the documents are signed, sealed and on their way. You had only tough, no-win options here Jake. For what it's worth, I think you did the best you could with what you had."

I stood. Shook his hand and walked out. I had only myself to blame, a huge check in my pocket . . . and a hole in my heart that has never healed.

Chapter 45

Butch was still reading old case files when I sat down at the desk across from him. "Find anything?" I said, as I lit another coffin nail, even though my throat was raw and sore from all the smoking, and my chest felt like a car was parked on top of me.

Hernshaw, face-down in a file folder, held up an index finger for a few seconds as he finished the page he was reading, then looked at me and said, "No. I haven't." He yawned and stretched and rolled his head around to get the kinks out of his neck.

"How long have you been at them?"

"Since before you left," Butch yawned again, looked at his watch, "about three and a half hours. Maybe a little more."

"Well, damn, are you buckin' for a desk job or somethin'," I said, and smiled, to let him know I was kidding.

He grinned. "Naw. Not yet. I usually wait a week or two for that."

I noticed several pink message slips and some cookies wrapped in wax paper. When I picked them up, the note underneath them read, *Thanks! I don't know what you did, but thank-you.* It was from Ann-Marie. The cookies were oatmeal with cranberries and walnuts mixed in them, and delicious. Butch and I drank coffee and munched until they were all gone.

Then we got back to business. I said, as I drained the last of my coffee, "What did you think of the Skin Ripper Case . . . or did you even get a chance to look at it?"

"I did," Butch said, as he chewed the last of his cookie. "It's pretty high profile. I don't envy you in the least. I think you've tried about everything that can be done without some kind of a break in the case.

And, I believe that book you found has something to do with it."

"Yeah. Me too. But what? Until I can read it, it's meaningless."

Hernshaw twisted his chair back and forth and thought about it. "I still think it looks like some kind of Hebrew . . ."

"It is, according to the Jesuit priest, Gianette, up in Denver. But, he said, there's hundreds of dialects and the problem is finding out which one it is in order to translate it into English."

"You believe him?"

I thought about it for less than a second. "No. Something about him set my teeth on edge. I had to pull the book out of his hands. He wasn't going to give it back."

"That's interesting. Why do you think he was so hell-bent to keep it?"

"I don't know," I said. "But I thought he coveted the manuscript, like a miser loves money . . ."

Butch handed the Skin Ripper Murder Book back to me. He picked up the cold case files and started walking away, then stopped. He turned and said, "Maybe it would be a good idea to find a Hebrew speaker, see if they could read the manuscript. You've got nothing to lose."

"Good thought. I like it," I said. I reached for the phone book, while Hernshaw disappeared down the stairs on his way to the file room, where more cold cases lay waiting to be reexamined . . . maybe even reopened if some new clue, some new witness, or some new kind of science came along to root out the evildoers and lay the victim ghosts to rest. I hoped so. Though, *in a perfect world there would be no cold cases. Hell, there'd be no murders—because there wouldn't be any evil . . .*

I dialed the number for Doug Sikes Photography where, as usual, his wife answered. "Hi Rhonda. This is Jake McKern. I was calling to see how my project is coming along."

"I dunno Jake, but I'll go see," she said. "He's been working on it all night, and I'm pretty sure he's doing something with it right now. I'll go ask him. You wanna hold on the phone?"

"Yeah. I will . . ." I started to say 'thanks,' but the phone clunked down and the sound of footsteps, followed by doors opening and closing and a small dog yapping was all I heard.

"Jake?"

"I'm here Doug."

"I was up until about four a.m., so if I sound a little goofy, that's why."

"I understand. And thanks for all your hard work and effort."

"You're welcome. I'm almost done with the halftones, so, if you wanna come get 'em and take them to the print shop, he'll knock them right out for ya. Said he'd have them done by late tonight or early tomorrow morning,"

"That would be a great favor to the case and the CSPD. I owe you one Doug. I'm on my way."

Less than twenty minutes after that, the tired photographer handed me a file box full of halftones, ready to go to press. He said, "You know where O'Shay Printing is located?"

"I'm the police," I said. "I know where everything is."

"So, you say. But I'd try the 1000 block of North Nineteenth Street if I was you. He knows you're coming; I called him already."

I made my good-byes, took the box, and made a beeline for the west side of town. From Sikes's Studio on North Union, the quickest way to get there was on Uintah Street, which pointed west like an arrow, right at the heart of the big granite mountain the white European settlers named Pikes Peak. I made it there in record time, running at a pretty good clip in light traffic.

Mr. O'Shay himself was on the phone, standing behind a long linoleum-topped customers counter when I walked in with the halftones. He cupped the phone with his right hand over the receiver. "You McKern?"

"Yeah."

"Leave it on the counter. Come back tomorrow around eleven. Three copies. You want 'em in loose leaf binders or just metal clips?"

"Clips," I said. "Like a manuscript. And you've got to be careful to keep 'em in order. There's no page numbers."

"I know," O'Shay said, his brogue as thick as churned butter. "Sikes told me. Pay when ya pick 'em up. I don't do no billing."

I nodded, put the precious box on the counter and left to find some lunch. I remember thinking as I got in the car, *Jeeze, what would he have acted like if I had some kind of a snobby-assed British accent . . . he talks and looks like he came here straight out of time. I wonder if he even had a part in The Rising on Easter Sunday, back in nineteen and sixteen. He sure has the eyes of an old warrior.*

My stomach growled, reminding me that it was way past time to eat something nutritious. I still had a whole afternoon of sleuthing to do on the telephone, trying to find someone to read Sorwell's Manuscript . . . and trying not to think about what I'd done that morning in the City Attorney's office, or the check that was nestled against my chest, where it was burning a hole in my conscience and making me feel like Judas Iscariot.

Chapter 46

Since I was already in the neighborhood, I stopped at Roger's Bar on West Colorado Avenue, where I had a hamburger sandwich with cheese, tomatoes, and onions on it, plus a basket of french-fried potatoes and a couple of glasses of draft beer to wash it all down with. I popped a couple of pain pills and swallowed them with the last of the beer, left three-dollar bills to cover the tab and leave a decent tip, then headed back to the station.

I took a moment on the way in the front door, to speak with Officer Magness, who was still manning the public desk, and enjoying himself from the looks of it. I said, "Rags, could we have a quick word . . ."

He looked up at me, "Hello, Jake. What's goin' on?"

I leaned on the counter. "You know that Jim Dunlap put in his papers and quit . . ."

"Yeah. The cracker motherfucker won't be missed neither. There's a rumor going around among the patrolmen saying you had something to do with it. That true?"

"Not a bit," I said with a straight face. "But I wanted to give you a warning to be on the lookout for him when you're off duty, out and about. Lt. Patterson told me Dunlap said he'd, *'See me around.'* The Loot thought it was a threat. I don't. But I wanted you to hear it from me in light of your history with him—just to be on the safe side."

Magness grinned, said, "Thanks for the tip-off, Jake, you're bein' more of a friend than some of my own kind. But don't worry about me. Black folk are always watchin' their ass, lest some ofay fool like Dunlap be tryin' to sneak up on 'em."

"Rags," I said, "You are one of a kind. And I'm damn glad we're on the same side."

"Me too, Jake. Me too. Y'all take care."

"And you as well." I turned and went upstairs, while Magness picked up the phone that had just started to ring.

Hernshaw wasn't back at his desk when I sat down at mine and began to sort through the new batch of message slips, stacked on a pile in the middle of my desk. The first one was from Gianette in Denver, and marked 'urgent' by Ann-Marie. I dialed the long-distance operator, gave her the number, and listened, as she rang it up.

The person who answered was a grad school assistant to Gianette, who told me that the Reverend Father was coming to the Springs in the middle of next week. He would be here for a few weeks, giving a series of lectures, sermons and talks at various colleges, high schools, and churches in the area, as well as some in the steel mill city of Pueblo, plus Trinidad, the coal mining town down by the Colorado-New Mexico state line, if time allowed. He'd be staying in the rectory at St. Mary's church in Colorado Springs, where he was planning on meeting with me and translating the Sorwell Manuscript. The last item the aide told me, was that Gianette would reach out once he got settled in with Father Ray O'Reilly, the priest at St. Mary's Parish.

Well, whooptie fucking-doo, I thought. *Who gives a tinkers damn.* I shook my head in disbelief at the hubris of the man in the clerical collar, and went through the rest of the messages, to see if any of them needed immediate attention. They didn't, but two caught my eye. The first was from Gilda Arkady, and the second came by way of Lenny Bragg at the *Gazette Telegraph*. He wanted to talk to me about 'Something important' and asked 'Would you make contact ASAP.' Gilda wanted to let me know about an upcoming visiting professor. I called her first. And, wonder of wonders, she answered. I said, "Gilda, it's Jake McKern, returning your call."

"Hello, dear man. I wanted to let you know that the college has a visiting professor coming at the end of March to give a lecture about his experiences in a Nazi death camp during the war. His name is Chiam Leviwitz. He was a prisoner at a place called Buchenwald, and he's one of only a handful of survivors. Anyway, I thought he might be of some help in your murder case somehow."

The skin was prickling at the back of my neck and the hair on my forearms was standing to attention. There were too many coincidences all of a sudden . . . and I don't believe in coincidences. They only happen in novels and in the movies, not in real life. I said, "It sure wouldn't hurt if I could talk to him. Do you think he might know anything about what's in the Sorwell Manuscript?"

She hesitated for a moment, then said, "Interesting question. I don't have the answer. Other than both of them being concentration camp survivors, I don't know that they have anything in common. I guess it's possible . . ."

"All I can do is ask. Thanks Gilda, for letting me know about this. Will you keep me in mind when he gets here?"

"Yes. Absolutely. It'll be in the newspapers too."

"I'll watch for it," I said, and we rang off. I looked at the Bragg message for a moment before I wadded it into a ball and dropped it in the trash. Then I lit a cigarette and sat there, thinking about why all these different and opposing—but somehow connected—forces were coming together at the same time in Colorado Springs. Minutes later, I still had no answers . . . only a creeping suspicion something bad was going to happen . . . and soon.

I sighed, put out the cigarette and pulled the battered old phone book from the bottom desk drawer, started to do some yellow pages reconnaissance. I was looking for ideas—trying to find that certain someone who could make sense of the Sorwell Manuscript and tell me if it was worth all the trouble.

Then, proving that luck was better than planning, I struck gold on the third call when Rabbi Saul Risenberg answered the telephone. It was almost as if he was expecting me and we were old friends. After I told him who I was, explained what it was about and why I needed assistance, he was intrigued. Then I said, "The copies will be ready tomorrow at a little before noon. I can bring one anytime after . . ."

Rabbi Risenberg said, "No. Not then. It's Shabbat. I have services and obligations to the congregation all day."

"What's Shabbat?"

"It's the Sabbath. Saturday is the holy day of the week for Jews."

"Oh. I didn't know. Would Sunday work okay?"

"Absolutely. Come at noon. We'll have lunch and see if I can be of help to the CSPD."

I surely hope so, I thought. *The Skin Ripper Case will be the end of my career if it goes into the 'open-unsolved' files . . .* I kept on worrying and hoping and wishing and daydreaming all afternoon about a positive outcome, one that would allow me to keep my promise to the Sorwells . . . that I would find their killers and get them justice.

The last thing I did that Friday was to call Nurse Gloria and ask if she'd like to go out for dinner and a movie. I had more than three years salary in my pocket, a load on my conscience, and much to share with her.

Chapter 47

The deaths of legendary Texas wildcatter 'Big Jim' Curdy and his wife, Jody Belle Curdy, were made public in a press release from the Chaparral Oil Company in Houston, Texas late Friday afternoon. Corporate attorney and official company spokesman, Preston Lee Grinder held a news conference at company headquarters, accompanied by the Curdy's only daughter and the sole heiress to the Curdy fortune: Imogene Elizabeth Curdy. Grinder read from a prepared statement and took no questions afterward, saying only that "Further announcements would be made in the coming days, no changes were expected in the company's operations and all contracts will be honored to the letter." Oil prices closed mixed on the New York Merc at $28.13 per barrel of light sweet Texas crude on the news, and were trending slightly higher on world markets in after hours trading.

I pushed the newspaper off to the side and stirred my coffee, lit an after breakfast smoke and watched Nurse Gloria, as she came back to the booth. She sat next to me, took my left hand in hers and said, "Thanks for dinner and all this too, but we can't eat out all the time . . ."

"I know. Wanted to treat you, is all, for being so nice to me when everything else in my life is so crappy."

"Quit feeling sorry for yourself Jake, and things will get better. You'll see," she said as she nestled closer and squeezed my hand.

"I hope you're right. But on top of everything else, the Skin Ripper Case is wearing me out. Captain Duncan's on my ass about it, the Chief's on his and the Mayor's on the Chief. Everyone wants the Skin Ripper caught and brought to justice. Including me. But there's nothing to follow up . . . no clues, no leads . . . no nada."

"Maybe the manuscript will be what solves everything for you."

"Let's hope so Gloria. It's the only thing left at this point that might help."

Our waitress came over, topped off our coffees and left the check. I dropped a dollar tip on the table and paid the cashier, who sat on a stool behind the counter next to the front door, as we walked out.

It was late, when I left Gloria at her house, where we said our good-byes at her back door with Buddy Boy, merowing and rubbing against our legs, anxious to go inside after a long night of carousing, marauding, and fighting. Gloria unlocked the door and Buddy squeezed in and disappeared on the run. She giggled and said, "He's really gonna be mad when he finds out there's no cat chow yet."

"I see where I stand in the social order around here," I said, as I leaned down and kissed her one last time.

"Call me Monday. I've got the day shift today plus I'm covering tonight for a friend. I'm scheduled for Sunday too. Then I have Monday to myself."

"I will. Be well, Gloria."

"You be careful, Jake."

I headed straight over to the printer's shop. It was still a bit early, but I was hoping that the manuscripts might be done when I drove into the parking lot at a few minutes before eight that Saturday morning.

I put the car in park and was reaching for the ignition key to shut the engine off when the radio crackled to life. "Dispatch to any available unit, Officer needs assistance at Twenty-First and West Cucharras Street. Shots fired."

I keyed the mic. "McKern to Dispatch, I'm at Nineteenth and Uintah. Responding." I hit the lights and siren in the unmarked police car as I tore out of O'Shay's parking lot, anxious to help a fellow officer in trouble.

When I got to the scene, I found Officer Donnie Brearley crouched behind the front fender of a patrol car in the middle of the block, trading occasional potshots with a suspect, who was firing from the front window of a small, two-story clapboard house. I slid to a stop behind his unit and duck-walked with my .45 in hand, over to where he was crouched beside his left front wheel. I said, "Donnie, are you hit?"

"No. I'm okay. Twisted my ankle is all, when the suspect opened fire on me."

"How many in the house?"

"Two. Shooter and his wife, so far as I know. He was busy beatin' the shit out of her just before I arrived. One of the neighbors heard a woman screamin' and called it in, but there ain't been a peep since I got here."

"Think she's still alive?"

"Dunno. Been hard to tell very much about what's goin' on in there with him shootin' at me."

As if on cue, another round boomed from the house and thunked into the patrol car.

I yelled out, "YOU. IN THE HOUSE . . .

"COME OUT WITH YOUR HANDS UP!"

The only response we got was two more chunks of lead, whacking into sheet metal.

I said, "Donnie, if you can keep him engaged out front here, maybe I could get in there from the back door and surprise him."

"It's as good a plan as any. There's an alley that runs parallel to the street, in behind all these places. You can drive your car down 'em."

"I know that . . . keep him occupied . . ."

I got in the unmarked, backed up to the end of the block and around the corner, the wrong way against traffic, until I passed the alley. Then I dropped it in drive, pulled into the entrance and idled past the backs of several homes. I stopped, left the car one house before the shooter's place, and eased out on foot. I crept by a garage that allowed me good cover to get into the backyard of the suspect's residence and up on the back porch, where an ordinary wooden door beckoned.

I heard an exchange of gunfire out front as I reached for the doorknob. I had my .45 ACP cocked, locked, and loaded in my right hand, my heart in my mouth and the dry taste of fear on my lips as I grabbed the door handle with my left. And sonofabitch . . . it opened.

Chapter 48

The door led to the kitchen. I stepped in, being careful to keep the leather heels of my boots from clopping on the linoleum, and eased across the galley floor on the balls of my feet . . . then headed into a short, dark hallway that went to the front room, where Donnie and the suspect were still battling.

I had my back to the wall and my pistol in a two-handed combat grip as I side-stepped, ever so slow and careful, toward the shooter in the parlor. I was so intent on the gunfight, I failed to see the body of a young woman. It looked as if she was shot in the other room, then crawled or dragged herself into the hall, where she died, huddled face-first against the baseboard. I slipped in the blood that was pooled around her and went down on my side, but managed to hold on to the .45 auto with my right hand and kept watching the front room, where the killer had closed all the curtains and window blinds . . . except for the one he was shooting through.

"Who's there?" He said, as he cranked off another round at Officer Brearley.

"Police. Put down your weapon and show yourself with your hands up. Do it now."

I heard a clunk as he let go of something heavy, then the sinister double click of a pair of hammers being cocked. He said, "In a pig's ass I will," and charged into the hallway with a sawed off double-barreled twelve-gauge. It was pointed straight at me.

I didn't hesitate. Didn't think. Didn't give him the chance. Put a pair of 225 grain Super Velocity hollow points in the center of his chest . . . and dropped him like a rock.

He pitched over backwards with a look of utter surprise on his face, touched off both barrels of the Remington as he went, and blew a fair-sized hole in the back door. He hit the floor in a heap, both eyes wide open and his feet in the dead man's cross.

My heart was beating so hard I thought it might explode. I was breathing in rapid, hyperventilating gasps, my ears rang and I was so sick to my stomach it felt like I might puke at any moment . . . yet I was alive. And that was a wonderful feeling. I wanted to rejoice. Shout. Sing. Cry. But I did none of those things. I'd never been so close to dying—not even in the war—so I just laid there, sucked air and thanked God for my deliverance.

What seemed only an instant later, the place was full of uniformed officers with guns in their hands and questions on their minds that came at me in rapid fire fashion.

Are you hit? Where are you hit? and *Who's blood is all over you?* being the most often repeated until Sergeant Andy Claypoole appeared and asserted his authority to establish command and control of the scene. Soon after, he had a perimeter cordoned off and guarded by a pair of uniformed officers, while some others were beginning to canvas the neighborhood for witnesses. I was left in a dim hallway with two bodies, the coppery scent of spilled blood and the tang of cordite in the air. It smelled like death.

My left side was soaked in blood. I had it on my pants, shirt, boots, and hands, as well as some on the front of my leather bomber jacket. The khaki slacks and sports shirt were goners. There was too much bloodstain to ever get out, but I thought that my boots and jacket could be saved.

I was at the sink in my stocking feet when Lt. Patterson and a heavyset, cigar smoking old dinosaur of a homicide dick named Wilson Bell came into the kitchen after inspecting the carnage in the hallway. Patterson said, "Jake, you look like you've been in a knife fight. You hurt anywhere?"

I looked up from rinsing the last of the blood out of the cuff of my A2 jacket and said, "No, Loot, I'm not. I didn't see the victim in the hallway . . . slipped in the gore and went down on my left side. All the blood belongs to her."

Bell—who'd been on the force since the mid-thirties, gazed at me with the eyes of an old campaigner who's looked at too many tragedies like the one in the other room—and said, "When did the suspect enter the hall?"

"Right after I fell."

"What happened then?" Patterson said.

"The suspect yelled. I told him I was the police. Commanded him to surrender. He came at me with a twelve-gauge. We fired. He missed. I didn't."

"Who shot first?" Bell said.

I finished washing and drying my hands, looked at him and said, "You got any more questions?"

Bell took the cigar out of his mouth and pointed at me with it. "I just ast yuh—who shot first?" Then clamped the stinker back in his jowls.

"And I asked if you had any other questions," I said as I sat on a kitchen chair and pulled my cowboy boots on. I stood. Watched and waited.

Lt. Patterson tried to defuse things. "No Jake. No more questions. But write it up and have it on my desk today. You'll have to interview with Chief Budd and Captain Duncan."

"Yessir," I said, as I pulled my jacket on. I still had blood on me, but thought I was presentable, at least. I didn't know when I'd be able to get back to the house on Seventh Street for a fresh set of clothes.

Bell glared my way for a moment, took the cigar butt out of his mouth and turned to Lt. Patterson. With his back to me, Bell pointed over his shoulder with a thumb and said, "You gonna pull his gun and badge?"

"No. I'm not. That will be up to the Chief."

"You pulled them from Magness just a few days ago under the same circumstances—an officer involved shooting."

Patterson's face flushed. I could see the anger building up in him as he said, "What's your point Detective? Do you have something more to say . . . something else you'd like to add?"

To my surprise, Bell went all in. He said, "Magness is colored. This boy's white. Some might see that as preferential treatment, in light of what's goin' on with the Civil Rights Movement 'n' all."

I opened my mouth to speak, but Lt. Patterson beat me to it. "You're outta line Bell. First of all, McKern is an experienced and decorated officer with an exemplary record in the line of duty. As such, he's entitled to the benefit of his rank and experience and the proper use of force in a deadly situation, unless the Chief's inquiry determines otherwise. Magness, on the other hand, was still in his probationary period and not yet a sworn officer in the department."

"As far as that other crack of yours is concerned, unless my eyes deceive me, you and a number of others are living proof that there's no color barrier on the CSPD. I resent your insinuation . . . this ain't Alabama and Bull Connor isn't the man in charge here. You say something like that in my presence again and I'll bust ya down to school crossing guard. Understand?"

"Yessir."

"Questions?"

"No sir."

"Good. Go help Sgt. Claypoole and send Hernshaw in here."

I watched him leave by the kitchen door. We didn't speak, but the look Bell shot back left no doubt he had more to say to me . . . a lot more as it turned out . . . and none of it was congenial. Not one word.

Chapter 49

While we waited, Lt. Patterson and I smoked and flicked our ashes in the kitchen sink and made small talk. We ran through the usual things—the lack of rain, the Pikes Peak Hill Climb and the Pikes Peak or Bust Rodeo—but then the conversation turned a little more serious. "What's got Bell all riled up ?" I said.

Lt. Patterson knocked the fire off his cigarette and stuck the butt in his shirt pocket. Then he said, "He's tired of ridin' in the back of the bus. Don't blame him either. I would be too if I was colored."

Butch Hernshaw came in the back door at that moment, so the Loot and I never finished our conversation. I wish we had. It would've been thought-provoking, I think.

As soon as the new guy stepped into the room, Lt. Patterson said, "Butch, I'm putting you in charge of both of these homicides. There's no doubt about who did what, but maybe you can find something about why the suspect in the hallway murdered his woman and did his best to kill two police officers. Any questions?"

"Yeah," Butch said. "Would you mind letting everyone outside know that?"

"Done. Anything else?"

"Don't let Officer Brearley leave until I've talked to him. Have the coroner and photographer been called?"

"They're all on the way," Patterson said. "Jake knows 'em. He'll tell ya who's who."

"Okay Lieutenant. I've got it," Butch said as he pulled out a notebook and started writing.

Patterson nodded at me and took his leave of us, going out the same door we'd all used to come inside.

Without hesitation, Butch looked at me and said, "Just how'n hell did you come to be here Jake? Seems to me the last I heard you were off for the weekend."

"I am. I was picking up copies of the Sorwell Manuscript at the print shop over on nineteenth Street when the call came in that *"Officer needs assistance. Shots fired."* It was pure chance that I was only a few blocks away with the motor running. Another two seconds and I wouldn't have heard the summons. I was reaching for the ignition key when the radio squawked."

Butch made notes, asked questions, had me walk and talk through the crime scene. Then we did the whole thing again . . . "Just to make sure I didn't miss anything," Butch said, as he filled page after page of his notebook with his crabbed and almost impossible to decipher style of personal handwriting.

As Butch put the last few words down and dotted the 'i's and crossed his 't's, the coroner's man, Doug Sikes and a fingerprint tech came in to start processing the scene, then tagging and bagging the evidence. As they got to work, I said, "Butch, are you done with me?"

"Yeah. For now, anyway."

"I need to get back to the printer's and pick up the manuscript copies before he closes."

"Okay. Go ahead and go. But let me know where you are in case, I need ya."

"After I'm done with O'Shay, I'm gonna go clean up and change. Then I'll be at the office, writing my report."

"See you there," Butch said. He went down the hall, talked to the coroner for a moment, then went out the front door . . . to talk to Donnie Brearley, I assume.

As soon as Butch entered the front room, I hustled out the kitchen door, around the garage and back to the unmarked I'd left in the alley. I wanted to get away from there before the publicity storm started. The last thing I needed at that moment was a bunch of newshounds biting me on the ass. I started the motor and drove down the alley to Nineteenth Street, then north to Uintah, where O'Shay Printing was located.

I could hear what sounded like a printing press running somewhere in the back of the building when I walked in and stood at the empty counter. Not long after that, O'Shay came out wearing an ink-stained apron, wiping his hands with a red shop rag. He stopped in his tracks when he looked my way and said, "Sweet sufferin' Jesus boyo . . . what befell ye then?"

I looked down at my sport shirt and khaki slacks, covered in blood, said, "The victim's . . . not mine. Went over to Cucharras and Twenty-First to help another officer and got involved. Otherwise, I'd have been here hours ago."

O'Shay nodded. "Saw ye come and take off again. Figured somethin' was afoot."

"Police work goes on all day every day without ever stopping. You call, we come. No exceptions. It's that simple."

The older man snorted, and said, "Well, let's just say my experiences with the peelers, umm, I mean the police, are most different—and not so helpful."

"I understand," I said, "my mother was in service in Dublin during the Rising. She was a young woman working with her mother for the family of a doctor who supported the IRA. She was pressed into nursing duties as the casualties started mounting."

"Did she now. I've some experience meself . . . but another time laddie. I'm sure you're wanting to change 'n' cleanup," O'Shay said. He reached under the counter brought out the box I'd carried in from Sikes Photography the day before and put it on the counter between us. It contained three double-sided copies of the Sorwell Manuscript, all neatly put into manila folders and bayonet clipped together on the left margin.

I pulled the topmost one and gave it a cursory glance. It was still unreadable but appeared to be intact as best I could tell, and all the pages were complete and legible.

O'Shay said, "Your halftones are in an envelope in the bottom of the stack."

"Thanks. And the invoice," I said, as I reached for my billfold.

"Right here . . ."

It totaled up to $27.82 with tax. "For three copies? That's almost ten bucks apiece . . ."

"Tis," the dour Irishman said. "And I only take cash."

I bit my tongue and kept my smart-assery to myself as I pulled bills from my close-to-empty wallet and forked them over. It was while I waited for Mr. O'Shay to return with my change, that I finally read the neatly rendered poster on the wall, behind where he'd been standing.

—Pick Any Three—
We can't do all four at the same time:

EXPERT WORK
FAST SERVICE
QUALITY MATERIALS
CHEAP PRICE

Over the years, I've thought of that sign and the clear message it conveyed a thousand times. It always brought a smile to my face when I did.

Chapter 50

As it turned out, I threw away all the clothes I wore that day. Shirt, slacks, belt—everything went in the trash or a burn barrel—even my boots, underwear, and leather jacket, which had bloodstains on the inside liner. I just couldn't bear the thought of walking around with that murdered woman's blood on me.

The lady's name was Juanita Rose Pacheco, according to Butch Hernshaw, who also told me that she was the seventeen-year-old common law wife of the man I killed in the gunfight after he refused to surrender.

"His name was Lukas Earl Batt," Hernshaw said, as we both sat at our desks doing paperwork on Saturday evening; wrapping up events and detailing our activities during the morning rowdy-dow and ruction, over at Twenty-First and West Cucharras Streets. "He was forty-one years of age and wanted in Mexico and Arizona."

"What for," I said, as I sat back from the typewriter and shrugged my shoulders a few times, trying to ease the ache out of them after being hunched over for so long.

"Suspicion of murder in Tucson, Arizona, armed robbery in Phoenix, eluding, resisting, vehicle theft . . ."

"Christ, he sounds like a one-man crime wave. What about Mexico?"

"There's where it gets real interesting. Kidnapping, robbery, arson, attempted murder, and jailbreak. Batt claimed that he bought the girl from her father three years ago, when she was just fourteen years old, for twenty-two silver pesos. Her mother claimed Juanita was stolen. Taken by force and carried away to *El Norte*, by Lukas Batt."

"I'd go with Mamacita's version," I said. "But what set things off this morning . . . do you know?"

"The neighbors said they began to fight sometime around dawn. He started beating her and the folks next door called us when they heard her screaming. Officer Brearley responded and the gunfight began. You came on the scene about twelve minutes after that, is all we know at this point. With both of the principals now deceased, it's probably all we're ever gonna know too. . ."

"Maybe." I said as I pulled my report from the old Olivetti and stapled it together. I signed and dated it, then put it in the center of Lt. Patterson's desk, where I weighted it down with his ashtray. I thought for a second, about using a few .45 caliber hollow points, but didn't. I figured the Loot might not appreciate the gallows humor, in light of the fact that I'd taken a man's life with the same type of ammo, earlier in the day. But the truth? The truth was—and still is—I had no remorse. Not then, and not now, for taking a pedophile and murderous sonofabitch like Lukas Batt off the board. He wasn't worth the price of a five cent reload in my book . . . then too . . . there's the undeniable fact that he was trying to kill Officer Donnie Brearley and me. The world became a little bit better place the instant Lukas Batt left it, in my opinion.

The last thing I did before I returned to an empty and cold house over on Seventh, was to go down to the evidence room. I jimmied the lock and went inside, to make sure the mockup of the Sorwell Manuscript was still on deposit. But when I knelt on the floor with a pen light clamped in my teeth and pulled the lid off the file box, there was no trace of the wrapped and bound metal box. It was gone. I remember wondering, as I closed and replaced the file on the shelf, *Who, amongst the members of the CSPD had taken it? And why? Who could I count on in a firefight like the one this morning, to have my back? Anyone?* Those thoughts kept bouncing around in my head as I checked Roscoe's ledger, to see if the Sorwell Manuscript had been signed out of evidence by anyone else . . . a fool's errand for certain. No one but myself—and whoever stole it—had laid a finger on the damn thing.

I locked the evidence room door and went home . . . to the house I no longer wanted to live in, where I made a peanut butter and jelly sandwich for supper, washed it down with several bottles of Coors beer, then had three of the pearl gray pain capsules for dessert. Next thing I knew, it was 8:30, the sun was shining and Sunday morning was falling all over the place.

After a couple of tries, I managed to sit up on the couch where I'd conked out last night, and realized I still had my boots, as well as all my clothes on. My head had a nine-inch nail in it, the phone was ringing non-stop and a TV Preacher was badgering me—and anyone else listening out here in the electronic haze— *"If you want to get from God, you gotta give to God. Want them prayers answered? You'd better support his church, here and now. Send your contributions—no amount is too small—to Post Office Box . . ."* And that was the moment, the holy roller's head exploded in a shower of smoke, sparks, and shattered glass as the beer bottle I'd thrown hit the TV screen and destroyed it.

I picked up the phone, heard a voice say, "Jake? Is it you? Are you alright?"

"Hi Gloria. Yeah. It's me . . ."

"And you're not hurt, not wounded or anything?"

"I've got a headache and I'm a little groggy. I just woke up. I had a few beers after I got home from work last night and took some pain meds for my leg."

"The gray ones . . ."

"Yeah."

"How many?"

"Three."

"With alcohol?"

"A few beers is all," I said as I surveyed the octet of dead soldiers on the coffee table, *Plus the one I chucked at the RCA . . .*

"You must have the constitution of a horse. Please don't keep doing this. Those things will really damage your organs. I can't stress that enough."

"You're right. I'll do better, be more careful. I promise. But why are you so worried if I'm okay?"

"Because of the newspaper, Honey. Your picture's on the front page. You're covered in blood."

Chapter 51

A little hair of the dog later—followed by a long hot shower and a shave, some clean freshly ironed clothes, shined boots, and a gray tweed sport coat just back from the dry cleaners—and I was starting to feel well enough to face the world again. When I clipped the gold shield to my belt and snugged the cleaned and oiled Colt into the shoulder holster under my left arm, I became a cop once more.

I took my old brown briefcase out of the closet, put two copies of the Sorwell Manuscript, a legal pad and a couple of extra pens inside, then closed it with the metal clasp and buckled its two leather belts. After taking a look at my eyes in the hallway mirror, I put on a pair of aviator sunglasses and headed out.

My first stop was the Waffle House, where Maggie Johnson met me as I took a seat in the last booth. "Jake," she said, "I'm glad to see you up and around, honey. Are you better?"

"Better than what, Maggie? Or who?"

"I guess you haven't seen the paper . . ."

"No. But I heard about it."

"I'll getcha a copy," she said, as she poured coffee for me. "What'll you have?"

"Some biscuits and gravy."

"Coming right up."

The Gazette got there before I took a second sip of coffee, and I saw right away why Nurse Gloria was so bent out of shape. Under a headline that read:

GUNFIGHT ON SPRINGS WESTSIDE
COPS BATTLE WANTED KILLER IN SHOOTOUT

Lenny Bragg wrote:

> *In a scene reminiscent of Wyatt and Doc battling Ike Clanton at the OK Corral, Colorado Springs Detective Jake McKern, and Patrol Officer Donnie Brearley shot it out early Saturday morning with a wanted desperado and known killer named Lukas Earl Batt at 21st and West Cucharras Streets. When the gun smoke cleared away however, Batt—who had just murdered his pregnant wife, Juanita Pacheco, aged 17—lay face down and dead in a pool of blood, with two .45 caliber slugs from McKern's Colt through his heart. (Shootout, Cont'd p8)*

A quarter-page photo accompanying the story, showed me sitting next to two dead bodies in the hallway of the house, just after the gunfight. I'm soaking in gore, looking dazed and holding that big pistol in my right hand. The caption underneath reads, *"McKern, still unable to catch the Skin Ripper, takes time out to help."*

Aww, shit, I thought. *Why couldn't I have gotten to O'Shay's one minute earlier and then I wouldn't have heard the radio call for help . . .* My better sense of self kicked in though, just as Maggie appeared with food and more coffee: *Yeah . . . and Donnie Brearley could have bought the farm because of it too . . .*

I took a bite of food I didn't really want, but figured I should eat something before heading out see to Rabbi Risenberg. I pushed the newspaper off to the side as one last thought hit me. *You can't choose fate—only deal with it.* I ate about half of the meal, left some cash on the table, then went to the phone booth to call Ma and let her know I was unharmed. After that, I headed for the northeast part of town in hopes of getting some kind of translating help with the manuscript. It was a long shot, but I had nothing to lose.

At that time, the city was just starting to push its boundaries evermore easterly, in both north and south directions, as most of the pioneering ranchers and farming families succumbed to the realities of modern agricultural consolidation, and the siren call of the land developers with boatloads of borrowed money. Rabbi Risenberg lived out there, in what was then the newest part of the Springs, where the bulldozers and loaders, the scrapers, hoes and graders were busy transforming God's own prairie into mankind's urban nightmare.

I lit an after-breakfast smoke, headed through the downtown area, and took Platte Avenue east, all the way to Circle Drive, then turned north. I stayed on Circle, out past Constitution Avenue and Maizeland Road, until it hooked back around into Fillmore Street. I made another turn onto Templeton Gap Road . . . and followed it for about a mile . . . to where the rabbi lived at the edge of town. It was a roundabout way to get there, but I wanted to take a look at the east edge of the city, see how far it'd seeped. It wasn't encouraging. The ooze of new construction was swallowing everything in its path with an insatiable appetite. It didn't look like it was gonna stop anytime soon either.

I had no trouble finding the Risenberg's place, and pulled into a circular driveway with a raised flower bed in the middle of it. The house was an L-shaped ranch style that looked into a dry creek bed on the west side and had an oversized two car garage on the south. The nearest neighbors were at least 100 or more yards away by my reckoning, as I walked up the brick-lined path to the front door. The man who opened it wasn't anything like what I was expecting. "Rabbi Risenberg?" I said

"I am he," a tall forty-ish and physically fit man who looked more Aryan than Ashkenazic said. "And you must be McKern. Come in, please."

"Guilty as charged, Rabbi."

"You can call me Saul. This is my wife, Naomi."

"Ma'am," I said, to the tall woman whose auburn hair was in a long braid that ran down the middle of her back, and was complemented by a pair of rainwater blue eyes. "Please call me Jake."

"Okay, Jake I will . . . if you'll use my first name as well," she said with a slight hint of an accent. Eastern European? Russian maybe . . . I couldn't tell.

But as if she could read my thoughts, Naomi said, "I am Polish. We both are. Saul and I survived Hitler and the Nazi's. We fought for the partisans. After the war we helped to found Israel. Fought the Arabs.

Were you in the war?"

"Yes. With the Marines. In the Pacific."

Saul interceded at that point. Said, "Naomi, please. That's enough. Let him get in the door,"

She shot him a look that I interpreted as an "I'm not done . . ." then gathered herself and asked if I'd like coffee. I told her I would and she set about making some, while her husband got mugs and napkins out.

While the coffee boiled, the three of us sat at the dining room table, where I started telling them almost everything, but not all, about the Sorwell Manuscript. I got the sense —as I answered their questions— that there was more to the couple than they were letting on. I had the growing feeling, coming from the reptile part of my brain, that Saul and Naomi were both warriors. By the time we'd finished the pot of coffee and they had looked over the copies of the manuscript . . . I was flat-out sure of it.

Chapter 52

"This is ancient Aramaic," Saul said, as he tapped the manuscript with an index finger. "Some call it Biblical Aramaic. It's what the Book of Daniel was written in."

Next to him, Naomi nodded her head in agreement.

"Can you read it?"

"Some. A few words here and there. It takes a scholar to fully comprehend it however."

"Are there any available here? What I really need is to get the document translated into English. The whole thing. As I told you, it may be the key to solving the Sorwell murders . . . or not. But it's the only possibility I have left."

Naomi said, "I'm curious. Why do you think that?"

"The apartment where they were murdered was ransacked. The killers were looking for something," I said, "and I think it was the manuscript. I only found it by accident, the second time I searched the place. Last of all—and I'm going out on a limb here—there's been a couple of attempts to steal it."

Saul picked up on the implication at once. He said, "Was it in CSPD custody at the time?"

"Yeah. It was. That's why I had these copies made."

"The original, hand-written copy," Naomi said, "you still, have it?"

"Yes."

Her husband said, "Is it safe? Do you have it secured?"

"Of course," I lied. Then said, "Why do you ask?"

A silent but pregnant glance passed between the pair of them before Naomi said, "Hand-written Judaica is rare, often old, and almost always significant in some way or another. We wouldn't be able to tell without seeing the actual document."

I decided to put a few more of my cards face-up, said, "I think you're right about two of your suppositions: rare and significant. But the age of it is questionable."

"How so?" Saul asked.

"Gilda Arkady, the Art History Professor at Colorado College, told me the book wasn't very old. 'A couple of decades at the most,' she said, based upon what she saw of the paper. The priest, Gianette is his name, is a Middle Eastern language expert. He said it was 'ancient.'"

"I can say with absolute certainty that it's not old," Naomi said.

"I agree," Saul added. "And it's easy to show you why. The manuscript was written over a long period of time, with different materials and tools . . ."

"Yeah," I said. "That's pretty obvious. Gilda even thought some of it was done in blood. Another section looked like ash, or charcoal."

Saul went on, as if I hadn't interrupted him and said, "But if you look at the last couple of dozen pages—even on these copies—it's plain to see that they were written by someone using a ballpoint pen."

"Yeah. So . . ." I said . . . and then it hit me like a runaway dump truck. *Ballpoint pens are a recent innovation.* "They weren't invented yet. They didn't exist until two or three years ago."

"Very good. You may now pass GO, and collect two hundred dollars," Saul said, with a grin on his face.

"Can't believe I let that one slip past me . . . I'm supposed to be the detective here . . ."

"Don't find too much fault with yourself Jake. Everyone makes mistakes, even Saul and I."

"Thanks for your kindness, Naomi, but overlooking the obvious makes me feel like a dope." I said. At the same time, I thought, *It also proves beyond a doubt that dear old 'Father Al' was lying through his teeth to me. Why? What's he trying to gain . . .*

"How well do you trust him?" Saul said.

"Who? Trust who?"

"The Jesuit, Gianette?"

I hoped my sixth sense wasn't failing me at the moment, but I was comfortable with the pair of them, even though we'd just met. I said, "I don't. Something about him set off alarm bells in my head. It was like there was another, whole different person behind the public facade he was presenting. I had to take the book back. He didn't want to give it up."

"Interesting," Saul said. "Are you aware of the stories about the relationship between the Nazis and the Catholic Church?"

"Only what I read in the newspapers and a few magazines. I followed the Nuremberg Trials when I was in college after the war, but that's all. Now that I think about it, I guess I don't know very much about it."

"That's not unusual Jake," my host said as he stood and headed for the kitchen. "I'll fill you in with what I know after we have something for lunch."

Naomi and I followed him and a few minutes later, we were all enjoying roast beef sandwiches with lettuce and tomato slices, along with another pot of coffee. It was a lot better tasting than the cafe food I'd been living on too.

We finished eating and were sitting around the kitchen table enjoying some after lunch cigarettes—me with my Luckys, while Saul and Naomi were both smoking the new filtered kind with cork tips—and drinking more coffee. For a few minutes at least, I managed to unwind . . . didn't think about much of anything . . . and had some moments of relaxed and easy peace. Such times have been rare in my life, and short lived, as they were that afternoon when Saul put out his cigarette and said, "About the manuscript . . ."

"Will you be able to translate it into English?" I said, as circumstance and reality, time, and situation, all poured down on me like buckets of cold, icy rain.

"Naomi and I have out-of-town guests coming from Israel in a day or two, and between them and us, I think we can manage it. So, the answer is yes, but it'll take another few days before it's transcribed. It would help to see the real document though . . . for nuance."

"Could you possibly try for Friday of this week?" I said. "I know it's asking for a lot from you but I think it's critical to know what's in that thing."

"We'll do the best we can Jake. It may turn out to be more important than any of us realize. We'll see. Right now, though, I need to fill you in a little bit about the relationship between the National Socialists and the hierarchy of the Catholic Church," Saul said.

Chapter 53

The three of us went into the living room at that point, where Saul bent down to light a fire that was already laid in the moss rock fireplace, because—in typical early spring fashion along the foothills of the Rocky Mountains—the warm sunshine of the morning had disappeared. The temperature dropped some thirty or forty degrees to the freezing point, while snow flurries pelted down from a gusting and lead colored sky. But a warm glow, along with the pleasant crackle and spicy scent of burning pinion, soon filled the room and held the outside world at bay.

As Naomi sat on the couch next to him, her shoes off and legs tucked up under her, Saul looked at me and said, "Jake, do you know what a ratline is?"

"Ropes," I said without hesitation, "for sailors to climb into the rigging of sailing ships."

"Yeah. But it's also a term that's used to describe an escape route."

"For rats . . ."

"Or for people."

"Such as?"

"Nazis and war criminals . . . from Europe to Argentina, the United States and probably a few other countries as well. Ever since World War II ended, certain Nazis have escaped from Europe—many thousands of them—via the ratlines established before the war ended."

"That's interesting," I said, as I looked from the burning logs back to Saul's face, "but I don't see what it's got to do with me . . ."

"Patience Jake," Naomi said. "You don't understand because you haven't heard everything. There's more to the story."

I noticed her almost imperceptible nod to her husband and wondered, *Who's in charge here?* as Saul resumed his narrative.

He said, "Certain countrymen of ours—Naomi's and mine—believe there's a ratline that ends here, in Colorado Springs. Abraham and Ruth Sorwell, and by extension you, may have stumbled onto its existence by accident. Proof of it may be contained somewhere in the Sorwell Manuscript. Thus, the attempts to steal it. We can't know for certain until the document is fully transcribed. It's as timely and important to us as it is to you."

I was hungover from too much alcohol and too many pain pills. My thought process was sluggish, and my brain wouldn't get fully in gear. I was having trouble grasping the enormity . . . and seriousness . . . as well as the full implications of what the pair of them had just revealed to me. Trying to buy a little time to get a better understanding of the situation and thaw my frozen mind out, I said, "Okay. I get the concept, but who's doing this? How? And why? Why here? What are these people doing once they get to the Springs? Most importantly—how many are here—are there more on the way?"

Naomi repositioned herself as I was babbling my questions and concerns. Now, she was tucked into a corner of the couch with her bare feet pressed flat against Saul's right thigh, and her eyes looking straight at me. I noticed the toes on her left foot flexing against her husband's leg. Then, just as I stopped asking questions, she flexed her right foot and Saul started to speak. I had a flash of insight, as I realized, *Not only is she in charge, she's watching me for tells and signs of lies. They both act like seasoned interrogators. I'm pretty sure they've done this before. You need to pay attention, Jake . . .*

Saul said, "I'll tell you as much as I can, but I don't have answers for all your questions. The people who are responsible for this are furtive and smart. They have to be wary and suspicious in order to survive. They can be ruthless when threatened and won't hesitate to resort to violence—beatings, kidnappings, and murder—even the extreme kind of violence that's meant to induce terror . . ."

"Like what Saul? And how exactly is it, that you know about all these things? It seems unlikely to me that you'd be involved in something so clandestine and global in scope while leading a tiny congregation in a small out of the way American city."

I was looking to Saul for an answer, but it was Naomi who spoke. She said, "You make assumptions at your peril Jake. These are deep and shark-infested waters we're in . . . don't underestimate our common enemies . . . and be prepared to accept help whenever it appears, in whatever form that comes your way. Last of all, be ready, willing, and able to fight at any time, in any place. It could mean the difference between life and death . . ."

"No offense, but do you have any idea how crazy all of this sounds to me? I came today, hoping to find some help translating an odd, handwritten diary that might be relevant to my first ever homicide case as lead detective—a case that's close to going into the 'open-unsolved' file unless something miraculous happens soon—and you're telling me to beware of bogeymen with evil intentions who are running something called a ratline, and may be lethal? I got your name out of the phone book . . . I only came here and met you by chance. There's just too damn much coincidence here for me to be comfortable . . ."

"But you were relaxed and at ease only a little while ago," Naomi said, "by your own admission."

The hair on the back of my neck stood on end. *How does she know THAT, for crissakes?*

"Tell you what," Saul said as he got up and poked the fire and added more wood, then returned to his spot on the couch, where his wife snugged her feet back on his leg. "Would you be open-minded enough to just listen to what we have to say, and form an opinion afterwards?"

"Reserve judgment, you mean?"

"Yes."

"Sure. I can do that," I said. But as I tapped out a fresh coffin nail and lit up, I thought, *You sound like an arrogant, ignorant asshole Jake . . .*

"Brace yourself," Naomi said. "Because it involves the Catholic Church."

Chapter 54

S aul took the lead again. He lit a cigarette of his own and said, "Are you aware that the current Pope, Pious XII, ignored what we're now calling The Holocaust, the industrialized murder of six million Jews—in addition to more than one million so-called undesirables: homosexuals, the handicapped and gypsies—by the Nazis, in what were called Concentration Camps?"

I paused for a moment, took a deep drag, and exhaled, thinking before I answered. Then said, "The camps are well publicized. They became common knowledge during the Nuremberg Trials, but I wasn't aware of the Pope's denials, to tell the truth. I guess I just never thought about it very much and assumed we were all on the same side."

"In a perfect world that would be true," Naomi said. "But in this one it's left up to each of us to decide how to behave and who we're going to be associated with. We have free will. It makes us responsible for our own actions."

"I get it. But what's that have to do with the Sorwell Manuscript?"

Saul took over. He passed the lit cigarette to his wife and put his right hand on her left foot. Then he said, "There's more we want to tell you, about some of the things the leaders of the church have been up to for the last dozen years or so, but we don't know where you stand. Are you religious? A practicing Catholic?"

I let out a short bark that passed for a laugh, "No. Neither one. I left religion and religion left me during the war. If anything, I guess you could call me a recovering Catholic."

My hosts looked at each other and seemed confused. But after a few moments, Saul said, "I don't understand the terminology. What do you mean?"

"It's a personal sarcasm," I said. "Means I'm getting over all of the dogmatic bullshit—pardon my French—that they pumped me full of when I was a child . . . the notion of original sin, sainthood, the confessional, the catechism, miracles and the liturgy among other things . . . and after what I saw in combat, I'm no longer sure if I even believe in God."

"Then I am sorry for you," Saul said. "Because it is a terrible thing for someone to lose their system of beliefs. Then they have lost their way in life—since they have no moral compass—and can no longer distinguish right from wrong. But that exploration, I'm afraid, will have to wait until another time, as we have other matters of a more pressing nature to discuss today. Wouldn't you agree?"

"I do, Rabbi," I said as I extinguished the cigarette I'd been smoking, "And I look forward to talking about the essence of God, and the nature of mankind with you."

"It will be interesting, I am sure," Rabbi Risenberg said, "as one old warrior speaking to another about the effects of armed conflict on religious faith."

Enlightening is more like it, I thought, *for how does any young man— or woman—go off to war, where they do what they do and see what they see, all while trying to stay alive long enough to make it home to kith and kin and a safe place to sleep at night . . .* What I could say for sure at that point in my life, was that I came back from the Pacific without a shred of personal belief in religion, and not much more than that in the idea of a Supreme Being. But over the years since then, God and I have come to an understanding. I no longer deny him, and he doesn't fuck with me . . . no plagues or boils or turning the wife into a pillar of salt for example, and we've been getting along pretty well.

Rabbi Risenberg and I saw each other a few more times that spring and summer, but never were able to have the philosophical discussion we'd talked about, because one or the other or both of us had more urgent problems to attend to . . . and then it was too late. In the fall of that year, Saul Risenberg died a warrior's death while on a covert mission for the IDF, the Israeli Defense Forces, against Fedayeen terrorists in the southern Sinai Peninsula during the Suez Crisis of October 1956. And although I knew him for only a brief while, he made a lasting impact on me—because I've thought about his moral compass metaphor tens of dozens of times over the years.

It was Naomi who snapped me out of my reverie and back into the moment that afternoon when she said, "Tell him what we know about the Austrians, Saul."

The two made eye contact and appeared to communicate in silence for an instant. Then, Saul nodded and said, "There's a region at the southeastern edge of Poland known as Galicia. Are you aware of it?"

"No," I said, feeling ignorant as dirt as I reached for the Skin Ripper notebook and started writing. "I'm not."

"It's a place that's been claimed, re-claimed and fought over for more than a thousand years." Saul said, as he drank some of the endless cups of coffee that kept appearing before us. He put it back on the dove-tailed wooden chest that served as a table and continued. "Galicia is where Naomi and I grew up, escaped from, and fought against the Nazis with the Polish Resistance during World War II. I'm giving you a small history of it, so you'll understand what we're dealing with. The area became a piece of the Habsburg, Austro-Hungarian Empire early in the 16th century. It remained a part of Austria until 1938 . . . when Adolph Hitler annexed it into Germany as a federal state . . ."

"The *Anschluss*," I said.

"Very good," Saul replied, while Naomi shook her head in approval.

"Wanted you both to know I'm more than just a tough guy with a pretty face and a potty mouth."

"Rest assured Jake, no one will ever take you lightly, doubt your authenticity or question your honesty . . ."

"That's alright Naomi," Saul said. "He was only making a joke. It wasn't a serious thought. And not meant as a statement of fact."

"Oh. I . . ."

Leave it to McKern to screw things up, I thought. Aloud, I said, "Sorry. That was my lame attempt at humor . . . which . . . as you just saw, I'm not very good at. Please go on Saul."

"Over the next three centuries the Habsburgs bled the province dry. They decreed that Galicia would remain agricultural, prohibited modernization or new investments, imposed punishing levels of taxation, and conscripted its young men to serve as cannon fodder in their many wars. The greatest irony of all was that vast quantities of oil were found there in the middle of the 19th century, but by the early 20th, or present century, the Galician wells had all been sucked dry. That was the Habsburgs. Then came the Nazis, and the "Final Solution" of Heinrich Himmler . . ."

"Final solution?"

"The eradication of all the Jews in Europe," Naomi said . . .

". . . And so, the Concentration Camps . . ."

"That's right," Saul said. "Along with the Waffen SS, in those black uniforms with the death head insignias, the gas chambers and the crematoriums that ran twenty-four hours a day, seven days a week . . ."

"It's like a living Robert E. Howard horror story," I said, referring to the Texas born pulp fiction writer from the 1920s and 30s.

"But all the more horrific because it was done on such an epic scale," Naomi said.

Saul resumed his narrative. "To give you an even more intimate idea of the slaughter that took place between 1941 and the war's end in '45 . . . there were about three million Jews—mostly Hasidic—living in Galicia, which stretches from the city of Lviv in the Ukraine, to Krakow in Poland, at the start of the war. From Krakow to the gas chambers at Auschwitz and the other nearby horror known as Treblinka, was a short, forty-five-mile trip west by railway. Of those three million, only ninety thousand or so Jews were still alive in Galicia when the Germans surrendered. Among their victims was every member of Naomi's and my extended families. Forty-seven souls in all, from our oldest grandparents to the youngest infants, no one was spared. We are the only ones left."

I was stunned. Knowing how much the murder of my sister had affected my mother, my youngest sister and myself, the pain that Saul and Naomi were enduring was unimaginable. I said, "No words can express enough sympathy, nor adequate condolences to be of comfort in the face of such barbarity and devastating losses . . . it's an unbelievable amount of butchery."

"For which the perpetrators are unrepentant, and whose only interest is in escaping the retribution they deserve in the here and now," Saul said, "and it's also where we come full circle . . . back to the Catholic Church, the Austrians and Galicia."

I looked from the fireplace to the big picture window, where huge feathers of wet spring snow were beginning to pile up on the grass and rocks and budding trees in the early April gloom, trying to process everything he'd just told me. Then, I turned my focus back to the two survivors on the couch and said, "What comes next Saul . . . where do we go from here . . . and most important from my perspective, how does it have to do with solving the murders of two people in Colorado Springs?"

Saul made eye contact with me, "In all honesty Jake, I don't know. But somehow, I think everything we've talked about is going to help solve the murders and stop an ongoing crime . . ."

"That's a leap I'm not prepared to take. I have to have facts and enough provable evidence to convince a judge and jury beyond a reasonable doubt."

"Would you hear me out?"

"Yeah," I said, as I reached for a fresh smoke and lit up while sneaking a peek at my watch. "I will."

"Good," Saul said. "It won't take long and you'll have a better idea about what's happening in the present because it connects some of the wartime authorities to current events happening here and now. Some of its guesswork, but we should know more when Frankel gets here . . ."

"Who's Frankel?"

Naomi said, "The company we're expecting in a couple of days. He's someone Saul and I worked with during the war with the Arabs in 1948, when the British withdrew from Palestine and the nation of Israel was born."

"He has access to a lot more information than we do," Saul said, "because he works for a man named Simon Wiesenthal, tracking down war criminals."

"Never heard of him," I said as I put my pen down, took a puff of Lucky Strike, and crushed it out.

"Not many have. But I'll let Frankel speak for himself," Saul said. "Right now, we need to finish up about the Austrians."

I picked up my pen, ready to write more notes.

Chapter 55

It was coming on dark when I left and headed for downtown. I had to stop a couple of times along the way to clear the windshield, because the snow was sticking on the streets by then and it was piling up so fast that the car's wipers couldn't keep the glass cleaned off. The white stuff would jam in the corners and wad up there, until visibility was down to almost zero. Then, I'd pull into the nearest parking lot and clean the packed snow with my bare hands. It was good in a way, because it gave me plenty of time to think about everything I'd learned that afternoon . . . and allowed for a chance to rub my eyes with the heels of my hands. They'd been watering most of the time I'd been in the car . . . due to the smoke from those burning pine logs and the smell of pitch in the fireplace, I guess.

The gist of what I'd heard from the Risenbergs in the last hour, was that Jews were a fraction less than twelve percent of the population in Galicia when the German army stormed into Poland on September 1, 1939. The rest of the inhabitants were about equally split between Roman Catholic Poles and Eastern Orthodox Catholic Ukrainians, plus a fractional number of German speaking Austrian overlords . . . the hereditary masters of the whole region. They were also aligned with the Pope in Rome and devout Catholics.

"We know for a fact," Saul said, "that two of the persons who were involved in the Galician genocide came from the region's Austrian elite. The first one was a lawyer and longtime National Socialist Party member named Otto Wächter. He was a *Gruppenfuhrer*—two star general—of the Waffen-SS, Governor of the Krakow District, and later the Governor of all Galicia. That fact alone makes him directly responsible for what happened . . . his signature is on the removal orders . . . and he started the mass movements of Jews from Galicia to the Auschwitz Concentration Camp. He worked directly for and directly with Heinrich Himmler. They were not equals, but I think they were familiars."

"The other evildoer is an Austrian Bishop of the Catholic Church named Alois Hudal. He lives at the Vatican in Rome, where he's been a long-time supporter, friend, and confidant of Cardinal Eugenio Pacelli—the man who is now Pope Pious XII."

"Bishop Alois Hudal is an enthusiastic and unapologetic supporter of Nazism, who wrote a book praising its virtues."

"Alois Hudal is also the father of all the Ratlines. He helped many high-ranking Waffen-SS generals escape . . . including Otto Wächter . . . whom Bishop Hudal protected, fed, and hid, disguised as a monk in several Italian monasteries scattered among the Alps for four years after the Nazi surrender. Wächter died in 1949, before he could get to Argentina. But we know that Hudal managed to get a number of others, including Josef Mengele—known as the *"Angel of Death"* for his medical experiments on human subjects at Auschwitz and Birkenau—away from the war crimes trials and safely out of Europe." Saul's narrative stopped at that point, as he closed his eyes and pinched the bridge of his nose in a simple gesture that spoke more eloquently of pain than words ever could.

After a few moments of silence, where we all lived alone with our thoughts, I remember Saul saying to Naomi and me . . . "The Poles can deny and claim they were forced all they want to, now that the shame and disgrace of what they did during the war has been exposed for the world to see . . . but as a nation they tend towards racism and bigotry in my estimation. I think they were eager to collaborate with the Nazis . . ."

"Not all of them," Naomi said. "We had plenty of resistance fighters . . . and look at how many Polish pilots flew with the RAF."

"An infinitely small number compared to all those who cooperated and supported the camps or ignored and denied them. Why do you think most of the gas chambers and crematoriums were located in Poland? Because people living there were compliant. That's why."

"Or maybe it was because they had all those Germans sticking guns in their faces . . . maybe that had something to do with it," I said. "You'd comply too."

"No." Saul said. "I. Would. Not."

"One of those who'd rather die on their feet than live on their knees . . . I come from a long line of them . . . they're buried all over Ireland."

"A luxury Naomi and I have not been afforded, as all of our ancestors and loved ones went up those industrial chimneys as smoke."

"Enough!" Naomi said. "Both of you. We're all on the same side here, with a common enemy. You're acting like a pair of roosters."

Saul looked at her and laughed without humor. "You're right, as you usually are Naomi. Sorry, I didn't mean to get carried away . . ."

"Me either."

"It's such an emotional issue it's not easy to discuss in a calm and quiet way though. My apologies to both of you," I said, while I thought: *Jee-sus Christ on a crutch, Jake. You sure know how to ask for someone's help.*

Not long after that I found myself full of hope, driving west on Fillmore Street with Saul's promise to attempt a translation of the Sorwell Manuscript as fast as possible, and somehow, I believed he just might succeed.

But it was Naomi's last words that kept ringing in my head. As the pair of them saw me to the door. She said, "I've been thinking about what you mentioned earlier Jake— about not believing in coincidence—and I understand. But, have you ever considered the possibility that it might've been *divine intervention* brought us together?"

It was self-contradictory . . . a paradox that defied reason and common sense. I've thought about it off and on for more than forty years . . . and I still have no answer. But in light of everything that was about to happen over the next few days, it was as true an answer as any we'll find while still on the green side o'the sod.

Chapter 56

First thing Monday morning, I called in and took one of my accumulated sick days, thinking I'd spend part of it with Nurse Gloria and the rest clearing up some personal loose ends—like the fifteen-thousand-dollar Chaparral Oil Company check I'd been carrying around for the last three days. But no sooner had Ann-Marie Fuchs said, "See ya tomorrow," and I put the telephone back on the cradle, it rang again . . . and my whole days scheme was shot in the ass while God laughed at the thought of me making plans.

Gloria said, "I'm sorry, Hon, but one of the other nurses was in a car wreck this morning and I've been called in to cover her shift."

"How bad was it?"

"Pretty serious. Her face hit the windshield, and she's got several broken bones. And I imagine she'll need a lot of reconstructive surgery too."

"Sorry to hear. Where'd it happen?"

"Down by Security is all I know. I'll call you later, maybe we can get together for a bite to eat somewhere. But I have to go. I'm already late."

It was a few minutes past six. I was sitting on the edge of the bed in my skivvies, rearranging the day's activities in my head and reaching for my first smoke of the morning when the damn thing rang again.

Wally Bailey said, "Drop your cock an' grab your socks boyo, you may want to hang on to your ass too, 'cuz we just got 'nuther'un . . ."

"Another what Wally? Quit talking crap and say what you have to say."

"The Skin Ripper Jake. The Skin Ripper's done it again. He's killed another person. You're catchin' it 'cuz you're lead on the first one. So says Chief Budd himself."

Which also makes me the perfect fall guy if it all goes to hell on a handcar like the first one, I thought.

Filled with unease and the creepy feeling of *déjà vu,* I copied the address and got busy. Left the house with my gut full of dread and headed for the crime scene less than ten minutes later.

North El Paso Street in the Patty Jewett area wasn't known for criminal activity. Tucked into a quiet pocket off east Uintah Street, it was a tranquil oasis of well-kept Craftsman style homes, huge old trees, and friendly neighbors. Adjacent to the golf course of the same name, and just a few blocks from the campus, the neighborhood was a favorite place for tenured Colorado College professors to settle down and nest . . . all of which made the police cars, flashing red lights and pha-lanxes of uniformed cops seem as alien as if a whole crew of Tommy Knockers—the bodies of dead miners who'd been buried alive—had popped up from their forgotten tombs in the exhausted coal seams that wormed their way like dark, subterranean capillaries throughout that part of the city.

A few early risers—fresh air friends and dog walkers—were start-ing to gather on the sidewalks, where officer Magness was keeping them back, when I pulled in and parked. A few of the bolder ones shouted questions at me as I made my way up to the house where an-other murder victim and mutilated body was waiting.

I climbed four steps onto the porch, where I nodded to Sgt. Clay-poole, who was just coming out of the front door. I said, "Morning Andy. Can you keep a lid on things out here, while I go inside?"

"Sure Jake. There's a detached two car garage out back with an apartment upstairs. Victim's in there."

"Same M.O.?"

"Pretty much."

"Anything else?"

"Yeah. Victim is a visiting professor from New York. Names Chiam Leviwitz. The house belongs to a history professor at CC."

I was making notes as Claypoole talked. When he stopped, I said, "Where's the homeowner and what's his name?"

"She's in the back of my patrol car. Her name is Zell Rodgers."

I looked up from my notebook. Said, "Guess I shouldn't have assumed. Put a couple of uniform cops to door knocking for witnesses and tell Mrs. Rodgers we'll be with her in a few minutes. Thanks. I appreciate it."

Claypoole looked at me for a moment, then said as I turned to go, "Me and Magness'll get names and information from the onlookers to . . . see if any of 'em saw anything."

"Good thinking Andy. I'll get it right eventually."

"We all gotta learn," he said, as he stepped away and headed down the sidewalk.

I went out back to the garage, hoping that the killers had made some small kind of mistake . . . anything that might lead me to them . . . and reminded myself for the umpteenth time. *Slow. The fuck. Down.*

Upstairs, the three-room apartment looked normal and neat enough when I first entered through the kitchen, but as soon as I turned toward the living room, a trail of blood leading from the bedroom to the bathroom gave the first indication of the violence that had taken place inside. Butch Hernshaw, Doug Sikes and the rest of the crime scene crew came in at that point, put on latex gloves and went to work. But after a few hours of looking through every inch of the place, they found only the partially flayed body of Professor Leviwitz with two bullet holes in the chest and one in the forehead, the same execution style killing as the Sorwells. The only difference I noted in my quick walk of the murder scene, was that Levitwitz had an unfashionable, long length of haircut, and he was wearing a coarse, full beard. There wasn't much else to see, other than the fact that his wardrobe consisted of some heavy black suits, white dress shirts, a pair of plain black shoes and a flat-brimmed black hat which would have been right in style a hundred years ago. It made me wonder if the professor was an ascetic of some kind, as I left Butch and the tech guys to do the fine sifting, while I went down to interview Mrs. Rodgers.

She was in the rear seat of Sgt. Claypoole's cruiser, looking anxious and forlorn when I opened the car door. She saw me and said, "Who are you and why am I stuck in here?"

"My name's McKern, Ma'am. I'm the lead investigator on the Sorwell case, and now I've been assigned to this one also . . ."

"The Skin Ripper? Oh, dear God."

Seeing her distress, I said, "The reason Sgt Claypoole put you in here is because we have to get a witness statement from you while everything's still fresh in your mind."

She clutched her housecoat together at the neck, shivered and said, "Am I in danger?"

I shook my head. "No. I don't think you are, but it's impossible to know for sure without more information. Tell me what happened this morning."

"Are you certain, I'm not going to be the fiend's next victim, young man?"

I was looking at her, trying to decide how tough to be, when a couple of tears slipped down her cheeks. They made me realize that she was scared . . . and her fear was bone deep.

Chapter 57

I was leaning on the roof of the police car with my other arm on the open door, talking down to the woman who looked older than my mother and frightened, so I kneeled instead, hoping to put her more at ease by looking up. "Truth is Miz Rodgers, no one knows for certain. But based on my experience and what I've learned so far on this case, I think we wouldn't even be having this conversation if you were in any danger, because whoever did that to Professor Leviwitz would have already taken care of business . . ."

"And I'd be dead?"

I nodded.

She said, "Thanks for the truth. Somehow it makes me feel better."

I could see Magness and Sgt. Claypoole admonishing the crowd to stay back, but it was getting larger, and with the swelling came more shouted questions I wasn't going to answer. "Tell you what," I said, "I think both of us would do better in a quieter setting. I'm gonna leave you here a moment and go get the car. I'll come back in a few minutes and take you downtown. That okay with you?"

"How would I get home . . . and what about my house, my keys and my purse?"

"Tell me where they are and I'll fetch everything and lock the door too."

"And bring me back?"

"Me or a uniformed patrolman will, yes ma'am."

I left Butch in charge of the crime scene, locked the house, and gathered her things, including, 'My blue raincoat and white sneakers in the front closet,' then headed down to the station at 220 East Kiowa

Street, where I hoped, Mrs. Rodgers could help solve some piece of The Skin Ripper puzzle.

Whether it was from nerves, or habit, she began talking before we even got to Uintah Street and never stopped. By the time we sat down at my desk in the bull pen, I almost felt as if I'd known her for most of my life, but learned nothing much about the case. Trying to get her back on track, I pulled out Agnes Bedwell's portable tape recorder and turned it on. I gave the time and date, the location and case number, then my name and badge number. I said, "State your name and address for the record."

She said, "Zelda Rodgers, North El Paso Street . . ." and we were off and running.

Before she could get distracted, I said, "What happened this morning?" as I put my notebook on the desk and prepared to write.

Zelda said, "The next door neighbor's dog started barking and woke me up. I like dogs, but this one's a nuisance . . ."

"Do you know what time it was?"

She thought, fidgeted, and said, "Can I smoke in here?"

I knew she used tobacco, because I saw the pack in her purse when I looked through it for weapons back at the house, before I gave it to her. I said, "Sure after you tell me what time the dog woke you."

"I think it was a little before three—maybe a little after—I'm not exactly sure."

"Why not," I said, as I pulled out a Lucky Strike of my own and tamped it on the face of my watch, then stuck it in the corner of my mouth.

"I had to use the bathroom and didn't look at the clock when I first got out of bed. It was a quarter after when I came back."

"Are you sure?"

"Absolutely," She reached in her bag and pulled out a smoke of her own.

I lit us both up and said, "Was the dog still making a racket Zelda?"

"Everyone calls me Zell. No. It wasn't, which is curious, now that I think about it, because I peeked out of the bedroom curtain and it looked like there was a light on in the apartment over the garage. That always sets it off. Bark. Bark. Bark. It goes on day and night, whenever anything moves out there."

"Did you see or hear anything else?"

"Not then. I went back to bed, but couldn't get to sleep again, just tossed, and turned. Then I heard a car start out in the alley and drive away."

"The time?"

"I don't know."

"Why not?'

"I had the covers over my head. I was irritated from lack of sleep . . . and no, I don't know what the clock read, but it was still dark outside, if that helps," she said as she inhaled, blew out a lungful of smoke and tapped her cancer stick on the ashtray we were sharing.

Thinking I wasn't getting any useful information, I changed the subject. "What can you tell me about Professor Leviwitz? Is he some kind of a holy man or something? Why the plain, old-fashioned looking clothes? Why isn't he staying in a hotel?"

Zell looked at me for a few moments—as if deciding how best to answer. Then she said, "Yes. He's Hasidic—an Orthodox Jew—who practices a strict religious life and adheres to a complex set of rules to live by. He's not in a hotel or staying at the college because it can't be sanctified, made clean enough in the spiritual sense, to meet his lifestyle requirements."

"Sounds complicated," I said, as I crushed out my coffin nail and continued with the notes I was making.

"It is," she said, adding, "I was his best option, in that I'm Jewish too, and although not Orthodox, I do observe the rules of the Torah and keep a kosher kitchen."

I found myself searching my mind for the right questions to ask. I was looking to get more clarifying answers from the enigmatic woman sitting alongside my desk smoking, and showing no emotion over the violent death of her tenant a few hours earlier. Her lack of concern was bothering me . . . but I didn't know why. At that point I closed my notebook and said, "Zelda—or Zell if you prefer—I'm trying to solve a complex and heinous series of murders that appear to be done by pros. They've left few clues and I'm struggling to come up with a solution. I need some help. Your help, if I'm ever gonna bring the bastards who did it to justice. If I can find out why, I can figure out who . . . but not without some leads . . . and so far, the only connection I'm seeing, is that all the victims are Jews who survived the concentration camps."

Zelda Rodgers sat forward in her chair and put out the cigarette without saying a word. Then she laid her left forearm on the desk with her palm up and said—as she pushed her sleeve back to display a six-digit number tattooed in blue ink—"It is an experience that was shared by more than a few of us . . . but we who managed to survive are only a smattering of the unfortunate millions who were taken . . . and I can say without a doubt, that those of us who are still among the living, saw and did things that are right out of one of Hieronymus Bosch's Nightmares."

Zell had given all the information she had relative to The Skin Ripper by then. After a few more perfunctory exchanges of addresses and phone numbers, I took her back to her house, so she could pack some things and go to a hotel for a few days while her place was still considered a crime scene.

There have been a few moments in my lifetime—after somehow coming into contact with the absolute evil mankind is capable of— that I have wondered why God doesn't just destroy the lot of us and start over. That day was one of them.

Chapter 58

After I left Zelda Rodgers at the back door to her house, I found Butch Hernshaw sitting in an unmarked police car out in the alley on North El Paso Street. He was making notes in a school composition book when I parked nose-to-tail alongside him and rolled my window down. He saw me and did the same. I said, "Anything new or different about this one?"

"It doesn't look like it," Butch said. "I think they were in and out in a hurry though. The victim's skin is mostly intact. It's been peeled off his front and back, but nowhere else. No other mutilation. Guess we'll know more after the autopsy . . ."

"If there's an autopsy. I just found out that Professor Leviwitz was an Orthodox Jew with a strict religious code. We may run into opposition from them is my guess . . . about desecration of the body."

"It's already been desecrated," Butch said as he lit a cigarette.

"True. Anything from the neighborhood canvas?"

"Sgt. Claypoole hasn't told me anything—not a word." Butch said, then looked down at his notebook and went on, "But I'll be surprised if they do. This is the weirdest damned case I've ever been on. It makes no sense. The killers are organized, unafraid and ruthless—the victims are targeted—that much is apparent to me. But what I can't figure out is why. Why three old people? What's the reason?"

"When we find out, we'll be able to close the case and mark it solved. The only commonality so far is that all three survived the death camps during the war."

Butch looked up and said, "Think that's why they were targeted?"

"Dunno. It's one possibility. It may also have to do with that book

I found. We should know more about it in a few days. Father Al—the Jesuit Priest—Gianette, will be here soon and I'm working on a second possible translator as well." I wasn't telling Butch everything. I thought, *Yeah, and until I find out who's taken the dummy manuscript, I'll keep the cards close to my chest . . .*

"Butch, I don't want to run the gauntlet of reporters and news folks out front, in order to speak to Claypoole. Would you let him know I'll catch up with him later . . . last of all . . . will you make sure Mrs. Rodgers leaves here unchallenged. I'll meet you back at the shop. See the place is secure and that we have keys for it. There's something personal I have to do. I've been putting it off for too long." *I just hope the damned thing is cashable,* I thought . . .

The Chaparral Oil Corp check was ready to break into three pieces from being folded and carried around in my breast pocket for so long. When I presented it to the teller's window at the bank, she didn't think it would be honored. "In any case," the woman said, "I don't have enough authority for approval of a check that large, you'll need to go see Mr. Brickell about it. He's the person in charge, and he'll have to okay it."

Twenty minutes later, I was ushered into a wood-paneled office where Michael J. Brickell, Vice-President, Colorado Commercial Bank, greeted me with a handshake and a smile. He said, "It's a pleasure to finally meet the man who saved the bank last year. I hope you've recovered completely."

My leg was killing me, but I wasn't gonna admit it. We did a little more chit-chatting and then got to it. "I need to put this in the bank," I said, as I passed the battered check across the desk.

"You know this is ten days old and in poor condition too."

"I've been busy."

"What's it for, if you don't mind me asking?"

"Is that important?"

"I'm supposed to ask. It's due diligence."

"It's a divorce settlement." I said, "And that's all I want to say. Are you going to accept it or not?"

Brickell smiled. "Probably. It's an awful lot of money. We have to be careful. Give me just a minute. I have a phone call to make and I'll be right back." He left with my check and closed the door behind him. I wondered for a moment, if I'd see him—or the money again—probably my dumbest thought of the month, because he was back in less time than it took to write this compound sentence.

Mr. Brickell sat down at his desk and smoothed the mangled check on the blotter. He said, "There's no problem. The check's fine. I'd advise you to open a new checking and savings account though, and close your old one. After talking with the other bank officer in Houston, I'll let you deposit it as a cash item too."

"What's that mean?"

"No hold on the funds. You can draw on them immediately. No waiting for the check to clear."

I shook my head in wonder. "Thank you. What do I have to do now?"

He wrote something on the front of the check and said, as he handed it back, "Give this to my assistant. Her name is Patricia. She'll see that all your banking needs are taken care of . . . and thanks for using the Colorado Commercial Bank."

Less than an hour after that, I walked out of there as the owner of a new savings account with $10,000 in it, a new checking account containing most of a year's salary, the Note and a Security Agreement marked 'Paid in Full,' plus the title for a '56 Chevy convertible that had been shot up and burned to ashes by the Lee Roy Morgan gang last November. They were attempting to rob the payroll for the Air Force Academy campus that's being built north of the city. The car was new. I'd just picked it up at the dealership, hadn't driven it two miles—or put insurance on it yet—and I've been making payments on it ever since. Pain is the price of ignorance. I'm living proof of it.

I called the station from a pay phone in the lobby and talked to Ann-Marie. She said that Butch and Claypoole were in the house, writing their reports, and that Lt. Patterson was looking for me. I thanked her and got Butch. I said, "Find anything?"

"No. It was pretty much the same as the last one on Tejon Street."

"Okay. Have you eaten?"

"No."

"Me neither. I'll be there in a few minutes with chow." I stopped at the Busy Corner Café, over at the intersection of Pikes Peak and Tejon, ordered a half-dozen hamburger sandwiches, then asked the counter-man if someone could bring them—hot—up to us at the Police Station. Gino said either he or his wife would be happy to. I paid for the food, left a nice tip, and headed for the PD, wondering, *What's the brass want with me now* . . .

Chapter 59

When I got to my desk in the bullpen, it was almost three in the afternoon. Butch and Andy Claypoole were busy writing reports, and there was a larger than usual stack of pink message slips vying for my attention, sitting in a neat pile on the middle of the blotter. I moved them off to the side as I sat down, looked over at Butch and said, "Food will be here shortly. Gino's bringing it from the Corner Cafe."

"He can't get here fast enough. My stomach thinks my throat's been cut."

I started to light one up, thought better of it, and put the cigarettes and lighter on the desk alongside the message slips. I smiled as I said, "Well damn, Butch and do ya think you could tell me the news before ya pass out then . . ." in my mother's Dublin accent.

"That's just it Jake, there's nothing to say that you don't already know. They came. They killed. They skint. They left. And that's all folks . . ."

"Canvassing the crowd and the neighborhood didn't yield anything either," Claypoole said, "exactly like the first one."

We'd just started looking through our notes for any similarities, or differences, from the first murder scene over on Spruce Street, when Ann-Marie walked in carrying a cardboard box filled with foil-wrapped hamburgers. She put it down on my desk and said, "The guy who brought this wanted me to let you know the french-fried potatoes are on the house, and he asked if someone could please bring the mustard and ketchup bottles back. There's also some fresh coffee. I just made some. And Jake—you need to read through your messages—I think a couple of 'em are important."

"Will do," I said, "and thanks for the warning," while I watched

Butch and Claypoole divvying up the food. Then, all three of us got busy eating as only the very hungry can. When we finished, Claypoole left and went off shift, while Butch and I smoked, drank coffee, and went over everything we knew, thought, or even suspected about the Skin Ripper murders, all to no avail. We didn't find any new information. We had no clues. Butch went home to his pregnant wife and three kids. I stayed at my desk for a while longer, frustrated about the case and my inability to solve it, until, also mentally tormented by what my personal life was become, I finally gave it up and left for a walk around the block to try to lose the blues . . . and clear my head.

I left through the Kiowa Street door, across from the front entrance to the city auditorium—home of the Lon Chaney theater—turned west, and then north on the sidewalk up Nevada Avenue. I strolled past the replica Statue of Liberty on the courthouse lawn. Then paid my respects to General William Palmer, who sat like a colossus on a giant bronze stallion atop a huge granite plinth, smack-dab in the center of the eight-lane intersection at Platte and Nevada Avenues, where he's been cursed by generations of motorists who were forced to navigate their vehicles around him. I've always held that it's an odd legacy for the man who was not only a Civil War hero for the Union, but also the builder of the Denver & Rio Grande Railroad, as well as the founder of the city of Colorado Springs. But like he always did, the General and his horse ignored me and continued looking to infinity as I lit a cigarette, turned right on Platte and again on Weber Street . . . now walking south on the final leg of my journey.

I was almost to the cop's parking area behind the station when I stopped to put out my cigarette. I stood at the curb, field stripping the butt, when I looked up and saw the prettiest car in the whole damn state of Colorado being installed on the showroom floor of the Chevrolet dealership across the street . . . and like a moth to a flame, I stepped over for a closer look . . . and that's where all my common sense and willpower just evaporated.

The vehicle was a cherry red sports car called a Corvette. It had a red leather interior with bucket seats and a manual floor shift transmission, plus a V8 motor that throbbed with power under the hood. It wasn't a very practical thing to own or drive, but none of those details mattered at the moment, because that gorgeous machine spoke to me somehow, and lovestruck as a sailor answering the siren's call, I was consumed by lust. I had to have her.

About two hours later, after negotiating with Mike Hillman, the General Sales Manager, and some cajoling on my part, the '56 Corvette I named 'Scarlett' was mine. My checking account had taken a serious hit, but I didn't care. I was happy for the first time since I could remember. The feeling didn't last long.

Chapter 60

With nowhere to go, and nothing to do—Nurse Gloria was exhausted and the Corvette was being prepped for delivery the next morning—I decided to go back to work and slug through the messages I'd ignored earlier. It turned out to be one of the best choices I'd made all week.

I turned on my desk lamp, lit a smoke and pulled a dozen pink slips to my front. Five of them from Father Al, four were sent by Lenny Bragg and marked 'urgent' and 'extremely urgent—please call immediately.' The last three were reminders from Ma, my dentist, and the date for the deposition in an old case that was led by Wilson Bell. Thinking it was time we had a few words after what he'd written about me, I called Lenny first. There wasn't any answer at his home number, so I dialed his direct line at the newspaper . . . and whattya know . . . he answered, even though it was close to eight o'clock in the evening. I said, "It's Jake. What's so urgent?"

"Information," Lenny said, "I know you're PO'd about what's been written in the column and I don't blame you. But we need to talk right away and face-to-face. Can you come here?"

"I can, but why should I?"

"Because I may know who you're looking for . . ."

"For real . . ."

"Yeah."

"I'll be right there."

The Gazette-Telegraph offices at 30 South Prospect Street, were about a mile away as the crow flies, and only a little bit farther via the land route from where I sat at the cop shop. I hopped in my unmarked and entered the lobby of the newspaper less than ten minutes later.

Lenny Bragg was sitting at his desk, slumped back in a rough-looking wooden office chair, staring at his big Olivetti typewriter. I said, "That chair makes my back hurt, just looking at it."

Lenny pulled his feet out of the desk drawer he was resting them in, sat up and said, "This is indeed the iron maiden of office seating, designed by sadistic bastards to impede comfort, discourage good posture, and prevent long-winded discourse. How are you, Jake?"

"Still up to my ass in alligators . . . and the swamp ain't gettin' any lower Lenny . . . no thanks to you."

Lenny pushed his glasses up on his nose, put his hands on the desk and said, as he pointed with his chin, "Grab one of those chairs and I'll make it up to you."

I sat and without being asked, offered my friendly adversary a Lucky Strike, and we both lit up. I inhaled, sat back with my left hand cupping my right elbow, and waited with the burning coffin nail stuck between my index and middle fingers. It didn't take long.

Lenny edged closer, and said, "I think someone has been following me . . ."

"Why do you have that idea? And secondly, what difference does it make if you are? Do you have anything concrete . . . or is this some bullshit you've dreamed up to get me over here?"

He didn't answer right away, just stared at me through the bluish haze of smoke rising from our two cigarettes for a few moments. Then he said, "I'm not a kid. I'm a newsman. A reporter. I don't make shit up. And last of all, my grudge-bearing, once-in-a-while compadre . . . I know you were thrown to the wolves in the column, but . . . believe me, it wasn't my doing. Television is changing the news business. They report on things the same day it happens. We can't. It takes time to get the paper together, printed and delivered . . . but we're all competing for the same advertising dollars. So, the editors have decided to jazz the stories up with more detail, some opinion, and a lot more hyperbole. It's survival Jake. Don't take it personal."

I puffed and crushed my smoke in the dirty ashtray on Lenny's cluttered desk. "That's an easy rationalization for you to say from up here in your ivory tower, but let's see how you feel the next time one of you gets threatened and calls for a cop—and none comes. See what it's like. Then let me know what ya think."

I started to stand and leave, but Lenny stopped me. "Hold on Jake. Please. It's important."

"I'm all ears," I said, as I settled back down on my chair.

"I have a tail. I'm sure I do. It started right after I began looking into the background of the woman who's running the new ski school they've opened down on Cheyenne Mountain, next to the Broadmoor Hotel. She says her name is Ilse Müller, and that she's from a small town in Bavaria, where she grew up milking cows and skiing in the Alps . . ."

I shook my head. "Wait," I said. "What does this have to do with my case? And why do you care where she's from . . . what difference does it make?"

"Hold on. That's too many questions all at once," Lenny said, as he reached over and emptied the butt-filled ashtray into the metal trash can under his desk. Then he extinguished what was left of his smoke in the ash blackened and cigarette scarred glass ashtray, sat back in his chair and went on. "Do you remember the woman from KRDO TV, Agnes Bedwell? She's the one who had on a red coat and was working the crowd at the first Ripper scene . . ."

"Yeah. She did a news clip about the coming of the local ski area and the woman who would run the school there."

"Yeah. That's it. Anyway, the bosses here thought we should run an article of our own, a more comprehensive and in-depth one that fleshed out the who-what-where-when, and the job was assigned to me. I interviewed her last week, then started doing some background stuff, talking to coworkers, vetting sources, making sure I had it all correct . . . and things started getting weird . . ."

"How so?"

Lenny began pushing a stray paper clip around the desktop with his fingertips—as if he was trying to decide how to answer—then let out a sigh and said, "It started when I interviewed a man named Otto Felter. He's the groundskeeper, the person who's the head of maintenance for the ski slope and the chairlift . . . and it almost seemed like he was her lieutenant, or something . . ."

"What gave you that impression?" I said, "Or, maybe I should ask, why do you think so?"

"Because he was over-protective. Whenever I was chatting with her, Otto Felter always managed to be hovering around somewhere within earshot. I know he was eavesdropping on us. He didn't even try to hide it."

"So, he's nosy. Maybe it's jealousy, a love angle of some kind or other."

"I didn't get that impression—it was more like he was her body-guard. I know he was carrying a gun too. There was a bulge near his right hip, under his shirt, which wasn't tucked into his pants."

That got my attention. I said, "Are you absolutely sure of it Lenny? And positive he was concealing a pistol . . . not a tool belt or something?"

He looked grim when he lifted his eyes and gazed into mine. "I'm absolutely certain Jake. I know what I saw . . . it was a 9-millimeter Luger Parabellum . . . the kind German Officers carried."

I was making notes as fast as I could write.

Chapter 61

My senses went on high alert in an instant. I didn't know why at the moment, but felt somehow that what Lenny had just told me was going to factor into the Skin Ripper case in some way. I said, "How do you know about German pistols?"

"I was sixteen when my older brother parachuted into France in 1944 with the 82nd Airborne. He sent a Luger home to me before he was killed at the Battle of the Bulge. I'm intimately familiar with them."

My mind was starting to churn up a ton of possibilities. I said, "Tell me about the shadow you picked up. When did you first notice it?"

Lenny thought for a little bit. "It was Saturday afternoon. I had been all over town doing errands and stuff, and I kept noticing this gray Volkswagen. I didn't think anything about it at first, but I started seeing it in all the same places I was going. From the post office, to the library, to the bank . . . there it was."

"Did anyone approach you?"

"No. No one threatened me either. And whoever's doing it isn't the least bit shy—I almost think they want me to know they're keeping an eye on me."

"Or maybe," I said, as my gut gave out a loud rumble, "someone's trying to intimidate you from nosing around any more."

Lenny couldn't have missed the rude noises coming from my stomach. He said, "Would you like to go grab a bite, and I'll tell you the rest of it . . . I'll even buy. Pay you back some, for all the cigarettes I've bummed."

"Wonders never cease," I said. "Lead on."

"I know just the place."

I followed Lenny in his little British sports car, over to a hole-in-the-wall diner and greasy spoon called the Chimes Cafe on East Platte Avenue, where we walked in and had the place all to ourselves. We sat at the counter, and saw a short order cook, who was sitting on the ice cream freezer reading the paper. He looked up, saw us, and said, "Lenny Bragg—if you ain't got no good news—go away."

"The food here's not good enough for you to be running paying customers off, Louie. How's your stroke?"

"Smooth as silk, baby. Smooth as silk and pretty as a new puppy."

Lenny laughed. "Jake, meet Louie Hankins, chief cook, and dishwasher of the Chimes Cafe—as well as the biggest pool shark from here to the New Mexico state line. Louie, this is . . ."

"No need Lenny. I recognize him from the newspaper. Louis Hankins, Mr. McKern . . . Screwy Louie to everybody who knows me."

"Just Jake is okay," I said, as we shook hands. "I'm not anybody special."

"Whatever you say mister. What can I get you gents?"

Lenny said, "How about a couple bowls of your Hot Rod Chili with some sweet cornbread and two coffees."

"Sounds good to me," I said, "but why's it called 'hot rod chili'?"

"'Cuz the first time I ever made it, I got a little too enthusiastic with my spices and the first customer who tasted it said, 'Damn! That stuff's like swallowing a hot iron rod.' I tamed the recipe some, but I liked the name and kept it."

Lenny said, "It doesn't exactly hurt that Louie runs around town in a '36 Ford three window coupe with a full-race flathead in it."

"Is it maroon?"

"Yeah," Louie said, "with black fenders."

"I've seen it once or twice," I said. "It's a good-looking ride."

Louie acknowledged the compliment with a smile and a nod of his head, then went back to the grill to get our food. As soon as he walked out of earshot, Lenny pointed to a row of empty booths along the opposite wall. "Let's sit over there," he said, "where we've got more room for you to make notes."

We moved and settled in, just as Louie came back with two mugs of coffee and some milk in a little metal pitcher. "I'll have your chili up in just a minute."

I sat with my back to the wall, facing the windows that looked out on Platte Avenue and watched, while Lenny took off his overcoat, then laid it on the seat next to him. When he got done smoothing his hair with his hand, I said, "Okay Lenny. Let's hear it. Why do you think you've solved the case . . ."

Lenny stirred sugar in his coffee. Then he said, "I told you that I think I may know who did it . . ."

"Well," I said. "It's come to Jesus time. Stop fiddle-fuckin' around Lenny . . . do you have anything or not?" Lenny looked at me then, and I realized that it wasn't recalcitrance holding him back from speaking . . . it was fear. "What's eating you?"

He looked away for an instant, then locked eyes with me and said, "I'm in over my head on this one Jake. Nothing checks out. Nothing's real about Ilse Müller, Otto Felter, or any of the rest of the crew down there. Her official narrative—which she reconfirmed when I spoke with her—says that she was born and raised in the southern German region of Bavaria, in a tiny little alpine village named Kempershafen, close to the Austrian border. She took a lot of pains to describe the place in great detail, telling me of her neighbors, friends, and the scenery . . . going on and on about the mountains and the skiing. But when I tried to pin down the exact location—I asked 'What's it close to,' and 'About how far is it from Munich or Nuremberg'—she'd get evasive or change the subject."

"Did it seem to be rehearsed," I said, as I looked up from my notebook, where I'd been recording everything, Lenny Bragg was telling me.

"Yeah. A little bit, but listen to this—because here's the real kicker—I went to the Penrose Library and checked . . . there's no Kempershafen, anywhere in Bavaria."

"The war?" I said.

Lenny shook his head. "Nah. There never was any such place, before or after."

"You're positive?"

"One hundred percent. I'm not only positive, I'm dead certain. I also have the gut feeling that those people have some kind of connection to, or involvement in, the Skin Ripper case . . ."

"I appreciate your instincts Lenny, but they won't get an arrest warrant signed."

"No. They won't. But that doesn't mean you can't go talk to them yourself."

"For what purpose? I can't accuse them, or anyone, without a damn good reason. How long do you think I'd have my job if I went off half-cocked down there and Ilse Müller complained to the hotel owners . . . who called the mayor . . . who called Chief Budd?"

"I know, Jake. I know," Lenny said, as he tried to balance the salt shaker on its edge. "Cops and newspaper reporters each have some of the same problems . . . but it makes us resourceful. And determined. You'll think of something. I'm sure of it. Because I know in my bones that those people are holding a lot of secrets. They stink of it."

I was processing his—Lenny's—opinions and sipping my coffee when Louie came out and served our food. It was halfway good chili, but it had beans in it, which just ain't right. I've always held the position and the notion that if I wanted to eat beans, I'd get me a pot full of 'em. And if I'm hankering for some chili con carne, then that's what I want. Beans in the chili is the equivalent of a felony in my opinion. It's something dreamt up by the Yankees to bedevil those of us with southwestern sympathies and Tex-Mex predilections at our table . . .

Such were my private thoughts about a free meal of pretty good chili, when Lenny and I said goodnight. I thanked him for my supper, and we sort of buried the hatchet . . . at least as much as two natural-born adversaries are able to. It was actually more of an uneasy truce.

Chapter 62

Hot rod chili my ass. That stuff kept me tossing and turning and kicking the blankets on and off all night. And when I did manage to nod off for a few, all the demons I've ever known slipped out of the cracks in my conscience, and twisted my dreams in knots with reminders of old misdeeds. They hammered me with guilt . . . so much so that I finally gave up the notion of sleep and went into work at a little before six a.m.

When I came to the door at the police station, Wally Bailey looked up from his new copy of *Manly Men* magazine and said, "Well ain't you in early boyo. Tough night, was it?"

I looked at him for a second as I pulled out a cigarette and lit it. I inhaled and blew smoke his way, then said, "Not bad Wally. You keep improving your mind by reading stuff like that. And good luck with the next nymphomaniac you get your paws on," pointing to the lurid byline of the pulp magazine in his hands. He was looking at the cover and sounding out the five-syllable word with his finger as I headed up the stairs. *Kee-rhist,* I thought, *and the sun ain't even up yet . . .*

The message slips were right where I left them. Ignoring the whole pile, I got some crappy leftover coffee and tried to wake up, then started working on writing a couple of days worth of daily activity reports. I knew it was only a matter of time before Captain Duncan started crawling up my ass with an ice pick again, and I wanted to be prepared.

I was so focused on what I was doing, I didn't even notice George Patterson approaching. He came into the bullpen, walked right over to the corner where Butch Hernshaw and I had two gray metal desks shoved together and said, "Jake, come to my office. I need to speak to you. Now."

I followed him to his cubicle and without being asked, shut the door, leaving us almost touching chests in the cramped and airless space. I stood, more or less, at attention, and waited in silence . . . wondering why he had such a bug up his ass. It didn't take long to find out.

Lieutenant Patterson took his seat behind the desk, leaving me in limbo, and feeling stupid, as I watched him shuffle files for a bit before finding the one wanted. He said, "Sit down Detective and listen up. This is your official notification that the Department is considering you for demotion back to the rank of uniformed patrolman, due to the lack of progress on your first, and current case, number, 56-00-27RH and 56-00-28RH, commonly referred to as 'The Skin Ripper.' Your probationary period is indeterminate, and subject to change, at this time. Do you understand?"

He looked at me as I nodded and said, "Yes."

"Sign here. It acknowledges that I've briefed you and given you a copy."

I leaned over and scratched my name on two different copies, watched as Lt. Patterson did the same. He noted the time and date, then handed one of the pages back to me. I took it and said, "Is that all?"

"No. It's just the formal part Jake. Sit down and I'll tell you the rest . . . the informal part. It's cover our asses time for the higher-ups in the Department and you're the designated sacrificial goat if the case doesn't get resolved. There's a lot of pressure being brought to bear behind the scenes from the public, especially the moneyed ones down in the southwest part of town, adjacent to a certain five-star hotel."

I remained standing, said, "And what about you Lieutenant . . . are you an ally or an adversary? Off the record, of course. Do I dare confide in you, or are you the conduit to Captain Duncan and whoever else is trying to sabotage me? And just how in the fuck do I solve a case with no clues . . ."

Patterson's face was red and the veins were starting to rise up in his neck as he looked at me and said, "Easy there Hoss. I'll stand for a little insubordination, but you're gettin' way past the limit. I've got a job to do, same as you. Today it was to give you this message, which I did. How you take it is up to you—because I'm not your friend or your foe—I'm your boss. And I'm a survivor. I've got a wife, kids, and a mortgage to pay . . . and I'll see to all of them 'cuz that's what I signed up for. You took on this case. Now you're suffering the consequences. Get on with it."

He was right. There wasn't anything else I could think to say. But as I turned to leave, Lt. Patterson said, "Oh, and Jake, just so you know, Chief Budd's going to a leadership conference for police officials out in Reno, Nevada. He's leaving this afternoon and he'll be gone for the next ten days. Captain Duncan will be acting chief while he's away."

And the hits just keep on coming I thought, as I made my way back to my desk in the corner. The time was eight o'clock in the morning and my phone was ringing off the hook when I got there.

Chapter 63

"Homicide, this is McKern."

"Hello Detective. It's Alphonso Gianette, Father Al here. I was wondering if we could get together later today. I've some ideas about the manuscript you asked me to look at, but it would help if I could see the original . . . instead of this copy you've provided."

"Sorry Father, on both counts," I said. "I'm tied up on other police business all day today and tomorrow, plus, the District Attorney has that book entered into the chain of evidence. I can't even get in to see it."

I could hear him fussing around with something, then the scritch of a match, followed by a wet suck of breath, as he set fire to one of those god awful stinking black cigars. Then he said, "How disappointing. The manuscript, I'm sorry to say, had not much else in it so far as revelations go, other than what I've already told you. But the original, as I've also said, would help with nuance, idiom, and dialect to some extent. I'm afraid I've gleaned all I can from the copy. Call me if you get an opening, timewise. I'm staying in the rectory with Father O'Reilly at St. Mary's for the next few days."

"Will do Father, and thanks for the call. I'll be in touch." I said, but as I nodded to Butch, who'd just shown up with a couple of white paper bags that looked a lot like coffee and something to eat, I was thinking, *I've heard a ton of lies in my life, but if bullshit was music, you, Father Al, would be hotter than Alexander's Ragtime Band . . .*

I hung up the telephone and watched Butch produce breakfast for the pair of us. "Thanks, Amigo," I said as he pushed a cardboard cup of java my way, and then raised the ante with a couple of chocolate covered cake doughnuts. We ate and sipped while I filled him in on most of what Lenny Bragg told me, as well as everything Lt. Patterson had just piled on too.

Butch tipped his cup up to catch the last few drops, then tossed the empty into the trash and said, "He sure is the master of incentives ain't he. Whatta we do now?"

"Be damned if I know, Butch, other than to start all over . . . approach it as if it's a new case and . . ."

"You mean re-interview everyone? Go back and retrace everything we've already done? I can't think of anything less productive. How about one of us goin' on over to the ski school and checkin' for ourselves?"

"Check what?"

"I dunno. See if that Felter guy is really carryin' a German pistol maybe. Or watch how they act when somebody with authority shows up."

I chewed the last bit of my doughnut and drank the last of the coffee while I watched Butch light a cigarette. As he did, I said, "That's a good idea, but we're not ready to do it yet. We still have to figure out the why of the murders first. If those folks are responsible, I don't want them to know we suspect 'em yet . . ." And my phone started ringing.

I picked it up, said, "McKern, Homicide," and waited.

"Jake, it's Mike Hillman. Your car's ready."

I was so focused on the events of last night and this morning, I'd forgotten about it. "Thanks Mike, I'll be right there. Did you put the top on?"

"Yeah Jake. We did. It's been winterized and we filled it with gas . . . we also threw in a free set of floor mats. You're all good and ready to go."

"I'm on my way," I said, as I put the handset of the accursed instrument back on its cradle.

I looked at Butch, who had a bewildered expression on his face. "It's okay, pard. That was personal and all fun. I have to go pick up something, but I won't be gone very long. Would you cover me for a few?"

"Sure, so long as you tell me about it when you get back," he said with a grin on his face. "And tell me her name."

"Scarlet," I said over my shoulder, "like in the movie," as I hit the stairs and left.

It was a short walk out the back door, through the parking lot and across north Weber Street to the Chevrolet dealership. I said hello to the receptionist and headed straight to Mike Hillman's office. Thirty minutes later, I put the key into the ignition switch of my new Corvette, fired it up and drove north on Wahsatch Avenue, all the way to Cache La Poudre Street, before turning around and heading south, back down Nevada, and returning to work. It was an enthralling—but oh, so brief—span of absolute freedom, surrounded by the leathery smell of new car, the throb of a big V-8 engine in my ears and the feeling that I was the master of everything in sight . . . if only for a few minutes.

Butch was all agog when I showed him the car. He asked me a million questions—even after I told him about the terms of the divorce from Imogene, along with its carrot stick provision because she wanted it to be over and done with in a hurry for her own personal reasons. I didn't want to go into any long explanations about why I took the deal, for purposes of my own. It was complicated. Distancing myself from Mo made me happy . . . being forced out of my son Scotty's life is a hurt that still drives me to my knees. I didn't want to go anywhere near that pain with my partner, or anyone, at work.

"I've always wanted a sports car like this," Butch said, as he sat in the driver's seat of the Corvette admiring the interior. "But with a wife and four kids that ain't gonna happen. Not in this lifetime."

I stood up from where I'd been loafing on the roof of the low-slung roadster talking to Butch. I started lighting a cigarette and said, while my colleague peeled himself out of the factory hotrod, "Well I guess we've all got different roles in life, and yours is being a father. And who knows, maybe one of your kids will grow up to be a doctor, lawyer, or someone famous."

Butch got out. He rubbed the small of his back, snorted and said, "You wouldn't think so if you could see those little hellions runnin' around the house screechin' and fightin' with each other, tearin' the house up, terroizin' the poor dog and momma's cat . . ."

"Oh, hell Butch they're just being kids is all."

"I'll see howya' feel after you've been around 'em for an hour or two."

We laughed and joked and ribbed each other like that, all the way back to the door and up the rear stairs . . . where we were met by Ann-Marie Fuchs, who said, "Jake, I've been looking everywhere for you. There's a couple of men here to see you, downstairs at the info desk. They seem like foreigners of some kind."

And just like that . . . I was once again up to my neck in murder and mysteries.

Chapter 64

When I reached the front desk at the police station, I found Rabbi Risenberg and another man he introduced as "An associate from Israel," whose name was Solomon Frankel, waiting for me. I noticed as we shook hands, the stranger was tanned, sinewy and fit, of indeterminate age, with calloused hands that gripped like a vise and a piercing gaze which seemed to look right into my heart and character. His face was what told the story however—Solomon Frankel was a warrior, a hard old campaigner who had seen many battles and fought many fights. He looked like what he was . . . as I later found out . . . a highly placed member of the infant nation's clandestine service known as the Mossad.

"Is there somewhere we can talk in private," Rabbi Risenberg said.

I could see Olfield, the desk sergeant, soaking up every word. I had no reason to not trust him, but at the same time, I suspected everyone I worked with—except Butch—of trying to sabotage me. I said, "Yeah. Come with me," as I headed out the door onto Kiowa Street.

On the sidewalk, Frankel said something in a language I didn't understand, and Rabbi Risenberg answered in what I assumed was the same tongue. I decided to nip it in the bud. Said, "Saul, I don't know what language you're using and it makes me uncomfortable. Would you mind staying with English, please."

"Sorry Jake. Not at all. We were speaking Hebrew, which is the official language of Israel. I don't get much chance to use it here. I'm also fluent in Russian, German, and Yiddish . . ."

"I was telling him that I like Colorado Springs. He's lucky to live in such a beautiful city, but it's hard, I think, to keep kosher in such

238

a place with not-so many Jews. I too apologize. We didn't mean to be rude."

"Already forgotten," I said, but I was all alert and on guard. I pulled out my cigarettes and offered them around.

"We're here Jake, to make you aware of some terrible events—war crimes and crimes against all humanity—which took place during the war, over in Europe. They happened during the late 1930s and 40s in Germany and Poland."

"I know about the concentration camps. Saul, Naomi and I talked about them . . ."

"Which ones?"

"Polish. Auschwitz in particular." Saul said. "We also filled him in somewhat, about Galicia and the connection between the Catholic Church, Pope Pius XII and Bishop Hudal with the Nazi hierarchy."

"Okay. Good. Are we ready then, to tell him the rest?" The Israeli said, as he smoked one of my American cigarettes and talked about me in the third person . . . as if I wasn't standing right there, in front of him.

I sucked down a lungful of Lucky Strike tobacco smoke while the two of them compared notes . . . and started to do a slow burn. Said, "Tell you what fellows, why don't I just go back to what I was doing and leave you here, able to say whatever you want about me . . ."

"Oh. No. Jake. Please. Time is short. We don't have much and everything we're doing is important . . . to you, me, Solomon and both of our countries. Hear us out. You won't regret it. But we can't do it here, like this, on the sidewalk."

"We could go to the library, it's only a few blocks from here, over on Cascade Avenue and Bijou Street," I said.

"Too quiet and too public," Frankel said.

"Restaurant?" I said, thinking of the Waffle House.

"Sure," the Rabbi said, "that'll do."

I pointed to my unmarked, nosed in at the curb and said, "We can take mine if you want."

"I'd rather follow you," Rabbi Rosenburg said, as he and Solomon Frankel got into a white '48 Ford station wagon with wood paneling on the sides. Ten minutes later we were all seated in the last booth at the Waffle House, where the new waitress named Florence Sue was on her way with three cups of coffee.

"If youse want somethin' else, just lemme know," she said as she left our coffees and the check. "I'll bring it right over."

We nodded our acknowledgement and Rabbi Risenberg thanked her on behalf of the group. Then we got down to business.

Frankel said, "I've seen the copy of the manuscript Jake. I've read it in its entirety and I only hope you have it somewhere safe and secure and protected, because it's a unique work that was complied and written over a period of several years—at the risk of death if discovered—by some Jewish prisoners in a place called Buchenwald. It's a detailed account of atrocity on an industrial scale, with names, dates, and descriptions. Some of the responsible individuals have been tried and punished. Many others have not. They've escaped to other countries, died, or been forgotten. A handful of them were overlooked, and are now prominent public persons who would do anything to suppress or destroy the document in order to protect their names, reputations, and fortunes. You're in possession of something explosive. The only thing saving you from torture and death is the fact that until now, it's been unreadable . . . and a lack of organization on the part of our common enemies."

I lit another cigarette to cover my growing angst and unease. "Wait a minute here," I said. "What common enemies? How do you know any of this? And lastly, who the hell are you? You're asking me to take an awful lot at face value . . . so let's back up and fill in a few of the many blanks."

Solomon Frankel let his guard down for a moment, and looked at me with enough anger in his eyes to start a brush fire. Rabbi Risenberg must have seen it too, because he put his hand on the other man's forearm. He said a few words I couldn't understand, then turned to me. "I asked for his patience. You are two alphas, who have the same goal in mind and both want to lead . . ."

I glared at the pair of them without looking directly at either one and said, "Look, I've got a serial killer running around loose in my city. He's responsible for butchering three victims that we know of, and people are terrified. I'm being publicly humiliated on a daily basis by the press, criticized and threatened by my bosses, and sabotaged at work by an unknown enemy who's doing his best to make sure that I fail. I'm not able—and not willing—to accept any more horseshit from anyone. You said you've read the diary . . . let me know what it has in it. Show me, tell me, point me in the right direction . . . just give me the information to catch the sonofabitch."

Now, it was my turn for Saul to put his hand on me, and ask for perseverance. He said, "Your frustration is evident Jake, and understandable. But try and comprehend Frankel's and mine. He's a full colonel in the Israeli Secret Service. It's called the Mossad, and he, like you, is a detective—but on a different scale. He and his teams are assigned to work with a man named Simon Wiesenthal to track down Nazi war criminals . . . anywhere in the world, at any place they may be hiding . . . and bring them to justice. Frankel is trying to capture the murderers of millions; men, women, and children. They were butchered in industrial fashion, with machine precision, most of them selected upon arrival and force marched into gas chambers disguised as showers, their dead bodies thrown into crematoriums and burned. Some of the strongest were forced into hard labor until they dropped dead, others, the most attractive, were used as sex slaves in bordellos, a few poor wretches were chosen as human guinea pigs for pseudo-scientific experiments without the benefit of anesthesia . . . while scores of the most unfortunate ones were tortured to death for sport. Some had their skin removed and made into lampshades. Individuals with interesting tattoos were especially vulnerable to that last one. None were spared. Jews who came by the trainload were packed into cattle cars so tightly that many died standing up. All of them left as smoke and ashes in the wind."

I felt like I was going to vomit.

It's not easy for a sane person to think in intimate detail about the blood soaked and wanton killing of another human being—the mind recoils, the senses repel the idea, the gut churns and threatens to disgorge its contents—as the act unfolds in the imagination, step by step.

The slaughter of innocents by the millions is an act of such depravity that it can only be appreciated by the utterly insane.

Those two sentences, if accepted as truths, make mass murder a most difficult subject to write about, and to read about, for all of us who profess faith in a supreme being and who have a moral core to guide us in life. I have always believed in the concept of good and the power of evil, but I had no inkling of their sovereignty over the lot of us mortals until that day of enlightenment. When Frankel and Rabbi Risenberg finished talking with me that early spring morning . . . I was a changed man.

Chapter 65

I looked down the mostly empty row of booths for a moment, watching the early lunch crowd begin to drift in; thinking about the revelations of the past few days as I reflected on the ever-growing scope of the case; my brain was whirring and click-clacking, selecting, and rejecting possibilities, alternatives, and outcomes. I sipped from my cold coffee and said, "Who was Sorwell?"

The Rabbi said, "He was an ordinary man, caught up in the horror of what we're now calling The Holocaust. Before the war, before Hitler, and before the National Socialists, he was a scribe . . . an artisan who created hand-written Torahs, or Jewish bibles, on parchment scrolls that were used in synagogues. His work was highly sought after and prized. It was beautiful calligraphy . . . and perfect. He survived the camps by making himself useful, creating documents for the higher-ranking Nazis, writing ledgers and records for the SS Cadre, and creating exquisite greeting, holiday, and birthday cards for the lower ranks of guards. He traded his skills for things like an extra crust of bread, or a piece of meat in his soup, a warmer shirt or anything else that would help him to survive . . . and live to tell the tale of 'The Beech Woods,' or Buchenwald, in the German language. It's where the poet and writer Goethe—who wrote *Faust*—was from, and a purposefully chosen location, because the National Socialists disapproved of him."

"Why?"

"He was a liberal who favored too much freedom in the Nazi's eyes."

"Did Sorwell create the manuscript I found in his freezer?"

"Yes. He was also the one who smuggled it out of Europe and into America." Frankel said, as he lit a cigarette with a paper match from a book of them that he picked up at the register when we came into the café.

"Is it written in Hebrew?"

"A scholarly, archaic form of it, yes."

I popped the question I'd been waiting to spring . . . "Then why can't anyone read it, or is everybody lying to me?"

"I can answer that," the Rabbi said. "The same as Leonardo da Vinci, Abraham Sorwell was left-handed . . . and like the Renaissance master, he wrote his notes in backwards, or inverse script. Solomon here, deciphered it rather quickly with the aid of a mirror."

"Would you be willing to transcribe the manuscript into English and type it up for me?" I said, as I took out a fresh coffin nail and lit up, in order to cover my growing unease.

Frankel smiled. Rabbi Risenberg said, "We thought you might say that, and the answer is yes . . . but we hope you'll trade the real manuscript for the translation. We intend to use it as evidence during trials in Israel of some of the perpetrators, as they come up."

"Why bother? Here in America the lawyers would object and get it thrown out of evidence as hearsay, or gossip." I said.

"Not in the war crimes trials," Frankel interjected, "in which I have been involved many times . . . because Sorwell's manuscript is the declaration of an actual victim who was, as well, an acute observer and recorder of the atrocities taking place there. All such first-hand documents are not only exceedingly rare, they are considered almost sacred—voices from the grave—and as such, they are irrefutable. You will see for yourself when you read it."

I smoked for a minute, and refrained from saying a single word. Waiting.

After a few moments, the payoff came when Rabbi Risenberg said, "I have the translated document in my briefcase. Naomi, Solomon, and I worked around the clock to get it done. It's in a three-ring binder out in my car."

"Let's go," I said, as I laid a dollar bill on the table to cover our coffees and a tip.

Out in the parking lot, Saul took the driver's seat of the '48 Ford Woodie, I got in on the shotgun side and Frankel stood guard, slouched against the right front fender, where he was smoking and watching the other vehicles as they came and went.

Saul opened the briefcase he pulled from the floor of the backseat and removed a fat blue binder that he handed to me with both hands. "I think you might want to see the last ten pages right away. That's where Sorwell laid out in detail what he saw here in Colorado Springs. Frankel and I think it's the reason he was murdered."

I put out my half-smoked cigarette in the ashtray on the dashboard and took the notebook that looked to be more than two hundred fifty pages in length. "Is this the original, and do you have a copy?"

Risenberg nodded and said, "Yes. To both of your questions. We made carbon copies. It's all detailed on the title page. We also included sworn, notarized statements that it's a true and accurate translation . . . which will be verified by anyone who can read archaic Hebrew, with the aid of a mirror."

"I can keep this?"

"Yes. It's our show of good faith, in the hope that you will in turn, give us Sorwell's manuscript. It is a document that is beyond price to our young nation."

I thought there was sincerity in his voice, and recognized the gravity of the situation I had just been thrust into. I processed it all for a bit, then said, "If Sorwell and his wife were killed because of the manuscript; can we assume that Professor Leviwitz was murdered by the same person because of the similarity? If so, why? How does he figure into things?"

Frankel said, "According to Sorwell's writings, Leviwitz was also a survivor of Buchenwald, where they both suffered at the hands of a woman named Ilse Koch and her assistant, a young medical student named Helga Fischer. Sorwell thought he'd spotted her, called his old prison mate, Leviwitz, in an attempt to confirm his—Sowell's—suspicions. Read it for yourself and decide."

"Seen who?" I said, "Koch or Fischer?"

"Fischer. Ilse Koch is in a West German prison, doing life without parole for her deeds during the war. We suspect, by the way, but cannot prove, that Helga Fischer may be the illegitimate daughter of Ilse Koch."

"How'd you come to that conclusion, and more importantly, why does it matter?"

It was Risenberg who answered me. He said, "In talking with Abe Sorwell . . ."

"Hold on a second," I said, "what do you mean, 'In talking with Sorwell? Did you know him?"

"Yes. He and Ruth came to shul—synagogue—on occasion, and he spoke with me about his life and times. It's not in the manuscript, but he told me that Helga looked like Ilse, spoke like her, and had similar mannerisms—much the same as a mother and daughter. In addition to that, Helga always deferred to Isle, always carried out the older woman's commands without hesitation and invariably acted in a respectful and obedient manner around her."

"Do you believe him . . . think he's right?"

"Based upon his candor and frankness, yes. I do. Plus, when you think about it, how could anyone who didn't lose their mind from the pain and trauma of the experience, ever forget the face of someone who'd tortured them? I know I wouldn't."

"Do you know if the two of them, Sorwell and Leviwitz, ever met in Colorado Springs?"

"No. I don't."

"Did Sorwell ever say where he saw Helga Fischer . . . or when?"

"Yeah." The Rabbi said, "he did. At the new ski area, down on Cheyenne Mountain by the Broadmoor Hotel, where she was calling herself 'Isle Müller' . . . two days before he and Ruth were murdered."

I did everything in my power to keep a poker face . . . but I was seething inside. I let the silence linger for some moments, then said, "I have to wonder, Rabbi, why you failed to mention the fact that you knew Sorwell when I first brought the diary to your attention . . ."

Risenberg looked down at his hands on the steering wheel before turning toward the passenger's seat. Locking eyes with me, he said, "The short answer is that I didn't trust you. The history of the Jews is rife with acts of betrayal . . ."

"As are the annals of the Irish."

"Yes. But the nature of the crimes we're dealing with here is not only murder on an unprecedented scale, it's evil of a magnitude that, until now, was unimaginable."

It was an unassailable truth.

I thanked the Rabbi, and told him I'd be back in touch as soon as it was humanly possible, then nodded at Frankel, who said, "Time is short, be quick about it," as I got out of the white station wagon and made my exit.

Chapter 66

With a hundred different and conflicted thoughts careening around in my head, I gimped up the walk onto the porch of the home I rented on Seventh Street and let myself in. Kicking aside the mail that had been shoved through the slot in the door, I went straight to the bookcase, pulled out the brown paper covered copy of my so-called 'college theses, and breathed a sigh of relief. After what I had just learned of its importance, there was no way in hell that Sorwell's manuscript was ever going to be out of my direct control for as long as I had possession of it. Now, when I held the book, it felt somehow, as if the weight of seven million murdered souls—and the responsibility for bringing a measure of justice on their behalf— rested in my hands. It made the hairs on the back of my arms and neck stand up.

Shaking off the willies, I got to work. The leather briefcase I'd carried since I had been a student in college was right where I'd left it, on the top shelf in the hall closet. I stuffed in a new legal pad and some pencils, packed in Sorwell's manuscript, plus one of the copies Doug Sikes made, and Frankel's translation. It was crammed with all that I hoped would be needed to break the Skin Ripper case wide open. By then I was starting to have a lot of discomfort in my leg, so I popped one of the gray pain capsules nurse Gloria gave me and drank some water straight from the kitchen faucet before leaving the house and heading back to the P.D.

The parking lot behind the station was full, so I left my unmarked over in the alley by the City Auditorium and walked in the front door of the Police Department at about ten minutes before noon. I nodded to Gene Olfield at the front desk, and headed upstairs with the briefcase in hand.

Butch Hernshaw was in his seat across from mine, chatting with Ann-Marie Fuchs when I got there. I said, "Hello, you two. What's the news?" as I stowed the leather case on the floor under my desk and sat down.

Ann-Marie said, "You look like you're feeling pretty good Jake."

"I managed to get some sleep last night for a change."

"Well, it must have done something good for you. Because you look better than you have for a while. And by the way, that priest, Gianette's called several times too. He thinks someone is following him."

"I don't think that's true, and I don't want to talk to him right now. Would you mind telling him to leave a message again?"

"Nope," she said, as she went back to her station by the top of the stairs.

"I think she's got the hots for you."

"Don't go there Butch. Not even kidding. I'm eleven or twelve years older than her and she's trouble I don't need."

He grinned. Said, "Ouch. A little touchy are ya?"

"No, it ain't that. I've got too much on my plate at the moment . . ."

"Speakin' of which, Gloria Martinez is looking for ya too. She's called on your private line a couple of times this morning while you were gone with those two foreigners. What'd they want?"

Before I could answer there was a loud commotion, as Wilson Bell and another old dinosaur named Jack Gander, shoved, and wrestled a resisting, arguing, and fighting young man whose hands were cuffed behind him, into a chair beside Wilson's desk. Neither one of them was being very gentle about it and the prisoner started cursing at the pair of red-faced and sweaty detectives. Without a word Gander turned, picked up a phone directory with both hands, then spun around like a whirling dervish, and hit the kid upside the head . . . knocking him off the chair, down onto the floor . . . where he started to weep and curse.

Butch and I rose up in unison and went to aid the stunned detainee. While my partner tended to the kid, I stepped in front of Gander as Bell watched open-mouthed, and said, "That's enough Jack. Why don't you and Wilson go have coffee someplace. We'll take care of the prisoner."

Bell said, "Thanks Jake. But me'n the Goose'll do what we're paid to do. This one's 10-62 and 10-69, plus evasion, resisting, attempted murder and whatever else I think of."

Rape and child abuse. I felt sick to my stomach at the image it conjured in my head as I nodded to Jack and turned back to my own business.

Butch heard the 10 codes too, and without saying a word, uncuffed the prisoner's left manacle and snapped it into the eyebolt on Bell's desk.

When we were both reseated at our own places, I looked at my partner and said, "Chief Budd would never condone abuse of a prisoner. Neither do I. But I happen to think that asshole had it coming."

Butch was quiet for a moment while he lit a cigarette, then said, "Makes two of us. Molestation of kids is one of my white-hot buttons that don't need pushin'."

"We agree completely," I said as I lit one of my own . . . hoping he couldn't see my hand trembling when I put flame to tobacco, while visions of my murdered sister Catherine danced in my head.

Shaking the old nightmare off, I looked at Butch and said, "Those two foreigners you saw waiting for me earlier may have done us a huge favor and translated Sorwell's manuscript . . ."

"Really? What's it say?"

"Dunno. I haven't had a chance to look at it yet. But if what Rabbi Risenberg told me a little while ago is even half true, it may hold the answers we've been looking for."

Butch looked away, then turned and locked eyes with me. "Will it solve the case?"

"It'll give us motive and put actual names in our hands. Sorwell may have seen someone . . . here in the Springs, who was responsible for—and committed—some of the atrocities at the Buchenwald concentration camp."

"No shit?"

"None."

"Well get it out. Let's see it. Let's read the friggin' thing."

"Not here Butch. I ain't lettin' the translation out of my sight. I can just see us, somewhere in the midst of reading it and some kind of commotion starts up, like it did just now. We have to leave, and the whole damned enchilada disappears. It was only good luck and fortune that put the manuscript back in our hands when you picked the one random locker in the whole entire place that you did."

"So, what now Jake . . ."

I took a look at Ma and the Goose and their prisoner, then said to Butch, "Here's what I want you to do . . ."

Chapter 67

I called Gloria, intent on killing two birds with one stone. When, surprise, surprise, she answered, I said, "It's me. Are you gonna be there for a while?"

"Well, hello to you, Mr. where-have-you-been-my-honey . . . and yes, I'll be here for a while . . . all day in fact. Why do you think I've already called you twice times?"

"I was hoping for that. I've got something to show you. I'm on my way."

But before I could hang up, Gloria said, "Is it smaller than a breadbox?"

"What? No. It's not. You'll like it. Say 'bye.'"

"Bye . . ."

I hung up before there were any more chances to chit-chat, grabbed my briefcase and a fresh pack of Luckys from the bottom desk drawer, then headed for the stairs . . . where I met Butch, on his way back from the men's. "I'm going over to the westside and some place quieter, where maybe I can read what's in the manuscript," I said. Then added, "I left ya a phone number, just in case. And lastly, would you kindly retrieve Sorwell's book from the evidence room and keep it handy? I've got a copy to work from, but I think we should have the original when I go to the acting chief."

"I agree," Butch said. "And I'll review the case material and make sure it's all in order while you're gone."

"And Butch . . . anybody asks, tell 'em I'm out tryin' to get it translated. I'm not ready to let it be known that it's already been done."

"Okay, Jake. I'll take care of it. Good luck."

"Thanks," I said, and headed out the rear door of the station, to where that new Corvette was waiting.

When I got to the back lot however, the first thing I noticed was some wise-assed cop had stuck a parking ticket under the driver's side wiper blade. I folded it in half and stuffed it in my shirt pocket, intending to deal with whoever wrote it later. It wasn't the end of the world, just an irritant I didn't need at the moment.

I got in, tossed the briefcase into the passenger's footwell, fired up the motor and sat there for a moment, luxuriating in the sight, smell, and sound of my new sports car. Then I stuck it in first gear, idled out onto Weber and headed down to Colorado Avenue . . . feeling like the King of the World.

The drive to Gloria's place was magical—and over with almost as soon as it got started. I parked on Kiowa Street in front of her house, went to the front door with briefcase in hand and rang the bell. I heard footsteps, followed by her voice calling, "Who's there?"

"Fuller brush man."

The door opened and Gloria waved me in as if I really was a door-to-door salesman, then closed it with a bang and jumped into my arms—where she started kissing my neck and face. The sudden movement caught me by surprise. I dropped the briefcase and wrapped my arms around her in a bear hug, while she put her hands on my cheeks and kissed me on the mouth in such an enthusiastic manner, she left no doubt as to her intentions. When she finally came up for air, I said, "I guess that means you're glad to see me," as I lowered her back down on her feet.

She giggled. "Yup. I am. Seems like an awful long time since we've laid eyes on each other. All we do is work."

I picked up the briefcase and said, "That's because you're right . . . and, sorry to tell you this, but I've brought some with me. I needed a quiet place to do a little homework, plus, you're what's been keeping me from going crazy Gloria. I've missed you, more than I can put into words."

She pulled me down to her level and whispered in my ear, "Me too honey." We hugged for a bit, just appreciating each other's embrace and the comfort of another human body, warm and close.

When we separated moments later, we both started to speak at the same time. We laughed and I ceded the moment to Gloria. She said, "Would you like some coffee? I'll make us some."

"I would, but I want to show you something first. And yeah, its bigger than a bread box . . . but you're gonna need your coat. It's outside."

Gloria pulled a buckskin leather jacket that had fringes on the arms, the back, and across the front from the entryway closet and slipped it on. "Nice coat." I said, as I opened the door for her.

She stepped out, locked the deadbolt, and turned to where I stood at the top of the porch steps. "So, what's the big sur . . . prise . . ." fell out of her mouth as she saw the red Corvette at the end of the walk. "Is that it? How'd . . ."

"It's a complicated story. I'm gonna tell you, while we take a ride. Hop in." I said, and opened the door for her, then put the briefcase in the trunk before climbing into the driver's seat. "So, what do you think of it?"

"I don't know yet. I've never been in a new car before."

"Saw it yesterday afternoon." I said, while the big V8 rumbled to life, "And bought it last night," as we pulled away from the curb and took off. I drove us west, through Manitou Springs and up Ute Pass, all the way to the village of Woodland Park, where we dropped in at a little café for a quick lunch and a pit stop, while I told her everything about Imogene, Scottie, the Curdy's, Chaparral Oil, Preston Lee Grinder, the bribery money, and my part in all of it.

Gloria was a patient listener, who let me get everything off my chest without interruption or comment. When at last I wound down to silence, she said, "I'm glad you've finally told me Jake. It's been obvious to me; something was eating at you besides the Skin Ripper case. I thought it was me, that I was just an easy lay and a free drug supplier. It made me feel cheap. Used. I thought about breaking it off with you. Several times in fact. But something held me back. And I have no idea what it was. You're the only man I've ever loved. The only boyfriend and the only person I've ever slept with or made love to willingly, and with all my heart. You're it for me. The one and only and forever."

We were on our way back to the Springs, almost to the hamlet of Green Mountain Falls as she poured her heart out to me—and that was when the road got so blurred, I couldn't see to drive. I pulled the car off on the shoulder of the road, where we sat for a time in silence . . . with the motor throbbing, with Gloria's hand in mine . . . and with a lump in my throat that was so generous, I could not speak.

Chapter 68

We rode together in a comfortable quiet, just holding hands and listening to the muted sounds of the Top 40s on KVOR radio, all the way back to Gloria's place on West Kiowa in the Old Colorado City area. When I turned off from Colorado Avenue onto 19th Street however, she said, "Honey, would you please park in back, instead of on the street, so that nosy old biddy across the way, Mrs. Kelley, doesn't have anything to gossip about."

"Sure. Be glad to." I said, then made a couple of right and left turns and dropped into the alley that ran between the rows of houses. I parked next to her garage, where we got out together.

"What now, Gloria? Where do we go from here?"

"Who says we have to do anything honey. Let's just enjoy each other's company for a while and see what happens. This is pretty new to both of us—our relationship I mean—and I don't want to mess it up by moving too fast . . . doing something we'll regret later."

"I agree. And I believe you're right. We have our jobs to think about too," I said, as the enormity of my first-ever murder case came down on me like the weight of the world once again.

I retrieved my briefcase from the trunk of the car and we headed down the hill on the path through the copse of Siberian Elms that grew in profusion along both sides of the alley, and into the backyard . . . where a young Hispanic man was sitting on the back steps, smoking a cigarette, while Buddy Boy kept a wary eye on him from his perch atop the old green couch. When they saw the two of us crossing the lawn, the man stood, holding his straw hat in his hands, and the orange cat ran over to the back door, where he sat merowing to be let in.

Gloria touched me on the arm and said, "It's okay. Jake. He's here for some medicine for his wife. She's pregnant and malnourished from the journey here. The desert dehydrated her and I'm trying to help her keep from losing the baby."

I nodded to the man, and went up on the porch while Gloria and her patient's spouse conversed in rapid Spanish. After a few moments she joined me and unlocked the door, let the three of us into the kitchen, then disappeared down the cellar stairs into the basement, where I could hear her making noises and rattling things around as I rummaged through her cabinets, gathering the gear to make coffee.

Gloria came back up the stairs carrying a small paper bag, just when I was lighting one of the burners under the coffee pot. She saw what I was doing and said, "Good idea. Find everything?"

"Yeah, except for the cat. He's after something to eat."

"Under the sink. I'll be right back, as soon as I give these to Joachim."

I located a ten pound "Pikes Peak Brand" lard pail, right where she said it would be and found it filled with dried cat chow when I removed the lid. I fed Buddy and left him a saucer of milk, pulled the boiling coffee off the flame, and set it aside to cool.

Gloria was still outside, so I got the translated version of Sorwell's manuscript from the briefcase, poured myself some coffee and settled down at the kitchen table to read. Even for me—a combat veteran and experienced cop—it was emotionally draining right from the start. By the time she came back in the house, I was a little more than halfway into the disturbing memoir . . . with its accounts of barbaric, pseudo-scientific experiments, I was sickened by what I was seeing . . . but compelled to continue reading at the same time. I skipped over to the last fifteen pages, trying to find out why Solomon Frankel had referred me there.

The orange cat had finished his food and jumped up on the bay window, where he was busy washing his face with his paws and sitting amidst all the ferns, begonias and ivies that were thriving in the afternoon sun. Buddy stopped and watched for a moment, as the woman whose house he shared came inside, then curled up in a ball and went to sleep. When she saw me, Gloria said, "Sorry honey. That took longer than I thought. I was having a hard time making him understand the regimen I was giving his wife. She speaks no English. He barely does . . . and neither of them can read any language. How's the coffee?" She added, while taking off her jacket and hanging it on the back of the other chair before pouring herself a cup and sitting.

"It's passable," I said, as I watched her and tried to figure out how I was going to say what I had to say next, about the risks she was taking, without starting a tiff.

She took a sip, said, "Honey, this is good. If you want to taste crappy coffee, come by the hospital some night."

"Or the Police Department any time . . ."

"How's that going?" Gloria said, and pointed with her chin at the loose-leaf binder in front of me.

I hesitated a moment, thinking before speaking, trying to decide what to say . . . or not say. Then went with, "This is the most difficult thing I've ever read. It's a first-hand account of depraved indifference to human life and suffering on an industrial scale, that was written by a man who was witness to his entire family being murdered—along with nearly everyone he knew and thousands of others—for no other reason than they were born into a hated race and religion. It's horrible."

Gloria looked over the rim of her coffee mug and said, "Do you have to read it all? Can't you just skim through, or outline it maybe?"

"Wish I could honey, but it's the key to the Skin Ripper case. At least three people have been murdered because of what's in this manuscript, and for all I know there may be others. The people who did the crimes in here represent the essence of evil. They have to be held to account. Their crimes are crimes against the world."

"I thought the Nuremberg trials did that."

"That brought a few of them to justice, but according to Rabbi Risenberg and Solomon Frankel, there's thousands more who've escaped. They claim that there's Nazis living all over the world under fictitious identities."

"Maybe so, but it's not up to you to catch every one of them Jake."

"No, no it's not. Only those who are here, in Colorado Springs," I said, just as the phone in the hall next to the stairs came to life.

Chapter 69

Gloria picked it up on the fifth ring. Said, "Hello . . .Yes, he is. Sure . . . Just a moment." She laid the receiver on the little table and came back to the kitchen. "It's for you. Some guy named Hernshaw."

I could see the blurred shapes of cars moving along Kiowa Street through the etched glass and leaded panes of the front door as I picked up the telephone and said, "Hello Butch. What's the news . . ."

"Hell's a poppin' Jake. Duncan's on the warpath 'cuz you're out-of-pocket, Andy Claypoole's out lookin' for yuh too, because that priest, Gianette, the one who's been callin' here every half-hour . . . he's been shot."

"Still alive?"

"Barely. He's over at Memorial, in the emergency room. Docs say he ain't gonna be with us much longer by the looks of it, and he's hollerin' for you. Refuses to talk to anybody else. Says he knows who the Skin Ripper is. Lt. Patterson is with him right now, tryin' to coax him to spill, but he won't. You'd best get over there pronto."

"I'm on my way. And thanks, Butch, for calling with the update. Maybe I'll keep my job after all."

"*De nada,* Jake. Good luck."

I hung up the phone and went back into Gloria's kitchen, where she was sipping coffee at the table. When she looked up, I said, "Good news, bad news honey. We may have a break in the case, but I'm the only one he'll speak to. Bad news is that he's in the ER at the county hospital with gunshot wounds that will likely be fatal. I need to get over there on the double."

"Memorial has some of the best trauma doctors in the state," Gloria said, as she helped me stuff the translation, and all the other paraphernalia I'd spread across her breakfast nook back in the briefcase. "If he has any chance of survival, they'll save him," she added while I closed the flap and buckled the straps on the satchel.

I looked at her for a moment, just wanting to capture her image in my mind, then broke the spell when I said, "Would you be okay driving me downtown in the Corvette? My police car is in the alley by the auditorium and I need to get it. Then, I'll call you whenever it winds down at the hospital and we'll figure out the car swap-a-thon. Okay?"

Gloria stood, put her buckskin jacket on and said, "Would I be okay, tooling around town in a brand-new, bright red sports car? Well. Hell, yes honey. I'm ready, willing, and rarin' to go."

We had to spend a few moments re-adjusting the driver's seat so she could reach the pedals, but other than that, Gloria fit so well in my new car, it was almost like the Corvette was made for her, and we were downtown only minutes later. "Stay on Colorado until we get to Weber Street before you turn," I said. "I want us heading west on Pikes Peak, so I can get out by the bus station and walk up the alley. I don't want to draw any attention, if we can help it."

Gloria started laughing as she downshifted, hung a left and zipped up Weber, where we caught a red light. Waiting for southbound traffic to clear, so we could turn, she said, "Honey, in a bright red car that looks and sounds like it's going ninety miles-an-hour standing still, you're gonna attract attention. There's no way around it."

"I meant from the other cops . . . about leaving my unmarked unattended, out in the alley. We're not supposed to do that."

"Why not," Gloria said, as she double parked next to the bus garage on Pikes Peak Avenue.

"Its against city policy because of possible theft or vandalism." I said as I unwound myself from the passenger's seat and got out. Then I leaned back in. "I may be a while. I'll call, if possible, but don't worry. Okay?"

"Yeah. I'll see ya when I see ya honey, but I'll miss you in the meantime. Be careful."

"Always. Bye," I said and closed the door. She looked me in the eye, sent an air kiss my way, then dropped the clutch and took off. I hustled up the alley to where my unmarked was sitting, got in and headed for the county hospital on the double.

Nothing had changed at the patient care center since I'd last been there. The parking lot was full, with every space occupied and cars prowling around like hungry beasts, looking for any hint of someone about to leave; and bumper to bumper on all the surrounding side streets. The solution for me—and all the cops—was to pull into the Emergency Room entrance, park in the first ER DOCS ONLY slot, throw my OFFICIAL POLICE BUSINESS placard on the dashboard by the speedometer, and walk in as if I owned the place. And once again, it worked like a charm.

I went up to the nurse's station at the check-in desk, showed my shield and asked for the whereabouts of Gianette, the Jesuit priest and gunshot victim. The charge nurse, a tiny woman whose name tag said she was Susie Miller, heard me and took over. She said, "Follow me Detective," and led the way through a confusion of small rooms and down a maze of short hallways, to an isolated area with a windowed space where several medical personnel were performing various trauma procedures around a hospital bed containing a bloody Alphonso, 'Father Al' Gianette. Sitting outside the room was a uniformed cop I knew, named Dirk Kloss. I nodded to him, just as Susie tapped on the glass door, announcing our arrival.

Seeing me standing there waiting, Lt. Patterson came out at once. Ignoring Susie, he looked at me and said, "I don't know where you've been, but it's high time you got here Jake. Gianette's leaking blood faster than they can pump it in him, and I don't think he's gonna make it much longer. He's been calling for you ever since he was found in Palmer Park by a couple of hikers. Says he knows everything and wants to confess. You better get in there."

"Any idea who plugged him?"

"If he does, he didn't tell me."

I thanked Susie, who waved over her shoulder as she headed down the hallway, while I shouldered my way into the intensive care area, where all the beeps, dials, doctoring, and pandemonium was taking place.

Chapter 70

I smelled blood the instant I opened the door. It seemed like it was everywhere in the small room, and visions of the medics and corpsmen and blood-soaked marines I'd encountered on Guadalcanal, rose up behind my eyes and flashed like bolts of nighttime lightning as I stepped into the room.

Other than a few scattered premonitions, I'd never in my life experienced anything that could be considered unworldly, or paranormal until that day. But as soon as my body entered the room, some kind of heightened awareness came over me. I tingled from the roots of my hair to the tips of my toes, and felt like I'd just come into close proximity with a high-voltage electrical field. It was the oddest thing to either feel back then—or try to describe these many years later—and they were only the beginning of all the unusual events on that late afternoon of strange phenomena.

When I neared the footboard of the bed, Gianette's eyes popped open and his body jerked upright—like a marionette with some broken strings—into a sitting position. He said . . . in a voice that sounded a thousand years old and cut to bone, "Finally, you're here McKern. I have much to say and little time left. Clear the room. Everyone go. You too, Father Ray. Leave now." Then, trance-like he closed his eyes, fell back on the bed, and waited for his demands to be met.

I hadn't noticed Father O'Reilly, who'd been administering the sacrament of last rites, because he was a small man and practically hidden by all the medical equipment. He stepped out from the middle of the bank of monitors, wearing a blood spattered alb, frayed clerical collar and shiny black suit. When he passed by, he shook his head and said,

"He's almost gone, yet Father Alphonso refuses to unburden himself to me, so that I might see him off to Heaven with a clear conscience. Says he'll only confess to you, Detective. Call me if he does, so I might give him absolution."

"Is he lucid?"

"Mostly. He slips in and out of consciousness, babbles on occasion, and loses his train of thought sometimes. But see for yourself," Father O'Reilly said, as he made the sign of the cross and added "Bless you my son," as he followed the hospital personnel out of the room.

As soon as the door closed, Gianette's eyes reopened. "Come close McKern. My voice is fading and I have much to tell before I am taken."

"Who shot you?"

"A man named Felter. He's the one who repairs the machinery at the skiing place on Cheyenne Mountain, over by the zoo and Will Rogers Shrine."

I pulled out my notebook, and started writing, putting everything down on paper as fast as the dying priest uttered it. "Why did he shoot you—and where?"

He ignored my question. Blood and salvia leaked from the corner of his mouth as Gianette's words spilled out. "I am, like Lucifer, fallen from grace and goodness and God's own mercy. I have forsaken my vows to the holy Catholic Church and turned away from the light to embrace the darkness. I am an evil man, in league with evil men. I have committed evil deeds in furtherance of misbegotten schemes that are the fruits of a diseased mind and an insane ideology. I am become that which I once abhorred . . . and it has cost my immortal soul. I am bound for perdition, sentenced to die a repeated death of fire at the hands of foul monsters . . ." Gianette's speech slowed at that point, and became unintelligible, then ceased altogether.

He's out of his mind, I thought as I waited, hoping he'd reanimate long enough to tell me about the Skin Ripper.

Nothing happened for what seemed like an eternity of minutes in my head, but in real time, he came back to life only moments later. Drawing a shaky gasp of air, Gianette said, "I am part of a secret cabal within the highest-ranking members of the Pontiff's inner circle of advisors. We are less than a dozen in number, but exercise great influence with His Holiness, and determine much of the doctrine which issues from the Holy See. We supported the ideology of Adolf Hitler and the Third Reich, and we endorsed the Final Solution in its entirety. I am also a committed fascist; as I was before the war, during the war and since the war. I abhor communism in all its forms and detest those in the church who espouse it, whether they be nuns, priests, bishops, or cardinals. They should all be lined up against a wall and shot, in my opinion, lest their ideas begin to spread."

It felt like my brain was bleeding after hearing the filth that was spewing from this supposed man of the cloth; who was educated and ordained; a representative of the church founded by the Apostle Peter. My mind was still reeling as Gianette continued. "Since the war ended, my brethren and I have used our positions to facilitate the escape of the Reich's leadership and soldiers, as well as some of its ardent supporters, doctors, and scientists. Unfortunately, we couldn't save them all, but thousands are living new lives as they await word . . ." His eyes closed and he sagged back on the bed again.

I haven't gotten anything about the Skin Ripper . . . and it's hard to tell if he's gonna last long enough to do so, ran through my thoughts as I waited and watched for any sign of a reawakening. It came a few seconds later.

Just as he had the first time, Gianette's eyes opened, he sat up in the same spastic manner and said, "I'm here McKern. Not going to die until he says so."

"He who?"

"Behind you. The Archangel Michael is waiting to cast me into the flames for my apostasy—and he's growing impatient."

I looked over my shoulder. "I don't see anything. There's no one there."

"Because he's not here for you."

"Why did Felter shoot you?"

"My commitment was wavering, in their eyes, I know too much; they are preparing to leave the area and scatter, dispersing, and so they wanted no witness of their presence here . . . It might have been any one, or all those reasons . . . or none of them. For who knows what lurks in the minds of fanatics? Felter is a former Waffen SS Commando who spent much time on the Eastern Front before being reassigned to the prison camp at Auschwitz and put in charge of the guards. He is a formidable and implacable enemy. Never underestimate him . . ."

Gianette's speech ended as his body spasmed, arched, and thrashed like a hooked trout—while his eyelids fluttered, his teeth chattered and all the machines he was hooked up to began flashing alarm signals. I thought he had died . . . but he reopened his eyes one last time.

"Who are the others?"

"Ski area. All . . . them."

"Is Felter the Skin Ripper?" I said, as the air in the room seemed alive with electricity that had the hairs on my arms and the back of my neck standing on end.

"I'm counting . . . It's almost . . . It's no . . . It's . . ." Gianette babbled through gritted teeth and bloodless lips, while the discharging of blue static energy from some unseen, unknown source sparked and crackled and built up again in the small space. The atmosphere became so alive with charged particles that it was becoming harder and harder to breathe. It smelled of ozone and lightning as he said, "Get out now McKern before its too . . ."

I was almost to the crash bar on the door when the sonic boom came and the lights went out as bolts of pure energy sizzled around me, all throughout the room.

Chapter 71

I smacked through that door as if my life depended on it. Behind me, the ICU ceiling lights were back on, the room smelled like electricity and all of the monitors hooked to the figure on the bed were going haywire, because Gianette had flatlined. He was dead.

The hospital loudspeakers were calling for 'Dr. Blue' as the ER personnel shoved past me in their haste to get back to Gianette's aid. But their efforts were wasted. There was not any way that the fallen priest could be revived. He was officially pronounced a few minutes later.

"Where's Patterson," I said to Officer Kloss.

"He left. Right after you went in there."

"Did you see what went on just now?"

Don stared at me for a long hard moment, said, "What do you mean?"

"The lights going out, the crack of thunder and a lightning bolt?"

"Are you kidding? Nothing happened. You talked to him until he expired. Are you okay Jake . . ."

"Oh yeah. Thanks for your help out here. Guess you can go back on patrol. I'll go deal with the brass."

I have never talked about what went on in that room until this very day. Not once. Not ever. But, so help me God, it happened just like I wrote it. I know what I saw. And those events convinced me that logic and science and rationality are helpless to explain all of the incidents which take place between here and whatever comes next when we die.

All the way back to the police department, I kept going over everything Gianette had said. Not everything made sense, but he did tell me who the shooter was, and that would be enough to get a murder warrant for Otto Felter. Putting together his dying declaration with the information Lenny Bragg had offered, plus the Sorwell manuscript, I thought I had the solution to the Skin Ripper case. It was either Felter, or someone else in the crew at the Cheyenne Mountain Ski School. But my money was on the man himself . . . Otto Felter . . . and the only way to know for sure, was to round them all up and to get their statements on the record. The larger issues like ratlines, false identities and the aiding and abetting of war criminals by high officials of the Roman Catholic Church was for someone a lot higher up the chain of command to figure out.

I noticed that my unmarked police car seemed to have a little bit of play in the front end. It sort of wobbled in turns and wouldn't go in a straight line without constant correction, even where the city streets went in a beeline. I put it down as just the difference between that new Corvette and the Ford sedan loaded with gear in the trunk. I made a mental note to check the air pressure in all the tires on my way home . . . something I never did.

Filled with optimism, I parked on Kiowa Street and went in the main door of the station on the double. From his post behind the front desk Sgt. Olfield said, "Chief Duncan's on the warpath Jake, and he's lookin' for you in particular. You'd best go right on over. I'll call and let 'em know you're on the way."

"Thanks Sarge," I said, thinking, as I headed past the stairs and down the hall to the Chief of Police's domain, *Wonder whatever happened to 'Acting Chief?' Sounds to me like Duncan's taking liberties he's not authorized . . .* but by then, I was in the lion's lair . . . with no idea of how much license he was ready to use against me.

When I entered Chief Budd's outer office and waiting area, I nodded to his assistant and said, "Hello Mrs. Cary. Sgt. Olfield said Captain Duncan wanted to see me ASAP."

"He does. I'll let him know you're out here . . . And I'd better warn ya, he's not in a very good mood."

"What's the problem?"

She looked around the empty room as if checking for eavesdroppers, then said, "You didn't hear it from me, but Duncan is after the Chief's job. He's trying to show that J.J.'s not up to the job while he's out there in Reno with all the other top cops . . . And I think it has to do with your case."

"Well, forewarned is forearmed, I guess. Thanks for telling me. At least I can brace myself now," I said.

"I hope so. Are you ready?"

I nodded. Mrs. Cary pushed a button on her telephone. "Detective McKern's here Chief . . . Yessir . . . In a few minutes . . . Yessir."

"Do I have time to hit the head?"

"Sure," she said as she put the phone back in the cradle.

I left on the double. On a whim, I rushed up the stairs to my desk and retrieved the department issued Smith & Wesson six-shot revolver from the top drawer and clipped it on my belt, right behind the gold badge. I looked over at Butch, who was staring open-mouthed, and said, "No time to explain. I'll call you later, but keep everything to yourself, if you can."

Hernshaw nodded as I beat feet back toward flag country and the wrath of Acting Chief of Police Duncan. Handicapped by my bum right leg and the Colt .45 auto stuck in the small of my back, I walked into the Chief's outer office just in time to hear the intercom at Mrs. Cary's elbow come alive and the growl of Fred Duncan's voice as he said, "Okay, Betsy. Send McKern in."

She stood, reached over, and patted me on the arm. "Chief Budd will raise the roof over this. He'll be back in four more days. Just hold on until then."

"Thanks," I said, as she led the way to open the door to the Chief's office. I walked in like a Marine: tall, proud and ramrod straight . . . Came to attention, threw a stiff salute, and held it. Said, "Detective McKern, reporting as ordered."

Captain Fred Duncan, the Acting Chief of the Colorado Springs Police Department, returned a sloppy, lackadaisical, and indifferent acknowledgement of my show of respect. Without preamble he said, "I'll have your badge, gun, and the keys to that fancy-assed Chief's car you've been running around in McKern. You're not the Chief. I am. In fact, as of right now, you ain't anything but suspended without pay, pending an investigation into your failure to produce any results on the Skin Ripper case, and, in addition, your actions in two recent shootings, each of which resulted in a civilian death, plus, the destruction of a city-owned 1954 Chevrolet sedan. You'd better get a lawyer."

"Yes. Sir." I said, while I thought for a second, about stepping forward and knocking the self-important asshole into the middle of next week, as the rage monster howled and thrashed at the bars of his cage inside me and I gritted my teeth until the urge to commit violence faded, then disappeared.

"Any questions?"

"None," I said as I laid the car keys, badge and department issued pistol on the Chief's desk. I made a show of opening the cylinder, ejecting all six bullets, and putting them in my pocket before I turned and left without another word.

Chapter 72

"What now Jake?" Butch Hernshaw asked.

"I don't honestly know," I said, as I got a few personal things from my desk. "To tell you the truth, I'm still trying to wrap my head around the fact that I'm no longer a cop. I can't think very straight right now."

My ex-partner watched, as I took a snub-nosed .32 caliber Saturday night special from its bottom drawer resting place and slipped it into my jacket pocket. Then I stood, reached over, and shook his hand. "It's been a pleasure working with you."

Butch looked like his dog had just died. He said, "What should I do about the case?"

"See what happens. Maybe wait for orders. I think Duncan and Lt. Patterson are trying to cook something up . . . jump my case maybe. Be patient, you'll be told," I said. I sat down and reached in my shirt pocket for my cigarettes. When I did, I remembered that damned parking ticket some smart-ass left on my car.

But when I smoothed it out on the desk, I saw it wasn't what I first thought. On the bottom of a blank traffic ticket, Rags Magness had scratched out a hasty note:

Jake—
When I was on patrol last night, I saw your un-
marked in alley by auditorium. I kept watch on it
best I could, but was busy nite downtown. Had sev-
eral fights and drunks to run in. Sometime around
0230 I seen somebody messing around with it—do-

*ing something underneath the front end. I'm sure
it was my old T.O., Jim Dunlap. I'd recognize the
fat-assed cracker anyplace. You might take a look
at car. When I come back, he was gone.*

Rags

"Look at this," I said to Butch, and passed the note over to him.

He read, grunted and pushed it back without comment, watching while I fired up a coffin nail. When I shook the match out and took a drag, Butch said, "What's that about?" pointing at the note with his chin.

I exhaled a lungful of smoke and thought for an instant, of telling him everything that had happened—but then I'd have to give up Ann-Marie's confidence too—so I just shrugged my shoulders and said, "Beats me . . . but the car drove weird on the way back from the hospital. Felt like the tires needed air or something."

I could tell from his facial expression, that Butch knew bullshit when he heard it. But all he said was, "What yuh gonna do about it?"

I grabbed the phone and dialed the Chief's office. When Mrs. Cary answered I said, "Ma'am, it's Jake McKern. Could I speak to Captain Duncan?"

"I'm sorry Jake . . . but he took off as soon as you left his office . . . in the car he confiscated from you. Said he was going to meet Lt. Patterson, but didn't tell me where."

"There may be a problem with the vehicle, I just read a message Officer Magness left me this morning. He said the car may've been tampered with. And it drove funny on the way back from the hospital . . . felt like the tires had gone soft and it didn't steer right either."

"I'll try and get in touch with him, but it's way past time for me to leave. Chief Budd gets irritated if I put in overtime."

"Would you please leave word with dispatch? And I'll pass the note on to Detective Hernshaw."

"Sure. I'll do my best. Good luck, Jake. I'll fill the Chief in as soon as I hear from him. About everything."

I thanked her and hung up.

I put the ticket in an evidence bag and signed and dated it before handing it to Butch and watched, as he did the same and added the time, all without being asked. I said, "Dunno if we'll ever need that, but keep it someplace safe, would ya."

"Don't worry Jake. I'll see to it."

"Thanks," I said as I took a drag and exhaled. "And by the way—did you pull the original manuscript from the Evidence Room, like I asked?"

Butch looked up. "No, I didn't. Guess I haven't seen yuh, or had a chance to tell you, but when I went down to get it, the evidence box was empty. There's no trace of it."

"Didja raise hell . . . make a fuss?"

"Oh yeah. I made sure everybody, from Roscoe to the Chief, heard about it."

"What do you think happened to it?"

Butch got angry. Said, "Whoever it was that tried to steal it the first time, come back for seconds and got it. I'd like to cut his nuts off . . ."

"At least we have a copy Butch."

I looked around the room one last time and hoped I'd see it again . . . then got up and walked out. Stone-faced, Butch watched in silence.

It was almost 7:30 when I limped up to the door of the empty house I still lived in, over on Seventh Street. The walk from the P.D. to the near westside had taken about an hour because I had to stop and rest my right leg once or twice. But that was okay. It gave me a chance to think.

I called Gloria first thing, to let her know where I was, and ask if she would come get me. "Of course," she said. "Have you eaten?"

"No. Not since Woodland Park."

"Okay. I'll be there in a few."

A few turned out to be almost an hour, but she brought a cardboard box with a thermos of hot beef stew, another of coffee and several grilled cheese sandwiches wrapped in tin foil. Most important of all, she handed over the keys to the Corvette, which had my briefcase with Sorwell's manuscript inside, secured in its locked trunk. I couldn't eat a bite until I had it in my hands.

I filled her in on most of the events of my afternoon between mouthfuls, while Gloria drank coffee and smoked. When I told her about

Captain Duncan suspending me, she said, "He'll come to regret it."

"What makes you say that?" I asked, as I finished eating and reached for my cigarettes.

"I think you've solved the case."

"Yeah . . . but now I have to prove it." Then I yawned.

"It's been a long day for both of us," Gloria said. "The badder news is, I have to be at work by six o'clock tomorrow morning."

I got the message. "Let's go," was what I said as I picked up the briefcase and keys, and held the door for her when we got in the car.

After a long kiss goodnight on her back porch, I hugged her tight, said, "I don't know about tomorrow, Gloria, where I'll be, or what I'll be doing, but I'll try my best to call you sometime . . ."

"I understand. Stay safe Jake. You're my one and only now." Then she went inside without another word.

I was almost to Tenth Street and Colorado Avenue with the briefcase in the seat alongside, when I made the decision that changed everything.

Chapter 73

Looking back now—given the wisdom that comes with age—it seems almost incomprehensible to me that such a momentous, life-affecting decision was made in so spontaneous a fashion . . . but it was. I did it. And even though it was based upon shaky, unreliable, and emotional reasoning that some might think was stupid—as well as possibly seditious—I was bound and determined to go ahead with it anyway, because I thought it was the morally right thing to do. And so, I was about to assist agents of a foreign government to carry out an operation on American soil, by giving them Sorwell's manuscript. I weighed the pros and consequences in my head, all the way out to Fillmore Street and Templeton Gap Road . . . and they scared the crap out of me.

The white Ford station wagon and a one-ton Dodge farm truck with stake sides were parked in Risenberg's circular driveway when I tooled up in the red Corvette. Motion activated lights came on as I walked up to the reinforced front entrance, and a few moments later a shadow flitted behind the peephole. I heard locks and bolts being drawn, then the door was opened by the Rabbi himself . . . holding a big automatic pistol down by his right leg. "Whoa there hoss," I said, holding the briefcase up with both hands. "I come in peace."

Saul moved past me and looked outside before he closed the door. He pointed the gun at the floor with a two-handed combat grip, and eased the hammer down before he spoke. "What are you doing all the way up here Jake . . . why didn't you call first?"

"It was a spur of the moment decision on my part. Why all the hardware?" I said, nodding at the gun.

John Dwaine McKenna

"You first . . . Why are you here Jake?" The Rabbi turned face-to-face with me. Still holding the weapon, he was blocking me from entering further into the house, where somewhere, I could hear the sounds of several male voices talking. "Are you here in an official capacity of any kind?"

"No. Saul. I am not. I'm here to help. I've been suspended without pay. I have no badge, no gun, and no authority. I am armed though. And I won't give it up without a fight. You'll have to come and take it . . ."

The moment of silence that followed stretched, then lengthened until it became more than a simple pause, and I realized it was a judgment. Risenberg was trying to decide if he could trust me enough to take me into his confidence. I didn't flinch, didn't look away and didn't move a muscle or twitch an eye while the world stood still, and time seemed to stop.

It started again when Naomi said, "What's in the briefcase Jake?" She was standing in the shadow of an unlit hallway, partially hidden behind a corner, sighting down the barrel of an M-1 carbine that was braced against the side of the wall.

I was a goner—bracketed in a crossfire that would mean instant death—if a gun fight ever broke out. *Who ARE these people,* I wondered as I stood there, mouth agape, too surprised to be shaken. I said, "I gave up the notion of living forever a long time ago, when I was an eighteen-year-old grunt marine, fighting the Japanese in the Pacific. Pointing a gun at me isn't intimidating. It just pisses me off. Either use 'em or lose 'em, otherwise I'm leaving. I came here in good faith . . . now I'm not so sure."

Naomi was first to react. She stood, pointed the rifle at the floor and said something to Saul in a dialect of some sort, that I didn't recognize. He turned, listened until she finished, shrugged his shoulders, and holstered the pistol in the harness he wore under his left arm.

"What's going on here? Why the hostility? And why the foreign lingo, which I don't appreciate being used in my presence . . ."

Without another word Naomi turned and disappeared down the hall with the short rifle under her right arm. Saul turned to the side and said, "Come in Jake. I hope you bring good news."

I stepped forward into the living room, where I could still hear voices. Then they ceased, and were replaced by a woman. It sounded like Naomi, but I couldn't make out what she was saying and decided to ignore it. "I have Abraham Sorwell's manuscript," I said, as I turned toward Risenberg. "I came here to give it to you."

Saul looked in my direction with the biggest, most shit-eating grin on his face that I have ever seen on another human being. "You won't regret it. Come with me." He said and started down the same dark hallway his wife had used just moments before. My subconscious was urging me to flee. So, ignoring the lizard brain fight or flight instincts from deep inside, with my survival senses screaming, with adrenaline pumping into my bloodstream and with my heart beating out a Krupa drum tattoo . . . I followed him into the unknown.

Chapter 74

At the end of the hallway was a set of carpeted stairs that led down to an unfinished basement . . . where wooden crates of small arms and ammunition marked *U.S. Govt* were stacked along the walls. In the center of the room, sitting on folding chairs around a ping-pong table, was Solomon Frankel and three of the most lethal looking hombres I have ever put eyes on. They were all focused on Naomi, who stood in front of a roll-away chalkboard, just like a college professor lecturing her students. They all turned their attention our way when the Rabbi and I clomped down the stairs.

Addressing Frankel, Risenberg said, "Jake brought it."

"The original, hand-written one?"

"Yeah," I said, as I put the worn old briefcase on the table and opened it. I reached inside, pulled the leather-bound record that represented so much pain for so many, and put it in front of the Israeli operative. "The metal box Sorwell kept it in was gone. I believe whoever stole the decoy from the CSPD Evidence Room has it."

"What decoy? What are you talking about," Naomi said.

I told them again, about someone at the PD stealing—or attempting to steal—the manuscript from the evidence locker.

Frankel started leafing through the diary, while Naomi addressed the other three men in the same foreign tongue she'd used upstairs.

Seeing my look of discomfort, Risenberg said, "She's speaking Hebrew. It, and Russian are all these men understand. She's telling them about the treasure you've brought to us. They're Jews, who fought the Germans at the battle of Stalingrad, and then on the Eastern Front as the remnants of Hitler's forces retreated . . . while the Holocaust was taking all of the rest of their families. Afterward, they made it out of post-war Europe, to fight in the Middle East, helping to establish the nation of Israel. Now, they work for Solomon, tracking down escaped Nazis all over the world."

"And they're damn good at it," Frankel said, as he closed Sorwell's Manuscript with care and placed it within reach of everyone at the table. He added, "I also want to thank you—personally, as well as officially—for delivering this artifact into our hands. It is a national treasure . . . a hand-written, first-person account of daily life, and a witness to the atrocities that took place at one of the most infamous of all the Nazi death camps—Buchenwald. It's all the official recognition you'll get. Unofficially however, I have access to the sort of information that's only available to high level operatives on a need-to-know basis that I'll share with you, anytime you need it. This number," he wrote something on the back, then handed me a business card for an import-export company, based in the Israeli port city of Haifa, "will put you in touch with me, anywhere on the globe. Only a handful of people have it. Two of them are heads of state."

It was heady stuff, and almost overwhelming to think that I was being put on the same plane, or an equal footing at least, with a couple of heads of state . . . I didn't know what to say or how to react for a bit, because it was so far over my head. But I finally snapped out of the fugue long enough to mutter a humble acknowledgement. Said, "Thank you Solomon. I won't abuse this," as I put it in my shirt pocket and buttoned the flap. Then I picked up the briefcase and turned to leave, heading for the stairs.

"What's the matter Jake . . . where do you think you're going?" Saul said.

"Back to my house, to get some sleep and try and figure out what to do, now that I'm no longer a cop. It's been a helluva long day," I said, and yawned again, a big jaw cracking one that I tried, but failed to cover up with a forearm.

"I don't think you want to do that."

"Why not, Saul? Is that a threat," I said, as I realized how bad my tactical situation would be, outnumbered by six to one.

"Because we're getting ready for an operation and we could use your help," the Rabbi said. "It's about the Skin Ripper. We know who it is . . ."

I stopped in mid stride, turned to face the group and took a closer, more careful look at them. Each one was dressed in well used combat boots, faded green fatigues bloused into the tops of their footgear, and each of them was armed with army-issue .45 caliber ACPs that had suppressors screwed onto the business end. Neither Frankel, nor Risenberg, had introduced, or even acknowledged the three commandos to me. They all sort of matched each other in appearance, except for their hair. The first was bald, while his two mates both had close-cropped short black hair. The third one however, had a half-inch wide red scar that zig-zagged along his right temple, from his eye to the back of his head. Whatever hit him there had also clipped off the top third of his right ear. To myself, I named them 'One,' 'Two,' and 'Zorro,' who all turned out to be hellaciously good fighters when the bullets started to fly. But at that moment, I looked at Risenberg, Naomi and Frankel for an instant, then said, "How do you know who he is? What's all this about . . . and how do you propose to carry out an armed operation on American soil . . . this isn't a two-bit backwater run by some tinhorn despot and his brother-in-law . . . it's the mightiest country on earth."

Frankel looked at Saul and his wife, then said, "If you would, let me take this."

Naomi answered for both of them. She nodded, "You may . . . but remember that it's me, who represents the Israeli Government here. Be careful what you say. Time is short. Saul and I will handle the loading of the truck with the three Russians and a pair of volunteers while you brief him."

Chapter 75

Frankel and I went upstairs and sat at the kitchen table, while downstairs, I could hear the movement of crates and men at work. Frankel saw me listening and said, "There's a lower entrance with an overhead door that you couldn't see from where we were sitting. Another truck, with a driver and helper from the synagogue was waiting for us to finish our meeting and load out. You walked right into the middle of everything."

"What's with all the military equipment down there? How'd you get it, and why?" I said, and yawned again before I could stop it.

"Why? Why's the easy part," Frankel said as he removed a fresh pack of Lucky Strike cigarettes from a pocket on his sleeve, pulled the cellophane strip and peeled the top off. He tamped them on the table, offered one, and I lit us both up with my old Zippo. Then I sat back, smoked, and waited for him to resume. It didn't take long.

Frankel exhaled a cloud of nicotine fumes and said, "Our leaders think we'll soon be at war with Egypt and its Arab allies. And because there's a world-wide embargo on arms sales to Israel, we've had to go out and get them wherever we can. All the weapons that you just saw were bought at Army Surplus stores by Naomi, Saul or other Jewish patriots who support Israel in any way they can—monetarily, influentially, or by actual deeds. We have bills of sale for everything down there, plus a helluva lot more that you didn't see. It's all being gathered and sent to a central shipping point, where it's loaded aboard an ocean-going vessel. The ship will leave soon, and make some other pickups, then head out for the Middle East."

I leaned forward on the chair, said, "What about the Skin Ripper?

Is it Felter? Is he the one?"

"No, not him. Her. The ski school instructor. Ilse Müller. Her real name is Helga Fischer. She's the illegitimate daughter of Ilse Koch—also known as *The Bitch of Buchenwald.*"

"You told me about her at the Waffle House two days ago. What I want to know is, how are you so sure that she's the Skin Ripper?" I said, as I tapped the ash from my cigarette and waited for his answer . . . or a tell that he was lying.

None came for a bit. Frankel drummed his fingers on the table and turned away, then looked me in the eye and said, "She has a documented history of torturing prisoners in the camps by flaying them. She learned how at her mother's side. Sorwell wrote about it in the manuscript."

"Where? I didn't see it."

"Then you didn't read the whole diary. It's somewhere around page 200."

I thought, *He's right. I stopped reading about halfway and skipped over to the last twenty pages—where Sorwell identified her.* I said, "I didn't read to that point, the subject matter was becoming disgusting to me. The depravity . . ."

I could sense the disapproval in Frankel's eyes, but he simply continued, "As far as her identity is concerned, we have extensive records from the camps that we've collected piece by piece, from sources all over the world which contain personnel files with physical descriptions, fingerprints, and photographs . . . it's a lengthy, slow, and tedious process to go through them all. But now we have found hers, Felter's, and two of the others in the group. It's her. We followed Helga and her henchman until they left some used coffee cups at a café and lifted prints from them."

"When?" I said, "and where?"

"It was two days ago, at the chocolate shop on Tejon Street. Seems Helga has a sweet tooth."

"Michelle's. I had lunch there not too long ago with an art professor, when I was still trying to figure out what Sorwell's Manuscript was. She was a charmer named . . ."

"Gilda Arkady," Frankel interrupted. "She's the one who got the fingerprints for us. She's a Russian Jew whose family escaped the U.S.S.R in the late '20s, just before Stalin's great purges of the 1930's."

I yawned again, involuntarily, couldn't help myself, and soldiered on. Said, "So, Gilda's part of your group—a spy?"

"No," Frankel said, "she's not. But Jews everywhere are expected—and usually willing—to aid Israeli interests whenever asked by someone like me. On another note, what's the matter with you? Why do you keep yawning like that? Are you able to go for a few more hours?"

"Oh yeah. I'm tired is all," I said as I drowned out the last of my cigarette. "I got up at six this morning. Been going ever since."

The man from the Mossad looked at me for a moment, with all the intensity of a desert lynx, assessing the chances of catching a long-legged jerboa that was a couple of jumps out of reach. Then, through a haze of cigarette smoke, he said, "I can fix that, but you'll pay a price when it wears off."

"What kind of price?"

"A physical one," Frankel said, as he leaned toward me to put out his cigarette in the same coffee mug that I'd used. It too, went out with a wet 'ssst,' before floating back up in the dregs, like a dead body in a dark pond. "You'll feel great, like you could go for days at full speed . . . but then you'll crash like never before. It will be the baddest, worst headache you can imagine, one that nothing—except time—will fix."

"How much time?" I said. "Would I still be able to function like usual?"

"Recovery depends on the quantity of pills you've eaten and the duration you've been going on them. But you'll still be able to do everything you'd be doing with an alcohol hangover."

I yawned again, said, "You ever used it?"

"Yeah, on a number of occasions, like now, when rest is a luxury, you can't afford. It was discovered by the Germans during the war. They gave it to their troops before battle."

I made another impetuous decision that I came to regret later. Said, "Okay. Give me some."

Without a word, Frankel got up and went out of the kitchen, leaving me sitting there alone and listening to the grunts of men lifting heavy objects, while I wondered . . . *What the hell am I getting myself into?*

Frankel came back in less than five minutes and handed me a small glass vial with some white pills in it that looked like ordinary aspirins, only smaller. He said, "What's your height and weight?"

"Six four and two forty."

"Start with three," he said, while he pulled a tumbler from a wall cabinet over the sink, filled it with water, then went on, "and drink this," as he handed it to me.

I unscrewed the cap from the small glass bottle, tipped three of the harmless looking little round balls onto my hand, threw them into my mouth, drank the whole glass of water . . . and changed my life forever. Because that was the moment, I first tried amphetamines.

In just a few heartbeats my senses got sharper, the world sped up and Frankel droned on about the ill effects of misuse. "Don't forget what I'm telling you." He said, "No more than eight in a 24-hour period. They can be addictive."

I nodded as if I agreed, but in truth I wasn't hearing a word he said. At the time, I thought I was eight feet tall and bulletproof.

Chapter 76

A ll of a sudden, I had so much energy that it took a conscious effort to sit still. To cover my unease, I pulled another cigarette from the pack Frankel left laying on the table and lit up. Then I cut right to the chase. Said, "What are you planning on doing tonight? Where do I fit in? How do you know that Ilse Müller is the Skin Ripper . . . I don't have a badge anymore but if we have proof, I can get her by a citizen's arrest and Felter too for the murder of the priest Alphonso Gianette I heard his deathbed confession I . . ."

Frankel reached over the table, jabbed a calloused finger into the nerve ganglion in the hollow of my left shoulder, and sent a bolt of pain down my arm that hurt so bad I couldn't move a muscle or speak for a few seconds. At the same time, he said, "Stop. You're babbling. Not making sense. You have to focus. Look at me and concentrate."

I began to regain the use of my arm and started to figure out where I was going to smack the bastard—then realized—it was the drug speaking, not me. I relaxed. Put my energy into loosening my arm and shoulder muscles.

Solomon watched me, then said, "Sorry to do that, but there isn't any time to waste. The people we're after—Müller, Felter and the other three are all war criminals and international fugitives who've been able to evade capture and trial for more than a decade. They're ruthless fighters who'll give and expect no mercy . . . plus . . . they're preparing to leave the area and we have no idea where they might be headed."

"I understand. I fought fanatic Japanese soldiers who were indoctrinated—maybe infected is a better word—with the Samurai code of Bushido. It's about self-discipline, courage, and loyalty to the emperor.

So much so, that they never surrendered. Fought to the death. It was them or us. Somebody was gonna die."

"I expect this will be the same kind of a fight. Be ready."

"I am."

Frankel looked at me. "Do you know where the road to Williams Creek Ranch is?"

"Yeah. It's about fifteen miles south of Colorado Springs. Probably closer to twenty-five from out here, on the north side of the city. Why do you ask?" I said, while I tapped cigarette ashes into the coffee mug, we'd been using for a communal butt can.

Frankel watched me do it with a look of distaste, but didn't comment. Instead, he said, "How long will it take us to get down there?"

"From here, at least the best part of an hour. We'll have to navigate through a lot of city traffic and stop lights."

Frankel nodded in understanding, had nothing more to add . . . Downstairs, I could hear a series of bangs, metal-on-metal scrapes, grunts and what sounded like male voices cursing . . . then an overhead door slid home with a thud. Next, came the growl and cough of a diesel engine starting up, followed by the noise of a heavy truck grinding up through the gears as it pulled away. Naomi, Saul and the three Russians humped back up the stairs and joined Frankel and me, filling the kitchen to capacity. It became too confining, so while Saul set out making coffee for everyone, Naomi ushered the rest of the group into the living room.

After all of us found somewhere to sit down, Frankel said, "We're heading for a place that's about an hour from here." He nodded to me and continued, while Naomi translated for the three Russians. "Jake knows where the place is and the best way to get there. We're going after the woman who calls herself Ilse Müller, plus Otto Felter, and the three underlings. You can expect stiff resistance and fortified positions. We'll have the element of surprise, but they're on familiar ground. We need to get in, find the woman and get out, as fast and as efficient as possible . . . because a firefight will attract unwanted attention." Frankel looked at me. "Okay. Jake, show us where it is and how to get there."

All eyes in the room were on me as I pulled a blank writing tablet and ballpoint pen from my briefcase and put them on the coffee table.

I started speaking and drawing a rough map at the same time. "We'll leave here and head downtown on Nevada Avenue. It turns into State Highway 115, once we pass the city limits, south of the Broadmoor Hotel and Cheyenne Mountain . . ."

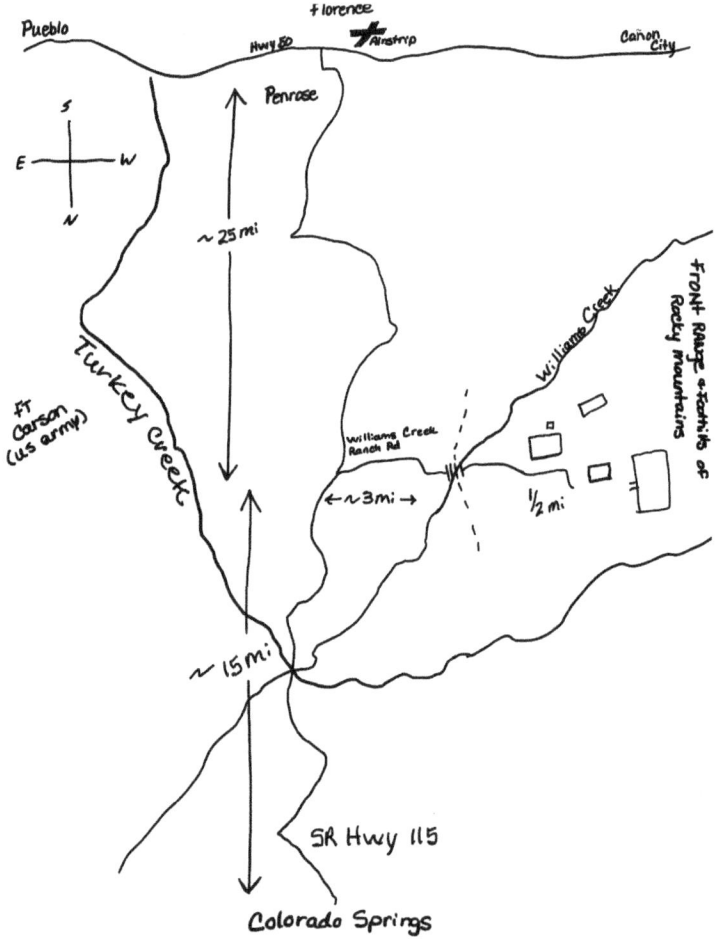

"How far from there to Williams Creek Road?" Naomi asked.

"About fifteen miles," I said. "At that point, it's another three or four miles of dirt road to get into the ranch itself. It's an old pioneer cabin, built by one of the last mountain men—a fur trapper and indian fighter—named Jim Williams. Legend has it that he knew Kit Carson

286

and Quanah Parker, but it's a fact that he bred horses and mules which he sold to the U.S. Government during and after the Civil War."

"We'll pass through a fence and cattle guard here," I continued, as I drew a dotted line and four short parallel lines. "Then, it's another quarter of a mile to the house—here on the left—and the barn is thirty or so yards up the drive on the right. There's a bunkhouse and a few other smaller buildings too . . ." I noticed Zorro touching Naomi on the wrist to get her attention. He leaned over and said something to her in Russian. She looked in my direction. I said, "Yeah, Naomi . . ."

She said, "They want to know if it's uphill to the house and barn from the fence line."

I nodded, said, "Yes. The house sits on top of a little knoll. So do all the other buildings and the barn. Each one of them is uphill from the road."

I watched Naomi translate. Zorro looked serious at first, while One and Two were smiling. But as she continued with what turned out to be a rather long-winded answer in a foreign language, the faces all began going the opposite way . . . until One and Two were dour and glum . . . while Zorro was laughing out loud and pounding his left palm with a right index finger that was as big as a hammer handle, in the age-old 'cash on the barrelhead' sign. He said something in rapid-fire Russian to Naomi, who laughed and turned to me. "He said to thank you. He just won a hundred dollars from his two pals when you told them it was uphill in both directions to the house and the barn."

"It is. They both sit atop little hills."

Another burst of Russian from Zorro to Naomi ensued. She laughed again and shook her head, then looked at me and said, "The bet was 'It can't be so unlucky for us that we have to fight uphill in two directions at once! He," she nodded at Zorro, "said it could."

They were still arguing amongst themselves minutes later, when Risenberg showed up with a gallon of coffee and a platter of roast beef sandwiches. I wasn't hungry. Just sat there smoking a cigarette and drinking coffee while I watched them and wondered what it was about Russian humor that I didn't get.

Frankel saw me and said, "Don't worry. They never pay their bets anyway."

Chapter 77

I was about halfway through the cigarette, watching the others eat, drink coffee, and argue amongst themselves. Frankel came over and sat by me, munching on half of a roast beef on rye and holding a mug of black coffee in his other hand. He sipped, swallowed, and said, "The pills inhibit your appetite. Don't forget to eat, or you'll run out of energy and drop."

"I'm good. My girlfriend fed me just before I came over here."

"That's fine. But listen to me—I know what I'm talking about. Risenberg has a bunch of these wrapped in wax paper. Put one in your coat pocket and eat it later."

I indicated I would with a nod of my head, drank some coffee, then said, "I'm curious. How'd you get the location of that whole bunch, and so much information so damn fast?"

Frankel ate the last bite of his sandwich before he answered. Then, he looked at me with a wolfish grin and said, "Not all Jews are doctors. Some are accountants, bookkeepers, and attorneys. I have the names of all five people at that address, their social security numbers, W-2s, tax returns and occupations. They're all employees of that big hotel as maintenance workers, or—get this—florists. And all of them entered the United States as a war refugee or a displaced person without citizenship . . . and each one was sponsored by a high-ranking member of the Roman Catholic church in Austria, or at the Vatican itself. It makes for a lot of interesting reading."

"I hope I get the chance." I said, as I extinguished the coffin nail, stood up and walked over to the fireplace and back, trying to stretch my legs and get ready for whatever was coming next.

Zorro made the first comment. He rose from his seat on the hearth and crossed the room. He stared at the hand drawn map for a bit, memorizing its features . . . then looked at me and said something that Naomi translated as, "Where do we get out from this place?"

"Same way we got in," I said. "There's only one road."

"Then what?"

Frankel said, "We go back to the airport in Colorado Springs and take off."

"Take off . . . how? In what? Are you all flying commercial?" I said, wondering for the first time, how do four, or possibly more, individuals travel around together . . .

"We have our own airplane and pilot, and I can also fly it if the need arises." Frankel said, "It's old and ugly . . . but dependable. We have traveled all over the globe in it."

"It's just sitting out there?"

"At the General Aviation Terminal, all gassed up and ready to go. All I have to do is call Moshe, the pilot, and he'll have the props turning and the engines warmed up, ready for immediate takeoff."

The antique clock on the mantle chimed eleven times. I looked over at the group of Israelis and thought for a moment, then said to Frankel, "I'm not sure that's a good idea Solomon . . ."

"Why not? We've done it that way dozens of times before."

"Think about it," I said, as I went back over to where the hand-drawn map was resting on the coffee table. I pointed, "It's at least fifteen miles back to the city, then another six or seven to get out to the airport, over on the east side—and all the while, traffic will be getting heavier—and people getting curiouser. The odds of being stopped by the cops become ever greater the farther you go."

"At four or five o'clock in the morning?" The Israeli operative said, as he reached for the same pack of Luckys that I'd pilfered from, only minutes before.

"Oh, yeah. Colorado Springs rises early. We've got military installations on the south, east and north ends of town, that all start the workday before dawn. Then there's cooks, milkmen and shift workers like the newspapers and hospitals. Believe me—I've done a lot of graveyard tours and midnight patrols—there's always a lot of pre-sun-up activity that you don't want to get involved with."

"What's your solution then?" Frankel asked, as he set fire to the cigarette.

I took a deep breath, pointed to the map, and said, "There's a small airstrip right here, on Highway 50, between Penrose and Cañon City. I don't think it's lighted and I know it's not open at night, so it's damn sure quiet. It's a bit further in miles, but a lot less conspicuous."

"Do you have any idea how long the runway is, or what types of aircraft are using the place?"

"Anything I say is just a guess, but I've seen different kinds of World War II planes down there—all propeller driven, both one and two engine types."

"No big, four engine bombers?"

I shook my head. "No."

"Do you know what the landing surface is?" Frankel said, as he scribbled notes on some paper, he'd pulled from the pad I'd drawn the map on. He checked the spelling of the small Fremont County towns with me, then went into Risenberg's office to make some phone calls, after I told him I didn't think that it was.

As soon as Frankel got up to leave the room, Risenberg waved me into the group of others, where he and Naomi were drawing up the plans for a military style assault on a civilian target here on American soil . . . where I was about to throw in with them . . . and to hell with the cost. Whether it was my burning desire to see justice done—no matter the personal price I might have to pay later—or just plain insanity, I've never been able to figure out. But a few hours later, we were all fighting for our lives.

Chapter 78

When our small posse reassembled itself at the intersection of Williams Creek Road and 115 south, it was apparent right away that my reckoning of the distance and the time it would take to get there, had been off by a country mile. It was coming up on 2:30 a.m. and according to the speedometer in my Corvette, we'd gone almost thirty miles since leaving Risenberg's place out on Templeton Gap . . . Proof as far as I was concerned, that the landmass of Colorado Springs was growing like a malignant tumor in the heart of God's own Great Plains.

Frankel, who rode with me, was silent for most of the trip. Filled, I assumed, with command worries—of methods, men, and materials. I left him to it, while I concentrated on my own concerns: *In seeking justice, was I being unjust? An outlaw? Turning into that which I abhorred?* I knew Otto Felter had shot and killed the Nazi priest, Alphonso Gianette. I could've gotten an arrest warrant signed, based on Father Al's dying declaration . . . but then I was suspended by the acting chief before I could have it sworn out . . . which took away my authority. Then there was the problem of Ilse Müller—or Helga Fischer—and her three merry men. I knew they were the ones who'd killed and mutilated the bodies of Abraham and Ruth Sorwell and the visiting professor, Chiam Leviwitz . . . but the hell of it was I couldn't prove it. There was a ton of circumstantial evidence, but not one single shred of tangible proof. Now, they were trying to disappear, escaping in another vanishing act like they did after the war. And, on top of everything else, was the fact that someone at the CSPD had tried to sabotage the Skin Ripper case at every possible opportunity. My frustrations were boiling over, so much so that I was about to resort to vigilantism. I fretted and seethed, waffled, and argued with my inner self . . . all the way down to the old road that led to Williams Creek Ranch.

Then it was time. I had to buckle up and put my war face on.

We pulled our three vehicles up the switchback where the ranch road met the blacktop, and parked in a meadow that overlooked Highway 115, about fifty feet below. There, besides Frankel and me in the Corvette, Naomi and Saul Risenberg were in the Ford station wagon, while Russian Two drove the one-ton farm truck with Zorro riding shotgun and Russian One perched in the middle, over the gearshift stick. I noticed when I walked past it, that the stake-sided vehicle had two courses of hay bales stacked in it and was roped and covered with a green canvas tarp. I hadn't seen the load back in the Springs, because the truck was backed in and parked facing the street. *Maybe you were too tired to look around,* I thought. *But you'd better wake up. Inattention will get you killed.* I took Frankel's vial of pills out and swallowed two more amphetamines. Five minutes later, I was loaded with nervous energy, my heart was racing full out and I was itching for the action to start.

We gathered around the hood of the station wagon and Frankel took charge "Our objective is the woman, everyone else is secondary. She'll be in the house." He stopped talking and looked my way for a moment then added, "What can you tell us about it Jake?"

"Not as much as I'd wish for a mission like this. It's been ten years since I hunted deer down there, and then I was on horseback . . ."

Frankel interrupted me, said "Saul and Naomi have already gone over the tactical part. Be specific and brief. We're running late and we need to retain the element of surprise."

I nodded. "Understood. The house is an ax-cut log cabin that's been modernized and added-on over the years. It's one big room with a couple of bedrooms tacked on to the rear. There's a single door and a hallway in the middle that leads to a privy out back and each bedroom has a small window."

"Big enough to escape through?" Naomi said.

"Maybe. I can't really remember. But I'd assume that Otto Felter will be in one of those two bedrooms . . . probably the one closest to the front door."

"I agree," Frankel said. "What about the bunkhouse?"

"Other side of the road, about midway between the house and the barn is all I can tell you, I only passed by. Never was inside."

"Okay," Frankel said, "We'll go in two teams of three. Saul, you take Russians One and Two and hit the bunkhouse. Jake, you're around the back of the main house while Zorro and I go in the front. Naomi, you're our rear guard. Stay here with the sports car and do whatever you have to in order to keep the road clear. We'll be in a hurry when we come out. You men be quick, be quiet, be vigilant, check your equipment and fight hard. Your country and the souls of millions are looking to us for justice."

Those last three sentences seem corny and trite from the comfort of my study these many years later, but back then, juiced up on dope and about to head for the unknown . . . I took it all to heart.

As I handed her the keys to the Corvette, Naomi smiled and said, "I'll look great in this, don't you think?"

It was the only time I can remember her being less than dead serious. "Like a million bucks," I said. But I was thinking at the same time, *And cheap, compared to my raven-haired Nurse Gloria.*

We started up Williams Creek Road by starlight, with the station wagon in the lead and me behind the wheel. Frankel rode shotgun in the backseat with the windows down and a twelve-gauge pump between his knees. I had a Thompson submachine gun with a thirty round stick magazine on the seat next to me, and we both carried .45 caliber pistols in shoulder holsters. I also had spare clips for both guns in the pockets of the army field coat I'd exchanged for my leather bomber jacket that was now in the trunk of my car. Saul and the Russians were all armed in similar fashion, courtesy of the equipment cache that was now on the way overseas in the hold of a tramp steamer.

Without headlights, it was slow going on the unfamiliar one-lane dirt road, but I managed a steady pace that brought us to the fence line and the cattle guard after about thirty minutes . . . where we stopped to take a last look before going in. There were no lights on that we could see, and the house, bunkhouse, and barn were all quiet as we got ready to move up. We left the Ford station wagon parked outside the break in the fence, facing the highway with keys in the ignition and ready for a fast exit.

Our approach was precise and well organized to begin with. Frankel and Zorro and I were on foot in front of the farm truck. Risenberg was at the wheel, and Russians One and Two stood in the bed with M-1 Garand rifles. We were formidable, quiet, and confident until we'd closed about half the distance to the historic ranch house . . . That's when the dogs came.

Chapter 79

Without warning, two big German Shepherds came streaking out of the darkness like a couple of black and tan rockets. All teeth and bad attitude, they were intent on destroying us.

Our skirmish line had Frankel at the left flank with Zorro in the middle and myself on the right—which was where the first attack came. One moment I was trying to make out the terrain in the absence of light, and in the next I was knocked ass over tin teacup, fighting with a monster that was trying to rip my left arm off. The Thompson fell to the ground as the shepherd clamped down with its razor-sharp teeth and I could feel blood flowing down my forearm. The dog snarled and shook its head, shredding my flesh through the sleeve of the jacket. The pain came then, as I screamed and thrashed and rolled and punched and kicked with a ferocity born of desperation that I hadn't felt since my first hand-to-hand combat with a Japanese soldier.

The angry beast was getting the best of me when Zorro bashed it on the head with the barrel of an M-1 carbine stunning the animal and knocking it away from me. Dazed, the dog was getting set to re-attack when one of the Russians in the truck shot and killed it. At the same time, a boom from the shotgun in Frankel's hands, followed by the thump of a carcass hitting the ground, informed us that the other attacking animal was down and presumed dead. Other than my arm, which continued to bleed, we were all okay, but we'd lost any chance of surprise.

There was still about a hundred yards to reach the cabin itself, plus another twenty-five or more to the bunkhouse. We had to pick up the pace or risk getting pinned down. I bent over and retrieved the weapon I'd dropped, worked the bolt to check the action and cleared the muzzle, making sure it was free of any dirt or debris . . . then ran to catch up with my two companions, who were zig-zagging their way up the slope toward the homestead.

Risenberg meanwhile, had floored the old farm truck and was kicking up dust and gravel as he sped towards the bunkhouse with Russians One and Two hanging on in the bed. They were almost to the door of the barn-like structure when the first bullets hammered into the cab. Outside lights came on from a pole midway between the bunkhouse and barn, and stayed on just long enough for me to see Russian Two, followed seconds later by One, disappearing into the darkness. Risenberg dove out of the driver's seat and took cover on the ground behind the front wheel. More rounds pinged into the front, back and sides of the truck before someone shot out the pole light. At the same time, some other somebody opened up on us with a machine gun from the cabin, and I had problems of my own to deal with.

I hit the ground, hoping for cover and sent a half-dozen bullets in the direction of the main cabin that was now only fifteen yards in front of me. I rolled to the side, jumped to my feet, and ran left for two steps, then right for three more, while squeezing off short bursts from the smoking Thompson. I could feel my heart pounding in my chest. I smelled the oil cooking off of the gun barrel and heard the percussive pops of small arms fire to the front of me as my companions engaged the bad guys in a hot firefight.

I made it to a wall of the house, stood with my back to the logs catching my breath for a moment, then began edging around toward the back door. I was almost there when the sound of a furious gun-battle came from inside, followed by a long, sustained burst of machine-gun rounds . . . then nothing. The log cabin went quiet as an abandoned grave.

I was at the side of the screened back door, reaching for the latch when the lights came on and the inside door opened without warning. It blinded me for a moment and wrecked my night vision. I put a hand to my face in an automatic reflex, just as Frankel said, "STOP HER JAKE."

Still not seeing, I stumbled in front of the screened door at the exact instant Ilse Müller bashed into it from the inside, twisting the ancient thing off its hinges and leaving the pair of us tangled in the debris.

Quick as a feral cat, the woman who was responsible for so much pain and so many deaths sprang to her feet and started screaming obscenities, while I was still on my ass in the twisted mess of ripped window screen and pieces of the busted door. She was raising her hands, holding a .32 Beretta in a combat grip, and leading it toward my face. I didn't give her a chance to get a shot off. From the seated position, I hit her in the ribs with a left hook that had all I could muster in it . . . and caught her by accident across both forearms with the barrel of the Thompson at the same time, as I swung it for balance. The pistol went to the ground, while Ilse Müller fell against the door casing with a moan, holding her left wrist and trying to catch her breath, which was coming in short gasps.

Frankel grabbed her left arm and pulled her upright, then snapped handcuffs on while she spewed out a never-ending series of curses.

I disengaged from the wreckage of the door and pushed it to one side, so I could reach down with my handkerchief and pick up the .32 auto. I wrapped it in the white cloth and stashed it in an inside pocket, then looked at Frankel and said, "What now Solomon?"

Before he could answer, a series of back-and-forth gunshots rang out. In the near distance I could hear another gun battle happening. Then Frankel said, "You guard the prisoner. I'm going to help capture or kill Felter. Then the others. We've got to end this."

Chapter 80

Ilse Müller looked at me with eyes so full of rage, she could've stopped a clock with them as I stepped inside and closed the wooden outside door behind me.

Frankel said, "Don't take your focus off of her. Don't listen to her, and for the love of God, don't believe anything that comes out of her mouth." Then he slipped out of the same door I'd just entered through.

My leg was killing me. I needed to get off of it for a while. I motioned with the gun under my arm and my chin in the direction of the main room and said, "Move," to the prisoner.

"Where do you want me to go?"

"The front parlor," I said. "Nice and slow. No sudden moves."

She was a tall and trim woman, lithe and fit from skiing, who looked to be in her late thirties or early forties. She was barefoot, with her blonde hair in a braid that reached the middle of her back, and wore a granny style flannel nightgown. *Even with her hands cuffed behind her,* I thought, *I'm gonna have a helluva time if she decides to run . . .* Lucky for me—owing probably, to the fight in the doorway and the punch I laid on her—she didn't. It's the only time in my life that I've ever hit a woman on purpose, and I'm not proud of it . . . even given the circumstances. I only mentioned it here for the sake of veracity, and to keep the story straight.

She sat down on the wooden rocking chair I pushed to the center of the room, where I could keep watch on her. With scorn and the haughtiness that only a certain type of highbrowed elites are capable of displaying on their faces, Ilse Müller watched, as I pulled one of the kitchen chairs over, then sat facing her with the Thompson across my knees and the front door in plain sight. Outside, the sounds of gunfire were punctuated by the booms of a large bore shotgun as the shootout continued unabated.

I changed mags in the Thompson, and noticed when I did, that the old one was almost empty. There were only two rounds left in the clip. I started to put the used magazine in my pocket when a heavy back and forth exchange of gunfire erupted somewhere close, then ceased. The door opened and a bloody Otto Felter crashed through—followed by Solomon Frankel, who had blood on his left shoulder and a Colt pistol in his right hand. "Felter?" I said, as the Israeli knelt next to the fallen man.

"Dead."

"You?"

"I'll be okay. I've had worse."

"And the others?"

"Don't know," he said, "I think we both need some medical attention. All of us are trained medics and there's first aid supplies in the station wagon. We'll be okay."

I nodded, said, "I haven't been able to look around in here. I think we should."

"Agreed. I'll guard her. You do it, but be quick. We have run out of time."

I stood, handed the machine gun to Frankel and began the search for evidence, while he began interviewing Ilse Müller in her native tongue.

The place was a rectangle, constructed of hand-cut, peeled and adzed lodgepole pines at least a hundred years ago. It was a basic, no-frills shelter and as such, didn't offer a lot of opportunities to conceal anything. The fireplace had no loose stones, the mantle was solidly put together, nor did the chimney or the hearth come apart. I moved on, into the bedrooms.

The first, a man's, was Spartan—a place where a monk lived. It held only the basics; a bunk, a small wardrobe with some empty wire hangers and a change of clothes, one straight-backed chair and a side table. I tossed it fast and found nothing but two hunting knives and some empty boxes of ammo. I threw the mattress on the floor and spotted a small wooden box under the bed. I put it by the door jamb, next to a duffle bag that held army work clothes, a pair of boots and ammo for a nine-millimeter Parabellum. I left everything on the floor where I'd dumped it and moved on to the other bedroom . . . where I found some of the answers to the Skin Ripper case.

Chapter 81

The second bedroom belonged to Ilse Müller and contained more frill, but it too was packed for a quick departure. Only a few more hours and all of them would've been in the wind by the looks of things. The four-drawer dresser was empty and a large folding trunk—the kind used by experienced travelers—stood on one end next to the door. It was open down the middle, with four drawers in a stack along one side and a space on the other for hanging clothes.

The first drawer I pulled out was filled with cosmetics, nylons and under garments . . . the kinds of things anyone on a trip would have in their luggage. The second one contained ski gear, shoes, and a pair of books. They were both written in German, so I couldn't read them, but I recognized the first as *Mein Kompf*, or 'My Struggle'. . . Adolf Hitler's autobiography. The second one appeared to be a treatise of some kind—a dissertation perhaps—on the art and practice of human tattooing. I reasoned that out from the multitude of photographs which illustrated the text. I flipped through the pages, taking note of the variety of primitive, and painful looking uses of sharp objects or needles to drive ink under living flesh. It was eerie stuff, weird and creepy . . . but the last few pages stopped me cold. The pictures showed how to skin a human being, remove the hair, and tan the hide in order to preserve the folk art depicted in the dermal layers. With bile rising in my throat, I tossed the book back where it came from, and closed the drawer. I took a deep breath and pulled out drawer number three. That's where the depravity began.

On first glance, I saw surgical tools. All wrapped in neat bundles, and encased in velvet carriers that had slots sewn into them for each tool. They were rolled up and tied with ribbon. Untied and uncoiled, the stainless-steel clamps, tweezers, pliers, scalpels, forceps, retractors, bone saws, probes, and shears of different sizes gleamed in the incandescent light as they lay there, ready to heal in the hands of a physician or surgeon, or commit an atrocity when employed by a monster like the woman in the front room.

The rest of the drawer was filled with pieces of tanned leather of different sizes, that had been laid flat, then rolled into a cylinder. Curious, I picked one at random and flattened it out. The leather was a light tan in color—and, just like the cover of Sorwell's manuscript—it was soft, supple, and about twelve inches wide by fourteen long . . . that's when I saw the five-digit number tattooed in blue ink and realized I was holding the skin of a human forearm. I put it down and counted forty-seven additional pieces of leather. Worse still, under the leather, in manila envelopes were dozens of glossy black and white photographs depicting the entire process . . . from victim to finished product: art deco lampshades and leather-bound copies of *der Führer's* autobiography.

Nauseated, I closed that drawer and braced myself as I pulled open the bottom one. It too was filled with horror.

Packed tightly in foam rubber and straw, were three dozen medium-sized sealed and watertight specimen jars. They looked to be high-quality—like a scientist would use on field trips—and each one contained what looked like flayed human skin in various stages of the curing process. I was stunned. The evidence right there in front of me told the truth of the crime. There were more victims of the remorseless, evil woman in the other room. A lot more. But where were they? I was closing the drawer and thinking about how to get an answer to that, when Zorro stepped through the door.

The big Russian Jew with the long scar on the side of his head had blood on his face, shirt, and left hand. He smelled of gasoline and had dirt, pine needles and more blood on his coat, but no injuries as far as I could see. He said something to me in Russian or Hebrew . . . and pointed to the door. "Frankel?" I said.

"We have to get out now," he answered from the front room.

"You need to see this. Can you call Zorro out there to watch the prisoner?"

Frankel said something in one of the throaty guttural languages the big man understood, and just like that, as quiet as a whisper in church, Zorro melted out of the door and was gone.

As soon as he started to leave, I reached in drawer three and grabbed the leather swatch with the five-digit number tattooed on it, and one of the envelopes of photographs. I secreted them inside my shirt on the non-bloodied side, only a fraction of a second before Frankel came into the room with the Thompson submachine gun in his good hand.

"Here's everything we need to prove her guilt." I said

"Tell me," Frankel said. "There's no time to sift through all of it," as he nodded at the open wardrobe.

I gave him a short version of its contents.

"Close it up and ready to move. There's a Mercedes sedan in front of the house. You and Zorro put it in the back." Then Frankel was gone as well.

I had the trunk shut, latched and was busy securing the leather straps around it when Zorro returned and gave me a hand. Together we wrestled it to the front door and out on the porch. I left him to it, went back inside to fetch the small wood box from Otto Felter's doorway. *I sure hope this is worth the effort it's taken,* I thought, as I stepped over his dead body.

Chapter 82

Out front, Zorro had dragged the trunk down the slope that passed for a lawn to the driveway, where he and Russian One were heaving it up into the open boot of a Mercedes-Benz Sedan.

"Where'd this come from," I said, indicating the late model black luxury automobile with a nod of my head.

"We commandeered it," Risenberg said from the back seat, where he was holding a pistol to Ilse Müller's ribs. She sat in the middle of the seat with her hands cuffed to the front, still wearing the flannel nightgown, and looking angry enough to burst into flames.

"Where from?" I said, looking at the plush, red leather seats and wood inlaid dash.

"It was parked in the barn with the keys in the ignition and a full tank of gas. You drive. Take us back to the highway."

"And the others?"

"Russian One's with us. Zorro's with Frankel and Two. Let's go."

Zorro disappeared without a sound. One got in the car next to the prisoner and I slid behind the wheel. I looked at Ilse Müller and said, "Ilse Müller, I'm placing you under Citizens Arrest for suspicion of the murders of Abraham Sorwell, Ruth Sorwell and Chiam Leviwitz."

She looked at me for an instant, then spit in my face.

Her hatred rattled me, but it was her act of defiance that bothered me the most. *You're on thin legal ice here and you know it—and so does she—because no matter how you slice it or dice it or try to evade it with a tinhorn 'citizen's arrest' maneuver, kidnapping is still kidnapping.*

I wiped her saliva off with my good sleeve . . . the clean one . . . turned around and started to figure out how to drive the fancy German vehicle.

I'd found the parking brake and released it, kicked in the clutch, and fired up the engine when Risenberg said from the back seat, "It's a four-speed."

"On the column? Where's the reverse?"

"Pull all the way back and up. Then a regular H pattern with first gear at the top left."

"Got it," I said as the big car eased forward with the power and grace of a panther. I caught a faint whiff of smoke. It got heavier fast as it filled the air with tar and ash that stung our eyes and made breathing difficult. I looked in the rearview mirror, saw thick white smoke pouring from the cabin and bunkhouse, while flames were already shooting from the roof of the barn.

"Don't stop the car," Risenberg said.

I headed for the cattle guard and the break in the fence line where Williams Creek ran through a steel culvert under the road, never able to peel my eyes from the rearview mirror, where I watched the tinder dry historic old buildings going up in flames forty feet high, while sparks and embers and chunks of ash the size of wolf paws lifted off from the inferno and settled into the tops of the evergreens and conifers that grew in abundance, right up to the edge of the pasture.

"That's gonna start a forest fire," I said, as we passed the gate and started to pull over by the white station wagon. The fire was growing in the distance, and I could see the old Dodge Brothers farm truck rumbling towards us at the same time. It looked a lot worse for wear, with bullet holes everywhere, no window glass or windshield and trailing a plume of blue smoke.

"Do. Not. Stop. Keep driving until we get to the highway Jake . . ."

Maybe it was just my imagination, but I could've sworn at that point, something cold and hard—like a pistol barrel—brushed the back of my neck, but when I reached up with one hand, there was nothing there. I put it down to stress, exhaustion, or maybe . . . well, I'd rather not think about what that implied. Another time and place I might have made an issue of it, but not then. I just drove on through the scrub oak and sage, the cedars, the wild currant and mountain mahogany bushes that grew in such profusion all along the high desert and near foothills of the mountains I hold so dear. And while I drove, I kept one eye on the washboard road in front, and the other on the growing conflagration behind us and imagined what would be left, this time tomorrow.

There wasn't any conversation as the Mercedes rumbled over the unmaintained lane, which left me brooding to myself and trying to justify my extralegal activities—but I couldn't find any easy way out. I was wondering if I'd survive prison when the red Corvette came into view and we were at the end of the road.

"Stop next to Naomi," Risenberg said. "Set the brake and get out of the car. Leave your window down halfway and the motor running."

"What about her?" I said.

"Talk to Frankel," he said.

I pulled up beside the Corvette and got out of the car. Behind me, the headlights of the white Ford station wagon were coming fast, but there was no sign of the Dodge truck as the smoke and the flames further to the west continued to grow and expand.

Naomi was standing next to the front bumper of my car when we stopped. She said, "Did you capture Helga Fischer alive?"

I pointed over my shoulder with the good thumb, said, "She's in the back seat, shocked, angry and scheming, but alive and well."

"What happened to your arm?"

"Dog attack. German Shepherd," I said, as she dropped the keys into my hand.

"I'll need to look at that, but not now. Are you able to drive?"

"Yeah," I said, just as Solomon Frankel slowed to a stop and called me over.

Chapter 83

"We need to get out of here," Frankel said through the open window. The station wagon was covered in dust and had a bent front bumper, but otherwise looked to be in good condition. The motor was still so quiet, I had to listen for a moment, to realize it was running.

I said, "About ten miles down the road, there's a place to pull off and park on the right side. It's got a big billboard with different kinds of tourist attractions on it that'll make a great place to regroup, do some first aid and figure out what the plan is for our prisoner."

"Agreed. I'll go first. Put Naomi in the Mercedes and let her bring up the rear. Tell her to stay back. Don't attract attention. Go," he said, as he drove away, out on to Highway 115, where his taillights vanished like a magical illusion.

I watched his lights wink out and made my way back to where Naomi waited by the pair of cars. I told her what Frankel said, adding that I had a towel in the trunk of my car to wrap my arm in to stop the bleeding. Without a word, she got in the black sedan and followed the Ford wagon. What I really wanted was a chance to get out of the army field jacket with the .32 Beretta in the pocket and to stash the manilla envelope of photographs and the piece of tanned leather under the rubber mat on the floor of the trunk. It wasn't a very good hiding place, but it would have to do. I wrapped the pistol in the liner I took out of the bloody field jacket and tucked it behind the driver's seat. I grabbed the leather bomber jacket I'd purchased to replace the one I threw away after the shootout on West Cucharras Street, slammed the trunk lid and jumped in the driver's seat. I tossed the jacket over to the other side and keyed the ignition.

When the motor started and a blast of warm air poured from the heater vents, it was as welcome as a letter from home during the fighting overseas. I was chilled and couldn't seem to get warm. *Probably because of your arm,* I thought as I drove down to the blacktop . . . where I opened the throttle and kicked it into high gear, intent on overtaking the Mercedes, which was about a mile in front of me.

My arm was a mess. I hadn't realized just how bad the dog wounded me until I got out of the field jacket. I could see a pair of deep gashes about four inches long on the underside of my left forearm, and several puncture marks plus smaller rips in my flesh, both on top and bottom that were all leaking blood or other fluids in a steady drip. I turned the interior light off and tried not to get anything on the seats.

There were no oncoming headlights in the northbound lane when the Corvette blew past the big sedan at close to twice the speed. Naomi flashed her high beams in my mirrors in annoyance, and I slowed down to just over the posted limit, keeping her well back, but always in sight. We made it to the billboard turnout fifteen minutes later.

I waited for them to catch up and turn off, then followed the sedan into the parking area, getting there in time to see Frankel coming back down the telephone pole with a lineman's handset hanging from his hip. He walked to the black sedan, where Risenberg and his wife were getting out and Russian Two was taking his place alongside Ilse Müller. Zorro climbed in the front passenger's side and turned to face the prisoner. I could just make out Zorro reaching back and a struggle of some kind breaking out. I turned to go over and investigate, but Frankel restrained me. "What's going on," I said. "Are they abusing her?"

"No," Risenberg said, "they're checking her mouth for a cyanide capsule. We don't want her to escape after all of the trouble we've gone through to capture her."

I'd been anticipating and dreading this moment for some time . . . and on top of that was the fact I was starting to fade physically. I was woozy from lack of sleep, overexertion, and dope sick from all the crap I'd ingested over the last hours. I looked at the pair of them and said, "I put her under citizen's arrest before we started down here. The Müller woman is my prisoner. I said so in front of witnesses . . ."

"Who don't speak English," Risenberg said, "and won't back you up."

Frankel said, "Easy Jake. There's a time and a place for everything. Right now, you are about to pass out. You need to let Naomi have a look at that arm. She's the closest thing we have to a real medical doctor. You've lost a lot of blood."

"I'm alright," I said, as the pair of them steered me toward the Ford station wagon, where Naomi had the tailgate down, with an Army battlefield medicine cabinet and trauma kit open. I sat down and she started tending to my wounds with a small flashlight in her mouth for an examination lamp.

Frankel lit a pair of cigarettes and passed one to me. I thanked him and took a drag, sucked the smoke deep into my lungs and said, with the raspy voice of a long-time nicotine fiend, "I appreciate all you've done to help Solomon, every one of you. I couldn't have solved the case without your help. I'll say it to the whole damn world . . . but there's a dilemma here. I've got a responsibility to speak for the Sorwell's, professor Leviwitz, and all the people of Colorado Springs I swore an oath to. I have to take her in."

Frankel looked at me with the saddest eyes I've ever seen, then said something to Risenberg in Hebrew, or Russian maybe. It could even have been Arabic for all I know . . . but it made me feel as ignorant as a pail of common dirt. Whatever it was, they were worried. I could see it in their faces and demeanor. They stopped talking. Risenberg tapped the face of his watch, then went to the Mercedes where he spoke with Zorro.

Frankel said, "You're due a better explanation than this, but I can't risk the lives of our men, the prisoner, or even our mission. If it were discovered that we Israelis carried out a covert mission on American soil, the consequences could destroy our young nation and result in never-ending war in the Middle East and elsewhere. That woman over there," he pointed toward the black sedan, "has murdered three people that we know of, here in Colorado Springs. There's no doubt of that. There's no doubt because Sorwell's diary proves it, and it's backed up by the physical evidence you've collected. But she's also guilty, directly or indirectly, of hundreds—perhaps thousands—of others in Europe during the war. She's helped to murder whole families . . . men, women, children . . . Ilse Müller is guilty of crimes against humanity and the weight of those killings is greater than the murders of a handful. The voices of six million souls crying out for justice will have to come first, because we humans are fallible and incapable of judging the evidence of evil on such a huge scale. That is a duty reserved for God . . . and Him alone. Here on Earth, the murders of the multitudes will outweigh the killing of the few, because it is all we are morally capable of."

Naomi, who had been doctoring my left arm the whole time, did something to it that hurt a lot. I winced. She said, "Sorry Jake . . ." I was looking at her when something stung me in the right trapezius and everything in my world went dark.

Chapter 84

I woke up, disoriented, and confused, in a hospital bed with an IV drip in my right arm. I found the call button that was taped to the pillow, pushed it, and waited for something to happen. It didn't take long before a nurse in a starched cap and white dress entered the room. She said, "Well hello there. Welcome back."

"Where am I? How long have I been here?" I said, as I tried to sit up.

"Easy does it there. You're in Cañon City. This is St. Thomas More Hospital. You've been in here for a day and a half. You were dropped off by a nice lady and her husband, who found you about a mile north of Penrose. They said it looked like you stopped to answer the call of nature and got attacked by some kind of wild animal that chewed up your left forearm. You remember anything like that?"

"No. Not really."

"I'm not surprised. You were pretty drunked up when they got ya here . . . and stinking of whiskey. You're lucky that pretty red car of yours is still in one piece is all I can say. Better mend your ways cowboy."

"Where is my car? Do you know?"

"It's out there in the parkin' lot, front and center, right where that nice tourist lady left it. Everybody's been admirin' it. The keys are in the drawer of the nightstand, along with your belt and pocket stuff."

"What about my clothes?"

"In the dresser, all washed and folded for you."

"And what do I have to do to get out of here?"

"You have to talk to Dr. Battle. That's whose patient you are."

"Where is he? When can I see him?"

"Not him. Her. Dr. Battle is a woman, and a great physician. All her patients love her . . . but I gotta warn ya, she doesn't take no grief from nobody. She'll be here soon, on her late rounds."

"Okay."

"You need to drink water. I'ma go get you some. Think you could eat?"

It had been two days since Nurse Gloria's stew and sandwiches. My gut rumbled. I said, "Yeah. I'm hungry."

There wasn't any clock that I could see, which left me with no idea what time it was, but I guessed late afternoon, and I wanted to be out of there as fast as possible. As it turned out though, there was no need to hurry; Dr. Battle came in and laid down the law. She wouldn't agree to release me until I had a night's sleep and a solid meal or two without alcohol or any sort of illicit drugs. It was a good decision on her part, and good advice too . . . the same things Gloria had been warning me about. But the problem was, not quite healed, my right leg still throbbed with pain, all day and all night. It never stopped. Not ever.

When I told her about it, Dr. Battle said, "Stop drinking. Take a daily multivitamin and eat a balanced diet with more protein in it. Drink milk. Those changes will help, but nothing will completely heal all the damage you've inflicted upon yourself. Now, let's talk about your arm."

"What about it?"

"I'm not buying that 'a wild animal attacked me' story."

"Why not?"

"Because it doesn't make sense. A wild animal bold enough to go after a human wouldn't stop at one arm. It would have to be starving or rabid. I'll listen to what you have to say, but if I don't like it, you'll have to take rabies shots for thirty days and I'll have to fill out a report. That will bring an inquiry because public health is at risk. Am I making myself clear?"

"Yes. But it's not that simple."

"Why not? After putting forty-five stitches in that arm, I deserve an explanation, and I'll have one before we finish."

I thought for a moment, and said, "Can I trust you Dr. Battle?"

"Of course. Why wouldn't you? I kept you from bleeding to death and put three pints of whole blood back in you . . ."

"I meant can I trust you with secrets? I said it's complicated, and it is, but it also bends the law somewhat."

She looked at me for a moment as the impact of that sunk in and she processed the information. Then she blinked and said, "I will not commit a criminal act of any kind. I don't even know for certain who you are. You haven't got any identification."

It's all in my briefcase, which is locked in my car . . . I thought . . . And just what I was hoping for. Out loud I said, "Let's try another way. Would you be willing to trust me?"

"Probably not. You've given me no reason to. I'm busy. I have other patients to see. Say what you have to say. Get to it or I'm gone."

"I think you already know who I am—my picture has been all over the news. But, I'm asking you to let me remain John Doe and allow me to leave here tonight for the sake of everyone. I'll send payment anonymously. I give you my word on that, and I'll do so right away . . . you won't have to wait for it."

"Why should I do something so one-sided and outlandish? I can't see any reason for me to do that young man. We'll need to begin the rabies shots without delay."

My anxiety was rising with each passing moment. I decided to go for broke. Said, "Are you aware that up in Colorado Springs a series of murders have been happening?"

"*The Skin Ripper Case?* It's all the entire staff's been talking about for the past month. This isn't a very large facility. Everyone knows everyone and I, as well as the other doctors, hear nothing but speculation about it. People are worried and scared."

"I can promise you two things, Dr. Battle. The first is that, as of the night before last, the Skin Ripper is done, absolutely unable to commit another murder in Colorado—or anywhere else. The second promise is that I was not bitten by a rabid animal. It was a German Shepherd police dog, trained to attack on command. The animal is dead."

The nurse had cranked the bed into a sitting position so I could eat. I watched as the light of recognition began dawning on Dr. Battle's face. She said, "Oh, Now I see, you're that det . . ."

"Don't Doc. Don't say it. You'll put us into that part where the limits of the law get bent."

"I understand Mr. Doe," she said, as she made a series of notations on the clipboard attached to the foot of the bed. "I hope the hospital doesn't have to absorb another five or six hundred dollar loss due to indigent services. You're recovering very well. I'll have the nurses come in a few minutes to remove the IV. Get a good night's sleep and there's no reason you can't be out of here. Your amnesia should go away after a while, but you'll have to monitor it. I want you to call me in a few day's—say a week or so—and let me know if your memory's better." She fished a business card from her lab coat, wrote on it and put it in the nightstand, along with my car keys. "A pleasant evening to you sir," she added, then turned and was gone.

Two hours later, during the evening shift change, I followed her out the door. I slipped away . . . into the night and back to a fractionally better world where the demented Helga Fischer, aka Ilse Müller, aka The Skin Ripper—a monster who terrorized thousands—no longer existed. I was proud of that . . . even without an arrest to show for it. In such an imperfect world, it would have to be enough.

Chapter 85

I stopped on the outskirts of town, at the first open place—a Frontier Gas Station with the familiar "Rarin' to Go" sign that depicted a cowboy atop a rearing horse. While the attendant filled the tank, washed the windshield and checked the oil, I got my briefcase and looked in the trunk. Everything was as I'd left it, and it all went into the case. I got change for some bills so I could phone Gloria and let her know I was okay. She answered on the third ring, while I pumped coins into the pay phone. She said, "Oh, Jake, I've been so worried . . ." Then before I had a chance to say a single thing, she was angry. "Why didn't you call me?"

"I couldn't. I . . ."

"Why not? And where are you? Do you have any idea what it's like for the one person you most care about in the world to just disappear like this? My phone's been ringing off the hook with people looking for you. Butch Hernshaw's called at least half-dozen times. Lt. Patterson and Wally Bailey too. What's going on Jake? Why are all those people so anxious to find you? Have you done something wrong? When are you coming back . . ." She finally ran out of questions and stopped to take a breath.

I said, "I'm in Cañon City. There weren't any phones where I was. I'm headed back to the Springs and I'll explain everything when I see you . . . okay?"

"What about all the phone calls?"

"If they try again, tell them I'm on my way. Do you have any idea how everybody got your phone number?"

"I think Butch gave it out, but I don't really know."

"You better now?"

"Yeah. I was just crazy with fear that something awful had happened to you."

"Me? Never. It's the bad guys who've got to worry. And besides honey, it wasn't any worse than trauma surgery, was it?"

"You asshole," she said. But I think she was laughing as she hung up the phone.

I broke the connection, got a dial tone and called the Robbery-Homicide desk at the CSPD. When Ann-Marie Fuchs answered, I asked if I could speak to Butch. She said, "It's good to hear your voice Jake. Hang on . . ." then she disappeared in a flurry of telephonic clicks and hive noises.

Two seconds later Butch said, "Where the fuck are you Jake . . ."

"Cañon City. What's it to you? I'm a civilian now, remember? That sonofabitch Captain 'Acting Chief' Duncan, fired me . . ."

"Duncan's dead, Jake."

"WHAT . . ."

"You heard me right . . . Captain Duncan's dead. Chief Budd came back in the early hours of the morning. He flew on a special flight from Reno in a military jet, courtesy of some Air Force General . . ."

The telephone operator came on and said, "Please deposit forty cents for the next three minutes."

I stuck my last quarters in the pay phone, heard "Thank you sir, go ahead."

"What'd you say, Butch? Go fast. I'm outta change. Tell me about Duncan."

"He was responding 10-100 to his house for some sort of personal problem and plowed into the ass-end of a ten-wheel dump truck loaded with gravel for the Air Force Academy. Rumor has it that he was doing seventy-five or eighty miles per hour, and the truck, about thirty-five. No skid marks either. He was driving Chief Budd's old car . . . the one he confiscated from you earlier in the day."

"Truck driver?"

"He's okay. Burned his hands and arms trying to get Capt. Duncan out. Traffic guys think the car was tampered with. They're lookin' at it now."

"Any word back on it yet?"

"No. Too soon. Rumor mill says the brakes and front end were tampered with. We'll know soon. Meanwhile, *Kemo Sabe*, Chief Budd wants to see you ASAP. Patterson says he thinks the Chief wants to reinstate you. Get here fast."

"Tonight?"

"Yeah. We've got all hands on deck right now. Everybody's here."

"I'm on my way," I said, and hung the phone up, just as the operator began asking for more money. *Damn!* I thought, *Ma Bell's as relentless as the Catholic Church about squeezing coins outta poor folk . . .*

I paid the pump jockey for the high-test, got behind the wheel and took off for the Springs like Stirling Moss through the Alps during the Italian Grand Prix. I parked in front of CSPD on East Kiowa Street about an hour later, waiting at the front desk for Wally Bailey to return to his post. He waddled out of the public restroom a couple of minutes later, busy pulling up his galluses. He belched, scratched his backside and began reading the pulp magazine he'd had stuck under one arm. Then he stopped dead in his tracks when he finally noticed me.

"Wally," I said, "good to know you're still living up to the highest standards of public service and representing the Springs Police Department with such style and grace."

He looked at me with an expression that was somewhere between a smile and a sneer and said, as he sat down, lifted a leg and passed gas, "Well if it ain't ole MIS-TER McKern . . . and how's life among the germs Jakey?"

"Ever interesting, chum . . ."

"I ain't cher chum. G'wan up. The Chief's lookin' for ya boyo."

"Wish me luck."

"In a pig's arse."

Like old times, I thought, then headed for the inner sanctum wondering what my life would be like in another couple of hours as I trudged down that seemingly endless hallway, wearing an army surplus store leather jacket to cover my wounded left arm and carrying a beat-up old briefcase with its hard-won and priceless exonerating evidentiary material. The only thing I was sure of at the moment, was that I'd never surrendered to evil.

Epilogue
One year later

The ramifications of the Skin Ripper case were many and far-reaching. The entire city of Colorado Springs was affected, and nowhere was it felt more than in the Police Department, which got a top to bottom examination and cleaning. Heads rolled, promotions were made and departments were modernized as the people in charge awakened at last to the fact that the Springs was no longer just an oasis for the fabulously wealthy, or a playground for the rich and famous from the big eastern and midwest megalopolises. They recognized we were a small city that was fast becoming a big city . . . and with it would come the problems associated with urbanization. The upshot of it all is that each and every resident of Colorado Springs and El Paso County is forced to accept constant growth and eternal change as a condition of living here.

As far as the characters in this story:

Imogene Curdy—ex-wife number one—is now listed in the financial news as one of the richest women in America. Rumor has it that a fall wedding is planned, for her and her long-time fancy man, Preston Lee Grinder. (Yeah, shocked me too. Some detective . . .) The same rumor mill also says that my son, Scottie has been sent off to a private school back east somewhere. I'm trying to get more information.

Lenny Bragg wrote a series of articles about the Skin Ripper Case, the ratlines into the Springs and the Israeli efforts to bring Nazi war criminals to justice—all based upon my exclusive story. He's in the running for this year's Pulitzer Prize for investigative journalism, and he has offers from three national newspaper chains.

Gilda Arkady now teaches art history at Notre Dame University in South Bend, Indiana.

S. William "Wild Bill" Tournillon, Esq., still represents the City of Colorado Springs in legal matters, and continues to clean everyone's clocks at the Friday night by-invitation-only poker games at City Hall.

Tyler Myers has completed basic training and is now a seaman apprentice aboard a US Navy warship somewhere in the Pacific, where he is an electrician's mate and learning about world geography by visiting various ports-of-call.

Michael "Mike" Brickell continues as a Vice President at the Colorado Commercial Bank. He's been trying to interest me in a fifteen-acre piece of property out on Templeton Gap Road that the bank is going to foreclose on early next year. He says it'll be a great investment for me. We'll see.

Harry Bucklin was re-elected to serve another term, but has his sights on bigger things in the state capitol—if not Washington D.C.

Dr. Alta Chapin, the pathologist, runs the El Paso County Coroner's Office in all but name. She's self-sufficient, capable and respected by all who deal with her.

Hizzoner, Robert "Mayor Bob" Eldridge is still the mayor . . . and intends to stay there forever from the look of things.

At the Colorado Springs Police Department:

Captain Frederich Duncan was buried in Evergreen Cemetery with full honors. Cops from all over the state attended.

Captain Edward Hoffman, Wilson Bell, Jack Gander, Roscoe Gifford, Sgt. Billy Olfield, and a handful of others were all retired from the P.D., several of them forcefully.

In one of the big surprises to everyone, Chief Jasper John "JJ" Budd, resigned and retired after forty-five years of honorable police work and dedicated service to the community. Before he left however, and while he was still the Chief of Police, Chief Budd hired his replacement, a top cop by the name of Dan Sherman, from somewhere in North Dakota. Big Dan turned out to be a helluva good Chief.

George Patterson was promoted to Captain. Andy Claypoole made Lieutenant, Amos "Rags" Magness made P2, Ann-Marie Fuchs got married and quit. Betsy Cary became Executive Secretary to Chief Sherman, and Wally Bailey is still scarfing down doughnuts while reading smut on the front desk during the night shift.

Butch Hernshaw and his wife Sallie, welcomed their fourth daughter, Lora, into the world August 13, joining her sisters Jane, Ann and June. Butch has turned out to be a damned good detective and an even better partner.

Ex-cop Jim Dunlap was arrested and charged with First Degree Murder for the death of Captain Duncan, and is being held in the El Paso County Jail awaiting trial. In one of life's sublime ironies, it was evidence provided by the man Dunlap abused, Officer Magness, (i.e. his note on my windshield) that provided the evidence to indict him.

The three Russian-Israelis I named, "One, Two" and "Zorro" along with the prisoner, Ilse Müller—or Helga Fischer if you prefer her real name—all disappeared. Saul and Naomi Risenberg went in mid-August, and I never saw any of them again.

Butch however, has a lot of contacts in the Fremont County Sheriff's Office. He went down to Cañon City last fall, where he bought a dozen hamburgers at the Owl Cigar Store lunch counter, then dropped in at the Sheriff's office for some bad coffee, lunch with the officers, and a chat. The deputies said that on the same morning a certain 'John Doe' was brought into St Thomas More Hospital, calls started coming in about an out of control forest fire in the foothills around the Williams Creek Ranch area. The deputies were sent out to investigate reported sightings of a battered old C-47 cargo plane that dropped down out of the clouds and darkness just before daylight and landed at the dirt airstrip a few miles to the south of town on Highway 50. The witnesses stated that the plane taxied to the far end of the runway where it was met by a black sedan of some sort. It appeared as if several people and a large box were quickly put aboard. Then the plane took off and disappeared to the west over the Sangre de Cristo Mountains just as a rain storm moved in. The automobile was also gone by the time the deputies got to the scene. The scuttlebutt said it was taken to a scrapyard in Pueblo and destroyed. It was all very frustrating to the law enforcement community, Butch told me afterwards. Then he lit a smoke and smiled when he said, "But what really pissed 'em off was when they hotfooted it over to the hospital for an interview with John Doe. Deputy Byrnes told me, 'But that sumbitch had scarpered off, slick as ya please. Nobody seen him go neither. He was there one minute and gone the next' . . . Would you happen to know anything about that Jake? Anything to help?"

"Nope. Not a single thing." In all the years I knew him, that was the only time Butch mentioned my lost day and a half. We never spoke of it again . . . something I've always been grateful to him for.

There is one thing however, that continues to occupy my thoughts and keeps me from sound, restful sleep at night . . . and that is the fire set by the Israelis as we pulled out of Williams Creek. The last I saw of the old place was an inferno and getting worse by the minute. It was spreading fast, and given the terrain, I thought it could burn ten to twenty thousand acres or more . . . plus there were the bodies of Otto Felter, and the other three, all dead from lead poisoning somewhere in all the fire mess. But nothing—other than a few ashes—was ever found. By the time the fire crews had battled their way into the old homestead, nothing was left of the dried buildings and the rain that was coming down in sheets had scoured most of the area clean, then washed it all away, down a raging William's Creek . . . which was at flood stage and still rising . . . as if the land were being purged of the evil which had been there.

Deuteronomy, fifth book of the Old Testament, is the first of more than thirty references in the Bible to the Jews as "The Chosen People." The events—as well as the astonishing coincidences—at the Williams Creek Ranch have caused me many hours of contemplation throughout the decades . . . until I no longer question the veracity of that claim.

Solomon Frankel goes on with his work for Mr. Wiesenthal as they track down and drag escaped Nazi war criminals and murderers, kicking and screaming, out of their hiding places to face the justice they are due. I hear from him on occasion, when I receive a small can of "Virgin Olive Oil" from the Golan Import Co, Ltd. in Haifa, Israel. In it will be a translated file from Interpol—the International Police Agency— about some Nazi or other who'd come through on the church's ratline and wound up somewhere in, near, or close to my jurisdiction, here in Colorado. There were less than a handful in a span of many years, but each one was stunning in terms of its revelation. Frankel is the one who informed me of Risenberg's death in the fall of last year. Indeed, the Rabbi died as a hero . . . with a weapon in his hands while fighting the avowed enemies of his country. For a warrior such as him, it was a good death.

As for myself, the Skin Ripper Case has never come to any kind of a satisfactory conclusion, because I was never able to bring her or any of her cohorts into court, or put them in prison for murdering three elderly citizens of Colorado Springs, and the Nazi priest, Alphonso Gianette. I had to be content in knowing that 'Ilse Müller' faced a judge, jury and the hangman in Israel as payment in full for her crimes. Say what you want, it was a fitting end, and a fitting price, for such monstrous deeds as she was guilty of committing.

There were no secretaries, police brass or witnesses of any kind in Chief Budds's private chamber that night . . . only he and I were present. He greeted me in a neutral voice that gave no clue as to his thoughts, or his reasons for the early and dramatic return from Reno. I couldn't tell if he was angry or indifferent; not even by guessing, or with one of those notorious hunches I was known for.

I thought, *What the Hell, I'm a civilian.* Said, "Could I use the phone? I'm expected and I don't want her to be worried."

Chief Budd pointed toward the table surrounded by eight leather chairs at the other end of the office. A black rotary dial telephone sat on the end facing his desk. "It's an outside line. Be quick."

"Thanks. I will sir."

I left my briefcase on one of the two wingbacks at the front of his desk, walked over and dialed. When a sleepy voice made a noise on the other end, I said, "Gloria, it's me. I'm at the police station talking to Chief Budd in his office . . .

"No. I'm not under arrest. He asked me to come in . . .

"I don't know yet, but soon . . .

"Okay, I will . . .

"I promise . , ,

"Okay honey, I have to go. He's waiting for me . . .

"You too. Bye."

I hung up, returned to my seat facing Chief Budd. He said, "Tell me about the case."

"Do you want the long or short version?"

"I want it all," he said. "From A to Z. Start to finish. No bullshit, no music . . . just the facts." Then the Chief busied himself with the selection, trimming and lighting of a big Cuban Corona from the humidor on his desk. He sat back in his leather chair, smoking and waiting for me to begin.

I opened the briefcase, pulled out my notebook and began to speak, starting with the callout from Wally Bailey, and didn't stop until the moment I walked into his office, and backed it all up with copies of the daily activity reports Captain Duncan forced me to write. I also showed the Chief a copy of Sorwell's Manuscript, the translation, and capped it off with the photographs and sample of tanned human skin with its Auschwitz tattoo. Last of all, I produced the .32 caliber Beretta automatic pistol. "I personally took this away from Ilse Müller during the shootout at the Williams Creek Ranch. I think it's the one used in all three murders."

The Chief spoke for the first time in more than three hours. "That is one helluva tale, son. In all my years of law enforcement I ain't never heard one like it. And I'm concerned about a few of the things you just said, so I want you to go back and tell me again, what all you know as to any foreign agents operating hereabouts, or organizations dumping former Nazi henchmen into Colorado Springs. And finally . . . who, how and why . . . is someone in this department attempting to sabotage an ongoing investigation? I'll have somebody hang by their balls for that, I swear to Christ . . ."

I went over all of Chief Budds' concerns a couple of more times that morning—and with Chief Sherman as soon as he took office—but without any conclusion either time.

The debriefing was over at that point. It ended in the gray light of the false dawn, that brief few minutes just before the sun rises over the eastern plains of Colorado like God's eye opening in the endless nothing, when the Chief took my badge and service revolver from his desk and handed them over to me. As they touched my hands, he said, "Your undercover work has been exemplary Detective McKern. You've proven yourself to be a dedicated and brave member of the Colorado Springs Police Department who has performed meritoriously while on a secret mission that, unfortunately, brings no recognition, other than this: I'm hereby putting a Letter of Commendation in your jacket and officially promoting you to the rank of Sergeant, with our heartiest appreciation. Congratulations."

One thing about the old Chief, I thought, as I received the equipment and stammered out my thanks. *He sure knows how to sling the blarney . . . no matter what the circumstances . . . But I'd hate to ever, ever be on his shit list. And that's a fact.*

Then, all I had left to do was get back into Gloria's good graces. I wasn't sure of the reception I was in for.

In the earliest minutes of a few cloudless days, if the humidity is just so in Colorado Springs, when the sun finally rises, for a short bit of time it turns the massive face of Pikes Peak a rosy pink color that seems to glow with its own spectral light. It's awe-inspiring, and a thought-provoking sight for anyone fortunate enough to get a glimpse of it . . . and I am no exception.

I saw the 'Shining Mountain Sitting Big' that morning as I turned west on Colorado Avenue and headed toward Gloria's house, and it put me in a pensive frame of mind. It made me think about how radically my life had changed in the span of just a few weeks; about how fortunate I was to have freedom of opportunity, the chance to work for good, and try and make the world a better place; to love who I wished and live how I chose.

I was full of hope and optimism about the future as I climbed the three steps up onto Gloria's porch, where Buddy Boy was draped over the back of the old green couch. He jumped down and ran to the door when he saw me, meowing to be let in and fed. I was in a jaunty mood as I took the key from its hiding place and let us both in. It didn't last.

Acknowledgments

I would like to thank Dwight Haverkorn for his good humor, patience and for sharing his endless amount of historical knowledge about the CSPD . . . as well as for answering all of my dumb questions with his everlasting good cheer. Any errors are mine alone.

The Skin Ripper has taken a significant amount of time to come to fruition. It would not have done so without the help and encouragement of my friend Bob Will, my right arm and assistant in all things digital—Lora Brown and her son Dillon, my physical therapist Kim Myers and her helpers Tyler Myers and Trevor Myers, good guy neighbor Mike Hillman, Israeli Scribe and West Bank resident Jonathan Lev, Bob, Jane and Hayden Battle, as well as Don Kallaus and all the gang at Rhyolite Press in Colorado Springs.

A special thank you to my wife June, whose understanding, help, patience, support, care and love got me through the down times. I would not be here without her.

Lastly, a shout-out and thank you to my almost-agent, Nat Sobel, in New York City. Your interest in me and my work . . . fueled personal dreams of first-class representation and a series of hardcovers that sustained me through illness, Covid, deaths in our family, and a thousand mile relocation. I will always be grateful.

John Dwaine McKenna is the acclaimed and award-winning author of *The Neversink Chronicles, Colorado Noir, and Unforsaken.* Find him at johndwainemckenna.com.

Look for Jake's next adventure:

The Shining Mountain

Summer 2025

www.ingramcontent.com/pod-product-compliance
Lightning Source LLC
Chambersburg PA
CBHW071203020726
47502CB00002B/521